RETURN ^{OF}_{THE} OLD ONES

APOCALYPTIC LOVECRAFTIAN HORROR

EDITED BY BRIAN M. SAMMONS

DRP

PUBLISHED BY
DARK REGIONS PRESS
—2017—

Not with a bang, but a scream © 2016 Brian M. Sammons
Around the Corner © 2016 Jeffrey Thomas
Tick Tock © 2016 Don Webb
Causality Revelation © 2016 Glynn Owen Barrass
The Hidden © 2016 Scott T. Goudsward
The Gentleman Caller © 2016 Lucy A. Snyder
Scratching from the Outer Darkness © 2016 Tim Curran
Messages from a Dark Deity © 2016 Stephen Mark Rainey
Time Flies © 2016 Pete Rawlik
Sorrow Road © 2016 Tim Waggoner
The Call of the Deep © 2016 William Meikle
Howling Synchronicities © 2016 Konstantine Paradias
Chimera © 2016 Sam Gafford
The Last Night on Earth © 2016 Edward Morris
The Incessant Drone © 2016 Neil Baker
Breaking Point © 2016 Sam Stone
The Allclear © 2016 Edward M. Erdelac
The Keeper of Memory © 2016 Christine Morgan
Shout / Kill / Revel / Repeat © 2016 by Scott R Jones
Strangers Die Every Day © 2016 Cody Goodfellow

Dark Regions Press, LLC
P.O. Box 31022
Portland, OR 97231
United States of America
www.darkregions.com

Edited by Brian M. Sammons
Cover image and design © 2016 by Vincent Chong
Interior illustration © 2017 by M. Wayne Miller
Interior design by Cyrus Wraith Walker

First Trade-Paperback Edition
ISBN: 978-1-62641-191-3

TABLE OF CONTENTS

NOT WITH A BANG, BUT A SCREAM

BRIAN M. SAMMONS

"The Old Ones were, the Old Ones are, and the Old Ones shall be."
—H.P. Lovecraft, "The Dunwich Horror."

That quote is where the idea for this book began. The Old Ones, the undying, cosmic entities that H.P. Lovecraft gave birth to, and other authors would expand upon, in what would one day be known as the Cthulhu Mythos, have captivated my imagination since I first read about them. They are titanic, beyond comprehension, eternal, and inevitable. Because they are so truly alien to us, their motives are unfathomable and that adds to their horror. You have no idea where they're coming from. Unlike the Devil, they're not in a cosmic chess match with the Almighty for our souls. That doesn't stop the cults that worship them like gods from sacrificing victims in their name. Unlike raging beasts, they don't want to consume us out of hunger, as they are beyond such petty physical concerns. That doesn't mean they won't gobble a few people down just because they enjoy the taste. They don't kill for sick, sadistic pleasure like a psychopath, for if the Old Ones have any emotions at all—and that is debatable—they are certainly deeper and more complex than any that we can relate to. Although they do seem to have other baser impulses that they indulge in from time to time, as Lavinia Whateley could attest to. But even then there seems to be purpose in their actions. Every action a step forward in some grand plan. Whatever could that be?

And the Old Ones *shall* be.

Unlike many horrors in fiction, the Old Ones can't be beaten or escaped. Death and taxes have nothing on these immortal beings. At best humanity can only delay their inevitable return, only slightly from their point of view, and then only at great cost. They are more than a force of nature; they are that mysterious force behind nature that we think we understand, but when we're honest with ourselves we admit that we do not. Cannot. Not really. The Old Ones are beyond us in every way imaginable. And they. Will. Return.

While I love horror fiction in many forms and flavors, my favorite kind of terror tales are the ones about inescapable horror. If the family moving into the haunted house only heeded the signs and "got out" their ordeal would be over. If the teens at the summer camp trusted their instincts and didn't go off alone to investigate a strange noise, the masked slasher would never get them. If people facing vampires only acted during the day. If those being stalked by a werewolf would only believe "those old stories" sooner rather than later and get some silver. If the kids at the prom hadn't been assholes toward the weird, creepy girl with the massive telekinetic powers. But there is no such scenario for getting out alive and well when dealing with the Old Ones. One day, they will return, and then that's it for humanity or, at the very least, life as we know it. Sure, by great hardship and sacrifice you may postpone that day for a little while, but it's still going to happen. There will come a time when the Stars are Right, and when that happens....

Well, that's what I wanted to explore with Return of the Old Ones, and I wanted to look at all aspects of it. So I began with: What led up to that final day of reckoning? What were the signs? Who played a part, however small, in the ushering-in of a new age, and who tried to oppose it, however ineffectually? Was there a moment when humanity could have once again delayed their own demise for a few more years and failed to act? Was this the last few ticks of the great cosmic clock before the Stars were once again Right?

Then I wanted to look at that fateful day when the world shook, the wall between realities crumbled, and the Old Ones stepped through and returned for once and for all. What would people do in the face of such a momentous event? Would mankind go gentle into that not-so-good night, or would they rage against it? Would humanity come together at last or, more predictably, turn on itself in one last orgy of fear, hate, and violence? And then there were the individual stories I wanted explored. The "Where were you when ..." moments that would go unremembered in whatever future that was to follow.

What of that future nightmare life would become after the Old Ones returned? Who would survive? How would they survive? In addition to the more usual post-apocalyptic survival stories, how would having living "gods" walking the face of the Earth affect people mentally? Spiritually? Faith, one of the things humanity could always turn to in time of crises, would be shaken to the core, gone, and redefined. Would the world as it once was become myth? Just tales parents living in the dark shadows of uncaring deities would tell their children to give them some glimmer of hope? Would half-remembered truths that the world wasn't always this way and half-believed lies that one day things would get better be the new bedtime stories? And for those that did live in the new world, what price would they pay for existence? What bargains would they make with their new overlords? How would mankind have to evolve when the Old Ones returned, and would they still be recognizable as humanity?

Questions. So many questions. I asked those questions to some of the best authors writing in weird and horror fiction today, and I was amazed by the answers they gave me. Each told their own unique tale of cosmic apocalypse. Each had their one take on which Old Ones would come back first, how they would breach the boundaries between their world and ours, and what would be the aftermath. For every scenario I could have thought of, I received a multitude of others that never occurred to me. Some were as black as the darkness between the stars. Some offered the faintest glimmer of hope, something to cling tightly to, something worth fighting for.

Here are those answers, those stories. Nineteen very different takes on what happened on the days before, the day of, and all the days that followed the Return of the Old Ones.

Brian M. Sammons
March 12, 2016

In the Before Times

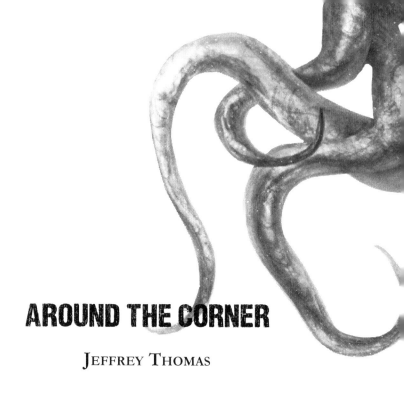

AROUND THE CORNER

JEFFREY THOMAS

Coming in from the summer glare outside, the darkness within Unit 3 of the Trinity Village Apartments was like having a black cloak thrown over his head. A vague purplish afterimage, like a negative impression of light, throbbed in the darkness like a great jellyfish pulsing at the bottom of the sea. It didn't help that Franklin was suffering a throbbing headache from having had too much to drink last night, it having been Friday. Though, drink or no drink, these headaches had been pretty frequent lately, for the past couple of weeks occurring just about every other day. He remembered having endured debilitating headaches as a kid, though it was one of the few things he recalled from his childhood.

The smells of the building's hallway, a mix of food cooking behind the closed doors that lined it and industrial-strength carpet cleaner, didn't do much for his headache, either. Muted bass-heavy music and TV firefights provided an aural complement to the miasma.

Before his vision adjusted to the sudden contrast of subterranean gloom, he detected a low muttering close by, like the forlorn whispering of a ghost. Franklin turned toward it, and from out of the murk a human shape took form. A diminutive, elderly white woman stood in front of the elevator, poking its button and murmuring to herself fretfully, all the while casting nervous glances at Franklin as she no doubt had been doing since the moment he entered the hallway. One would think he was the first African American man she had ever seen, though that could hardly be the case at Trinity Village. He vaguely recalled having seen her before, but if so he hadn't paid her much mind.

"Not working?" he said to the woman. Though he lived on the third floor he seldom used the elevator himself, even when he carried a fistful of plastic shopping bags from the market as he did now. He didn't spend his lunch breaks in the company gym just so he could ride elevators when he didn't need them.

"No," the old woman said in a childishly self-pitying tone. "It won't open."

Franklin strode to the elevator and pushed its call button himself. "Looks like it's stuck at the top floor."

"That's where I live." She looked down at her two-wheeled folding shopping cart, which was laden with plastic bags of her own, and moaned piteously. "Ohhh ... what am I going to do?"

"Fourth floor, huh?" Franklin said. "I'll bring that up for you, but can you climb up there okay?"

"Ohhh ... I'll try, I guess."

They entered the stairwell beside the elevator and proceeded upstairs slowly, Franklin carrying his own bags in one hand and dragging the cart after him one jouncing step at a time. "God damn," he said under his breath. He had told the old woman to go first and she kept looking back at him as if she expected him to suddenly rush back downstairs, claiming her supplies as his own. When they reached the third floor he said, "Let's just wait here a sec so I can drop off my groceries. It'll be easier." He left her cart beside her on the landing, jogged down to his own door, unlocked it and left his bags just inside, then returned to the woman so they could mount the next flight. This time, instead of dragging the cart, he picked it up and carried it in both arms. When they reached the long, dimly-lit hallway of the top floor he set it down on its wheels again.

The woman was wheezing and mumbling to herself, eyes closed and bracing one hand against a wall bearing the faded traces of graffiti that had been inadequately scrubbed and painted over. "Hey," Franklin said to her, "you okay, there?"

She cracked her eyes and started a little as if seeing him for the first time. Finally, she pointed. "The last door."

"We're almost there, then." He continued pulling the cart for her and forced himself to walk ploddingly to remain at her side as she shuffled along. The wheels squeaked as if complaining after their ordeal on all those steps.

The old woman had begun scanning the apartment numbers on the right side of the hallway as they passed, her face scrunched in confusion. She stopped once, abruptly, to look back over her shoulder, then at a door on the left side of the corridor, then resumed walking. Seeing this, Franklin asked, "Are you sure you're in the right building, ma'am? This is Unit 3. Did you want 1 or 2?"

"I know what building I live in," she groused. "But I think someone moved the numbers on these damn doors." She stopped again, at the last door on the right. "This should be my apartment," she said. "10D!"

The number stenciled in gold on the dung brown door was 8D … D referring to the fourth floor. Franklin knew there were ten apartments on each of the four floors of the three buildings that made up Trinity Village, for a total of one hundred and twenty apartments, though there were one, two, and three bedroom units. His had only one bedroom, as he and Jess had never had children and now even Jess was gone.

"Hang on," Franklin said, abandoning the cart for a moment and continuing a few steps further. Just ahead, the hallway took a ninety-degree turn to the right. Coming to this corner, he entered a little dead end. It didn't have an equivalent on the third floor or he'd have seen it, since his apartment was 9C, the last door on the left. This unlit corner had an oddly angled ceiling such as one might find in an attic, and he supposed that was because they were just under the building's roof. The tapered, folded look of the ceiling and walls reminded him, oddly, of paper airplanes he had made as a boy, or of origami. The smell here was intense and unpleasant—maybe from some dish the woman had burned recently, such as fish—and it aggravated his headache, giving it a sharp nudge like a baby kicking in the womb.

Two doors stood close together along the inner wall just around this corner. The nearer of the pair bore the number 10D. The other was a metal door stenciled *EXIT*. Each floor, according to code, had to provide two means of escape should a fire break out. He never used the back stairs himself, though, as the residents' parking lot and even the trash dumpster were at the front of Unit 3. The ceiling slanted so close to this exit that he figured the door must barely clear it when it was opened.

Franklin poked his head out from the miniature hallway and gestured for the woman to join him. "Here you go, ma'am … it's right here."

"What?" She waddled over suspiciously, perhaps afraid he meant to lure her into an attack. Holding back a few steps, she grimaced at the number on the door as he pointed to it. "That's not my apartment!" she protested.

"Ma'am, you got your keys on you, right? Just try it."

He backed out of the bent little section of corridor to give her room as she drew close to the door and dug a keychain out of the pocket of her house dress. She inserted a key, the lock clicked, and the door swung inward. The woman pushed it in further warily, as if still expecting some sort of wired booby-trap to go off. Meanwhile, Franklin retrieved her cart and brought it to her.

"So … your place, right?"

"It looks like it," the old woman said, but she didn't sound convinced. She reached back and took the handle of her cart, her gaze so fixed on the interior of the apartment that she never looked back to thank him. Her door creaked shut and locked from the inside.

Franklin sighed and turned away, and as he did so found himself facing another woman, standing in another doorway: that of apartment 9D in the opposite wall. The apartment just above his. This woman, though also short in stature, was much younger. This woman he knew for sure he'd never seen before, because she was attractive and he'd have remembered her. He took her to be Mexican or from Central America, with lustrous black hair and oversized dark eyes that were capped with sexily drooping lids. The pupils of her eyes were dilated like twin eclipsed suns, their whites very red, and he suspected she'd been smoking weed though he didn't smell it on her. Still all he smelled was that stench like burnt fish.

When he met her gaze she giggled, and he took that to mean she'd witnessed his exchange with the elderly woman from 10D. He grinned and jerked his thumb over his shoulder. "Pretty crazy, huh? I think she must have that Oldtimer's Disease."

"You shouldn't make fun of her," the young woman said. Her voice was vaguely accented. "I'll bet you've forgotten some important things in your life, too."

Franklin stared at her for several seconds. She had to be new here and couldn't possibly know anything personal about him; even his longtime neighbors knew nothing of his history. She couldn't have meant that statement in the way he had heard it. He regained his smile and said, "You kidding me? When I'm her age I'll be lucky if I know my own name. By the way, it's Franklin." He extended his hand.

She regarded his hand as if amused by his gesture, but finally took it and said, "My name's Reyna."

"Nice to meet you, Reyna." He let go of her small warm hand reluctantly. "You new here?"

"We've been here a couple weeks now."

"You live alone?"

"I live with my family." He noticed then how she stood blocking the door, which stood half closed behind her. "I have a big family."

"Yeah, you got one of the three bedroom deals, huh?"

"Yes."

"Reyna?" a woman's voice said behind her. "*Quién es ese?*"

Reyna glanced over her shoulder. "*Sólo un hombre que se pierde.*" She looked back at Franklin and giggled again, then slipped backwards through the door and closed it. He heard it lock, as the old woman's had done.

Franklin shook his head. "She crazy, too," he said to himself.

A loud, drawn-out creak behind him caused him to look in that direction. He thought it was the old woman opening her door again, maybe to belatedly thank him, and leaned toward the corner for a peek. He saw that her door was still shut, as was the exit to the rear stairwell, but an undulating and amorphous smear of purple light hung in the air in the dark of the corner.

His headache stabbed him anew. God, he needed to get himself to his own place downstairs, take a few ibuprofen and kick back to watch a movie. He knew his eyes were only superimposing that restless purple light against the shadows, and yet it looked more like it was lurking back there *amid* the shadows, half submerged. Or rather, half emerged.

A dull heavy *boom* awakened Franklin, its echoes dispersing along his nerve endings. He sat up on his sofa wild-eyed, while the TV still blathered nonchalantly.

His body told him it had experienced a shudder or vibration, perhaps of a mild earth tremor, but there was no lingering evidence to support this. Aside from the TV, his darkened apartment lay still around him. Late afternoon had stealthily progressed into deep night while he slept.

He pressed the heel of one hand into the center of his forehead and croaked, "Jesus." The pain hadn't abated; was if anything more profound. Maybe he needed some food in his belly, and to hydrate.

That boom. He suspected now he had been dreaming. His dreams, he was certain, often tried to send him coded messages. These distorted dispatches from his subconscious were all he had in place of critical memories.

Yes … he must have been dreaming of the bomb. A bomb of water-gel explosive that had been dropped from a helicopter onto the roof of the house where his parents and other families—both black and white—had lived together, as the culmination of a long standoff and shootout with the police.

Not that he remembered any of the details himself, despite having been in that house at the time, but he had read of the incident years later online.

In the shootout and resultant fire, numerous people living in the bombed house had been killed, Franklin's father among them. His mother had survived uninjured to be committed to a psychiatric hospital, but had later committed suicide by self-immolation, as if desiring to die in the manner of her husband.

And he, only five-years-old when the police raid occurred, had been given by his grandparents to a deprogrammer, in whose home he had apparently stayed for several months.

He had no memory at all of the deprogrammer, and his grandparents had never explained why a five-year-old, whom one would assume to be very malleable and resilient, would require such radical brainwashing. His grandparents, both dead now, had angrily refused to discuss any of it when he was growing up, except for an occasional frustrated exclamation. Once his grandmother had referred to the deprogrammer as an "exorcist." Another time his grandfather, his father's own father, had shouted, "It's *good* the police killed them, before those evil fools called up the devils they worshipped!"

As a teenager, less afraid of his grandparents and less willing to let the matter go, he had persisted, "You'd think the cops wouldn't drop a bomb like that, after that thing with MOVE in Philly only five years before. Knowing what happened that time."

"You fool," his grandfather had replied. "Where do you think the police *got* the idea? They *wanted* that to happen again!"

He swung his legs off the couch but sat there in the fluttering blue TV light for a few minutes longer, giving his heart a chance to slip back into its regular rhythm. It was then that he realized he was hearing another sound that he had thought was part of the TV program that had been running obliviously while he slept. He reached for the remote, muted his television, and listened.

It was coming from the floor above, muffled through the ceiling: a number of voices speaking—or was it singing? —in unison. The words sounded to be in another language, though he couldn't say if it was Spanish. Well, of course it had to be Spanish, right? That was what Reyna had spoken in earlier today with that other woman behind the door.

Sounded like quite the Saturday night party up there. Maybe tequila and weed were the guests of honor. Despite his headache, he kind of wished pretty little Reyna had invited him to join them.

Each of the three units at Trinity Village had a laundry room in the basement, and Franklin liked doing his wash late on weeknights when there was less competition for machines. He really only ever used the elevator at the front of the building on laundry night, but he found it was still out of order, so he had to carry his overflowing basket down all those flights of steps.

When he scuffed in his flip-flops into the long basement room with its low ceiling, smelling of the underground, he discovered only one other person in there: a neighbor from the second floor named Vondra. Vondra snorted when she saw him come in, folding the last of her clothes atop a table. "Well, look at this sad lonely man. Are you still moping for that big white girl of yours, Franklin?"

He said, "Nice to see you, too, Vondra." He started loading one of the machines.

"Honest to God, I think men like you would rather date the fattest white girl in the world than the sexiest black celebrity. You see, the racists make you ashamed of your own kind so much you can't bear to be with a black woman. You got to try to show them you're just as good. Meanwhile, fine-ass black women like me are raising our kids alone. I think you must hate yourself for who you are, Franklin."

"I don't hate myself, Vondra," he said mildly as he poured detergent into the slide-out drawer. "Hell, I don't even hate you."

"Huh." She patted down the neat stacks of clothes in her basket, hoisted it up and started past him for the doorway and the steps to the ground floor. "Shit, I thought your big ole Jess came back here to see you a couple nights ago when I felt the building shaking." She laughed at her own joke.

Franklin looked up. "Hey, wait up. You mean you felt that, too? That ... boom or whatever? I thought I just dreamed it."

Vondra paused in the threshold. "Yeah, the building was shaking, just for a second or two."

"Earthquake maybe, huh?" he said.

"Guess so. Night, Franklin. Hey ... maybe you should come down and have a drink with me sometime when the kids are asleep."

"I would if you weren't so mean, Vondra."

"You mean you would if I was more fat." She cackled all the way up the stairs.

He sighed and wagged his head as he started feeding quarters into the machine. As it started up, he slid more quarters into the second of the two machines he'd loaded. The vibration of the two washers quivered up through the soles of his flip-flops and seemed to spread up his ankles, his calves, like a swarm of centipedes inside him racing for the ladder of his spine ... racing for his brain, so that they might start chewing into it and get another headache going.

For some reason, the vibrations made him glance around at the basement room uneasily. There was a padlocked door, probably with supplies or maybe water pipes or circuit boxes behind it, and one window at the far end past all the washers and dryers. To the right of the window, the wall took a turn into a tight little corner. He knew what was there, though he couldn't see it from this angle: a fire exit. It was locked from the outside but sometimes tenants propped it open, no matter how much the landlord threatened with flyers posted on the corkboard over the folding tables, so that they might let in cool air or stand outside and smoke while they waited for their clothes to wash or dry.

Franklin stared toward that dark corner. He knew there was only an exit back there. Not a low, weirdly-angled ceiling. Not a pulsing blob of purplish-blackish light … or anti-light.

"Hello, Franklin."

He whirled around, startled. For a microsecond he had thought the voice had emanated from within the corner.

It was Reyna, carrying a plastic basket of clothes. She set it down atop the washer nearest to the door she had just passed through. It being a sweltering summer night, the laundry room itself like a sauna, she wore cutoff denim shorts and a tank top. With her hair in a ponytail her neck was bared. Oh, all that coffee-with-cream-and-sugar skin. Vondra had him wrong. It was *all* good.

The timing seemed fortuitous, just the two of them alone down here late at night; he thought they'd have a chance now to become better acquainted. But no sooner had Reyna set down her basket than a tall, slim man in his early twenties, with short red hair and a sprinkling of freckles, appeared in the doorway behind her also carrying a basket. At first Franklin took him to be another of the tenants on his own, but Reyna faced him and said, "Just put that down right here, hon."

The young man said, "Right, sure, just put it down." He placed the basket atop the machine next to Reyna's, then stood towering over her awkwardly as if awaiting another command.

Reyna smiled at Franklin and said as if in explanation, "James is autistic."

"Oh … yeah? Are you his, uh, caregiver?"

"No, he's just my buddy. Right, James?"

"Right, I'm your buddy," James echoed.

Franklin was surprised. He'd assumed all the people, however many "all" constituted, living with Reyna in her apartment were of the same nationality. Apparently that wasn't the case.

"And he has superpowers, too," Reyna boasted. "Don't you, hon?"

"Right, I'm like a superhero." James flexed the muscles of his slender arms, smiling, but without making eye contact with either of them.

Reyna explained to Franklin, "When he first came to us with his mom when he was small, James could recite every word and imitate every sound effect in a Disney movie. But we figured he could do even better than that, so we worked with him, and now James can memorize every word in a book. Not just one book, either, but a bunch of books. Our family moves around a lot, because we do our work in all different cities, in all different states. So it isn't easy to bring a lot of books around with you. With James, we don't have to worry about that. He can recite anything we need for our work." She turned toward the tall young man, who had begun weaving from foot to foot, flapping his hands, smiling toward the ceiling and chuckling deeply to himself as if amused at some secret thought. "James, recite for me from page 984. You know the book I mean."

James started speaking in another tongue, while still weaving side-to-side and flapping his hands, though a bit more quickly than before, and still gazing at a point beyond the ceiling.

"What language is that?" Franklin asked Reyna. It sure wasn't Spanish.

"That's the language of the Naacal people," she replied.

"Huh." He didn't want to admit he'd never heard of them. But it did sound like James was speaking in an actual tongue, as opposed to just speaking in tongues.

"That's enough, hon," Reyna told him, holding up a hand to cut him off. "Good job. He's such a sweetheart. Family is everything, Franklin. Like they say, it's greater than the sum of its parts. Our individual lives are small and meaningless, but united we can have more of an impact on the world and bring about something greater than ourselves ... something that lasts where we don't. Haven't you ever wanted to be part of something bigger, Franklin?" Before he could answer—and he did open his mouth but paused for wont of words—she went on, "I get the feeling that you once did belong to something bigger, but you've forgotten about it. Once you were innocent, more open and in tune with the universe, like James is. But you lost that. I understand ... it happens to most adults. But there are ways to get back to that clearer vision, that bigger picture. You have to open your mind. That's what our family does ... we're all about opening doors. And for you, I think that *remembering* would be the first step to that." She smiled over at James. "You're great at remembering, aren't you, James?"

He chuckled, weaving.

"Well, I think maybe I'm not ready to be part of a family yet,"

Franklin said uncomfortably. "I kind of like being on my own right now." He didn't admit to missing having a woman live with him. That he missed Jess.

"You should still come upstairs and visit my family sometime. I'd be happy to introduce you." She started pulling handfuls of clothing out of her basket and shoving them into the front of her washer. "I think you'd like them. I'm sure you'd fit right in."

"Yeah, maybe sometime," Franklin said, but he found himself becoming less interested in Reyna by the moment, regardless of her motherly gentleness toward the autistic man. He watched her feed more clothes into her machine. So far everything she had put in was black. In fact, it looked like most of the items in her basket were the same type of long black garment. He gestured toward the next batch she pulled out into her arms. "What are those—robes?"

Reyna paused to look down at the black bundle she held against her chest and giggled, as she had giggled that other day in her doorway. "Yeah. We use them for parties."

"Halloween parties?"

"Something like that."

"Okay." Halloween was several more months away. Franklin remembered the sounds he had heard Saturday night, that he had taken for a party. Now he wasn't so sure. Those voices he had heard speaking or singing in unison … had that been in the "language of the Naacal people," too?

"Wonderful things are going to happen very soon, Franklin," Reyna told him. "You really should be a part of it, directly. Alone we're just like ants, but together we can make a difference that will change things forever. We're all going to die someday anyway, so why not do something of *gran importancia* that'll have an effect on *everything*— something that we could never accomplish by ourselves? Because by ourselves we're nothing. Right, James?"

"Right, we're nothing." He clapped his hands rapidly, then went back to flapping them.

Franklin started edging toward the doorway. "I hear ya—it's good to have something to believe in. Well, got some things to take care of while my clothes wash, Reyna. Nice to meet you, James."

"Don't be a stranger, Franklin," Reyna said, cocking her head seductively. "*Please* come and see me sometime, will you?"

"Sure, I'd like that. See ya around." He escaped into the little hallway that took him to the stairs up to the ground floor. To himself he muttered, "Crazy damn born-agains."

Sometimes he found copies of *The Watchtower* left on the laundry room's folding tables or pinned to the cork bulletin board, but he figured Reyna and her family were into something different from that. Whatever it was, he didn't want to know. Despite his efforts as a younger man to learn what it was his own parents had been involved in, lately the more gauzy scraps he thought he remembered of his boyhood the less he wanted to remember.

He wondered how Reyna had sniffed those traces in him. Was she sensitive to some nervous vibration he didn't even realize he generated?

He sat in his apartment channel-surfing and almost dozing off. When a half hour had elapsed he went back downstairs to switch his clothing to the dryers for an hour. He dreaded finding Reyna and James still there, but they weren't. Their own machines were still running. He hoped to get his business done and dash out of there again before they returned. However easy on the eyes Reyna was, he had had enough of her talk of family and changing the world.

As he pulled his damp load out of the second machine he had filled, he found an item among his clothing that he had not put in there himself. Slick, black, and heavy as the flayed skin of some sea creature, he recognized it as one of the hooded black robes that he had watched Reyna load into her own machine. He knew its presence was no accident. He understood she had sneaked it into his machine as a playful gesture of invitation.

"Fuck that," Franklin said, and he tossed the robe into one of her two empty, waiting baskets before he left the basement.

A loud scraping sound caused Franklin to jolt up straight on the sofa, to the realization he had fallen asleep waiting for his clothes to finish in the dryers three floors below him. The TV, his only constant companion, was playing a nature program. A chambered nautilus, spiraled like a symbol for infinity, hovered above the carcass of a lobster, upon which it was feeding. The TV's soft murmur explained that a nautilus could have up to ninety tentacles.

Maybe the narration had gotten into and influenced his sleeping mind, because he had been dreaming that his mother was showing him pictures in a great old book spread open in her lap. Though her face and hands were crisped charcoal black, and only smoldering wisps of hair remained on her peeling head, her eyes were undamaged and shone at him both dark and bright at once. She smiled with motherly gentleness at the five-year-old Franklin and pointed to an illustration of a seated creature or entity with a bulbous head bearing three eyes on either side, and many long tentacles where a nose and mouth would be in a human. His mother had been saying to him, "The more voices that sing together, the wider the doors will open. You have to learn to sing with us, baby. Soon you'll be singing, too."

The rumbling scrape he had heard had sounded like a piano or something else heavy being dragged across a floor. It had already stopped, so he couldn't be sure if the noise had come from the apartment directly above his own, where Reyna and her "family" lived, or from another location upstairs.

On top of being startled from his dream, he had awakened with one of his headaches in place, having seemingly slipped in like an intruder while his defenses were down.

He looked at the time. Almost midnight. His clothes would have finished drying almost an hour ago. And him having to be up at six in the morning to prepare for work. Startling noises, nightmares, and a headache. He grumbled a string of assorted profanities and pulled himself up from the sofa. At least it was unlikely he'd be running into Reyna and James at this hour in the laundry room, and he embarked for it.

Franklin found his warm clothes all neatly folded and stacked high in his laundry basket. Feeling more irritated than grateful, he hoisted the basket against his belly and carried it up all the flights of stairs to his third-floor apartment. Having set it down, he unlocked his door, shoved the basket inside, then paused at his threshold to tilt his head a little and listen, like a dog that appears to hear the sound of a ghost its master cannot see.

He hadn't heard another sound from upstairs, but just now he had seemed to *feel* a lingering echo of sound ploughed into the air like a scar.

He closed the door to 9C again and crossed to the other side of the hallway—to the metal door that led to the back stairs. The most direct route to the fourth and topmost floor of this unit of Trinity Village Apartments. He figured once he mounted the stairs he could crack the door a little and peek out, to satisfy the itch of curiosity. Though maybe curiosity was too benign a word for what he was feeling. It was more like a magnetic attraction, though there was nothing pleasurable in the sensation. If anything, his attraction to Reyna, up there, had quickly turned to an almost unaccountable repulsion. And yet, even now as his hand closed on the door handle she rose up in his mind's eye, smiling as if to giggle in that way of hers, the total eclipse of her eyes beckoning like those of a siren.

Having hauled the back stairs door open, he found the stairwell to be completely unlit. Where it spiraled down to the lower stories it was like a gaping well with no discernible bottom. He could imagine the light being out on one floor, but on all of them? Perhaps a circuit breaker pertaining to this portion of the building had been tripped. He held the door open so it wouldn't automatically close on its pneumatic cylinder, the light from behind him all that entered the shaft. He questioned whether it was worth feeling his way up in complete darkness to the next floor. Maybe he could wedge this door open, first?

Then, looking up, he noticed at last that it wasn't just darkness that lay at the top of the stairs leading to the fourth floor. The steps came to an abrupt end at a solid ceiling, with no opening through which to enter the level above.

Franklin recalled then, from helping the apparently senile old woman locate her apartment, that on the fourth floor the exit to the back stairs had been situated in that little space around the corner, not aligned with the rest of the doors in this stairwell. So there had to be another flight of steps behind the top floor's exit ... but if so, where did they come out? And why build these steps here only to terminate at a ceiling? Either the building had been poorly designed or its owners had deviated from the original layout at some point. Then again, he hadn't opened the metal door on the top floor. It could be that, in spite of being labeled *EXIT*, it didn't open onto stairs at all.

In the four years he'd lived at Trinity Village, he'd never had occasion to go up to the fourth floor until he'd aided that woman, but he must have descended this back stairwell at least a couple of times, for some reason or another. Why couldn't he recall if that were true? Was the increasing pain of his headache muddying his memory? If he had used it, he asked himself, wouldn't he have previously noticed the anomalous staircase that dead-ended at the ceiling?

From beyond the black pool of the ceiling he heard a teased-out, complaining creak. It was more than the sound a foot would make depressing a weakened section of flooring. More like the straining sound the mast of a wooden ship would make as that vessel listed on the swells of an approaching storm. Only the building settling in the stillness of night? Nevertheless, when the creak had subsided he realized an electric shiver of gooseflesh had flowed down his arms, and his headache had ratcheted up a notch.

Perplexed and unsettled almost to the point of disorientation, he let the door close and turned to gaze down the third floor's hallway toward the door to the front stairs at its far end. A moment later he was moving in that direction, like a drunken man trudging foggily in search of his way back home.

This stairwell was fully lit, and he crept up its steps quietly, as though he were a spy stealing up on an enemy encampment.

The fourth-floor hallway stretched out before him like a tunnel, as if he held the cardboard tube from a roll of paper towels to his eye like a child's pretend telescope. As he started forward, something odd about the corridor finally registered. The doors on its right side appeared to be spaced at least twice as far apart from each other as were the doors on the left side of the hallway, although he knew there would be five apartments behind either wall. He paused to turn and read the number on the door nearest to him on the right. 4D. He glanced behind him at 2D.

Once again he advanced along the corridor. At its terminus, on the left was the door to 9D. Reyna's place. Opposite that: the bend in the hallway, from this angle filled with shadow like the opening to a little cave.

After 4D there was only one more door before the sharp turn of the corner. It was 6D. No, there was no mistaking that the blank spaces between the doors on the right stretched much wider than those of the opposing wall. How could he have not noticed this the first time he'd been up here? Too distracted by helping the old woman with her cart?

Franklin reached the end of the hallway, and briefly regarded the closed and silent door labeled 9D before turning his full attention to the bend in the hallway, which he recognized deep inside was the source of the magnetic pull that had impelled him.

As if it had been holding off for him to face it directly, crouched back in the shadows of the corner space waiting to spring out at him like a jack-in-the-box, that same stench that was something like burnt fish but in the end wholly indescribable assailed him with the force of collision. He leaned forward, belly seizing, and rasped out a long, dry retch. His headache rocketed in enormity, and a ball of silently sizzling purple-black light materialized in front of his eyes.

Nevertheless, he couldn't take his gaze off the narrow side hallway that lay before him.

Three doors lined its right-hand side: the doors to apartments 8D and 10D followed by the metal door labeled *EXIT*. Part of his mind protested that he was certain the last time there had only been two doors in this wall ... that 8D had been the last of the doors *before* the bend...but he was unable to grapple with that thought directly. What gripped his attention more forcefully than the unknown stink or the mystery of the doors or the seething purplish light superimposed over his vision was the physical properties of the hallway itself. Not just its ceiling but the walls themselves now appeared to be constructed out of a confluence of angles so unlikely, perhaps even so impossible, that it pained his mind to view them let alone attempt to contemplate them. It was as though the dark matter of the universe, no man-made material bound by terrestrial law, had been utilized in fashioning this space before him. Angles that were folded and pleated, colliding yet intersecting, tortured and broken and brilliantly mended all wrong... not only in defiance of geometry but in perversion of it.

And somehow, those three prosaic doors still stood amid the chaos of converging planes. But the hallway no longer appeared to end after the last metal door. No ... it seemed to go on and on, funneling toward or *from* a blackness infinite and absolute. And the purple blob of light did not, in fact, float as an illusion within his eyes. It hovered outside of him, apart from him, there at the threshold of the black void beyond the door marked *EXIT*.

He heard a soft thumping, and a weak voice—the voice of an elderly woman—crying out, *"Help me! Help me!"* As near as a door away. As remote as another dimension away.

"The doors are almost open now, Franklin," said someone behind him. The voice was gentle and familiar. His mother's?

"Right, almost open," James repeated, also behind him.

"Add your voice to ours," Reyna went on. Her tone became exultant. "It's time!"

Franklin spun away without looking back at her, almost blinded by his headache anyway, only peripherally aware that Reyna and James were dressed in their freshly laundered black hooded robes. Having wrenched himself free of the magnetic grip, he surged away from it mind and body, racing wildly back down the fourth floor's hallway. He was whimpering, his throat seared raw by his one dry heave. Reyna seemed to be calling after him but he couldn't hear her over his pounding footfalls ... or maybe his mind *wouldn't* hear her. Maybe he was blocking her the way he had walled up the memories of his childhood all these years, as the deprogrammer had directed him to do.

He threw open the door to the front stairwell and thundered down its steps, the sound reverberating hollowly in the shaft formed of cinderblocks. One of his rubber flip-flops folded under his foot at one point and he almost tripped, almost pitched forward down the stairs, but fortunately he had hold of the handrail. Down one flight, then plummeting down the next, wheezing through his burned throat, waiting to hear the door at the uppermost landing squeal open and footsteps coming in pursuit, but so far there was nothing but his own noisy descent.

He had to get out of this building before the contamination spread further. Before it closed around him like a trap, and there were no doors but the doors that Reyna's family conjured.

As he descended, multiple tears began to open in the walls of the fortress the deprogrammer had helped him erect in his mind decades earlier. He remembered now, cloudily, how the deprogrammer had taught him to visualize the building of this structure, then once it was built had taught him not to be aware of its existence, like a desert stronghold lost under the sand dunes. Yet the breaches opening and widening in it now weren't so much random rips or cracks as portals unfolding open in complex ways like the flaps of a paper fortune-teller. As he envisioned the unburied memory fortress, against his will, he saw horrible purple-lighted faces outside these new openings, staring in at him. If faces they could be called. Each alien visage more horribly incomprehensible than the last. He could visualize these faces because his mother had instructed him even more indelibly than the deprogrammer. She had shown him these faces in books.

Still, even as these images welled up vividly from the depths of his unconscious, with the last dregs of his self-control he managed to keep his feet moving rapidly under him. As if he might actually be able to flee from himself.

In his blind panic, plunging down one staircase after another, he didn't realize he had gone beyond the ground floor with its front entrance to the building until he found himself in the hallway outside the laundry room. Rather than backtrack, he decided in an instant to follow through with his momentum, and he lunged through the laundry room's doorway.

At the end of the room was that little corner, and around its ninety-degree angle the fire exit door that locked from the outside, but which residents liked to prop open so they could stand out by the side of Unit 3 smoking while they waited for their clothing to wash or dry.

Franklin bolted across the room, skidded to a stop in front of the corner where the metal door stenciled *EXIT* should have been but wasn't, and straightened up frozen in place as if he had been pinned by the purple beacon of light that shone on him. That unearthly glow was rushing toward him through an infinitely long black tunnel, like the light on the face of an approaching train. Its onrushing wind blasted his face, as did the terrible stench driven before it.

Franklin opened his mouth wide and screamed, screamed, riveted there as the wind and stench strengthened and the purple-black light hurtled closer and closer. His screams, though, seemingly on their own morphed into the shouted words of a chant in a language other than English.

His mother had taught him these words from a book, long ago. He had never forgotten them.

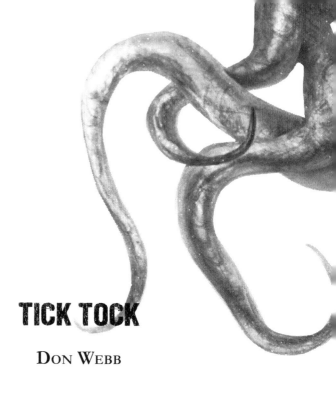

TICK TOCK

DON WEBB

If any humans had lived on in any meaningful way past the Night, John Cardenas' life trajectory would be seen as ironic. John failed out of the University of Texas twenty years ago. He has worked as an exterminator, apartment-leasing agent, vending-machine stocker and product demonstrator, and for the last four years for Eye-in-the-Sky. If you listened to late-night AM radio or to certain podcasts you've heard of Eye-in-the-Sky. If you visited their webpage with its bright purple eye above the pyramid design floating atop a silver saucer and read the free newsfeed, you would be up to date on excavations of giant skeletons, proof that we are living in a computer simulation, or the Big Foot love commune in Arkansas. Of course, for a few dollars more, you could subscribe and find out the REAL TRUTH THAT THE GOVERNMENT DOESN'T WANT YOU TO KNOW. Mainly this was about the plan to take away your guns, the tax on the Internet, and what really goes on in Area 51. This lively feed of the wacky, the scary and the plain untrue was largely John's work. He got to work from his North Austin apartment, he had a poker game once a week with five friends (of assorted races and sexes), and he had a newer car. He had benefits. It was a great job. Heck, he had basically done this job for free years before there was even an Internet. He had run a BBS called Shaved Truths that people with early PCs and external modems would call up to read paranormal news. Getting to be a "reporter" for Eye-in-the-Sky was the answer to a prayer. Not that John prayed. He had evidence that "god" was a meme created by the Babylonian elite to subjugate the masses. But for all of John's friends, it was a great fit.

He got out of bed about nine-thirty in the morning. He checked the Eye-in-the-Sky Facebook page, making quips at last night's posters. He read some of the better paranormal pages like Church of Mabus and Shaver Tron and shared their cooler stories. Then about ten, after his bowl of Applejacks, he began the day's "research." He looked at Fortean sites and occult sites and conspiracy sites. He checked Google News every hour. If he found something about the government it went into the paid feed; other stuff went into the free feed. He had lunch at one—always a large vanilla milkshake and a Spicy McChicken sandwich from the McDonalds three blocks away. He took a multi-vitamin and 2000 units of Vitamin D. At three he checked Facebook, tweeted some stories that he put on the site, and took a little nap. At six he wrote up whatever was interesting to him. He read books on cognition, world history, media theory, the occult, and the history of UFO sightings. He also read the classic paranormal writers—Fort, John Keel, Amos Carter, Pauwels and Steiger. He could handle dry academic stuff and mix it well with speculation from the '50s and '60s. On Sundays he called his mom in Flapjack, TX (English), and his grandmother in Mexico City (Spanish). He had a stable and uninteresting life despite the contents of his mind and his odd niche profession. Yet, without the aid of ancient texts, special training, or unusual genetics … he was one of the few hundred humans, whom in their own quirky ways, Opened the Gate.

John hosted the poker night at his apartment every other Thursday. On nights when he didn't he drove or walked about fifteen blocks to Don Bowen's small stucco home in the St. Johns' neighborhood. In the summer he walked. Don operated a small used bookstore out of his home, called Libby's Used Books. It used to belong to a man named Libby and be in a strip mall. It was one of the few used paperback stores in business. Don also rented out his garage apartment. He had inherited the house from his mom, and his expenses were low. He was John's supplier of old paranormal paperbacks. One night as John drove there, he had a funny scare. John was waiting at a light at the corner of two major streets, his car next to a large concrete storm drain. A piece of shiny Mylar (possibly from a balloon) blew into the drain. The silver caught the light from John's headlights. *Flash!* And it startled him. He almost jumped. He drove on to the poker game and expounded on the incident.

"It scared me because I never look down and to the right when I'm driving. I mean I have driven past that storm drain almost every day for eight or nine years. I never see it—especially if the street's dry and there is no rain going on. The drain could be the entrance to the world of Richard Shaver's deros, or the Xibalba of my Mayan ancestors."

John had decided he was Mayan in 2012. He didn't look very Mayan. Just a plump thirty-five-year-old Mexican-American with a thrift-store aesthetic.

"Or," said Don, "A storm drain."

"The point," John continued, "Is that the real unknown could be right under our noses and we would never know. Maybe we shouldn't be watching the skies or looking for government conspiracies. Maybe we should be looking at storm drains."

Phillip Blassingame, another poker player, said, "That would make your website a lot less fun—'The Daily Storm Drain Watch'—today a black and white tomcat was seen entering the drain about midnight. Is it a dero spy?"

"That's not what I mean," said John, "I don't mean that the drain is the entrance to another world. I think fear might be. A sudden flash of fear instead of the invisibility of the storm drain. You ever read about how the Aztec shamans couldn't see Cortez's ships?"

Mary Machworter shook her head.

"Supposedly," said John, "Back me up Don, supposedly as the ships sailed up to Mexico, the shamans knew something was up, but they literally couldn't see the ships because they had no scanning pattern for them. When the ships arrived with their cargo of white men and *horses*, for god's sake, they still couldn't quite make them out. "

"I'd read the story," said Don, "It's called "Inattentional Blindness"— look at that YouTube clip where they tell you to watch the basketball and you don't see the gorilla walk by."

"Yeah," said John, "Except I'm saying that the gorilla can't interact with you because you don't see it. What if fear opened a channel? What if it took down another brick in the wall?" He tried to make it sound like the Pink Floyd song.

Mary shook her head again, "But wouldn't that be a bad idea? Isn't better we don't interact with the gorilla?"

"Maybe the gorilla is the Bringer of Ecstasy," said John, "Maybe that's what he's waiting to do."

Don asked, "So what's your plan? Scare some people with a storm drain and hope God shows up?"

Which, in fact, was John's plan. He wrote it up on Eye-In-The-Sky as an "Experiment in Terror." He would draw people's attention to a hitherto-unnoticed object, and see what happened. He bought an Iron Man mask at the Dollar Store, and wedged it in the storm drain. It was shiny, and for the car parked in the right-hand lane, just visible as a face by headlight. It was far enough back to be a mysterious object. You could see a shiny face in the shadow. He took some photos of the mask, the mask by car headlight, and posted his theories. He parked his car on the cross street. He watched for hours. A couple of cars—once the passenger, once a driver - spotted the mask. But that meant nothing. He asked Don to ask his customers if they had seen anything weird in the neighborhood. He asked Phillip, Don's tenant in the garage apartment, to ask folks in the neighborhood if they saw anything weird. Nothing happened. Then a thunderstorm came, and the mask was washed down the drain. Oh well, as many people had said on Facebook, it was a badly designed experiment.

Two months later when a light rain had once again caused John to take his car, the mask was back. Or at least a mask. Or at least a shiny face. John decided that he would examine it tomorrow or at least the first day without rain, which proved to be Saturday. No mask. Well that was odd. Then a week later and weather caused another car trip. There it was. It looked to be a different mask. There was something odd about its proportions. The following day he went to snap a picture for his blog. No mask. Was someone putting it there at night? Some reader of his page, or a prankster following his own prank? He walked over that night with a flashlight. He couldn't just lie on the street and look in lest oncoming traffic roll over him, so he lay upon the top of the drain and leaned over. Three cars honked at him, and one driver shouted abuse. He could see the mask was much further in the drain than before. Perhaps tools had been used to push it in. Also it didn't look quite right; perhaps it was a different mask? Something was written in a fairly shaky hand near the mask. John first thought it was a magical inscription in some eldritch rune, but it turned out to be the words *"Thank You"* followed by another word obscured under the mask. He tried to get some good photos, but nothing useable could be made because of the odd angles involved. He talked with Don and Mary, and they drove by and looked at it, and Don suggested parking his car at the intersection and then using it as a shield from traffic, shooting some photos. Mary reminded him to put his hood up and put his blinkers on for extra safety. He did that the next night. The mask had moved slightly: the inscription now read, "*Thank You John.*" John's first hypothesis (after fifteen seconds of Wonder and Fear) was that one of the poker buddies had done this. He had not mentioned the location of his experiment on his blog—and it would be very hard to figure out what storm drain from the picture he had used. He texted his friends, "Haw Haw!" but none of them took credit.

And so weeks went by. John spotted the mask a few times, but the mystery was gone. Besides, he had been really busy. Weirdness seemed to be happening all over. There were bell sounds and booms off the Atlantic coast, the slime falls on those cultists in Argentina, and a nerd group claimed that pi was changing, Europa seemed to be leaving orbit, a massive something-or-other had been seen in the Arctic, there were Pacific earthquakes.... For the first time ever, the "fun" aspect of his job was slipping away. He had never believed all of it; heck, maybe not even most of it. He did believe that mainstream politics concealed a good deal of stuff, that mainstream science was spotty, and that humans didn't really have a decent grasp of metaphysics. He was beginning to wonder what to believe. Not in the sense of his clients, who could "believe" in Bigfoot, ESP, UFOs, the Trilateral Commission.... No. What to believe in like relativity, politics, love, good, and evil. The center had ceased to hold. He was even thinking of getting a real job and forswearing paranormal studies. Did posting reprints of John Kincaid's article "Was Bigfoot Lincoln's Father?" help anyone? Had he moved *homo saps* one centimeter closer to the Truth? Or was he the underpaid projectionist of a one-star B-movie in Plato's cave? John was in something of a spasm of self-hate as the light caught him at his storm drain. There were wreaths and candles—lit candles—on the drain. Objects of worship? Thanksgiving? Had there been an accident there, or was it connected in a sick way with the Iron Man mask? He turned on St. John's and pulled his car into a Texan market parking lot. He walked the half-block to the drain. There was a wreath of blue and white artificial flowers, three small white candles in jars, and in chalk in big letters—*THANK YOU JOHN CARDENAS*. He bent down to pick up the wreath. When he touched it a strong shock, not exactly electrical, not anything he had a name for, ran through him. He flinched and nearly fell. He could hear a bell in the distance, or was it a bark? A bell-like cry. For no clear reason he thought a very clear thought, "the cosmic alarm clock." He pulled out his phone to snap some pictures, and then put it aside in disgust. This was the problem. Focusing on this instead of education in Texas or the garbage island in the Pacific Ocean. If you divert all of human attention, all of human intent, away from mankind, you will break the center. All of the hatred and divisiveness in American politics. All of the decline of a civil civilization increased with more and more News of the Weird. He took the wreath back to his car. He was going to toss it on the green folding table they played poker on. As he drove the remaining eight blocks to Don's house, he had another clear thought—none of his friends did this. Logic might point to his friends gaslighting him, but this was beyond logic. This was the very crack he had meant to cause. Not with the damn Iron Man mask—with all of it—with eighteen years of focusing on the paranormal. He could still hear the bell. It was getting louder.

He parked in front of Don's house. He left the wreath on his passenger-side seat. Don was standing behind his screen door; the lights were on in his front room. Don looked worried.

Don spoke as John walked up the cracked narrow sidewalk to his two-step cement porch. "I've got troubles. Your kind of trouble." There was some anger in the possessive pronoun "your."

John already felt defensive, "Yeah? What kind of trouble?"

Don opened the door, "Come in. I'm sorry. I'm scared. I called off the game, but I didn't call you because I wanted you to come over. Come in."

As John walked in, Don took him by the collar and pushed him past the bookstore rooms to the tiny, greasy kitchen in the back. Several of the books had been pulled from the shelves, and something black seemed to be squirming under them. When John tried to stop and look at the strange scene, Don pushed him harder. The kitchen had had new green linoleum in Don's mother's day. Now it was shiny and mainly gray. There was a small kitchen table which once had false wood-grain, but now was brown with years of cheap furniture polish. Don had opened two beers, and he had chips and salsa ready on the little table. "Take a load off."

John pulled up one of the plastic-backed chairs. "So what problem you got?"

Don said, "I don't want you reporting this. I don't want to see it on your Facebook page. I don't want it on Twitter. Got that?"

"Sure, sure. What's happening?"

Don pulled up his own chair. For the next twenty minutes Don rambled on about the brightening of the Pleiades, the mass deaths of men in Tibet, the South Pole aurora phenomena, and the increase in coma cases. John had heard of most of these; in fact, he had blogged about most of them. He had no idea what his friend was getting at. He tried to interrupt, to share his new truth that it wasn't right or good or healthy to spend all of one's attention on such things. But Don went on and on, sometimes mentioning his reading habits as a boy and a young man. Finally he said, "You see, I never believed any of it. I saw how there was more weirdness every year, but I thought that was because there was simply a need for it. Now it's breaking."

John asked, "What's breaking?"

Don said, "Reality. Reality is broken. We can go in my front room, and I can show you where it broke. Well, a local crack, anyway. The break on this block. The Return of the Old Ones."

"What does that mean?"

"If I cover this table, my mom's old 'breakfast nook' table from Sears, with a newspaper, what do you see?"

"A newspaper?" asked John.

Don nodded as if encouraging a simple child. "No. You don't see a newspaper. You see stories: Governor said this, the President said that, the Pope said another thing. Two stars are getting a divorce. An embarrassing crime by a celebrity. Unrest in the Middle East. A sale at Jerod's. What do you not see?"

John ventured, "The table?"

Don smiled, "Right. But the table is older and bigger than the news. Mom bought this table in 1969. Dad spread his newspaper on it every day at breakfast. Then Mom did so after his death. Then when I got the house I kept my PC here and read the news. Stories about millions of humans for decades come and go, but the table remains. Now I read my news on my phone most days. So what can I see now?"

"The table."

"As a species we are beginning to see the table. And it ain't from Sears, and it ain't made for humans. It's older and bigger. Now I can show you the front room."

"Before you show me, can I ask you something?"

"Sure."

"On the way over here I started to hear this bell-like sound. Can you hear that?"

Don looked truly sad. "No, my apocalypse has no bells and whistles."

John followed him into the front room. Big bookshelves from Libby's Used Books dominated the front room. John knew that Don still had drop-in customers, although most of the business was online. The room had hardwood floors, Red Oak #3. Many of the books from the Science Fiction section were piled on the floor. Occult and "Metaphysical" likewise. The books moved up and down slowly, they were covering up living creatures. Don knelt down by the biggest pile. "Look!" he said, raising a handful of paperbacks.

On the floor were two black wet-looking creatures like a cross between a horned toad and an earthworm; they writhed as though in pain. "Look!" he said again. He took his right index finger and pushed through the flesh of one of the beasts. It had the consistency of pudding. A small part of the creature was easily scooped up. It was a homogenous blackness—no internal organs or bones. He flicked the nastiness off his finger, like a man gets rid of a booger. It flicked away and when it hit the floor reshaped itself into a tiny replica of the creature it had been sampled from. It scurried toward its parent, which promptly ate it. Then Don grabbed some of the books, "Look!" he said for a third time.

He fanned the books in front of John. The pages were blank. Old and yellowed but blank. No, that wasn't quite accurate; the front matter, the copyright notices and so forth were intact.

Don's voice began slow and even but broke as he said, "It started two days ago. Some of the books began sweating ink. At first I thought it was humidity; remember that killer fog we had Monday morning? Oh, that's right; you sleep then. At first I thought it was these two Lovecraft paperbacks. They're side by side (or they were). But then I noticed other books. All of my Lovecraft, my Ramsey Campbell, some Stephen King, all of my Phil Dick. Then a few books in the Metaphysical section: *UFOs in Colonial America* by Amos Carter, *The Mothman Prophecies* by John Keel. All my Charles Fort. Then some of my mythology books, an advanced math book I was holding for Phillip. I had no idea what to do, as you can see the books are worthless now. A few other dealers had the same problem. With the *same* titles."

John advised his friend to breathe.

"So," asked John, "Why didn't you report this?"

"I called up KEYE and they put me on hold and I played on my computer. I read the news. Did you know pi is changing? That's like a prime number missing, for god's sake. There are rumors that some of the dead are returning in Tibet, or that the rash of comas in Australia is much bigger than CNN says. In the face of that weirdness I'm going to report, 'strange paperbacks are losing their ink.'?"

"But the creatures," said John.

"They formed yesterday. Last night one of them crawled on my face while I was sleeping. I don't know if it was exploring me, moving mindlessly, or seeking to enter my brain. "

"We need to get you out of here. You can stay at my place."

"Oh, really? How many of these titles do you own?" Don broke into hysterical laughter.

"OK. OK. Let's get calm. We can get away from this. There's a Motel Six not too far from here. We'll go there, spend the night, and figure this out tomorrow."

"OK," said Don.

They went out to the car.

"What's this?" asked Don picking up the wreath.

"That's nothing. That's some trash I found. It has nothing to do with this," John lied. The ringing sound had grown more intense. John switched the radio on, picking an all-music FM station. Classic Rock will banish anything for a few minutes. It was ten minutes to the hotel. They had agreed not to watch the news.

Despite the level of fear, Don went to a snoring peacefulness quickly. John lay in the other bed thinking that he could do something. If he had helped crack reality, he could do something. He knew he wouldn't fall asleep. And then he was under.

He dreamed of sleeping in his own bed. Seven little men came in his room. Dwarves all wearing Iron Man costumes. They surrounded his bed, singing "Heigh Ho! Heigh Ho!" He couldn't move, but he could talk with them.

"Who are you?"

"Tough one to answer in your language John. We kind of liked your friend's label. The Old Ones. We have been around longer than you people. Anyway we're here to say thanks."

"That's it? You're just seven little men?"

"Then that would make you Sleeping Beauty." There was more than a passing sexual hint there.

"I don't believe you," said John very firmly.

"More to the point, you have ceased to disbelieve in us. We seven have always been here. Oh we're small potatoes, that's why we could come through a crack as small as you made. See, we're even a little human-looking—because we've been standing near the Barrier so long. We're not like the big things moving certain moons, or even the Door in the South. We're human enough to want to thank you for tearing the newspaper away. In a sense we're human enough to be sorry for what's about to happen in the motel room with you and your friend."

John woke, covered in sweat. Don still snored peacefully. It was all a dream.

Then John realized that there were seven little men standing in the room. At their feet writhed four of the spiked ink-worms. And like so many thousand, thousand humans in that hour, John screamed. Don woke and turned on the light by the bed. He started to laugh at the kids in their Iron Man costumes, but the seven little men took off their masks.

They weren't really human. Not. At. All.

for Joe Pulver

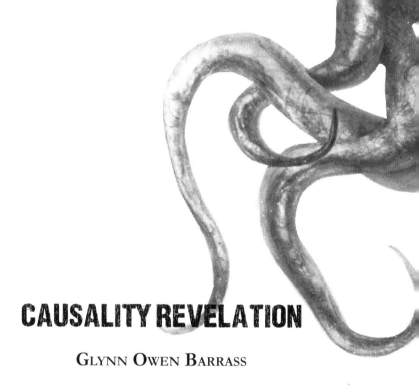

CAUSALITY REVELATION

Glynn Owen Barrass

Now

I failed her, the only one I ever cared about.

The streets were in chaos, the people fighting, screaming, while some took part in clumsy, demented orgies. The sky, Lloyd didn't like looking there, for the things that hovered and flew in that clear blue space were terrible upon the eye, and the mind.

He made space around a group of women engaged in kicking another to death and turned the corner onto his street, which thankfully was mostly clear of people. One wandering, confused soul, however, was a man he recognized: his neighbor Suliman.

Lloyd grimaced. *Damn, he's noticed me.*

The small olive-skinned man approached him with a panicked expression on his face. "The sky ... do you see angels?"

Lloyd tried stepping past him, but Suliman raised his arms, blocking his way.

"Why are they taking us, when only Allah tells them what to do? Are we being punished?"

Angels to some, Lloyd thought, and held back uneasy laughter.

Suliman's arms dropped and he turned away from Lloyd,

babbling in Arabic as he approached a car moving down the street.

With a shake of his head, Lloyd quickly took the final few meters to his house.

He heard a squeal of brakes and Suliman scream as he unlocked the door, but he slammed it closed without looking back. If his neighbor was dead, well, there were worse ways to go.

He rushed through the shadowy lounge to take the stairs beside the kitchen door three steps at the time, panting from the quick exertion as he reached the top. Straight ahead stood his bedroom door, Lloyd walking in without taking the usual time to prepare himself.

Sarah hadn't moved from the bed—the bonds he'd made with the ropes tight and unyielding, but she *moved* regardless, in ways quite impossible for a human being.

"Please just stay still," he begged, but she continued to squirm incessantly, fighting against the rope wrapped around her and the bed. Her movements weren't limited to her limbs, however, for the bare flesh of her legs, arms and face warped, expanding and contracting, her limbs and digits twisting in odd places. Her face was the worst. There the Program had had more to work with. Her rolling eyes wriggled around her face, her eyeballs expanding and contracting in random, alien movements. Sarah's mouth, when it wasn't disappearing and appearing elsewhere on her body, sometimes expanded so much it covered her whole face, a hungry, gaping maw that gibbered silently for release.

"Do I kill her?" he asked aloud, and wondered whether that would even work.

And I did this to her, transformed her into this travesty of life, her and the rest of humanity.

Seven Days Earlier

His wife, Sarah, sat channel-hopping, found it on BBC News. She put down the remote and watched avidly as the newsreader talked about the Internet phenomenon taking over website after website after its initial infestation of YouTube. From the other side of the room, he paused his current typing at his PC and watched the interaction, Sarah on the couch the receiver, and the television facing her the transmitter. He smiled grimly, with just a little pride.

Lloyd and an army of fellow acolytes across the globe had programmed Webdriver Torso piece by piece over many months before unleashing it. Code through dreams and visions, sent by a dreaming god. His smile grew as he listened to the television.

"Webdriver Torso, as most viewers will know, began as seemingly pointless eleven-second clips, all showing a series of blue and red rectangles, that were uploaded in their thousands to YouTube."

Pointless. He laughed and Sarah looked his way. Long, red center-parted hair, big blue eyes, round face. She smiled and returned her gaze to the television.

"—and each of the almost-hundred thousand clips, uploaded over a six-month period, follow the same pattern—ten slides, each with a red rectangle, a blue rectangle, and a computer-generated tone. There have been a variety of theories postulated, including one that the videos are a signal from aliens, or a digital version of spies' numbers stations, like the ones used during the Cold War to decode messages. Another outlandish theory is that it's a rogue artificial intelligence, spreading itself virally. Now that the clips have begun migrating onto other websites, replacing the clips already there, that theory is looking more and more like a reality. We now go to the BBC's technical expert, Stephen Becker, to discuss this phenomenon and talk about how the spread can be stopped."

It can't, Lloyd thought, and standing, walked over to the couch. He leaned down and kissed Sarah on the head. "I'm going for a walk, hon."

She turned, took his head in her hands and kissed him heavily on the lips. "Tea at seven," she said with a smile.

"Oh I'll be back before then," he replied and walked around the couch, taking his jacket and baseball cap from the hooks on the wall beside the front door.

"Later, baby," Sarah said as he left the house.

All going according to plan. Closing the door behind him, he stepped onto the pavement and examined his street. The sky was darkening just past sunset, the street quiet except for a few children playing around at the other end. He turned right, passing a few of the neighbors' terraced houses until he reached a junction. Lloyd paused there, looked around for traffic, and crossed the road. More terraced houses followed, the sounds of televisions vibrating through the windows making him wonder if they were watching the news like Sarah.

Soon he would have to do something with her, something drastic, for when the Program went full-exposure, he couldn't hope to stop her watching it with words. *Tie her up? Crude, but probably necessary.* He'd feed her, keep her clean, and explain it all when things were over. Reaching the end of the street, Lloyd approached and entered an area of wasteland, covered in the foundations of demolished houses gone to nature.

Walking through the grass, weeds, and stony foundations, he inhaled heavily, enjoying the scents of Mother Nature—a rare commodity in a town of bricks and concrete. He stopped, closed his eyes, and—

Thick fog permeated the air around him, damp and smelling of the sea. He turned, examined his new surroundings, and saw nothing but white in every direction. It reminded him of school, his first days there as a teenager, standing alone on the field and staring out at the swirling mist. Walking into it, he'd imagine it led to a different world, one devoid of discipline and rules.

"You're there again." The voice made him jump, but he knew he should've expected her.

He turned around to face a black silhouette in the mist, a silhouette that spoke with a strange yet beautiful humming voice.

"I was thinking about the past, and escape."

She nodded, a barely perceptible movement. As he had done before, he stepped forward to try and discern some features in her darkness. They were there, but shifting, moving so fast that they were in a constant state of flux. She raised her hand and he accepted it, a tingle of electricity shooting up his arm as they walked through the fog.

"How is the plan progressing?" she asked, and the tingling grew stronger, beginning to shake his hand.

"All good. My contact says infection is up to nine million computers in the UK alone. It's all over the news."

"All good," she repeated, and swayed her arm happily like a child.

They continued through the white world in silence, broken when a large, humped object appeared before them.

His companion said, "Ah."

Lloyd turned, looked at the shifting face and thought he detected a smile there.

"This is Cthulhu," she said. "Go; look," she added, and released his hand.

He stepped forward eagerly through the fog. As he walked it billowed and parted, giving him a clearer view of what he discovered was a bronze statue set upon a rectangular pedestal of malachite. The verdigris-spotted shape was humanoid and sat crouched upon its haunches. Its face, however, was far from human. Instead, it resembled an octopus with large, bulging eyes upon its swollen head. Its hands and feet terminated in claws, the former gripping its knees. Lloyd walked around it, and saw upon its humped back a pair of small dragon wings.

"This is the future, a world for the chosen," the silhouette said. "Two years from now. Why, you even helped construct this yourself."

"How … how can this be?" Lloyd asked.

"How are you here? You would call it a wormhole, an Einstein-Rosen bridge. We used it to reach you and the other acolytes in the beginning."

Lloyd smiled and laid a hand on the statue. It felt incredibly cold to the touch, so much so it began to burn, but he kept holding it, his anchor to a future he was helping to build.

"Tonight you start on a new phase," the silhouette said. "The infection must be brought to its peak if the Program is to remain on schedule."

He reluctantly removed his hand from the statue. "I want to see more of this world. Please, let me see it?"

The silhouette shook her head and said, "The future is still forming. Keep to the Program, and the mists, these mists," she raised her arms to indicate the white surrounding them, "will clear."

"What happened to your hand, honey?"

Lloyd was surprised at Sarah's observational skills; he'd gotten so much past her already. She stood over him as he typed away at the keyboard and he paused, examined the red mark on his right palm. "Maybe an insect bite, I think. A fly or some bug over at the wasteground earlier." He thought his lie was a good one, and it worked, for she replied, "Well there's some cream in the bathroom cabinet, and hey, don't work too late, will you?" She leaned over and kissed him. He felt her tongue and, getting the beginnings of an erection, pulled away and said, "I'll be half an hour, tops."

She kissed him on the forehead and headed for the stairs behind him. He heard her go up and enter the bedroom, and experienced a feeling of indecision. *Should I join her, or continue with the Webdriver Program?* It was a fleeting thought, the biological urge, for his responsibility to the Program had to come first. Ever since the visions started, two years earlier, first in his dreams and then in the strange, misty reality, he had lived for it.

Confident he wouldn't be disturbed, Lloyd closed the browser window he'd been looking at and reopened one in his bookmarks called 'Unlock Torrents.' The name was a lie, in fact; the link led him to a blank page with a box asking for two passwords. He typed those in and the window turned black before, in a small font, a list of other inductees to the Program scrolled down the screen.

There were users in Pakistan, the former USSR (these he knew, had been taking care of the macro viruses now filling electronic documents in computers worldwide), and users in America and the United Kingdom. The latter, him included, had been installing the boot sector viruses—particular files on unwitting users' hard drives that executed when they booted their computers.

With his mouse, he moved down the screen to the bottom left, clicked on an invisible icon, and brought up a list of the most recently infected users. Hundreds scrolled down the page, and some he saw, highlighted in red, were connected to news networks. Lloyd smiled. Quite soon, the networks would be fully infiltrated. Starting to type, he began the activation. The networks, as far as he had seen, had been silent about the virus attacking their own systems. Pretty soon, they wouldn't have a choice but to expose their infection.

Five Days Earlier

As Lloyd entered the house he found Sarah there to greet him with an excited expression on her face. She led him by the hand into the lounge before he even had the opportunity to remove his coat.

"You won't believe this," she said excitedly, and pointed at the television. A news channel was on, the newsreader, a well-dressed woman with short black hair and glasses, speaking seriously with a 'Breaking News' logo scrolling by beneath her.

"You just have to listen to this," Sarah continued, and having led him to the couch, sat down herself.

He followed suit and watched the news.

"They have been falling in the thousands," the newsreader said, "all across South America, with some isolated cases being reported in Mexico. The people, with no signs of previous symptoms, are being found in their beds unresponsive and, by most accounts, being described as being in a 'comatose state.'

"Argentina is apparently the worst hit by this mysterious illness, and we take you now to our correspondent there, Ryan Willis, who is present at an emergency conference held by the Center of Disease Control in Buenos Aires."

The scene changed to a harried-looking tanned man in a white shirt. His blond hair unruly, his shirt unbuttoned, he began speaking loudly but nervously into a microphone, trying to get his voice heard over the crowd surrounding him.

"… Willis," the man said mid-speech, "speaking to you from outside the Embassy of the United States. With the huge influx of comatose patients filling the hospitals of Argentina beyond their ability to find beds, and new victims being discovered hourly, the CDC has intervened with this impromptu conference. The representative, sorry, I don't know his name, is stepping up now."

The camera view moved from the correspondent to a sea of figures that stood facing a handful of men and women standing on large wooden blocks outside the embassy gates. It zoomed in on a tall, dark-skinned man dressed in a blue suit. His black hair was plastered to his head with sweat, and his expression was agitated.

"We will be taking questions later," he said into his microphone in a slightly accented voice, "but for now let me get a few things clear in regards to this emergency." He stopped, and a woman to his right translated what he had just said into Spanish.

"We are calling this a public health emergency, and have some instructions to give to you." The translator spoke again, then, "First of all I must address the rumors that have been circulating about this emergency being due to the spread of contaminated coca leaves, I—"

"Coca leaves?" Lloyd asked Sarah, and she looked at him with a wry smile. "Cocaine leaves," she replied.

"… no evidence of this, so I want to quell that rumor right now," the CDC spokesman continued. "Until we discover the cause of what we are tentatively calling an outbreak, I want to ask the people of Argentina to limit their contact with the afflicted and also, where possible, to limit their contact with large groups of people in enclosed spaces."

Cameras flashed as a roar of dissent rippled through the crowd. The translator tried to speak but was overwhelmed by angry voices.

The camera panned to the angry crowd then returned to the correspondent. More harried than before, his shirt's armpits and chest now bore dark patches. The man started speaking rapidly, but rather than listen, Lloyd leant back into the couch and put his arm around Sarah.

"Hey, someone's happy," she said, and he realized his mouth had formed a broad grin.

"Ah, I was just thinking about something I heard earlier," he lied.

It's spreading faster than I thought, Lloyd mused. His mood soured as he realized that now was the time to restrain Sarah.

"Hey," he said. "Let's go upstairs."

Sarah grinned and snuggled into him.

"Sounds like a plan," she replied.

Now

Lloyd sat with Sarah for as long as he could bear, mere minutes, before he found himself unable to look at, or hear, what was happening to her. He walked downstairs, found the remote control on the couch, and aiming it at the television, pressed the ON button.

It came on after a couple of seconds, a blue screen with a white box at its center displaying the words 'NO SIGNAL.' Checking through the channels revealed more of the same, and after going through twenty or so, he gave it up, tossing the remote back on to the couch.

A quick stride towards the PC, and Lloyd sat down, opening a browser window to Google.

The Internet works, but for how long? he thought and typed the words 'news headlines.' As expected, a list of the world's most recent horrors appeared onscreen.

'Coma virus' victims appear worldwide—States of Emergency called in over 70 countries.

Mass rioting in the USA as 'coma virus' victims walk.

'Coma walker' actions defy science—signals detected from human pylons—directed en masse to the South Pacific.

What is happening beneath the South Pacific Ocean?

All in the space of a week, no less than that, for the comatose across the world, those that had experienced heavy exposure to Webdriver Torso, had begun performing their part of the Program just a few days earlier.

Lloyd reread the fourth headline down. *What did happen beneath the South Pacific Ocean?* he wondered. *She'll know,* he told himself, *and she'll fix Sarah.*

Two Days Earlier

The instant Lloyd arrived home he went to watch television. He knew he should go see Sarah, try and placate her accusing expression as she lay constrained on their bed, but the guilt he felt …

Later, he thought, and flicked through channels till he reached the news ones, pausing on CNN to watch a distressed-looking female anchor, her blonde bouffant in disarray and her face pale beneath heavy makeup.

"—patients across the globe have begun getting up," she said, "although still unresponsive, and by some unknown urge have been gathering together to—"

He changed the channel, going through two more before pausing at Al Jazeera.

The video showed a woman seated in a tan Humvee. Dark gray top, mustard trousers, a dark red scarf covered her hair, the black ends of which waved in an unseen wind. Her skin was olive-colored, her face round, and her expression serious.

"—Subina Shresta speaking to you from Katmandu," she said, and climbed from the Humvee. The camera operator stepped back revealing the Humvee stood parked before dry, hilly terrain, spotted with small trees and bushes. The reporter paused, tucked the loose strands of hair into her scarf, and continued.

"The city has been heavily afflicted by the virus, and as such, the aftereffects, or should I say, *continuation* of its effects, have been greatly apparent." She turned and began walking past the car's bonnet. The camera followed, the handheld device steady, and the view changed to an uneven space of ground with green hills beyond.

Between the reporter and the hills stood a dark, wavering cone-shaped object.

She stopped some meters from the object and turned to address the camera.

"This is one of scores of these … fleshy pylons constructed by the coma victims." She turned and looked at the object behind her before turning back and continuing, "We'll go in now for a closer look."

The camera zoomed in.

"Oh my god," a male voice said, and the camera fell out of focus for a moment before showing the base of the pylon up close.

The thing appeared formed completely of human flesh, mostly of an olive hue but with other shades evident. Panning slowly up, the camera revealed buttocks, genitals, chests, and breasts, all melded together within the seamless structure. The solidified, mangled flesh also held faces, warped and melted into other body parts, some of the mouths twitching as if about to speak.

The camera zoomed out a little, showing the top half of the pylon tapering off to the tip.

The cameraman coughed and gagged.

"This is disgusting, and I don't just mean the smell," the reporter said. "There's something just so …" from the nervous tone of her voice, it appeared she had lost her composure. "They should destroy these horrors, burn them or blow them up or something."

The camera zoomed in to the base again. It followed movement, something that moved like a centipede but was, in fact, a row of eyes swimming through the flesh. They stared blindly as they traveled, then disappeared into a nearby, gaping mouth.

"I've seen enough," the reporter said, and a few seconds later, the view shifted to her anxious face.

A wail, high-pitched and echoing, made Lloyd jump in fright. He juggled and dropped the TV remote then stood, looking towards the stairs.

"What the … Sarah?"

The wail came again, the hairs on the back of his neck standing on end at the sound.

Lloyd bounded up the stairs, shoved the bedroom door open, and as the wail terminated, his blood ran cold at the sight of the woman issuing it.

Her jaw slack, eyes half-lidded, Sarah's pallor was deathly white.

"Sarah!" he cried and rushed around the bed towards her.

Her body twitched weakly, her flesh feeling clammy to the touch as he took hold of her limp hand.

How can this be? She was restrained when the Program went full exposure.

"Sarah, Sarah?" He lifted her by her shoulders, staring into glazed eyes.

She sagged in his hands, unconscious, comatose, infected.

Now

What preparations to enter a world of chaos, a world of insanity? Lloyd fastened the buttons of his jacket up to his neck, took a deep

48

breath, and stepped through the front door.

The street was empty. Not of detritus, for the flotsam and jetsam of humanity covered the length and breadth of it, but there were no people, just their bloodstains, their abandoned knives and clothing.

The early morning sky was dark, filled with black cinders of whatever conflagration had consumed the country overnight. If there were beings there, Cthulhu's kin and followers, their flapping progress was camouflaged by the ashes of the past.

Lloyd took his usual route. Turning right, he passed neighbors' houses, many with cracked windows and doors kicked through, and quickly reached the junction. The same evidence of carnage, and carnal rage, to his left and right, and, at the bottom of the street to his right, stood a flesh pylon, its tip moving, transmitting. His eyes lingered on the pylon for some seconds before he turned away and crossed the street.

More bloodstains, more vandalized houses, and before he reached the wasteground, he saw two more pylons there, flanking the path he was to take. Lloyd wanted to stop, turn back, but no; he had to see her, try and bargain for Sarah's return.

He entered the familiar scenery, walking between the pylons while staring straight ahead, his handiwork feeling more of a bane now than something to be proud of. Noises ahead paused him in his tracks, and Lloyd flinched at the sight of things once human, now naked deformed travesties, crawling away to hide beneath dead bushes and sections of collapsed building.

I wonder, did they reach the pylons only to find them full? Lloyd sniggered then stopped, his mood souring as he thought of Sarah. He continued towards the point the change usually happened, eagerly anticipating the mist.

Where is it? As he walked, he feared he'd reach the fence forming the termination of the wasteground without the transition even happening.

A white wave rolled beneath his feet, and Lloyd froze mid-step.

I'm here, he thought, and turned on his heels, expecting to find a world shrouded in white. Instead, he found the mist only covered the ground, but still, there she was, the shifting, female figure, no longer silhouetted and fully visible in the half-light.

"Sarah?" he said, and took a stumbling, confused step forward.

Her body was in a constant, spasming state of motion. A mouth appeared in the right place, then three mismatched eyes, one overly large and bulging, another blood red, and the final one, Sarah's. They resolved themselves on her forehead, and she spoke.

"We no longer need the bridge in your case," she said in a voice not Sarah's, but rather in the vibrating tone he knew from before.

"Sarah," Lloyd repeated, and all strength leaving his body, he fell to his knees.

"It was always you?" he asked hesitantly, and his eyes filled with tears.

"We thought it better to use someone you know," the Sarah-thing said. "We're not completely heartless." She stepped forward, breaching the gap between them.

"Not ..." Lloyd sobbed, confused and frightened.

"Shush," she continued, "Now that you've served your purpose as a human, it's time you joined the Program."

Crying quietly, he felt a shifting hand stroke his head.

"Pull yourself together. You have work to do."

Lloyd raised his head. Sarah was Sarah again. With the knowledge that his mind had finally snapped, he nodded and said, "Promise me I'll be in the same pylon as you."

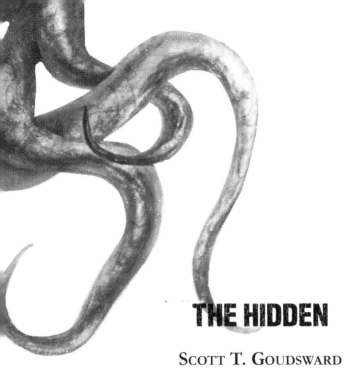

THE HIDDEN

Scott T. Goudsward

Thomas strolled behind the circle of chairs, hands clasped behind his back, brown eyes taking in everything and everyone. His steps were slow and deliberate to let the people gathered know he was there for them and standing behind them when they needed his strength and support. It was the close of the meeting. The group had been meeting there for years, in the basement of the museum. First as an AA group, then cancer survivors, and some twenty years later, still meeting. Different faces, different issues; everyone needed something.

The seated people took deep breaths and looked at each other, giving slight smiles and acknowledging head nods. The smell of dust, mold and burnt coffee hovered over the meeting place. Thomas had secured the room ages ago, and although the cast changed, he was constant. The current group was the last one he'd watch over.

And then there was Andrew.

Andrew was new to the group, not fully accepted or accepting. He stood in the corner, next to the stained six-foot once-white folding table and sighed. He kept a cigarette pinched between his fingers. His left eye twitched occasionally, out of nervousness or a physical thing, no one knew, or asked; it wasn't their business. Thomas glanced over, made eye contact, watched as Andrew's eye ticked, and he turned his gaze back to the group.

"Thank you all for coming," Thomas said and sidled between two of the metal folding chairs in the circle. "We all appreciate your words and concerns." He shook hands with each person in the circle, male or female. There were smiles and eye contact and that moment of physical contact for a show of strength. "Next week, there is no meeting here because, well, you all know why."

Thomas gestured with his arms like a symphony conductor, and the gathered rose, folded their chairs and stacked them neatly under a window crowded with cobwebs. Soft whispers filled the hall. Andrew stood and watched as they took their coats from the rack, pulled packs of cigarettes from their pockets and checked their cell phones for missed calls and texts. They all filed softly from the room, the whispers falling as they passed him in the corner. When they had gone, Andrew cleared the table of cups, napkins, and plastic spoons. The sugar and creamer pods went into a box for the next group. Finally, he slid a tray of mostly untouched cookies into a plastic storage bag.

"Something bothering you tonight, Andrew?" Thomas smiled that charismatic smile which allowed him to make that walk around the ring of chairs week after week: strength, confidence, stability. Something that everyone in the group savored.

"Nothing more than usual."

Thomas lifted the antiquated coffee-maker off the table and Andrew folded it and set it against the wall next to the chairs. Andrew stopped for a second to watch pairs of feet above on the street march back and forth through the dusty cobwebbed window. The window lined with webs reminded him of a giant monster's eye from a dream.

"Not much time left," Andrew said.

"Before?"

"Sunset." Andrew pulled a coat from the rack and slid it over his arms. Through the material of his shirt sleeves, the dark lines of his tattoos that ran from shoulder to wrist showed for a moment. "See you later, Thomas." Andrew placed the cigarette from his fingers in his mouth, and Thomas nodded in response. Then he pulled on his sweatshirt, covering his own array of dark green tattoos, obscured by the sheer shirt he wore.

Kathy stood in front of her metal monstrosity and smiled. She felt vibrant and excited from the meeting. The old barn she used for a workshop was alive with blaring music and strings of colored lights draped from the rafters. Up in the hayloft was a cot, small desk, and her laptop, for those long nights. Her "art" didn't pay the bills. Working at the auto-body shop downtown did.

She flipped up the visor and killed the flame on the welder. It looked ready to her, but the joints needed to be weight-tested and there was no one in town foolish enough to climb her sculpture, except for her. Kathy let the heavy gloves slide from her hands and land on the floor boards. Before the farm went bankrupt, the barn housed a dozen horses for breeding and training. The floor, once covered in hay and manure, was now saddled with plastic tarps. Burn scars like pock marks on a teenager's face dotted the floor from fallen sparks.

To the naked, untrained eye, it looked like a mesh of metal, steps and rungs, and shelves, all from salvaged metal. To her it looked like the gleaming exoskeleton of what might be a massive bird. Interspersed through the form were small platforms and ladder-like rungs used for climbing and standing on when welding. She knew they'd hold her weight, but she needed someone heavier. The farm was a wreck; no one worked the fields or herded cattle anymore. The corral was overgrown and the duck pond long dry. No one bothered her; that's why she had chosen this place.

Soon enough the barn would be full of people, gazing and gawking at her work. But first she needed to test the weight limits of the small platforms and add the leather. She carefully filled saddlebags with diving weights, slid the bags over her shoulders and climbed.

Ethel hummed while she rocked in her chair. Ella Fitzgerald crooned from a small radio on the table. Her fingers dexterously sewed at the tough green material in her lap. It was dark green and leathery, a mask for her grandson Andrew. The stitching was good and strong; it would last him a long time. As long as he needed it for.

Tony whistled at the girls walking down the street. One turned and smiled, the other flipped him off. He blew them a kiss and continued smoothing out the cement on the new sidewalk on his hands and knees with a flat trowel. His truck rumbled in the parking lot near him, churning the cement inside. There were wooden stakes driven into the corners of the molds and yellow safety tape woven between them. Still, some little asshole would scrape his initials in it, or some douchebag with a dog would leave prints in it. The back of his shirt rode up a little, exposing the bottom of some elaborate body art.

He stood to survey his work and smiled at the smooth cement. He had half a mind to put his own initials in the squares. *It's not like anyone would notice them.* He walked into the parking lot and climbed into the cab, pulled a sandwich from his lunch cooler and took a bite. He checked his mirrors and watched the wrecker pull into the lot next to him. He smiled and swallowed the sandwich.

"What's up, Rusty?"

"Nothing. What do you think?" Tony whistled at the fiberglass molds on the back on the platform of the truck, where wrecked cars normally sat. "You sure that shit is going to dry in time?"

"No doubt in my mind."

"Let's get this over with," Rusty spat. "I have a schedule, unlike the rest of you lot." Tony slid from the cab of the truck and went round the back. Rusty walked around to the front of the parking lot and watched the passing cars. Tony moved the cement chute to the first mold and, when it was in place, grabbed a spade from the truck and let the cement flow out into the molds.

"You sure you can get these off the back?"

"Less talking, more working." He looked at his watch, then the flow of cement. "Thomas has been planning this a long time. It won't be me to make him late." Rusty looked towards the museum and the tall spires added on in the 1960s and smiled.

Mary slid her glasses higher on her nose and pushed her mousy hair behind her ear. She pushed the book cart through the library, over-reactive and cautious of every creak and minor squeal of the wheels on the carpet. She flashed false smiles at the people who looked up at her as she walked by. Unlike the others in the support group, she'd never gotten inked: her skin was too thin, the chance of infection was too high.

She maneuvered the cart round tables and through aisles without thinking, the pathway ingrained in her mind. She'd walked it too many times to be anything else but habit at this point. Mary stopped at the elevator and waited patiently for the car to arrive. She fixed her sweater and pushed up her glasses. She looked at the display to see where it was and absently ran her fingers along the spines of the books.

"Going upstairs?"

Mary gasped and stepped back putting a hand to her chest.

"Sorry, Lynne, didn't see you coming. Guess I was someplace else."

"It's okay, sweetie. You didn't take the keys for the Trustees room." Mary smiled and took the offered keys as the elevator door opened. She stepped inside and let the glasses slide down her nose.

The second floor was mostly dark, underfunded and underused. She switched on the lights stepping from the elevator. Mary checked the security cameras: they were off, another causality of a crippling budget. When the elevator doors rolled shut, she pushed forward. The Trustees Room and Special Collections were only open a couple days during the week, when there were volunteers to man them.

She left the cart outside the door to the Trustees Room after unlocking the door. The books on the cart could wait. Even though she knew she was alone, Mary still locked the door. The room was a basic conference room: oval table, comfortable chairs—much more so than those the general public sat in. Glass display cases lined one wall, filled with artifacts from the city's history. The other side was a wall of bookcases locked behind heavy-meshed metal doors. You could look through the gratings to see what the books were and that was about it without the keys. The same keys warming to Mary's body temperature clenched tight in her hand.

She walked over to one of the locked doors and slid in the warm key.

Andrew stared at the street as he walked, keeping his twitchy eye hidden away from everyone, even though most everyone already knew about it.

He turned into the small diner and took a booth near the window. Not much later a plate of French fries and a chocolate milkshake were set down in front of him.

"Having second thoughts?" Thomas asked, sliding into the booth across from him.

"I did get this giant tattoo on my arm. Can never wear short sleeve shirts at the office again."

"I know there's a lot to think about and a lot to worry about."

"Only if you consider what we're doing."

Thomas slid his arms across the table, reaching for Andrew. Andrew pulled back, almost dumping the plate of fries.

"You're part of us. We need you, we need your strength."

"I know what I signed up for," Andrew said. He stood, took a last drink of the chocolate shake, and headed for the door.

"We'll see you at the barn, then." Andrew nodded and walked out. Thomas watched him walking away through the diner window, then pulled out his cell phone and picked at the fries while waiting for an answer.

Kathy watched the lights of the wrecker as it pulled away from the barn. Rusty needed to park it someplace "out of the way," which on the abandoned farm could be pretty much anywhere. Knowing him, he'd still find a way to block her in. The two molds were in place at the base of her "artwork." She smiled, looking it over again, up and down. It had held her weight climbing up and down the structure several times.

This was her masterpiece. What she'd be remembered for. The work for the local galleries had been hard work. But this would raise her to the highest ranks of the best sculptors in the world, in history.

"So this is it?" Rusty said coming back in.

"That's it."

"Don't look like much. Except maybe a scaffolding truck exploded."

"Fuck you, Rusty." Rusty laughed and rubbed her back. She stepped away grimacing.

"Still sore?"

"Yes, I just got that ink a few days ago."

"Want me to rub some lotion on your back?" He winked at her and licked his lips.

"I'd rather roll in salt, thank you." She sighed, looking at her creation. "It won't hurt much longer."

"You know it's your calling, don't you?"

"Yes, Gram, I do." Andrew took the mask from his grandmother.

"Try it on."

"Really?"

"I want to take a picture," she said. "You know how long I worked on that." She looked at the mask in her grandson's hands. "Your father used to sketch something like that. I bet I have his old books around here someplace."

"Thomas said we can't, not before the meeting tonight in the barn. It can only go on the head of the person it's meant for."

"Well, fine, then."

Andrew leaned down and kissed his grandmother on the cheek.

"What was that for?"

"In case I never see you again." He stopped on the way to the door and stuffed the heavy green mask in his coat. "The mask isn't for me. It never was. Dad used to tell me about my destiny. And although I'm part of this lunatic scheme, I'm not the focal point."

"There was no right time for this moment," Thomas said walking around the barn. His flock gathered around him, save for one. "No solstice, no equinox, no harvest moon or harmonic convergence. I know in most things, in history books, in the movies and stories, there's been an eclipse or a Hunters' moon." He raised his arms to those gathered. "The time is right. Right now."

The barn doors opened and every head gathered turned to watch Andrew as he skulked in, eye twitching in overdrive. He smiled nervously at the group and joined in the circle. They parted as Thomas walked to Andrew and hugged him.

"Have to be honest, I was worried."

"I think my Gram would be really disappointed if I didn't come."

He reached into his coat and pulled out the mask, looked at it in his hands, green and leathery, and handed it over. "Kathy, mind if I get an overhead view?" She shook her head partially in disbelief; no one had thought Andrew would show up for this. They had all known his father as children, all respected him, and all mourned his death.

Andrew went to the ladder and climbed up into the loft. He stood at the edge and watched as Thomas passed around his grandmother's handiwork. The statue was amazing and intimidating.

"What about the molds?" Andrew yelled down.

"Not too much longer," Tony said checking his watch. Mary walked over to Thomas, a blush decorating her cheek and handed him two old books stolen from the library. She pushed her glasses into place and stepped back into the gathered. Thomas smiled and ran his hands over the old leather of the books. He closed his eyes and stood still, as if absorbing the knowledge from the volumes.

"Fresh from the Trustees Room." Mary whispered. Then she took the keys and threw them into one of the stalls. As Andrew watched from the loft, Tony and Rusty went to work on the molds with hammers and crowbars. The fiberglass molds came apart easily. Tony stepped back as the pieces of the molds were pulled away. Andrew stepped back from the edge. It was all becoming too real.

The molds were five feet high at the top. Tony had spent weeks casting and forming and setting the forms. Spent god knows how much money to have the end molds made. And what stood before him meant more to him than his wife and kids. Thomas strolled over and draped an arm across his shoulders.

"They're beautiful." He looked up to the loft at Andrew trying to hide in the shadows. "Better come down now, Andrew." Andrew stepped into the light to see the concrete monstrosities. They were "real," he'd seen the sketches and notes in his father's notebooks, before taking them from his grandmother and turning them over to Thomas.

"Let's assemble. The Hidden become seen and become whole to awaken our sleeping God," Thomas said. Everyone in turn went to the metal work. The massive molded, clawed feet stood before them, and they climbed into the rigging of the framework. Kathy smiled, watching them. A tear ran down her cheek as emotions overwhelmed her. She was an integral part of something. Thomas had been saying it at meetings for a long time. And now she believed him.

The Hidden, the believers in the Great Sleeper, took their spots on the frame. Some at odd angles, others perfectly straight on the small shelves welded into the metal. Andrew was the last to take his spot on the outside of the rigging. Kathy climbed and secured everyone into place with the heavy leather straps that would have made any dominatrix moist. And then Kathy took her place next to Tony on the other side of the center. Mary climbed up into the middle of them and Thomas tossed her the mask.

In turn, as if on cue, they all took off their shirts. Men and women; there was no shame or embarrassment. Beer bellies, fat rolls, wrinkles, nothing mattered. No one was ever insulted in The Hidden. The men and women on the right side with long, detailed and dark tattoos of tentacles and claws and eyes on their right arms. Opposites of those on the left. Kathy snaked her arm around Mary to hold on to Tony. They were wings, what mattered to make this all fly. Mary slid the mask on to her head, covering her eyes and nose. Her mouth still showed. Not made of dyed leather like she'd been told, but dyed human skin.

Thomas set the books down on the barn floor and stepped back. Their Great God was taking shape. Soon the Sleeper would be back among them to take control of the Earth or destroy it. Whichever the great Cthulhu decided. Thomas pulled a double-edged dagger from his boot, with an ornate jeweled hilt. Not practical in a fight, but perfect for what he was about to do. Kathy closed her eyes as he climbed up the framework.

On her back was an exquisitely detailed wing. The matching one on Tony's back.

"Be strong. This is going to hurt." Tony squeezed her hand and Thomas started to trace the blade of the dagger around the outer edge of the tattoo. Blood flowed and dripped down the metal on to those below her. She stifled a scream, as Thomas set the knife down on a small shelf in the frame and then peeled the skin off her back, until the "wing" would be seen from below. He secured the flesh to a hook on the frame and kissed Kathy's cheek, who was fighting to not pass out from the incredible pain.

Tony wasn't as strong and screamed and screamed and finally passed out.

Those lucky enough to be in the path of the falling blood reveled in it, rubbed the steaming crimson on their bodies and faces with their free hands. Letting the blood coat and color their own flesh. Andrew looked on from his perch, excited and horrified. His father's notes never said anything about this.

Thomas gingerly walked back to his place in front of the skin and steel effigy. The books on the floor seemed alive; they hummed with submissive energies, waiting to be freed.

"And free you I shall" he whispered.

Andrew went to scratch, the ink on his arm suddenly painful and itchy. Despite that he'd had the tattoo for months, since Thomas had first contacted him. Mary grabbed his arm, holding him back, she was surprisingly strong for what he believed to be a meek librarian. He screamed as fiery pain raced up and down his arm, as if the blood itself had turned to sanguine flames.

Then it moved.

Not his arm: the tattoo. Flowing like seaweed caught in a tidal pool, liquid and graceful and beautiful. Mary released her grip on his arm as he calmed. He nodded to her and she flashed a smile. The others on the outside were all overtaken by the same calm that had captured Andrew. He watched their tattoos moving and flowing. The wings "flew" on their own accord, Kathy grimacing with each movement as the skin was torn a little more with each "flap." Tony was still providentially unconscious.

Thomas sat down cross-legged on the floor, the books from the library in front of him. He ran his fingers across the covers, leaving little trails of energy in the wake of his touch. Next to him was a stack of journals, which Andrew recognized straight away as his father's. They had been the heart of The Hidden since before Thomas had come around.

Thomas looked back at his effigy to the Sleeping God, to the Creator and the Destroyer. He felt the energy and the power building around him.

"My brothers and sisters, it is time." He looked at his crew, the librarian, the fry cook, the welder, and the mechanic. The lifetime student and the local journalist and all the others. Thomas gazed last at Andrew, who looked so much like his father it was reminiscent of his coming into The Hidden.

Thomas opened the book.

And the Earth shook.

Cthulhu had awakened.

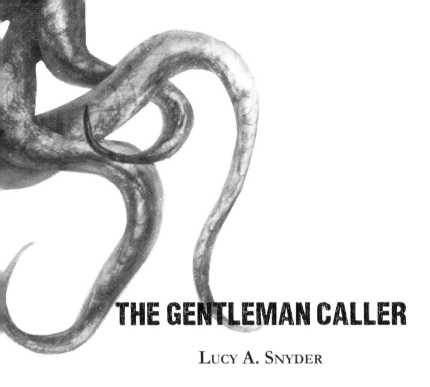

THE GENTLEMAN CALLER

Lucy A. Snyder

My back and ribs screamed at me as I leaned out over the armrest of the motorized wheelchair and slapped the round steel button again, harder. An eternity later, the front door of FoneLand swung open and I rolled out of the biting January air into the warm lobby.

The old man at the security desk peered out over his trifocals at me.

"Oh, sorry, didn't see ya, Janie. Woulda got the door for ya," Pete wheezed.

"S'okay." I forced my cold-numb cheeks into a smile as I drove down the beige carpet. Pete was a sweet old man, but God help us if anyone nefarious actually tried to sneak into the place.

The motor whined like a sick dog; rolling through all the snow outside was hard on the chair. Hell, it was hard on *me*. Even when I was healthy, if the temperature dropped below 20, the separation scar that ran the length of the left side of my body did nothing but ache.

Today, the cold made everything from my toenails to my teeth hurt. I'd carefully folded my legs up and wrapped them in part of the sheepskin rug I rode on to keep my butt free of pressure sores, but even so, my thighs and feet burned something fierce. Normally I didn't have any sensation down there at all, except for a dull, phantom itching when I had been moving around a lot. Probably something to do with my veins, which were bad enough that the doctors were always bugging me to get my legs amputated. They told me I could get a blood clot and die suddenly when I got older. I hadn't yet decided whether that would really be such a bad thing.

I still felt lightheaded and weak from the viral encephalitis that had laid me up for the better part of two months. Coming to work was probably not the smartest thing I'd ever decided to do … but I was so damn sick of watching TV in my assisted-living facility apartment I could cry. I wanted to be out around people, *young* people, not the eternally sick and dying.

Tooling around the snowbound parks and overcrowded malls weren't pleasant options, though. Going to my parents' house would have been even worse. So, that left work.

"You take care now." Pete's smile held an ample measure of pity.

Pity. I stopped the chair beside the elevators and stared up at my reflection in the round security mirror as I waited for the next lift. My face was as pale as the belly of some undersea creature. I supposed I looked normal enough from the neck up but no amount of blankets could completely hide that I was a deformed dwarf from the neck down: torso twisted and permanently hunched to one side, arms stunted. My legs looked like nothing more than useless spindles of flesh and bone, but they did help me keep my balance in the chair. And stylish baby shoes fit me fine. Today I had on a pair of glittery red ones just like Dorothy's magic slippers.

If only I could click my heels.

To the outside world, I looked like an eternal virgin. Nobody knew I'd been jilling off since I was twelve. The best present I ever got was a little battery-powered vibrator one of the young nurses' assistants gave me surreptitiously when I was spending an otherwise lousy sixteenth birthday in the hospital. She was just a few years older than me, full in the flush of hormones herself, and I guess she felt bad that I was never going to get laid.

Thing was, I *could* get laid. I *could*, dammit. If I was careful and saved up enough money, there was a local place that could rent me a pretty boy for a few hours. Word was it was a classy business with a no-theft, no-disease guarantee; the city had some of the best rehab hospitals in the country, so there were plenty of disabled girls and pent-up old ladies who wanted their services.

And, if I were willing to risk my safety, I wouldn't even have to pay for sexytimes. I'd been lurking on the BDSM FetLife site for a couple of years, more than long enough to know that people got turned on by the strangest things. If I started posting photos, I'd get a zillion meetup requests. Probably some of the pervs would even be nice. But it would be difficult finding anyone who saw me as a person and not a niche fetish.

But when you came down to it, I really didn't want a gigolo or a BDSM scenester. My ever-growing collection of toys did me fine. My rent-a-boy fund had taken a serious hit there, but thank God for discreet mail order. The biggest challenge was keeping my parents from finding my stash of schtupperware.

Neither they nor old Pete would *ever* imagine that I worked for FoneLand's fantasy line.

Once I got to work, I became Lady Rayne, a popular telephone mistress who got dozens of men creaming in their jeans each day. Some of my regular callers even sent gifts to her through FoneLand. Gifts to *me*, rather, but of course Rayne's fans didn't know that.

About a week before I got the encephalitis, a regular who said his name was Brandon sent me a real jade necklace. It was a gorgeous piece, but strange. The beads were etched all over in some kind of strange pictographic language that none of my Internet searches could decipher. The curvilinear carvings looked positively ancient; it *had* to cost serious money.

Brandon never wanted to talk about anything raunchy. He behaved like a perfect gentleman during our sessions, and he mostly just wanted to chat about movies and theatre. As our sessions went on, I had a hard time figuring out why someone as articulate and seemingly urbane as him needed to pay for conversation. And I was simultaneously intrigued and frustrated that nothing I said to him seemed to turn him on, yet my occasional attempts at dirty talk never offended him, either.

So, I'd considered sending the necklace back. I did feel a little like a fraud, even though I'd never asked for the present. But ultimately I decided to keep it. I felt ... special when I wore it. Prettier. More important. I'd worn it every day since I got it, except for when I was in the hospital and worried someone might steal it while I was asleep.

And, I told myself, why not keep it? Even if I had committed a kind of fraud, I figured that Brandon could never find out who I really was. The company had a strict information security policy, and nobody creeping around the parking lot was likely to picture me as the source of anyone's fantasies.

My callers were probably picturing a woman like my twin sister. Linda was a genuine beauty: tall, green eyes, deep red hair, long legs and an ample bust. Our parents were rich enough to afford the endless series of plastic surgeries Linda had needed after the doctors at Johns Hopkins removed me from her back a couple of days after we were C-sectioned out of our mother.

Linda got the ribs and kidney we shared. I was six months old before I even got a name. No one expected me to live, and when I lived, no one expected me to be anything more than a retarded cripple.

Maybe I'm being unfair, but I think Mom and Dad would have been happier if I'd been a vegetable. Then they could simply institutionalize me and forget that their lovely Linda had ever been two-thirds of a monster they'd spawned. They probably secretly wanted to give me up for adoption, but that would have been a faux pas of epic proportions for a family that made a big thing of donating to the March of Dimes each year.

Abnormalcy is not something my family suffers gladly. My father's life revolves around stocks and fancy cars and golf, and my mother gets freaked out if the silverware doesn't all match. If they ever found out I was working phone sex ... wow. I was saving that little tidbit for a general announcement at the next family reunion so that they'd be most optimally mortified.

Linda would *act* horrified but I thought she would be secretly amused. And maybe, just for a moment, a little envious. We were born with essentially the same brain, after all, but her weird side would forever remain in the closet hidden behind the pink taffeta prom dress of the Good Girl image our mother had thrust upon her.

I smiled to myself as I rode the elevator up to the tenth floor. Maybe I wouldn't go through with my plan for the reunion ... but it was an awful lot of fun to think about. Pity I could never dress the part; neither nasty boots nor corsets would ever fit me. Not without causing me a hell of a lot of pain, anyway.

I got off the elevator and rolled into the fantasy line offices. Zoe, a gangly rivethead who was one of my closest friends, was making herself some green tea at the coffee nook. She was dressed relatively conservatively in shiny black vinyl pants, tall Doc Martens and a black cardigan over an old Misfits tee shirt.

"Hey, Jane, how you doing? Didn't expect to see you back today." Zoe pushed her electric-blue bangs away from her eyes.

"The cabin fever got to me," I replied. "Figured I'd see if I could get through a half shift."

"So you're all better now?"

"Eh, sorta-kinda. Light still hurts my eyes."

I wasn't planning to mention the petit mal seizures I'd had since I left the hospital. The doctors assured me they would pass. I'd also had unusually vivid dreams ever since my feverish delirium; in some of them, I was a creature swimming through a sunken stone city in a deep ocean trench. I found that dream terrifying, and didn't want to talk about it. But most of my real-as-life dreams had been far too mundane to mention. Why bore poor Zoe by telling her I'd dreamed I was a night auditor at a hotel going over stacks and stacks of receipts? Or that I was an insomniac watching terrible late-night TV?

"But don't worry, I'm not contagious any more," I added.

"I wasn't worried." Zoe blinked slowly and smiled, her cheeks dimpling over her deep blue lipstick. "Just don't push yourself and relapse, ya know? It's been boring here without you around. No one to be rude with but the boys on the gay lines."

I threw a hand up against my forehead and pretended to swoon. "Oh, woe!"

Zoe giggled. "Get on in there, girl. The sweaty masses await their audience with the sultry Rayne."

I smiled and punched in at the time clock, then rolled down into the phone pit. Taking my place at an empty carrel, I put on my headset, logged into the computer, and tapped in my personal ID code to make myself available for calls.

I genuinely enjoyed working the fantasy line. It was far, far better than telemarketing in every way. Sure, I sometimes got the occasional abusive freak, but we were allowed to terminate a call whenever we felt uncomfortable. And I did sometimes feel sorry for the guys who called … many of them seemed sad and lonely. But I enjoyed the attention, and the challenge.

It wasn't just the acting—to be really good, you had to figure out how to keep them coming back for more. You had to really get inside a guy's head and figure out what he wanted to hear. I could size up a caller within the first ten seconds, and I regularly logged the longest calls in the center.

The phone buzzed, and I picked up.

"Hello, this is Rayne," I breathed. "What's your pleasure?"

"I … I wanna do something *really* dirty," the guy stammered earnestly. He sounded pretty young, maybe just barely old enough to be making the call. "I wanna do it … doggy style."

"Ooh, you want me down on my knees? But what if I want you down on *your* knees?"

Who the hell still thought doggy style was any big deal? The kid had to have led a massively sheltered life. I could practically imagine him sitting on his bed in his old church camp T-shirt and gray boxer shorts, heart pounding and sweat trickling down the groove of his back, his cock already hard from the excitement of doing something his Pentecostal minister father would never *ever* approve of.…

I suddenly felt dizzy, and had to shut my eyes against the vertigo. The jade necklace felt heavy and cold against my flesh.

When I opened my eyes a moment later, I was no longer in my phone carrel. I was sitting in the middle of an unmade bed in a messy bachelor apartment bedroom. Clothing littered the floor, and the walls were covered with Christian rock band posters. An old-fashioned phone handset was tucked uncomfortably between my chin and shoulder.

I looked down … and realized I was *in the guy's body.*

Am I having another seizure? I wondered. *Is this a hallucination?*

I stared down at the erect cock bulging beneath the thin fabric of his boxers.

I shouldn't do this, I thought.

But I laid the receiver on the pillow, reached down and started doing what my caller had probably been told his whole life was a sin worse than touching a woman against her will.

The flesh was more than willing. In just a few strokes, I came in a sweet hot shuddering spurt. I groaned loud in the guy's voice, and felt the come spatter against my chin and neck—

—the sudden dizziness was intense, and when I came to I was

back at my phone in the call center. Zoe was gently shaking my shoulder.

"Jane? Jane, you okay?" Zoe asked.

The call was still live. Through my headset, I heard the rustle of sheets, and then the guy's disoriented voice.

"What—what just happened?" he stammered. "I was in a dark place. It was so cold. I couldn't see *anything*."

"Everything's fine," I replied, trying to recover my composure as best I could. "Take a nice warm shower, and call back soon."

I clicked the call termination button on the computer screen, put myself on break, and turned to Zoe.

"What happened?" My voice shook. "What did I do?"

"You zoned out on us, girl. You started talking, and then you just sort of froze."

I winced, remembering how I'd moaned when I came. When *he* came. "Did—did I make any noise?"

Zoe shook her head. "Nope, not a sound until you came out of it just now. Don't know why the guy didn't hang up."

"Shit, I'm sorry. I—I still have little seizures." I knew full well that whatever I'd just had, it *wasn't* a seizure. "I thought I'd be okay. I think I need to go home."

After the shuttle bus took me back to Oakwood Tower, I went up to my apartment and hid under the covers of my bed with my cell phone. I stared at the bright screen in the muffled darkness. What had really happened at work? Surely it was some kind of hallucination … but I heard the guy's confusion. I *heard* it.

I wanted so desperately to know if it had been real. Wanted to know if I could do it again.

Could I enter the bodies of other people, live inside them? Experience life as a fully functional human being whose every waking moment wasn't a fight against pain? I knew it wasn't right to hijack somebody else's body. It might be a kind of rape. But if I had that power, would I be stupid to refuse to explore it? Stupid to refuse to take advantage of what little pleasure and escape the universe had offered me?

But how had this happened? Had my brain fever triggered something inside me? Or was something else going on? I couldn't be sure it was real, not yet. I had to call someone. Who?

An image of Linda immediately rose in my mind, followed by a complex wash of emotions. If anyone would understand my predicament, surely it was my own twin sister. I tried to ignore the tiny dark voice that told me that she owed me. She'd gotten everything in life that I'd been denied. If I called her, and if my new power worked, I'd finally be able to spend a few hours in the body I *should* have been born with. I could know what it was like to have a handsome, successful husband and a beautiful home in the country. To have parents who loved me and were proud of me.

I felt bitter tears welling in my eyes. Could I really do it? Did I dare? After walking in Linda's body and life, could I ever be happy again when I inevitably came back to *this*?

I finally decided that if I didn't do it, I'd spend the rest of my life wondering. Better to regret what I'd done than what I hadn't.

Two hours later, my sister finally answered her cell phone.

"What's up, Janie?" Linda sounded faintly impatient. "Is everything okay?"

"Everything's okay." I rolled my necklace's irregular jade beads between my fingers and closed my eyes. I could feel my sister's tall fine body, smell the perfume on her tailored clothes, feel the gold earrings bumping warmly against her neck....

"I just wanted to know what I should get Mom for her birthday," I finished. In Linda's voice. Linda's throat. My perfectly-manicured hand rested on a glass-topped coffee table, and I was sitting on a cream-colored leather couch. I disconnected the call on the new iPhone and surveyed my sister's domain.

"Holy shit. I've done it."

There'd been no dizziness, no vertigo. It was as if my consciousness were *made* for this body. I stared at her toned, perfect legs in their cream-colored tights. In my own body, I'd never been able to stand up, ever, much less walk ... and I wasn't sure how it was done. Could I make her body do it? Or would it remember how on its own through muscle memory?

I got my feet under me and slowly stood. The bones and muscles acted in practiced concert; the body *did* seem to remember. After my first tottering steps, I realized that the trick was to simply let the flesh do its thing and not think too hard about it. I went from room to room, touching the beautiful furniture, admiring the expensive art. I crossed through the airy, vaulted living room to the glass doors to the pool and Jacuzzi room.

The steamy blue water sparkled in the late afternoon light filtering through the fogged glass walls. Linda was an excellent swimmer. She'd competed in the butterfly and freestyle in high school and college, and had even gone as far as competing in an Olympic trial. I'd only ever learned how to float in case I fell into a pond or pool; I hoped Linda's body would also remember how to swim.

Had Linda ever gone skinny-dipping? If I had a great pool like this, I'd do it every day. And if I had a hot husband like hers, I'd do *him* in the Jacuzzi twice a day. At least.

I kicked off my sister's black patent leather flats, unbuttoned the hunter-green linen dress suit, shimmied out of the satin slip and peeled off her tights and lace panties. I carefully laid the clothes across the sailcloth seat of a nearby lounge chair and then stretched, enjoying the feel of my sister's supple joints and toned muscles.

There was a full-length mirror set into the wall beside the towel hamper. I stepped up to it and turned to look at Linda's back, tracing my fingers down the place where I thought my body had been removed from hers. There was no visible scar, only the faintest of indentations in the ribs beside the spine and a slight granularity and numbness to the flesh above the bone. I pressed my fingers into the indentation; no pain.

Feeling deeply envious, I abandoned the mirror and walked down the pool's steps into the water. I pushed off from the edge of the bottom step with her toes, my outstretched fingers slicing neatly through the cool blue water. Linda's body remembered perfectly well how to swim.

And it was glorious. Swimming in her body was every bit the pleasure I'd imagined it would be. I could walk, I could dive, I could push myself until I was gasping and still felt no pain.

As I backstroked the length of the pool, I heard the door click open. Linda's husband, Richard, stood in the doorway to the living room. Wisps of steam curled around his Italian loafers and the hem of his gray wool Armani suit. His hand went up to straighten his already perfectly straight red power tie, a gesture I recognized as a sign of nervousness.

"What are you doing?" he asked, his voice betraying more confusion than his courtroom-neutral expression did.

"Swimming. Want to join me?" I flicked some water in his direction.

The water droplets landed a yard away from him, but he took a step back as if he were afraid I'd ruin his loafers. Or as if he were afraid of *me*; he was staring as if he thought I'd gone slightly mad.

"Uh, no." He gave his tie another tug. "I have an important case in a couple of days, and one of the junior partners is here to go over the court documents with me. Please see that we're not disturbed. And *please* get some clothes on."

His cold tone and annoyed look told me that I should be ashamed of myself. Ashamed of my body. I felt a mortified blush spread across my face. Richard averted his gaze and stepped out of the room, pulling the glass door shut behind him with a stern click like a disapproving tongue.

What the hell? Linda was *hot*. Most guys in the city would jump off the north bridge to have a chance at getting wet and naked with her.

But my inner protestations did nothing to dispel the anxious lump in the pit of my stomach, the same lump I'd felt throughout grade school when the other kids taunted me. *Dwarf. Freak. Ugly.*

I splashed out of the pool and got a fluffy white towel from the hamper by the lounge chairs. *Dwarf. Freak. Ugly.* Tears welling in my eyes, I toweled off and got back into Linda's expensive clothes.

I looked around the beautiful pool room and felt disoriented, disconnected. This was all wrong. This was not my beautiful house, nor my beautiful life. Maybe Linda had everything I thought I'd always wanted, and maybe she didn't, but at that moment I mostly wanted to be back in my own bed.

"Get in, get off, get out," I muttered to myself.

I headed into the half-bath adjoining the pool room and locked myself in. Hiked up my skirt, slipped a hand down the front of my tights and ran my fingertips over the softly curling pubic hair. Nothing; not so much as a happy tickle. I circled my index finger over the hooded clitoris. The flesh was numb, unresponsive. Nerve damage. Jesus.

This is what our separation had cost her. I explored further to confirm my sweating fear: everything was too numb to feel pleasure. She *couldn't* come, at least not by any means I knew. I was stuck inside her. And where was she? If I stayed in her body, what happened to her consciousness? Was she trapped in that frightening cold, dark place the caller spoke of? And what would happen to my own body? Would it die?

I leaned against the sink, swallowing against my anxious nausea. No. I couldn't let myself panic. There *had* to be a way to get back into my own body. What was *like* an orgasm, but wasn't?

I'll take electric shocks for $500, Alex.

One of Linda's memories bloomed: Richard carried a stun gun. It was probably in one of the pockets of his winter overcoat. Supposedly the thing was powerful enough to knock a 300-pound man flat on his back but would cause no permanent damage.

I straightened my clothes and hurried through the house to the coatrack in the foyer. Droplets of melted snow glittered like tiny diamonds on the shoulders of one heavy black overcoat. I pulled it off its peg and riffled through the pockets. Leather gloves, cigarette case, restaurant receipts in the outside pockets—and in the inside pocket, something that felt like an unusually heavy cordless shaver.

I pulled it out and flicked it on. Blue electricity arced and crackled across the two prongs on the face of the stun gun. It was a wicked-looking device.

Where should I zap myself? Shoulder? Stomach? Side? I finally decided on my stomach. I sat down on the carpeted floor, flicked it back on, and plunged the gun into my midsection.

The pain was intense, even for someone as accustomed to pain as me. Every muscle in my body jerked spasmodically, uncontrollably. My hands flew up as I convulsed, and the stun gun tumbled away and landed under a chair.

After an interminable two seconds, the muscle contractions passed. I was sweating and dizzy and nauseated. Worse, I was still in Linda's body.

An hour later, I pulled up to the assisted-living facility in Linda's blue BMW. It was hard to suppress the full-on panic screaming inside my skull. Was Linda suffering in frigid darkness? I had to put things right.

I signed in at the receptionist's station and was hurrying toward the elevators when a man said, "Jane?"

I stopped, turned, and said "Yes?" before I could think better of it.

A man sitting in a chair by a huge potted fern set aside the newspaper he'd been reading (or hiding behind), stood, and smiled at me.

"Right on time," he said cheerfully. He was a white man of about forty, on the handsome side of average, and had graying blond hair and a long, angular face. His eyes were dark hazel. He wore a blazer and khakis and could have blended in almost anywhere.

I'd never laid eyes on him before, I was sure, but his voice was ringing all kinds of bells. "Have we met?"

His smile widened and he extended his hand. "We haven't met in person, no. I'm Brandon Wilks. We've spoken on the phone many times. And I believe you've been enjoying the necklace I sent."

My hand went to my bare neck. I wished I'd brought the stun gun with me. "I … I'm not.…"

He stepped closer and spoke more softly. "Not Jane? But you *are* Jane. You just aren't currently inhabiting her body. Don't be afraid; I'm here to help you."

"Do you know what's happening?" I asked.

He nodded. "I do, and I will explain, but I'm rather concerned about your body upstairs. They tend to not remain stable in the absence of consciousness. We should hurry."

He had an air of gentleness and competence, and frankly I was so frightened that I was ready to cling to anyone who had even a half a clue, so I took him up to my apartment.

We found my body unconscious where I'd left it in bed, my cell phone dead on my chest. Brandon pulled a stethoscope out of his blazer and listened to my body's heart and lungs.

"Are you a doctor?" I asked.

"I studied to be a physician, yes, but my career has moved in some interesting directions over the years." He pulled the stethoscope off his ears and hung it around his neck. "Your breathing is a bit shallow, but your heart seems fine. For now."

"That's good," I replied. "How can I get back into my body? I'm worried about Linda."

"As well you should be." He leaned down and removed his jade necklace from my body and held it out to me. "Put this on, please."

I stared at the necklace. "Why? What's going on?"

"A bit of quid pro quo, I'm afraid. I need you to use your gift to accomplish something for me before I can help you. Don't worry; it's quite simple, and won't take long."

I bit my lip and stared at the necklace. "I have questions."

"I'm sure you do," he replied. "But we both know you don't have time. Just do as I ask and I'll be on my way. You can even keep the necklace; it's the trigger for your powers, and with it you can sample other lives as you please. Or not; it's up to you."

I met his steady gaze. "Why me?"

"Yours is a family gift; it skips generations. Your mother, alas, she is not gifted by any definition of the word. I tested your sister first, when she came of age, but all the power rests inside you."

"You tested me?"

He smiled. "In our conversations. I could sense the potential in you, and I knew you'd be the one we needed when the stars were right."

I took the necklace from him and dangled it from my fingers, gazing at the strange carvings. "What is it that you need me to do?"

"I need you to help us make the world a better place." He pulled an older model smartphone out of his back pocket and scrolled to a contact entry. "Call this number. Enter the mind of the man who answers. Ask for Jebediah. Do what he asks. You can refuse if anything seems immoral or risky."

"How do I get back here?"

"He'll make sure you return. And then I'll see to it that you get back into your real body safely and Linda's soul is returned to hers."

I paused for a long moment.

"All right." I put on the necklace and took the cell phone from his hand. Pressed the button to dial. Focused on the tone.

"Barker. Talk." The voice was gruff and male. Maybe mid-thirties. Sounded bored and suspicious. I could picture the gray uniform and automatic weapon strapped across his muscular chest.

"Hello," I replied in Rayne's voice. "I know we haven't met, so this is crazy—"

Vertigo, hard and gut-churningly cold like being dropped from a plane through a hurricane into the Atlantic Ocean.

"—but call me, baby." My words, the gruff man's throat, tongue, and mouth. I was staring down at a scarred wooden desk, military surplus from the 1950s. A fluorescent light glared and buzzed overhead. I took a deep breath, inhaling smells of dust, metal, motor oil, and unwashed male bodies.

"Is Jebediah here?" I asked.

"Here," I heard behind me.

I turned, and saw a row of cells with heavy steels doors painted battleship gray. A pair of pale fingers wiggled through a barred window slit.

I approached the cell, Barker's boots ringing heavy and hollow on the damp steel diamond plate floor. Were we on a ship someplace? Barker's memories were a lot harder to access than Linda's had been. It was like trying to grab melting ice cubes with chopsticks.

"Took you long enough," Jebediah muttered.

"Sorry." I paused. "Uh, what do you need me to do?"

"Keys at your belt. Unlock the door."

"Right. Sorry." I shifted my automatic weapon to the side and found the key ring on a retractable cord. The third one I tried turned in the lock, and I pulled the door open. A small, slightly built man with close-cropped hair and a black eye stood there staring at me uncertainly. He wore a gray uniform similar to mine, but the insignia had been ripped off. His shirt was partly open, and I could see that his upper chest was covered in curvilinear tattoos like those on the jade necklace. His feet were bare and bruised.

"What now?" I asked.

"Can I borrow your knife real quick?"

I glanced down at my belt, and on the side opposite my keys I had a sheath for a fixed-blade fighting knife. A KA-BAR, maybe? "Yeah, sure."

I unsheathed the knife and offered it to him handle-first.

"Thanks, brah."

He took the knife and rammed it through the side of my neck.

I stumbled backward, the pain hot and intense, blood spurting from the severed artery, but then my knees gave out and I just kept falling, falling through vertiginous blackness—

—I thrashed awake in my bed at the assisted living facility, coughing, gasping for breath. The pain of being inside my old body was almost worse than getting stabbed through the throat. Linda lay across the foot of the bed, and for a bad moment I thought she was dead. But then she let out a little moan and stirred as though she were having a bad dream.

"You've done your bit, and so I've done my bit," said Brandon. "And now I must bid you adieu. I regret that I'll no longer be calling you to chat about movies; I'll miss our talks."

"Wait." I was dizzy on top of the pain; my body felt starved for oxygen, and it was hard to think. "That guy ... he *killed* me."

"Yes; that's the most effective way of returning to your body in the absence of ... other release."

What kind of a man had I unleashed on the ship? What had I just done? I felt sick.

"What's he going to do now?" My voice shook.

"Well, at this moment, I suspect he's preparing to launch a cruise missile from the defense contractor vessel. A little wake-up call for our Master to rouse him from his nap in the Pacific."

I blinked. "What happens when your Master wakes up?"

Brandon smiled enigmatically. "Oh, that's weeks off, I'm sure. A being of his magnitude won't be up and about quickly. In the meantime, enjoy the necklace. If you have any concerns that your actions might inadvertently ruin anyone's life ... don't. Trust me, nothing you do from this moment forward can cause any lasting harm."

SCRATCHING FROM
THE OUTER DARKNESS

TIM CURRAN

After two weeks of relative silence in which the pot of the world began to boil over, Simone Petrioux heard the scratching again. This time it came from within the walls. Sometimes it came from the shadows—particularly the shadows in the corners—and sometimes from behind her or the sky overhead. And sometimes from inside people.

"You have a marked hyper-aural sensitivity," Dr. Wells explained to her. "A form of hyperacusis. It's not unusual with those without sight. When one sense fails, others are heightened."

"But it's beyond that," Simone told him with a singular note of desperation. "I hear …strange things. Things I should not hear."

"What sort of things?"

She swallowed. "Sounds … things echoing from another place. *Busy* sounds."

He told her that auditory hallucinations were known as paracusia. Sometimes they were signs of a very serious medical condition. He did not use the word schizophrenia, but she was certain he was thinking it.

"Just because you hear things others do not does not necessarily mean there's anything there," he explained.

"And it doesn't mean anything *isn't* either," she told him. "Rocky hears it too. How do you explain that?"

But he couldn't, of course. Dr. Wells was a good man, she thought, but this was beyond him. Ever since she was a child, she heard things others could not. It ran in the family. It was something of a Petrioux family curse—like the blindness—the ability to detect sounds in a frequency beyond that of ordinary human hearing. Simone had been blind since birth. Vision was an abstract concept to her. She could no more describe her acute hearing to Dr. Wells than he could describe sight to her. Stalemate.

Of course, it really didn't matter.

Things had gone far beyond that point now.

Feeling very alone and very vulnerable, she listened for it to start again because she knew it would. There had been the two- week reprieve, of course, but now the scratching was coming again, and it was more frenzied and determined than ever. *Like someone's trying to get through*, she thought. *Trying to dig their way through a stone wall. Scritch, scritch, scrape, scrape.* That was the sound she kept hearing. It was worse at night. It was always worse at night.

Listen.

Yes, there it was again.

Scritch, scritch.

Rocky started to howl. Oh yes, he could hear it, and he knew it was bad. Whatever was behind it, it was bad. "Come here, boy," she said, but he would not. She found him over by the wall, fixated on the sounds coming from the corner. She petted him, tried to hug him, but he would have none of it. Beneath his fur, he was a rigid mass of bunched cables. "It's okay, my big boy, it'll be okay," she said, but he knew better and so did she.

The scratching sounded like an animal digging, claws scraping against a door, the sound of tunneling, determined tunneling. She cried out involuntarily. She couldn't bear it any more. Her greatest fear was that whatever was doing it, might get through.

Get through from where?

But she didn't know. She just didn't know.

Night—another abstract concept to the sightless—was a time she had always enjoyed the most. The noise of the city diminished and she could really hear the world. The gurgling of pipes in the ceiling. The gentle breeze playing at the eaves. Bats squeaking as they chased bugs around streetlights. Mr. Astano rocking in his chair on the third floor. The young couple—Jenna and Josh Ryan—at the end of the corridor making love, trying to be quiet because their bed was so terribly creaky (through the furnace duct she always heard them giggling in their intimacy).

But that had changed now, hadn't it?

Yes, everything had changed. These past few weeks, the night breeze was contaminated by a sweet evil stench like nothing she had ever smelled before. Mr. Astano no longer rocked in his chair; now he sobbed through the dark watches of night. For three nights running she had heard whippoorwills shrilling in the park, growing louder and louder in a diabolic chorus. Rocky howled and whined, sniffing around the baseboards almost constantly. And the Ryans … they no longer made love or giggled, now they whispered in low, secretive voices, reading gibberish to one another out of books. Last night, Simone had clearly heard Josh Ryan's voice echoing through the furnace duct, *"There are names one must not pronounce and those that should never be called."*

The scratching was persistently loud tonight, and no one could ever convince her it was hallucinatory. It came from outside, not within. Her nerves frayed, a frost laying over her skin that made her shiver uncontrollably, Simone turned on the TV. She turned it on *loud*. The voices on CNN were initially comforting but soon enough disturbing. There had been a mass suicide in Central Park. By starlight, two thousand gatherers had (according to witnesses) simultaneously slit their left wrists, using the gushing blood to paint an odd symbol on their foreheads, something like a stem with five branches. The police were saying they were members of a fringe religious sect known as the Church of Starry Wisdom. In Scotland, there had been arrests of a group—the Chorazos Cult—in Caithness who had gathered on the bleak moorland at a prehistoric megalithic site known as the Hill of Broken Stones. Apparently, they had ritually sacrificed several children, offering them to a pagan god known as "The Lord of Many Skins." In Africa, there were numerous atrocities committed, the most appalling of which seemed to be that hundreds of people had congregated at a place known as the Mountain of the Black Wind in Kenya and cut their own tongues out so that they would not, in their religious ecstasy, speak the forbidden name of their holy avatar. There were rumors that the offered tongues were then boiled and eaten in some execrable rite known as the Festival of the Flies, which dated from antiquity.

Madness, she thought. *Madness on every front.*

Christians called it Armageddon and began feverishly quoting from the Book of Revelation as, all across North America and Europe, they flung themselves off the tallest buildings they could find, smashing to pulp far below, so that the Lord could wash his feet in the blood of the faithful as he walked the streets of men during the Second Coming.

It was coming apart.

It was all coming apart now.

There was mass insanity, religious frenzy, mob violence, murder and genocide coming from every corner of the world.

Simone finally shut the TV off. The world was unraveling, but there seemed to be no root cause. At least none a sane mind would even consider.

The whippoorwills resumed their eerie rhythmic piping in the park, growing louder and louder, their cries coming faster and more stridently, as if they were possessed of some rising mania. Rocky began to whine in a pathetic, puppy-like tone. At the windows, Simone heard what sounded like hundreds of insects buzzing. It all seemed to be building towards something, and she was more afraid than she had ever been in her life. Now there were screams out in the street, hysterical and rising, becoming something like dozens of cackling voices reaching an almost hypersonic crescendo of sheer dementia. They resonated through her, riding her bones and making her nerve endings ring out. There was a power to them, some nameless, menacing cabalism that filled her head with alien thoughts and impulses. Now the walls … oh dear God, the walls were vibrating, keeping time with the voices and the whippoorwills.

Not out in the streets, not out in the streets, but from within the walls.

Yes, echoing voices from some terribly distant place and, as she listened, she could not be certain they were of human origin … guttural croakings, discordant shrieking, bleatings and hissings, and vile trumpeting, a reverberating lunatic chanting, hollow noises as of storm winds rushing through subterranean channels.

Dear God, what did it mean?

What did any of it mean?

There was a sour taste on her tongue and a foul stench of graveyards.

Feeling dizzy and weak, her stomach bubbling with a cold nauseous jelly, Simone fell to the floor, cupping her hands over her ears as the blood rushed and roared in her head, making it feel as if her brain was boiling in her skull. The sounds were getting louder and louder, the floorboards shuddering, the room seeming to quiver and quake like pudding. There were smacking and slurping sounds, the cries of humans and animals, of things that were neither … all of it lorded over now by a cacophonous droning that made her bones rattle and her teeth chatter. It sounded like some monstrous insect descending from the sky on droning membranous wings.

Then it stopped.

All of it ended simultaneously and there was only a great, unearthly silence broken by her own gasping and Rocky's whimpering. Other than that, nothing. Nothing at all. A voice in Simone's head said, *it was close that time. Very, very close, they almost got through. The barrier between here and there is wearing very thin.* But she had no idea what any of it meant. Between here and where?

"Stop it, stop it," she told herself. "You're losing your mind."

She pulled herself up from the floor, barely able to maintain her balance. The silence was immense. It was a great soundless black vacuum of the sort she always imagined existed beyond the rim of the universe.

She made it to the sofa and collapsed on it, wiping a dew of sweat from her face. With a trembling hand, she turned the TV on because she needed to hear voices, music, anything to break that wall of morbid silence.

On CNN, there were voices, yes, but they spoke of the most awful things, things that only amplified her psychosis … because it must have been a psychosis, she couldn't be hearing these things, these awful sounds like the veneer of reality was ripping open.

It was reported that several million people had made a pilgrimage to Calcutta to await the appearance of a dark-skinned prophet at the Temple of the Long Shadow whom they referred to simply as "The Messenger." Border skirmishes had broken out in Asia and the Middle East. There was pestilence in Indochina, bloodshed on the Gaza Strip, immense swarms of locusts blackening the skies over Ethiopia, and the Iranians had fully admitted that they were in possession of several dozen hydrogen bombs, each of which were equivalent to fifty million tons of TNT. With them, they would soon "ascend to heaven in the black arms of destiny" via a synchronized nuclear detonation which would bring about what they referred to as the symbolic "Eye of Azathoth." In Eastern Europe, a terror organization calling itself either the Black Brotherhood or the Al-Shaggog Brigade had been burning Christian churches, Jewish synagogues, and Muslim mosques, calling them "places of utter blasphemy which must be eradicated so that the way be purified before the king descend from the Dark Star and the Great Father rise from his sunken tomb...."

"Kooks, Rocky," Simone said. "This world is full of kooks."

The idea made her smile thinly. Was it at all possible that the human race was losing its collective mind at the same time? That instead of sporadic outbreaks of insanity there was a global lunacy at work here? She told herself it was highly unlikely—but she didn't believe herself.

That afternoon, the UPS man came to her door, knocking gently, announcing that he carried a parcel that had to be signed for. It was perfectly innocuous. He was delivering her new laptop with screenreader software ... yet as she made to open the door, a sense of fright and loathing swept through her as if what was out there was something hideous beyond imagining. But she did open the door and right away she was gripped by a manic paranoia and a mounting claustrophobia.

"Package for you," the man said, his voice cheerful enough. But it was a façade, an awful façade ... for there was something sinister and lurking just beneath his skin and she knew if she reached out to touch his face it would be pebbly like the flesh of a toad. Right away, she heard that dire scratching coming from inside him like rats pawing and chewing. In her mind, she sensed a spiraling limitless abyss waiting to open like a black funnel. A voice—his own, but ragged and wizened—whispered in her skull, *has she … has she … has she linked? Have the angles shown her the gray void? Has she seen the black man with the horn?* The voice kept echoing in her head until she felt a cool, sour sweat run down her face.

"Are you okay, ma'am?" asked the UPS man.

"Yes," she breathed, taking the parcel from him with strained, shaking fingers. "Yes, fine."

"Okay, if you're sure."

But deep within her, perhaps at some subconscious level of atavistic fright, she could sense a godless vortexual darkness opening up inside him, and a noxious stench like seared porcine flesh blew into her face and that dry, windy voice whispered once again, *show her, show her, it has been promised in the* Ghorl Nigral *as such … let her gaze into the moon-lens and gape upon the Black Goat of the forest with a thousand squirming young … let her … let her … find communion with the writhing dark on the other side….*

"Listen, are you sure you're all right?"

"Yes … please, I'm fine."

But she was *not* fine. She was blind and alone and a ravening outer darkness was spilling from this man, in diseased rivers of slime. She felt scalding winds and dust blowing in her face, a fetid odor enveloping her that was no single stench but dozens breathing hot in her face, with a fungous, gangrenous, nearly palpable odor.

He reached out to steady her, clutching her wrist with a flabby, leprous claw.

She screamed.

She could not help herself.

She slammed the door in his face, ignoring the whining and growling of Rocky. Physical waves of disgust and utter repulsion nearly paralyzed her, but she managed to reach the toilet as the vomit came out of her in a frothing expulsion. And crouching there on the bathroom floor, shuddering, drooling, her mouth wide in a silent scream, she could still hear that voice whispering from unknown gulfs: *eh, even now at the threshold, the veneer of the Great White Space weakens as the time of the pushing and the birthing draws near—*

Enough, by God, it was enough.

She went into the kitchen and made sure Rocky had enough food and water. He had touched neither all day. He was hiding under the kitchen table, trembling. When she reached out to comfort him, he snapped at her. *Even my dog, even my dog.* Feeling depressed and defenseless and without a friend in the world, Simone climbed into bed and tried to sleep. After a desperate round of tossing and turning, she did just that. Her dreams began right away. Twisted, unreal phantasms of limitless spaces closing in on her, of immense and shaggy forms that brushed against her, of monstrous pulpous undimensioned things moving past her, of crawling up winding staircases that led into nothingness, and being pursued through shattered thoroughfares of wriggling weeds set with monolithic towers that felt like smooth, hot glass under her fingertips, and a world, an anti-world of shifting surface angles where everything was soft and slimy to the touch like the spongy, mucid tissue of a corpse. And through it all, she heard a voice, a booming and commanding voice asking her to make communion with the darkness that awaits us all in the end.

A sinister, malign sort of melody was playing in the background, at first soft and silky then building to a harsh feverish pitch, an immense ear-splitting dissonant noise of bat-like squeaking and shrill creaking, bone grinding against bone, thunderous booming, and saw blades biting into steel plate, chainsaws whirring and jagged-toothed files scraping over the strings of violins and cellos … all of it combining, creating a deranged, jarring cacophony of disharmonic noise, filling her head, melting her nerves like hot wires, cracking open her skull like an eggshell until she came awake screaming in the deathly silence of her bedroom—

Soaked with sweat, shaking like a wet dog, she forced herself to calm down. But it was no easy bit. She was awake and she *knew* she was awake, but the terror and anxiety bunched in her chest did not lessen; it constricted more tightly. Her brain was sending a steady current of electricity to her nerves and the result was that her entire body was jittery and trembling. She had the most awful sense that she was not alone in the room, that another stood by her … breathing. She could hear a low, rasping respiration, a coarse, vulgar sort of sound like that a beast might make.

"Rocky?" she said in a weak, barely existent voice. *"Rocky?"*

Her voice reverberated around her oddly. The sound waves it created seemed to make the air around her vibrate. Her words bounced off the walls and came back at her like ripples she could feel on her skin.

She could still hear the breathing.

Terrified, she swung her legs out of bed and stood, instantly recoiling because the floor was not the floor but something almost gelatinous, a cool burning mud that was crawling with squirming things that began to slink up her legs. *Dreaming, dreaming, you're still dreaming.* But she couldn't convince herself of that. She reached out for the bed but it was no longer there. Panting, she stumbled towards the door and felt an immense momentary relief when it was still there. Something had happened. A pipe had burst or something and she was wading through shit, yet there was no odor save a dank, cellar-like sort of smell. She was in the short hallway that led into the living room. She pushed on through the slopping ooze. She reached out and could find no walls. The hallway seemed to have no end and no beginning.

"ROCKY!" she screamed in desperation.

Again, her words bounced around becoming waves crashing ashore on an alien beach and striking her with force in their reverberations. The air … warm, thick, almost congested …trembled like jelly. She kept moving, reaching out in every direction, but there was nothing, absolutely nothing to touch. That awful, degenerate breathing kept pace with her but its owner made no sounds as it glided along with her. Her head was throbbing, her temples pumping. A headache was gathering steam, its pain funneling out from the back of her brain to some excruciating white-hot spot on her forehead. There was an explosion of brilliance in her mind that left her reeling, it blazed like white phosphorus, igniting her thoughts into a firestorm of luminosity.

What?

What?

What is this?

Being blind since birth, she did not know sight. She could not conceptualize it. It was perfectly abstract in all ways to her. Even her dreams were of sounds, smells, tactile sensations … but not this. She saw for the first time in her life … a multitude of colors and images and forms like thousands of burning bright fireflies filling the night sky. And then, then she saw—if only for the briefest of moments—what stood breathing behind her. A man, a very tall man in a tattered cloak that crept with leggy vermin. He was staring down at her. His face was black, not African, but something like smooth, shiny onyx. A living carved mask. Two brilliant yellow eyes, huge and glossy like egg yolks, watched her. And then it was gone. Whatever had opened in her head had closed, and she nearly passed out.

The dark man gripped her with fingers like crawling roots and she let out a scream, one that seemed to echo from a distant room. Her hands, unbidden, reached out to him as they had done so many times in her life, finding a face that was greasy and soft like a gently pulsating mushroom. She cringed, but her fingers continued exploring despite the abhorrence that made her viscera hang in warm, pale loops. Beneath her fingertips, nodules rose and from each something worming slinked free. They crawled over the backs of her hands. One of them licked at a cut on her pinkie. Another suckled her thumb. Whatever they were, they came out of him in hot geysers, vermiform fleshy nightmares that gushed over her hands and brought a stench of death—old death and new death—that made her want to weep in her revulsion. Her fingers, seemingly magnetized to the face, continued exploring until they found something like a muscular, phallic optic stem growing from his forehead. It held a great, swollen, juicy eye that her index finger slid into, like an over-ripened plum soft with rot.

And a voice, a gurgling slopping voice that sounded as if it was spoken through mush, said, *"So thou might see and thou might make communion with the darkness that waits for all …"*

When Simone was next aware, she was sitting on the couch. She had no memory of getting there. She was in bed, she had nightmares, now she was on the couch. Her sense of smell, heightened beyond normal ken, gave her a sampling of the oily, sweaty, fetid odors that seeped from her pores in toxic rivulets.

The TV was on.

It was on the public-access channel. She never listened to public-access, but here it was. A man's voice was droning endlessly in great dry detail about the cult of the Magna Mater, Cybele-worshipping Romans, and the depravity of Phrygian priests. Little of it made much sense, from the dark secrets of alchemy to the thaumaturgical arts and necromantic rites, from Etruscan fertility cults worshipping the Great Father of Insects to nameless miscegenations that did not walk but crawled within the slime of the honeycombed subterranean passages of Salem.

"Was it not foretold?" the voice asked. "Did not Cotton Mather warn of it? Did not his sermons of those cursed of God, born of the tainted blood of those from outside, serve as an omen of worse things to come? Yes, but we did not listen! Was it not known to the mad Arab and his disciples? The time of the shearing and the opening is at hand, is it not? In *Al-Azif*—thus named for the sounds of night insects, some say, but in truth a cipher that prophesied the coming of Ghor-Gothra, the Great Father Insect—did he not tell us that Yog-Sothoth was the key just as the mad faceless god was The Messenger? Yes! Just as he hinted at the blasphemies of the Father Insect, who was the needle that would open the seams of this world to let the Old Ones through!" He ranted on about something known as the *Pnakotic Manuscripts* and the Angles of Tagh-Clatur and the Eltdown Shards. Becoming positively hysterical as he discussed *De Vermis Mysteriis* and the dread *Liber Ibonis*. "It was all there! All there!"

Simone wanted to turn the channel because these public-access stations were always infested with half-baked religious fanatics, but she did not. There was something here, something important. The voice told her that in 1913 there appeared a novel by Reginald Pyenick called *The Ravening of Outer Slith*, which quickly disappeared from bookshelves because of its horrendous nature, detailing a fertility cult worshipping a pagan insect deity. It was basically a retelling of the ancient German saga, *Das Summen*, which was hinted at in the grand, grim witch-book, *Unaussprechlichen Kulten*, and written about in detail by the deranged Austrian nobleman Jozef Graf Regula in his banned tome, *Morbidus Pestis de Resurrectus* ... the very volume which detailed the history of the Ghor-Gothra cult and the coming age of the Old Ones. Regula was convicted of witchcraft and sorcery for writing it and was drawn and quartered in 1723. No matter;, despite the suppressed knowledge of the cult, fragments of knowledge persisted in Verdin's *Unspeakable Survivals* and in the poem "Gathering of the Witch Swarm" which was to be found in Azathoth and Other Horrors by Edward Derby. "It was there—prophecy of the ages! Now He comes from the Black Mist to usurp our world and let the others in and we, yes, we, shall tremble in the shadow of the true progenitors of the dark cosmos that shivers in their wake. The 13th Equation is on the lips of the many and soon comes the Communion of Locusts, the buzzing, the buzzing, the buzzing ..."

Simone shut the TV off before she lost what was left of her mind.

She was hallucinating, she was paranoid, she was delirious. And listening to the ravings of madmen was not going to help her.

Do something! You must do something! The time draws closer! It is now!

Frustrated, scared, quivering in her own skin, she called good friends—Reese and Carolyn—but they didn't answer. She called friends she hadn't seen in months—Frank and Darien and Seth and Marion—nothing. No one was answering their phones. Why was no one answering? *Because they're gathering now in secret places, on hilltops and misty glens and lonesome fields to wait the coming of—*

That was insane.

Wiping sweat from her face, Simone called her mother. Mom was at the Brighton Coombs Medical Care Facility, a nursing home. Half the time, she did not even recognize her daughter's voice and when she did, she laid out a heavy guilt trip. *You shouldn't be living in the city alone. Terrible things can happen in those places. Your father would roll over in his grave if he knew.* The line was answered and thirty seconds later, her mom was on the phone.

"Mother ... how are you?" Simone said, trying to keep from choking up.

"Oh, Simone, my darling. I'm fine. How are you? You sound stressed. Are you eating enough? Do you have a boyfriend yet?"

Jesus.

"I'm okay. Just lonely."

"Ah, loneliness is a way of life as the years pile up."

But Simone didn't want to get into that. "I'd like to come see you."

"Oh! That would be just fine. I wish you were here now. We're all sitting in the sun room, waiting for the big event."

Simone felt a cold chill envelope her. "What ... what event?"

Her mother laughed. "Why, the stars will soon align and *they* will come through. The seas will boil and the sky will crack open. Cthulhu shall rise from the corpse city of R'lyeh and Tsathoggua shall descend on the moon-ladder from the caverns of N'Kai when the planets roll in the heavens and the stars wink out one by one. Those of true faith will be numbered and heretics shall be named ... you are not an unbeliever, are you, dear?"

Sobbing, Simone slammed the phone down. When something furry brushed against her hand, she nearly screamed. But it was only Rocky. It had to be Rocky ... then it moved beneath her hand with the undulating motion of an immense worm and now she did scream. She launched herself off the couch as that thing moved around her, making a slobbering, hungry sound.

She was hallucinating.

She had to be hallucinating.

Through the furnace ducts she could hear Josh Ryan saying, *"She crawls because she cannot walk, she hears but she cannot see. The sign ... she does not bear the sign."*

Simone pulled herself up the wall, standing on shaking legs. She heard the scratching again ... but this time, it was in her own head like claws and blades and nails scraped along the inside of her skull.

Scritch, scratch, SCRIIIIIITCH, SCRAAAAAAATCH.

The apartment was filled with a hot slaughterhouse stench of viscera, cold meat, and buckets of drainage. She could hear the buzzing of flies, what seemed hundreds if not thousands of them. And the scratching. It was very, very loud now, like giant buzzsaws in the walls and echoing through her brain.

The barrier was coming apart.

Shifting, tearing, fragmenting, realigning itself. She pressed a hand against the wall and felt a huge jagged crack open up beneath her fingertips. She touched something that pulsed within it—something busy and squirming like grave worms wriggling in some peristaltic nest. The buzzing was so loud now she could no longer think. Insects filled the room. They crawled over her arms and up the back of her neck. They tangled in her hair and lighted off her face, sucking the salt from her lips.

She stumbled from the living room and into the hallway as that great furry worm searched for her. Things touched her. They might have been hands, but they were puffy and soft with decay. Worming feelers came from the walls and embraced her, squirming over her face to touch her and know her as she had done so many times with so many others. A mammoth rugose trunk brushed her arm and her fingers slid through a heaving mass of spiky fur. She pulled away, trying to find the wall and succeeding only in finding a wet pelt hanging there that she knew instinctively belonged to Rocky. Her screams could barely be heard over the constant sawing, scratching noise and something like a great tolling bell.

Sobbing and shuddering, she fell to the floor and her knees sank into the floorboards as if they were nothing but warm, malleable putty. This was not her apartment; this was the known universe gutted and turned inside out, merging with another anti-world. She heard the roaring of monstrous locomotive mouths blowing burning clouds of irradiated steam. They shrilled like air raid sirens as the barrier weakened and the bleeding wound of this world split its seams and the nuclear blizzard of the void rushed in to fill its spaces. Her fingers touched snaking loops of crystalline flesh and things like hundreds of desiccated moths and mummified corpse flies rained down over her head. There was a stink like hot neon, shadows falling over her whose touch burned like acid. *The elder sign, child, you must make the elder sign, reveal the Sign of Kish.* Yes, yes, she knew it but did not know it as the air reverberated around her with a scraping, dusty cackling.

Though she could not see, she was granted a vision of the world to come. It filled her brain in waves of charnel imagery that made her scream, made blood run from her nose and her eyes roll back white in her head. Yes, the world was a tomb blown by the hissing radioactive secretions of the Old Ones who walked where man once walked, the skeletons of heretics crunching beneath their stride. The blood of innocents filled the gutters and putrefied bodies swollen to green carrion decayed to pools of slime. The world was a slag heap, a smoldering pyre of bones, and no stars shone above, only an immense multi-dimensional blackness that would have burned the eyes of men from their sockets if they were to look upon it.

Then the vision was gone.

But she could still see.

The crack in the wall was an immense fissure in the world, splitting open reality as she knew it ... and through the gaping chasm, through some freakish curvature of time and space, she saw strobing, polychromatic images of a misty, distorted realm and some chitinous, and truly monstrous form striding in her direction with countless marching legs. Something that was first the size of a truck, then a house, then what seemed a two-story building. She heard the nightmarish whirring and buzzing of its colossal membranous wings. It looked almost like some grotesque mantis with a jagged, incandescent exoskeleton. It was filling the fissure. Not only filling it, but widening it, its droning mouthparts and needlelike mandibles unstitching the seams of creation.

AL-AZIF, AL-AZIF, AL-AZIF, she could hear voices crying.

Hysterical and completely demented, she tried to escape it but one of the insect's vibrating skeletal limbs reached out for her and she was stuck to it like flypaper. Then it had her, flying off through trans-galactic gulfs, through shrieking vortexual holes in the time/space continuum.

She was dropped.

She fell headlong through a dimensional whirlpooling funnel of matter where slinking geometric shapes hopped and squirmed and then—

Her sight was stripped of meat, her soul a sinewy thing desperate for survival in some godless chaos. She crawled, slinked, crept through the bubbling brown mud and pitted marrow of some new, phantasmal unreality. Hungry insectile mouths suckled her, licking sweet drops of red milk, glutting themselves on what she had left. All around her, unseen, but felt, were crawling things and throbbing things and sinuous forms, mewling with hunger. She crept forward, razored webs snapping, cobweb clusters of meaty eggs dripping their sap upon her. She was trapped in the soft machinery of something alive, some cyclopean abomination, a gigantic creeping biological mass born in the night-black pits of some malefic anti-universe. She was crawling over its rotten fish-smelling jellied flesh, sliding through its oily pelt, a speck of animate dust on a loathsome unimaginable life form that dwarfed her world and filled the sky with coiling black tendrils that she could not see but could feel crowding her mind and poisoning the blood of the cosmos.

She was not alone.

Just one of many colonial parasites that crawled through the mire of the beast's life-jelly, swam its brine and foul secretions and oozing sap, her atoms flying apart in a storm of anti-matter and energized particles.

And then—

And then, it ended. A rehearsal, perhaps, for what was yet to come. She laid on the living room floor, drooling and gibbering, numb and mindless, giggling in her delirium. She wished only for night to come when prophecy would be realized and the stars would be right. There was a knob on her forehead, the bud of an optic stem that would let her see the time of the separating and the time of the joining, the rending and the sewing, the communion of this world and the next, as the Old Ones inherited the Earth and the Great Father Insect left his ethereal mansion of cosmic depravity with a swarm of luminous insects, and took to the skies on membranous wings.

As spasms knifed her brain in white-hot shards, the stem pulsated and pushed free, opening like a hothouse orchid so it could show her what was coming: that most holy of nights when the world of men became a graveyard and the cities, tombs.

MESSAGES FROM A DARK DEITY

Stephen Mark Rainey

Now:

Blair finally realized that the things lining the roadside were severed heads.

He had spent time in Iraq during a particularly violent spell, and if he were driving through Baghdad or Fallujah, he would have been just as disturbed, if perhaps less stunned. But this was Hinton, Ohio, a tiny smudge on the banks of the Ohio River. In every corner of the world, people made statements through violence, but in America's heartland, they rarely did it this way.

He slowed his Buick LaCrosse, keenly aware that the perpetrator might be watching him even now, intent on adding another cap to his collection. He counted nine of the awful things: three men, three women, three children, all placed neatly, about ten feet apart, on the road's solid shoulder. Only a few trickles of still-wet blood leaked out from beneath the cleanly sawn necks, and all bore expressions of vivid shock, as if they were still alive and pitiably aware of their condition. The dead he had seen in the Middle East never actually looked like that.

He brought the Buick to a slow halt, grabbed his camera, and clambered out, scanning his surroundings before moving away from the safety of his car. To the right, there was only high grass, a stand of oak trees, and a crumbling barn emblazoned with an ancient Mail Pouch Tobacco advertisement; to the left, a grassy slope led down to the banks of the river. He saw no other remains, for which he was grateful, and no one alive in his field of vision. When he thought about it, he could not remember the last car he had seen or which way it was traveling. This afternoon, he might as well be the only living soul in Hinton.

As he crept toward the nearest of the heads, which belonged to a young, possibly once-attractive woman, he drew his phone from his pocket, only to find no service. For the assignment he had just put to bed in Charleston—the busting of a deadly arson ring—he had opted to drive, rather than make the O'Hare–Yeager roundtrip, because he had wanted to stop in on his brother in Cincinnati. At the last minute, Jim had canceled because of a strep infection. Now this.

Unable to suppress his reporter's instincts for capturing a story, however ghastly, he braced himself and snapped several photos of the heads. If it came down to an assignment, though, he hoped Sibulsky, his editor, would put someone else on this one.

Fat chance.

Blair had witnessed many horrific sights in Iraq—particularly the bodies of children torn apart by shrapnel from homemade explosives and bullets from automatic rifles. But somehow *these* remnants of lives ended so brutally hit him like a vicious punch to the gut. It was the awful *awareness* in their eyes, he decided, both heart-wrenching and terrifying, as if the dead gazes portended for him an imminent, equally dreadful fate.

This place felt *sick*.

He had seen evil, especially overseas. People anywhere and everywhere were evil. But no location in his experience had ever felt like this—drenched in some tangible, noisome horror.

Photos done, he slipped his phone back into his pocket and returned to the car. He had a duty to turn this matter over to the local law, and he would. At this moment, to his profession, he felt considerably less committed.

As he started the LaCrosse, for a second or two, he thought he glimpsed something beyond the old barn: a hovering patch of darkness in the sky, like a hole punched in the fabric of the world.

A dark cloud.

No.

A black hole with soulless, spying eyes.

"What did Sibulsky say?"

"I didn't tell him."

"You serious?"

"Very."

Debra's hands on her hips, her head cocked quizzically at him, indicated that she thought his brain stem must have snapped. "You called the State Patrol and vamoosed? You?"

"I couldn't stay and deal with that."

"After the things you've seen?"

"This was the worst."

"Is it on the news?"

"Not that I know of."

"But you're checking on it?"

"Diligently."

Blair stepped around the wet bar in the corner of the living room and poured a second martini, very dirty, from the shaker. Debra followed and held out her glass, which he filled before turning to the window, wondering if he might again glimpse the strange image that had drifted into his field of vision several times since his discovery of the Hinton Heads. His 30th-floor apartment overlooked the Kennedy Expressway and the northern Chicago skyline, now ablaze with brilliant, kinetic light—a view that, as far as he was concerned, justified his spending more than a third of his income on his residence. He saw nothing unusual, other than a single, brilliant star in the sky, which must have been Mars or Jupiter, since no other celestial bodies besides the moon had the candlepower to cut through the city's canopy of smog and light pollution.

"Why do you keep looking out there?" Debra asked as she half-danced over to him and slipped an arm around his waist. "You're so preoccupied."

"I'm looking for a message from God," he said, with an ounce more solemnity than she would understand. "He doesn't seem to have left any lately."

"Something to ease the memory?"

That wasn't exactly what he was getting at, so he shrugged. "I think God's stopped watching because the movie's too nasty."

Debra's amber-brown eyes blinked away the remark. Every now and then, some remnant of her mostly forgotten Christianity asserted itself. "He doesn't stop watching."

There. At one o'clock. In the general direction of Lincoln Park.

A dark splotch. A black hole drilled in the midnight blue sky, from which *something* peered out at him, unseen except for a few barely discernible bubbles of color, a hue he couldn't quite describe, vaguely resembling a spider's bulbous eyes. As before, the thing existed for three seconds and then was gone, but his sporadic glimpses were just distinct enough to convince him it was not an optical illusion. The fact it had first appeared in Hinton might be coincidence or it might not, but somehow, insidiously, it brought to mind the dark days of two summers ago, when he was firmly entrenched in the atrocity that was the Persian Gulf.

He would remember why in his own sweet time.

He opened the sliding glass door and stepped out to what he called the Afterdeck: the sole remnant of a long-disassembled fire escape, a four-by-eight rectangle of iron grillwork anchored to the building's superstructure by a few bolts that looked rusty enough to pop under little more than his weight. Debra wouldn't set foot out here, but he had outfitted the platform with a table and lounge chair, and on pleasant evenings, he enjoyed reclining with nothing but 300 feet of turbulent air between him and Monroe Street. She knew when he went out there he had entered his own private world, and she let him be, if sometimes with more than a touch of anxiety.

Sipping his martini, he fixed his eyes on the northeastern horizon and the countless glittering towers that soared out of the sizzling ocean of light, hoping to take a bearing should the ghostly image appear yet again.

A steady breeze from Lake Michigan swept away the humidity before it could turn his skin to moist clay and, along with the alcohol, lulled him into a contemplative stupor. Every now and then, the grillwork platform would shift subtly, just enough to induce a touch of vertigo, and he wondered how long those old bolts in the wall would continue to hold. However, he enjoyed the thrill of the wind's tug and the perception that he was actually floating on a current of air, so the danger was more alluring than daunting.

He closed his eyes to enjoy the invigorating sensation, and when he opened them again, the moon had risen and the sound of traffic on the expressway below had changed from a slow, steady rumble to the occasional *swish-thrum* of vehicles passing by at high speed. His martini glass, empty, lay on its side on the metal latticework beside his lounge chair, and his chest felt heavy, as if something were pressing insistently down on him. Glancing northeastward, he half-expected to see a gaping pit in the sky, barely visible globular eyes peering out, their inscrutable gaze weighing on him like frigid stone. But there was nothing.

Except stars.

Holy God, the sky was full of them. Brilliant, multicolored jewels cutting through the greenish haze like smoldering embers that stretched from horizon to horizon. He'd never seen anything like it—at least, not in the city. Maybe in a far, distant desert, some years ago.

He sat up and nearly choked, and he realized the pressure in his chest was from a horrible, gut-wrenching stench, which hovered like a layer of thick, sulfurous smoke just above his reclining body.

"Fucking awful," he muttered, wondering what kind of hellish atmospheric cocktail had wafted to this altitude. He picked up his glass and returned to indoors, now dark and silent. Apparently, Debra had already gone to bed. The kitchen clock read 1:09 AM; five hours had flashed by since he had ventured out to the Afterdeck.

Age, alcohol, and fatigue, he thought. Traveling long distances wore him out more than it used to, and lately he'd been aware of a low, slow burn inside as the stress of endlessly delving into man's inhumanity to man took its toll on his mind and body. Lots of newsmen burned out quickly, especially now that the world had shrunk to the point that there was simply no such place as "over there." It was all one big mass of humanity on an aging, cancer-riddled sphere edging ever closer to its final days of existence.

He'd smelled something like that stench out there once before, he thought. But somewhere else, back in the past, never in Chicago.

He went to the bar, made himself a nightcap—a thing he had lately come to cherish like little else—and returned to the window to marvel at the inexplicable, star-stippled sky.

Two Summers Ago:

A few glimmers of light cut through the pulsating darkness that had become his entire field of vision, and, finally, he began to hear the sounds of mass confusion around him: haranguing voices, none in English; the grating rumble of HUMV engines; the distant, arrhythmic thuds of artillery fire—whether from the Americans, the Islamists, or both, he couldn't tell. It was heavy and constant. *So it must be ours*, he thought.

He was lying on his back on a rough, uncomfortable surface. As sight and hearing slowly returned, he took stock of every sensation, praying he hadn't been ripped half-apart by the nearby mortar blast. His back ached, but he didn't feel any other focused pain. He found he could move his hands and feet—*thank God!*—and apart from a dull pounding in his temples, he counted himself little the worse for wear. Overhead, he saw a cracked plaster ceiling; to his right, an open window, through which a few wisps of smoke trickled in; and to the left, a cracked wooden door, slightly ajar. There were no furnishings, and the walls were bare. At the moment, he appeared to be alone.

Soon, the shelling stopped, the motors faded, and the voices diminished until all he could hear was the soft whisper of desert wind outside. No further hint of incoming ordnance.

Thus reassured, he relaxed somewhat, a bit nervous about his unknown whereabouts, but still too dazed to worry much about it, at least for the time being. He was alive and seemingly whole.

He had no idea what had happened to Edward Hollister, the British journalist with whom he'd been traveling, or the young Iraqi translator, whose name he couldn't remember. He'd last seen them just before the shelling started—before the road had been completely obliterated by smoke and every vehicle and person in the convoy had scattered in search of cover.

He didn't remain relaxed very long. A new chorus of voices rose somewhere just beyond the window, and he sat up, slowly, carefully, wondering whether he had been brought here by friendlies or by murderous fanatics. But no—the window and door were open. If the Islamists had abducted him, they would never have left him unattended.

Or would they? Out there lay only miles of desert. He wouldn't get very far even if he were to walk out of here unhindered.

He rose to his knees, shuffled to the window, and stuck his head into the arid afternoon air. To his surprise, he found himself looking out over an expanse of blinding white sand from three stories up. Maybe he was in a mosque, or some vacant apartment building. From this vantage point, he couldn't see any other structures, but off to the right, he discerned a pale, thin ribbon that extended to the horizon, which he figured was the road his convoy had been traveling when the mortars hit.

Something on that horizon—which lay to the east, according to the sun—drew his attention and held it. A long, dark smudge, like a blotch of murky oil paint, had turned a portion of the powder-blue backdrop to yellow-brown soup. For a long minute, he couldn't figure out what he was seeing until he remembered having driven through western Indiana late one spring and seen something like it rolling across the endless, flat plain.

Dust storm.

A huge one, by the look of it.

A tremor passed through his gut, but he wasn't sure why. It wasn't just the approaching sand storm. Something here seemed wrong. *Evil,* even. As if more than danger lurked somewhere around him, hidden, waiting.

Plotting.

Now:

The next day when he saw the thing in the sky, it lasted for several minutes, occupying that same space above the horizon, becoming more substantial with every passing second, like an onyx-hued moon materializing through a thinning haze.

Debra hadn't seen it when he'd pointed straight to it. He doubted anyone else would either.

So he went after it.

Like a black star of Bethlehem, it led him northeastward until he arrived in a Wrigleyville neighborhood he passed through only rarely: an attractive, tree-lined residential street, quiet and restful, between Belmont and Addison. He knew when he had reached his destination because of the sudden tremor of cold, pure dread that passed through his body.

The same as in Hinton, Ohio.

And some other, still unremembered time.

An ancient, hulking church stood silently on a street corner, watching over the neighborhood with somber dignity, its tall spire thrusting skyward—toward the gaping black mouth that had climbed to a zenith directly overhead, occasionally revealing a shifting array of oddly colored orbs on which his eyes refused to focus.

He parked at the curbside, got out of his car with his camera and snapped a series of photographs. Hardly unexpectedly, when he looked into the preview pane to see what the lens had captured, he saw only azure blue sky and ruffled masses of a few altostratus clouds.

The implication nearly sent him into a screaming rage. That some portion of his mind had become unhinged and was causing him to hallucinate seemed sickeningly certain.

"What you s'pose that is?" came a cracked, dry voice from behind him.

Blair whirled to regard the speaker: a stooped, gray-haired woman who wore a moth-eaten overcoat and a ratty woolen scarf, even though the morning was already quite warm. A gnarled finger pointed, not to the sky, but toward the distant street corner to the north. At first, he saw nothing remarkable, but after a few seconds, he detected a movement among the tree limbs, just above the sidewalk.

A dark shape was gliding slowly earthward: a black cat pawing its way out of the branches and creeping down the trunk, he thought, until he realized, by way of comparing it to the car parked beside the tree, that the thing was easily larger than a man. It had a long, lithe torso and four spindly limbs, but he could discern only a black, featureless silhouette. When it reached the ground, it vanished behind the cars and did not reappear.

"An animal?" he asked, glancing back at the old woman, realizing he had failed to lift his camera for a shot.

"No. It came from outa that, up yonder." The pointing finger turned upward.

Blair's blood froze. He tried not to stammer, nearly succeeded. "You see it?"

"You think I'm blind? 'Course I see it."

Blair squinted, a little suspicious. "What do you see?"

"Don't get wise with me!"

"You mean the hole in the sky."

"Yeah. The hole in the sky."

The old woman's eyes shifted and turned north. Blair followed her gaze and again saw the black silhouette, almost a man, but not quite, and this time it began to dance.

Jerky, erratic. A puppet on strings pulled by a madman's hands.

Blair broke into a sprint, something he hadn't done in too many ages, and his lungs and heart protested after a hundred yards. When he blinked, the silhouette had again disappeared.

"No way."

As he passed a parked car, something caught his eye, and he stopped. There, half jammed into the grill, half hanging onto the asphalt: a shapeless mass, all pink and red, surrounded by a pool of liquid crimson.

No, it was not a child, it couldn't be.

A fractured, dripping skull hung from a few peach-colored, fleshy strands, its eyes glistening blue and staring vacantly skyward. Two crooked rows of teeth between bleeding, blistered gums grinned endlessly, and he heard a wheezing gasp, which seemed to come from the ruined figure hanging from the front of the car, though he knew it couldn't have.

This time he took photographs. Several.

He looked left, across the street, down the alley between two of the houses. From a tree in the backyard, barely visible, something small was hanging from a rope, swinging slowly back and forth, and for a couple of seconds, it appeared to wriggle helplessly.

To his right, from beneath the wooden stairs that led to the side door of a house, a small, ivory-white arm protruded, doll-like, but too clearly not a doll.

The odor that suddenly wormed down his trachea and expanded in his lungs was like an injection of brimstone. He turned, gagged, and emptied the contents of his stomach onto the sidewalk.

Sometime later, he struggled back upright and glimpsed the black silhouette pirouetting away to the north, where it vanished in the distance.

"You see?" came the voice of the old woman.

It was a little Clark Street tavern; he might have visited it a time or two before. At this hour of day, it was nearly empty. The bartender, a burly young man with a goatee and small but very bright emerald eyes, watched him curiously as he sucked down a bourbon on ice, its burn as beautiful as the caress of Debra's hand.

"Another," he said, passing back the empty glass.

"What did you see?" the bartender asked, his small eyes a little too intent.

"What makes you think I saw anything?"

"Intuition."

"I'll just bet."

"Lots of people lately. They see things, they come in here, they drink. Sometimes they talk."

Blair raised an eyebrow, but then his phone in his pocket burred softly.

"Yeah?"

"Why didn't you tell me about Hinton?" It was Sibulsky's voice.

"What about it?"

"You know what about. Did you get pictures?"

"Yeah. I got pictures."

"Somehow, I have not seen them."

"You will."

"I'm wondering why you didn't bring this to me straight away. And why—if you saw what you say you did—it hasn't been picked up by any of the majors. Or even social media."

"How do you know about Hinton?"

"I just talked to Debra. Wanted to know why you hadn't checked in."

He sighed. "Look, Ben. Don't even think of sending me back there. I can't go. Not now."

Sibulsky's voice turned sharp. "If this is something big, it belongs to you, Blair."

He hated where this train was heading, but there was no way to turn it. "Okay. Here's the deal. Something's happening here. In the city. I think it's part of the same thing."

"What the hell are you talking about?"

"Whatever happened in Hinton. It's here now."

"*That* calls for an explanation."

"Yeah. Later."

"This afternoon."

"Tomorrow morning."

Another long hesitation and a sigh. "Shoot me those pictures. Today. Now."

"I will."

He put his phone away and downed the last of his drink. He contemplated a third, but a lingering shred of reason dissuaded him. The bartender's little hyena eyes remained fixed on him.

"So what do people talk about here?" he asked.

"Black holes."

Blair barely kept his jaw from hitting the counter. "Black holes?"

"Yep."

"Have you seen a black hole?"

"Nope."

Blair leaned closer, the back of his skull buzzing. "So who has?"

"Nobody who claims to have seen one ever comes back."

He barked a laugh. "Well, I tell you what. When I find out what I aim to find out, I'm going to come back in here and have a drink. That, my young friend, is a solemn promise."

"I could use the business."

Two Summers Ago:

Footsteps echoed from somewhere beyond his room, and then the door burst open and four men entered, all dressed in sweat-soaked fatigues. Blair raised his hands, but they waved him down, speaking rapid gibberish that sounded reasonably friendly. At least they didn't seem intent on separating his head from his shoulders, he thought with some relief. One man was much taller than the others and had very dark skin, but bright blue eyes. Another one carried a primitive-looking radio-transmitter set, and he sat down on the floor, slipped on the headset, and began speaking in Arabic into the mouthpiece.

The two youngest, barely past their teens, pointed excitedly out the window to the approaching storm; the tall man, however, was watching it with grim fascination. The one with the radio seemed to be having trouble reaching his intended contact and finally shut it down, giving it a disapproving frown. Then he glanced at Blair and said in halting English, "Stay there, my friend. We find help for you after the storm goes."

Blair nodded and mumbled "Thank you," trying but failing to suppress his escalating anxiety. Outside, the great brown smudge had grown to cover the entire horizon, and he could now hear a faint, rumbling *whooshing* sound that grew gradually nearer and louder.

The man who had spoken turned, picked up his radio set, and disappeared through the door, his footsteps clattering away into silence. The others continued to gaze out the window, transfixed, as the thunderous rumble grew deeper and more menacing.

Soon, Blair could see the huge wall of brown sand and dust bearing down on his window: an endless series of huge, roiling columns that ascended into the sky and then collapsed, kicking up more sand, which, in turn, grew into towers, swirling and crawling and melting into an increasingly chaotic mass. In the center of the great cloud, a huge, black oblong appeared and seemed to expand slowly, like a mouth gaping wide to swallow anything and everything in the raging storm's path.

The two youngest men turned to face Mecca, knelt, and began to pray aloud, as if aware of the reek of *evil* that surrounded their little room. Their frenzied voices only added to Blair's apprehension. The air now felt charged with some dreadful electricity, and he detected a hideous odor—a nauseating mélange of sulfuric acid, ammonia, and rancid meat.

The tall, blue-eyed man remained standing and, if anything, appeared more captivated than concerned. Ignoring Blair altogether, he stepped closer to the window and began to speak softly, so softly that, at first, Blair could make out nothing he said. The words were guttural and ran together, but when they did become more or less clear to him, they sounded like "Ee-eye-ee-eye-oh, cuckoo who'll fool you, foe tag again, glue a gnarly toe tap."

Within two minutes, the winds died and the sandstorm collapsed upon itself, leaving only a few slowly rising columns of dark dust several hundred yards from their vulnerable window to mark its violent passing.

Without a word, the tall man turned and left the room, while the two young Iraqis shakily rose to their feet, exchanged shocked glances, and stared out at the now-empty desert. Finally, with what he took to be pitying looks at him, they followed the tall man out the door. Once again, he was alone in some tiny chamber in the middle of a God-forsaken land, feeling as if at any moment he might be struck down by the hand of some dark, unknown—unknowable—deity.

Now:

"Oh, God. It *is* a baby."

Debra's face was chalky as she handed the camera back to him.

"And nobody cared. It took the police forty-five minutes to get there, and then they wouldn't talk to me. No questions, no interviews, just a curt 'go away.'"

"That's awful. Horrible. But why do you think this is related to the other killings?"

He didn't want to tell her that God had said so in a message, or that God was looking more and more like a spindly black dancing thing that dropped from a hole in the sky. "Well, I had an interesting interview with a bartender. Where this thing shows up, people die."

"This *thing*. This thing that I can't see. That nobody can see—except for some people a bartender told you about."

Coming from her lips, it did sound ridiculous. "Something like that."

"You don't think the bartender might have been having a good one on you?"

"No."

He went to the sliding glass door to the Afterdeck and gazed at the afternoon sky. The sun blazed behind a thin layer of clouds, but an ocean of twinkling stars glittered across the azure backdrop. Overhead, Ursa Major and Polaris looked down at him with disdain, and closer to the horizon, Cepheus and Cassiopeia danced lewdly together in the sun's vain glare.

He snapped a few shots, wondering if the lens might deign to pick up more than it had when he'd photographed the hole in the sky. It didn't.

Debra joined him at his side, eyeing him thoughtfully. "So what's up?"

"Ever see a sky full of stars in broad daylight?" he asked.

"Is that what you see?"

He had never lied to her, but he could hardly stand to tell her the truth. "I wish I didn't. But I see stars, yes."

"So, what makes you—and those others—see things the rest of us don't? That the camera doesn't?"

"If I knew that, I'd know the rest of the story."

"Are you going to write this one?"

"Just now, I have nothing to write. I am now what we officially call investigating." He gave her shoulder a squeeze. "At least you haven't called me a liar."

Deep shadows surrounded her eyes. "I know you're not a liar. I wonder about your senses, though."

"I'd wonder too—if it weren't for those dead. Those were no hallucination."

She glanced distastefully at his camera and shook her head. "No."

105

He turned away from her and switched on the television, flipping through several news channels to see if any of the reports struck a familiar chord with him. They didn't. He needed to find others who had seen these things before he could start piecing together an even marginally cohesive theory. The bartender's revelation had bemused him, but beyond that, he hadn't been much help. But Blair at least had a location.

Eastward.

The camera's eye apprehended the bodies of the dead, but not the black hole or the stars in the daytime sky. The dead were real, all right; they just seemed barely to register to most human witnesses.

Blair noticed that Debra still stood with her eyes locked on the sky, so intently that he wondered whether the afternoon's stellar display had finally revealed itself to her. But when she turned away, her eyes barely held his, and her sad, heavy sigh indicated that she was vitally worried about him.

He spent the rest of the day trying to interview detectives at the Belmont District Headquarters, but after three fruitless attempts to see Lieutenant Ingram Trotter—usually one of his most reliable contacts at the department—he threw up his hands, went back to Wrigleyville, and walked the streets for two hours. With no sign of the hole in the sky or its attendant black dancer, he returned home, only to find an empty apartment and a note from Debra that she had gone out with her friend Sharon for the evening.

A night out with Sharon meant some serious commiserating, which often lasted until the following day. Chances were he would be sleeping alone tonight.

He dutifully flipped through the news channels, checked websites, every social media outlet, hoping for even a hint of some vindicating report. A story about the higher-than-usual number of random murders in Chicago and elsewhere raised his hopes slightly, but in the end, it was little more than a footnote to the major international news of the day. Then something drew his attention to the television screen during a report about corruption in the Justice Department, and his chest immediately constricted so that he could barely breathe.

A few blocks behind the cheerful-looking young woman narrating the story, a building was burning, and neither she nor the cameraman were paying it one moment's attention. And not a fire truck or other emergency vehicle anywhere to be seen. As the segment ended, the fire appeared to be spreading, while the news crew and a dozen or so bystanders went blithely about their business.

That was in Washington, DC.

Blair shut off the television, rose from the couch, and made himself a drink, barely able to comprehend the scope of what must be unfolding out there. Then, when he glanced out the window, he saw the stars: a billion of them, their jeweled faces flashing with sinister light behind a nearly opaque layer of haze. He automatically reached for his camera, before his brain had a chance to remind him of its futility. He paused, but then took the camera from the kitchen table, removed the flashcard, and plugged it into his computer, suddenly fixated on the fact that he had not bothered to examine his photographs except via the small preview pane.

Once he had brought the images up on his monitor, he selected the first shots he had taken of the sky—which by all rights *should* have pictured the black-hole thing—and began to study them at various zoom levels. In one, he now saw a faint oblong shadow hovering above the distant buildings—a vague suggestion of some airborne object that almost registered but didn't.

As if it had cloaked itself from the camera's eye.

He brought up a more recent shot of the afternoon sky and zoomed in on the seemingly empty field of blue, only to find an abundance of scattered pixels of slightly different hue than the rest of the backdrop. Then, by meticulously tracing the patterns of some of the off-colored dots, he was able to discern the shape of Ursa Major.

It was all there. Indiscernible to anyone who wasn't specifically looking for the signs in the sky, but there nonetheless.

A low, foreboding voice in his head told him that the source of the phenomena simply wasn't ready to reveal itself to a global audience. But it would be. Soon.

What the hell would happen then?

A little later, he went out to the Afterdeck with a fresh martini. He saw several fires in the distance but didn't hear a single siren.

Blair had only been asleep a few minutes when the creaking of the bedroom door drew him back to consciousness. His eyes opened only reluctantly, but when they found their focus, he saw Debra's naked body in front of the window, limned with electric blue. She slid onto the bed next to him and leaned down so that her hair spilled over his face. She kissed him lightly on the mouth.

"Surprised to see you," he mumbled.

"Wanted to make sure you were okay."

"How about you? You all right?"

"I'm okay."

"Did you cry on Sharon's shoulder?"

"You know better than that." Her eyes sought the ceiling. "But she …"

"What?"

"She saw something. Just like you."

He bolted upright and gripped her bicep with a taut claw. "What? What was it?"

"Stars," she said, grimacing. "Stars, during daylight."

"I've got to talk to her."

"Calm down. It's late. But she's going to come over tomorrow. You can compare notes then." Debra delicately extricated her arm from his grasp. "She's afraid."

"She's seen something else, then?"

She shook her head. "No, that's not it. Not really."

"Did you tell her what I've seen?"

"Not everything. Just about the stars. And the dead. That's what really got to her—the dead."

"Fires. Did you see any fires?"

She blinked questioningly. "Fires? No. What do you mean?"

"Buildings. Cars. Anything burning anywhere?"

"Not that I can remember."

He shook his head, his eyes moving to the window. "I think we're going to."

"You've got me worried now. And Sharon … I've never seen her like that." She searched his eyes for a long time. "What do you think is happening, Owen?"

"Something unprecedented."

"What? From *where*?"

He inhaled deeply and caught a faint whiff of sulfur. "A very dark place."

She pressed close to him, and he lay back, pulling her with him, cradling her head in his arms. He could hear his own heart clanging and feel Debra's pulse thudding in her neck. Still, her presence was calming, even as blood and adrenaline raced recklessly through both their bodies.

Finally, once her hand began to move down his chest, past his stomach, and then lower, the fires in his head went out for a time.

At some point, sunlight replaced the electric glow beyond the blinds. Blair opened his eyes and found himself alone in the bed, but he could smell coffee brewing in the kitchen, and he felt a warm rush of relief to know Debra was still here. Somehow, he feared she might have gone off again.

The coffee called to him, so he tugged on a pair of boxer shorts and set out on his quest. As he entered the dining room, he was surprised to see Debra standing in front of the sliding door to the Afterdeck, her head craned back slightly, her brown eyes reflecting the ten o'clock sun.

"Christ, Sibulsky's going to have my head," he muttered, moving toward her, wondering what caught her interest. But he stopped as she lifted a hand and pointed toward the door.

"I see them," she said softly. "God almighty, I see them."

His heart lurched, but he could only watch as Debra opened the sliding door and stepped out to the Afterdeck, her eyes never leaving the sky. He felt a faint twinge of unkind amusement, for she had only been out there once before, and that was with stark terror.

But the stars in the mid-morning sky had snared her completely, and now he saw them, ten times more numerous and far more brilliant than the day before.

They must be almost *right* by now, he thought, wondering where that peculiar idea had come from.

Right for what?

She slowly turned to look at him, her face drawn, defeated. "I see them," she said softly. "Are you happy now?"

For a moment, the omnipresent breeze seemed to dwindle and die, for the world went unnaturally quiet. Then, with a sharp *bang*, one of the bolts in the wall snapped, and one end of the Afterdeck dipped abruptly, pitching Debra off-balance. She threw out a hand to steady herself, but a second later came another *bang* and then a scraping sound, and the iron platform, railing and all, simply disappeared. He had been looking right into Debra's eyes, but now he was facing only sky—a vivid blue, nightmarish canopy splattered with millions of twinkling stars, like speckles of fiery blood hurled from a sun laid open by a vast, sweeping scythe. At the edge of his vision, something huge and black was hovering in the blue.

"Debra?" he said to the sky. "Wait. No!"

He lunged forward, gripping the door jamb to keep from following her down, just in time to see her fall terminate on the Oak Street sidewalk, his trusty old lounge chair following and shattering a half-second later.

There were several passersby on the street, but none of them stopped to look. One old woman did glance briefly upward, as if she might have felt a stray drop of rain, before continuing on her eastward shamble.

"No," Blair said again, as an odor like sulfur, ammonia, and rancid meat drifted to his nostrils. "She doesn't go out there. She just doesn't."

The odor intensified, and he stepped back into the room, pulled the door shut, and locked it, half-afraid he might forget and walk out there before it registered that his favorite retreat had collapsed into ruin.

The sun's light failed to reach into the living room, and there, shadows swirled like living, dancing thunderclouds. As the terrible smell burned sharper and more menacingly in his nostrils, he saw, standing before him, the black silhouette that had yesterday danced on the sidewalk in front of the old church. That was all it was—a silhouette, shaped vaguely like a man but with disproportionately long arms and legs, an elongated, misshapen bulb that might have been its head, and some kind of horn-like protrusion curling outward from its torso. It was tall. So tall it had to stoop to clear his ten-foot ceiling.

The voice sounded like mighty stands of timber splintering. "Until the stars come right, only a few shall spy us, and those only dimly."

As if it had merged with the swirling darkness around it, the silhouette lost its contours, became a shadow of a shadow, and Blair felt a frigid, oily wave rush past him, battering his face, drenching him with cold brimstone, and in that moment, he expected to be scattered to the four winds, swept into oblivion.

His lungs struggled for air, and it was with some shock that he realized the hideous odor had dissipated. His skin, however, felt coated with vile slime, and the unnatural darkness in the room only slowly gave way to light from outside.

Unsteadily, he made his way to the bar and poured himself a glass of straight gin. He threw it back, poured another, and then went to the sliding door to peer into the well of empty space that had swallowed the only things in the world that actually meant anything to him.

He tugged the door open again and stood on the precipice, wondering briefly if he should take one more step and add his body to the wreckage thirty stories below.

While he thought, he drank. And breathed in the acrid smoke that was rising from the countless fires that blazed in clusters around the city as far as his eyes could see. Smoke that was beginning to take form— vaguely resembling the dark deity that had briefly acknowledged his existence.

It was almost a relief when his brain registered, at long last, the rising wailing of sirens.

And screams.

From all over the city.

From all over the world.

Countless Summers Ago:

Fifteen minutes after the strange man had left, Blair heard the sound of a helicopter approaching, and, looking out the window, he saw a UH-1 Blackhawk bearing down on the building, and damned if that wasn't Ed Hollister leaning out its door, his eyes anxiously scanning the terrain. Somehow, he caught sight of Blair in the building's window and began waving.

Blair waved back, only to freeze in surprise. For one brief second, beyond the approaching bird, the bright daylight sky appeared full of stars. Endless, brilliant, insane, *dizzying* stars.

He looked away and then back at the sky. The stars were gone. A migraine coming on, maybe. Not surprising after all he had been through.

The vertigo passed quickly, but he knew he never wanted to see anything like *that* ever again.

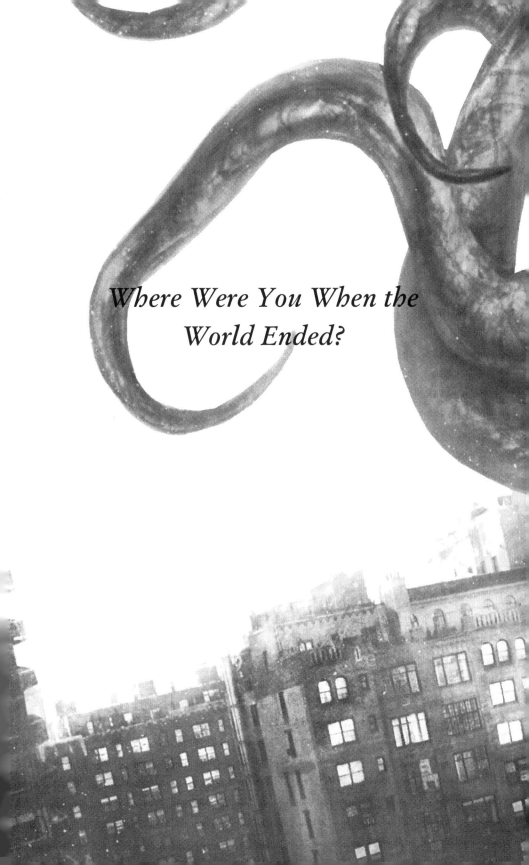

Where Were You When the World Ended?

TIME FLIES

Pete Rawlik

Pandora Peaslee sat up in bed and stared at her lover's silhouette. He was standing in front of the window, staring out at the Indian Ocean, watching the sun rise. The day was already hot and humid, and sweat glistened on his bare skin. He waved his hand over his head, shooing something out of his thinning hair. Sometime during the night the fruit flies had found their way in and were now busy hovering lazily around a table where a bowl of bananas, pineapples, and some things she didn't recognize sat slowly ripening into decay. It was December 26th, 2004, they were in Sri Lanka, and Pandora Peaslee had fallen in love with an alien.

His name had once been Vince Delarosa. He had been an underwater welder on an oil rig in the Arctic. He had died when his hard suit had cracked and freezing cold water had slowly leaked in. He had been in the water six hours before they finally pulled his body out and declared him deceased. They put him in a body bag and stored him in the meat locker. Two hours later he was screaming, but he wasn't Vince Delarosa anymore: the body had been possessed by an alien intelligence, one of a kind that had been known to the CIA for a long time. They were called the Yith, and for all intents and purposes they weren't much different than humans. They had better control

114

over their emotions, and they understood things about the universe, particularly the nature of time, better than humans did, but they could be reasoned with. The Yith were time-traveling aliens who were open to conversation and negotiations.

This was a good thing, because in the last eighteen months more than four thousand of them had suddenly taken possession of human bodies and become part of the human world. They brought with them knowledge, and sold it to governments and corporations alike. New chemicals, new medicines, new ways to harvest energy, and new ways to treat things that men had long thought incurable. There were treatments for HIV, Down syndrome, and even ALS. This knowledge didn't come free; it wasn't cheap—but it wasn't expensive either. The Yith seemed to understand the economics of things, how to balance price, returns, and market share. It had made them very wealthy, very quickly, and they liked to use that wealth.

Traveling, it seems, is what Yith did best, and when they did it, they did it *en masse*. In August they had gone to New York City for the Republican National Convention and to tour the Statue of Liberty. In October they had been to Rome and witnessed the signing of the European Constitution. But in November they had suddenly flocked back to their home base off the coast of Australia, and stayed there for two weeks. All staff, diplomats, and attachés had been asked to leave, briefly. The conspiracy nuts went wild.

Pandora's favorite theory from the wingnuts was that this was an invasion, that the Yith were coming to take over the planet; not through military force but by buying their way in. Of course, the public relations firm that had been hired by the Yith vehemently denied this, which, of course, was their job. They also denied all the other rumors that came down the pike. What they didn't do was ever explain why exactly the Yith were here. Any time they were pressed on the subject they simply released another piece of miracle technology or threw money at the issue. They were the epitome of vague, masters of the non-committal response.

As a CIA agent, Pandora knew the truth—or at least what the experts said was the truth. Incursions by the Yith had been documented for centuries, and according to files, they were mostly harmless. The expert opinion on the aliens was that they were time-traveling historians with a penchant for unusual events. By unusual, the files meant inexplicable. The Yith concept of what was an important event and what wasn't seemed to defy human logic. For the most part they shunned war but gravitated towards natural disasters. They recognized that certain things had value, but often left business details to be handled by their human agents. They were in many ways epicurean, enjoying food and drink and even sex, and a variety of other recreational activities. Some were avid readers, others loved music, or film, but very few seemed interested in sculpture or painting. Many were intensely interested in hiking, swimming, running, archery, and skeet. A few even had an interest in larger weaponry. They were a conundrum, but they paid well, so nobody minded that much; those who did were ignored.

And then there was the dead thing. All the historical incursions had been live individuals who had been occupied, sometimes for years, and then returned to normal, or as close to normal as possible. This large an incursion and using the recent dead was unprecedented. When asked about it, the Yith said they thought it was finally time.

Pandora had met Ys, Mister Ys, the thing that had occupied Delarosa, at a security interview. She found him charming, engaging, and even witty. When he had been cleared to enter the general population he surprised everyone by asking her to be his personal bodyguard. He had offered more money than she could refuse. Their first trip had been to the Library of Congress where he read her poems by Edward Derby. They had pizza for dinner, and two bottles of wine from a little shop on the edge of Chinatown. The next day they flew to Portland and had Dungeness crab and local-made craft beers at the Columbia River Brewing Company, before going to the Hollywood Theater to watch a marathon of Universal horror films. He could have watched these anywhere, anytime, but had, as he explained, wanted the theater experience.

Two weeks in, at a blues festival in Palm Beach, Pandora Peaslee had kissed him. He tasted like barbecue sauce, powdered sugar and apple cider. That night they made love. He proved insatiable, and the first man to truly understand and fulfill her own desires. Months later he was still as vigorous and ravenous as ever, and she simply couldn't get enough of him. Their schedule was often restructured to accommodate these extracurricular activities. Planes were delayed, but it didn't matter; the Yith paid well and so nobody minded. Given her sudden and fantastic new life, it wasn't surprising that Pandora had fallen in love. She was suspicious of course, about Ys, about her feelings, about his motives, about *his* feelings, but there was never any time for all of that. They were living for the moment, as if at any moment it might run out.

He turned to face her and glanced at his watch. Ys, like all the Yith, was obsessed with always knowing what time it was. He looked at her and a smile came across his face. "The Mission has arranged for a breakfast buffet on the roof; we need to be there by 07:00. We'll be going to the mountains afterwards: wear your cotton field shirt, jeans, hiking boots and that photo tog you bought in Budapest." He said it with an "H" sound, "Budapesht".

Ys was an avid hiker, and Pandora had gone with him on near-daily adventures, turning her lithe body into an efficient and tight machine. She wasn't muscle-bound, not by any means, but she was a lot more toned than she had been. She had more stamina now too, which allowed her more energy for a variety of activities. Pandora glanced at the clock, noted the time, did some quick calculations and pulled her lover back into bed. He didn't resist.

The first thing that Pandora noted as she stepped on to the roof was that, as usual, Ys had overbought, and had bought things that they hadn't really needed. There were two cubic yards of spring water bottles and dozens of coolers of ice. There was fresh fruit, still in mesh bags, in piles taller than a man, coconuts and bananas mostly. There were half a dozen machetes nearby. Next to that were several large propane grills, and an oversized fuel tank as well. Off in the corner was an iconic blue Porta-Potty. Several wooden crates were stacked about, their contents unknown, but large latches with ominous locks cried out for investigation. As she scanned the party she noted a large tent with solar panels, an oversized computer, a satellite dish, and several large televisions mounted about.

"What is all this?" she questioned her partner.

"Just a party," he responded without looking at her, "a very special party."

Her eye caught a strange kinetic sculpture, a huge thing, bigger than a man, comprised of mirrors and crystals and coils and rods of wire that seemed to be moving. She tried to see how it worked, how the various pieces fit together and influenced each other, but whenever she tried to focus on a particular component her eyes grew blurry and her ears began to hurt. She stumbled but Mister Ys caught her.

"Come this way Pandora; the morning excitement seems to have given you a touch of vertigo."

There was coffee. Not American coffee, not French coffee, not Cuban coffee, but a local blend of robusta concocted, or so legend said, by a British writer who had made his home on the island. It was rich and dark, but not overly bitter, and it lingered on the tongue and brought to mind the dark mysterious riches of the jungle. Pandora savored the bold flavor, then added a hint of cream. All around her, people, Yith, were savoring the dark liquid refreshment. It was then she realized that of the forty or so people at this little soiree only about five were human. The rest were alien minds occupying human bodies, bodies that had at one point been declared dead. She could tell by the bright blue symbol that had been tattooed on the left hand of every Yithian, a swirling symbol of curves that told everyone instantly what this thing before them was. Despite the tropic heat, the morbidity of the whole situation suddenly struck her, and manifested as a sudden chill. She grabbed a mimosa from a tray and tried to chase the feeling away. It was a prejudice deeply rooted in western culture: the dead should stay dead; they should not be hosts for other beings. Strangely enough, many other cultural traditions said just the opposite, and there had been a great debate amongst practitioners of Voodoo and Eastern mysticism about the issue. The Yith had remained silent—didn't even bother to attend.

At 7:20 one of the Yith, a woman who used the name Miss Trey, stood up and gently tapped her glass with a spoon, calling everyone to attention. As usual, the ever-polite Yith settled into their seats and were instantly still, like well-trained students at a private school. "Associates," her voice was crisp and clear, "A little over two hours ago the event we have been expecting occurred on time and in the predicted place. To enlighten our few human guests, a magnitude 9.2 earthquake occurred off the coast of Indonesia. As a result the planet is now oscillating at the predicted frequency and the rotational change

118

will be approximately 2.5 seconds."

All around her the Yith were eerily silent. Their attention was on the speaker, but they took in her news as if they were at an everyday morning brunch listening to a weather report or perhaps the scoring from a local cricket match. Only the five humans, herself included, seemed to take the news with a touch of terror.

"We have pictures coming in from affected areas." The monitors behind her sputtered to life and revealed scenes of terrifying devastation. Whole cities inundated with rushing water, with cars and small buildings completely submerged. The cameras showed no people. "The casualties will be immense. Indonesia is recorded at 167,000 with 500,000 displaced. Thailand, 8,200 with 7,000 displaced. India, 20,000 with 650,000 displaced. Sri Lanka, 35,000 with 516,000 displaced."

As those words left her mouth, one of the other humans, a man Pandora knew only as Jones, ran to the edge of the roof and looked out at the beach. When he turned back his face was pale and his eyes frantic. "I can't see the ocean!" he screamed. "It's gone, it just rolled away!"

A moment later Pandora heard the screaming. There was an immense rushing sound like a thousand jets all landing at once. The building shook, trembling as something unseen slammed into it. The lights flickered. Pandora stood to try and get to the side, to try and see for herself what was happening, but the building itself was no longer level. She lost her balance and fell to the floor, smacking her head against the bamboo mats that covered the concrete roof. As she lost consciousness she caught sight of one of the monitors. A tag at the bottom of the feed said *Indonesia*. The waters were receding, and with them came the bodies, a river of bodies mangled and entangled with the debris off some unknown third-world city. A city that looked quite a bit like the one she was in right now.

When she awoke there was an electric hum in the air. She could hear the sound of rushing water, and of debris, flotsam, crashing against itself and the building. In the background she could hear the voices of people, some talking, some screaming, some crying; it was a low murmur, a cacophony of human voices that filled the air in an indistinct drone. But beyond that organic sound of men living and dying, there was the decidedly artificial hum of some sort of machine that made the fillings in her teeth ache. As she stumbled to her feet she lost her balance and put her hand out to steady herself. It was met by a hand from Mister Ys, who put an arm under her shoulder and helped her to a chair. Without being asked he handed her a glass of water and knelt down before her, caressing her leg gently, reassuringly.

"Are you all right, Pandora?"

She looked about the rooftop and was shocked by two unusual sights. The first was that the kinetic sculpture of rods and mirrors was spinning, rotating, twirling at a frenetic pace. It was from this weird machine that the electric hum was emanating. The hum had a frequency, a rhythm that grew as the machine began moving faster, its mirrors and rods dancing about each other in complex elliptical orbits. The second thing that surprised her was that except for Mister Ys and Miss Trey, all of the other Yith were bound with strong rope, hog-tied so that they could not stand or use their arms. These prisoners were seated comfortably and carrying on cordial conversations with each other and the five humans, all of whom remained unbound.

"I'm fine," she muttered in response to Ys' question. "What's going on? Why is everybody tied up?"

Mister Ys sighed. "A measure taken to assure your safety. In a few minutes we will be leaving, and our former host bodies will become extremely dangerous." He handed her a machete. "You have to prepare yourself. The world is going to change. If you are to survive you'll need to change with it."

She felt the weight of the machete in her hand. "What are you talking about?" As she finished her sentence she saw Miss Trey open up a wooden crate to reveal a large cache of guns and ammunition. She looked up at Ys with her eyes full of fear and confusion.

"There has been an earthquake," reminded Ys, "and a tsunami. Hundreds of thousands are dead. Millions are injured and displaced. Over the next few weeks the priority will be to try and save and relocate a significant percentage of the world's population. Little to no attention will be paid to the cause of the quake, or its geological impacts. This is a mistake."

She opened her mouth but Ys shushed her. "The earthquake

has cracked the Plateau of Sung; seawater has seeped in. Even now something stirs in the depths of the Earth. Zhar and Lloigor may be dormant, but their spawn, that hideous, amorphous, polyphemic thing that men have no name for, will soon wake—and it heralds the end of the civilization of men. A strange city will rise in the Pacific, and from it shall burst forth the heirs of Xoth to pave the way for their father. The moon shall crack, the poles melt. Darkness will descend on the land."

Pandora shook her head at the madness of it all. "Old Testament stuff, dogs and cats living together."

Ys scowled at her levity. "You can survive, at least some of you. We've prepared a place in the mountains. There are maps and supplies here and on a few more rooftops where you'll find allies. It won't be easy, but you've been trained; trained all your life really."

There was a sudden peal of thunder. Pandora realized that it was the foundation of the building across the way cracking. The people on the other roof began to scream as their hotel began to crumble beneath them. She could hear the waters below as they lapped hungrily at the windows and terraces. She ran to the edge and watched as men fell into the swirling muddy waters and vanished from sight as if they had never existed.

"You've survived the tsunami," Ys whispered in her ear. "The waters will recede quickly. Use the supplies here to survive the next few days. Establish yourselves at the place we've prepared. It's very defensible. You should be able to keep out the anthrophages. A word of advice if I may: 'headshots'."

He suddenly had Pandora's attention. "Anthrophages?"

Ys pursed his lips. "Normally when we occupy the living, the departure process also replants the original mind, but these bodies were dead when we occupied them. There are no minds to replant. That fault in the procedure will create a biochemical error; a protein will misfold, and become self-replicating. You call these things prions. The prions will destroy most of the higher brain functions, leaving the bodies to become less than human, less than animals: they will be driven by only the most basic of needs. They will eat anything that moves, including humans. The process is infectious."

"Zombies. You're talking about zombies." Pandora's eyes darted to the bound Yith. "You've created a zombie plague."

Ys dipped his head in a kind of nod. "That is one way of putting it."

"Why?"

"We are moving. We've abandoned the past, all of us. There's nothing left of us back there. We couldn't leave human minds in our bodies; there would have been no one there to watch them, to help them, to explain things to them. So we used your recent dead. There were other options, but this was the most palatable to us all."

"This was Plan Number One?"

"Actually, this was Plan Number Nine," Miss Trey was suddenly behind him. She looked at Ys, "It's time," she said.

Ys nodded. "We have to go. I warn you, because of the chronal displacement, the prion replication process within a body is very rapid. It will only take moments for these bodies to become antagonistic. You should act quickly."

Pandora's emotions changed from fear to anger. "You knew about this. You prepared for it." Her mind was racing. "Did you cause this? Did you cause all these people to die? My God, were the wingnuts right? Is this part of your plan? Are you softening us up for an invasion?"

The alien time traveler shook his head. "The quake and tsunami were unavoidable. As for the deaths, yes we could have warned you, but the truth is it wouldn't make much of a difference. Over the next year, large numbers of people are going to die. We would have just been prolonging the inevitable." Pandora opened her mouth to speak but Ys raised a finger to silence her. "We're sorry, we truly are. We've enjoyed our time with you. We've done what we can to help you survive." He was walking away from her, and toward the strange whirring machine. "As a precautionary measure I and Miss Trey should be tied up like the others, but it takes two to operate the machine, to make adjustments. So I apologize for what this body will do later."

"I thought, we thought, thought that you were our ..." Pandora was stuttering, and out of words.

"Friends?" Ys shook his head. "We never said that, Pandora. You and yours assumed too much. You thought of us as friends, business partners, saviors, geniuses, historians, travelers, but you never realized, never suspected what we truly were."

"And what is that?" Pandora Peaslee yelled over the sound of the machine as it revolved and spun faster and faster and louder and louder. Mister Ys responded, and as he did Pandora collapsed onto the roof in stunned silence.

Around her the Yithans, both those bound and the two that were unbound, suddenly slumped down. It was as if they were puppets and their strings had suddenly been cut. They were still, horrifically still, for far too long. They were breathing, Pandora could see that, but it was so slow, barely perceptible. They almost looked as if they were peacefully sleeping. Then she remembered what Ys had said about the anthrophages and she also remembered the machete in her hand.

The thing that had been Mister Ys took a sudden breath, one that was echoed by the other Yithians scattered around the roof. His eyes opened and from his throat leaked an animal growl. He sprang at her, and Pandora swung the machete as he flew through the air. With a single blow she severed the head of her former lover and set it spinning across the roof, an arc of blood trailing in its wake. She spun around, letting the momentum carry her. Miss Trey had awakened as well, slower than Y's, Pandora buried the point of her machete into her skull. The former Yithian twitched and spasmed as the now-empty body adjusted to the fact that its brain was dead. It just needed a moment to remember to lie down and be still.

All around her Pandora watched as the few other humans systematically slaughtered the bound former Yith. It was a process Pandora could catch a distant image of being carried out on another rooftop just within her view. She hoped that all the others were as efficient as she and her new allies were, but she doubted it. From the sudden screaming and animal growls and howls that drifted in from distant unseen quarters those doubts seemed justified. In front of her the televisions still powered by solar panels and fed by satellites still showed the devastation that was inflicting the coasts around the Indian Ocean.

She grabbed the machete and wrenched it out of Miss Trey's skull. She looked at Mister Ys head as it leaked thick, black blood across the roof and thought about what he had said. "We're none of those things. True, we have characteristics of all of them, and we may be a bit morbid in our tastes, but being immortal there are very few pleasures left to us. We didn't come to invade, or study, or document your history. We travel through time to see the greatest shows the universe has to offer. We come to watch civilizations die. Some have called us morticians, caretakers at the end of worlds, corpse-flies, but the truth is, it is a lot simpler than that." He was smiling as the machine reached its full intensity. "We're on vacation, nothing more, nothing less; come to see the world of men be extinguished." As his knees gave out the last few words passed through his undead lips. "I suppose you could call us tourists."

Pandora grabbed a bottle of champagne and clipped the cork out with a swing of the machete. The pop and fountain of foam caught the attention of the five others who were still alive on the rooftop. "The guests have all checked out: time for the staff to raid the mini-bar and rifle through whatever they left behind." She took a swig from the bottle. "They had good taste in booze; let's hope that extends to their choice of guns." She took a swig from the heavy glass bottle, and then another.

Somewhere in the city, on a not-too-distant rooftop, there was a sudden eruption of gunfire. An automatic weapon was being used in short, controlled bursts. There was screaming. The gunfire stopped; the screaming didn't. Over the next few hours the pattern repeated itself. The gunfire and screaming spread; the gunfire stopped; the screaming continued. The screaming grew. It was only a matter of time before Pandora and her team had to either move or face what was out there, but the Yith had known that—for them it had always only been a matter of time.

The screaming was infectious.

And it was only the start.

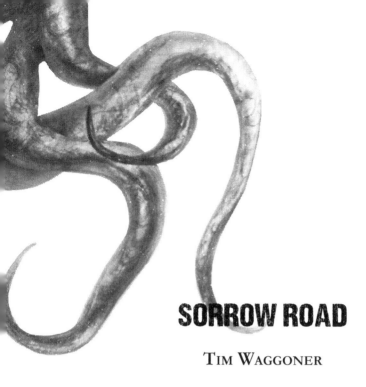

SORROW ROAD

Tim Waggoner

We've stopped.

Kris continued gripping the steering wheel, her foot pressing the gas pedal halfway down. But the engine made no noise, even though—she did a quick check—the key remained in the ignition, still turned to the on position. Gazing through the windshield of her Traverse van, she saw three lanes of cars ahead of her, stretching as far as she could see. Like her van, the other vehicles—all of them—were motionless. She turned to look out the driver's side window to see if the traffic on the northbound side of I-675 was still moving. It wasn't.

She reached up a hand to touch her cheek and found it wet. Why was it like that?

"Mommy?"

For the merest fraction of a second she didn't recognize the child's voice, didn't even recognize it as a human sound. But then a name bobbed to the surface of her consciousness: Danny.

She looked into the rearview mirror, reached up to adjust it to get a better view of the back seat. Her little boy sat strapped into his car seat, wearing jeans and a red-and-white striped shirt he called his *Where's Waldo?* shirt. His brown hair was mussed, which was normal, but his pudgy cheeks were white as bone, as was the rest of his face,

125

and that definitely was *not* normal.

"It's okay, honey. We're okay."

Her voice sounded strained, almost desperate. She knew something was wrong, felt it deep in the core of her being, but she had no idea what it was. She angled the mirror to check her own reflection and saw her face as pale as Danny's, her eyes wide and panicked like a frightened animal. No, not simply frightened. *Terrified.*

But what could've happened to scare both her and Danny so badly? They were stuck in a traffic jam, that's all. She couldn't remember stopping the car, but that was probably because she'd had a habit of daydreaming while driving.

Where *had* they been coming from? She couldn't—and then the details started coming back to her.

We'll need to perform more tests in order to be a hundred percent certain, of course, but the last thing I want to do is give you false hope.

The doctor moved a mouse, clicked, and the screen changed from a background displaying a cartoon aquarium—the words *Children's Hospital* spelled out on the side of the largest fish—to CT images of a spine.

Her first thought: *It's back.*

Her second: *My poor baby.*

Her third: *Fuck you, God. Just fuck you.*

Two years ago, a tumor had been discovered on Danny's spinal cord. The doctors assured Kris and Danny's father that they'd caught it early enough that surgery and chemo should take care of it. This afternoon, Kris had discovered how very wrong those doctors had been.

She remembered now why her cheeks were wet. She had been crying as they drove home from the pediatric oncologist's office. Something Danny had said had set her off. *Mommy, are they going to have to cut my back open again?*

Thinking about it now made her want to start crying anew, but right now she had something else to worry about, and no matter how strange or disturbing it might be, she was grateful for the distraction.

So … they had been driving and she had been crying when the van stopped. And not because she'd taken her foot off the gas and pressed the brake. Wasn't her foot still on the gas pedal? Wasn't the van still in drive? Ignition on but engine dead?

One moment she'd been cruising down the highway at sixty-five miles per hour, and the next ... she just stopped. There'd been no transition between, no slowing, no swerving, no being thrown forward and back by the van's momentum. They—and presumably the other vehicles on the road—had stopped instantaneously without any ill effect. Except for a broken engine, it seemed. She didn't bother telling herself it was impossible. She knew that. It didn't change the fact that it had happened.

She put the van in park and turned the key in the ignition to the off position. After a half-second of thought, she activated the emergency brake for good measure.

Danny had been silent since her attempt to reassure him, but now he began whimpering. She hit the release button on the seatbelt and turned around to face him. Tears welled in his eyes and his lower lip quivered. He squirmed in his seat as if he were trying to escape from it. She reached a hand toward him, intending to repeat what she'd said earlier, but before she could speak, Danny said, "They're here."

He burst into tears and began wailing.

Danny was still crying several moments later, but his wailing had become a soft keening that, despite its lower volume, tore at Kris' heart even more. She stood outside next to the van holding Danny who gripped her tight with both his arms and legs. He pressed his face to her chest and she could feel him tremble against her. He was a big boy for his age and she normally found him too heavy to hold. But now he felt light and fragile as an autumn leaf.

Kris wasn't the only one who'd gotten out of her vehicle. The highway was filled with people, all of them standing around, silent and expressionless.

We're in shock, she thought, but she had no idea why that might be. Sure, the way the traffic had come to an instant stop was weird as hell, no doubt. But strange as it was, she sensed that was the least of it. *They're here*. Why had Danny said that? What did it mean?

The silence extended beyond the people and the lack of traffic noise. There had been a fairly strong wind blowing, enough to make her keep both hands tight on the wheel as she drove. But now the air was still. More than that, it felt thin and lifeless. She inhaled, and although she took in a deep breath and felt her lungs expand, the air didn't feel nourishing. It lay flat and stale in her lungs and left a sour metallic taste in her mouth. She experienced a moment of panic when she feared she couldn't breathe whatever substance the air had become. But she forced herself not to give in to her fear. She had to keep it together—for Danny.

She shifted Danny—still trembling, still keening—to her left hip.

"Ow! Mommy, that hurts my back!"

Kris knew the growth on his spine wasn't large enough to be causing him discomfort yet. Still, she felt a stab of panic at Danny's words and loosened her grip on him so there wasn't as much pressure against his back. She then reached into her pants pocket for her phone. She wasn't sure what she hoped it might tell her. Maybe her husband or her sister had sent her a text about what had happened. If whatever it was was bad enough or big enough, maybe CNN had posted a story about it. If nothing else, she could call Kenny at work and let him know that she and Danny were … maybe not okay, exactly, but unharmed. But no matter how many times she swiped her thumb across the phone's screen, it remained dark. She looked up and saw that many of the people standing near her had had the same idea, and with similar results. It seemed none of their phones worked.

She slipped her phone back into her pocket and repositioned Danny so she could hold onto him with both arms once more. Danny's keening had been replaced by soft sobs. The sound seemed distant, though, as if it were coming from a dozen feet away. A trick of the weird air? Maybe.

"Kris?"

She barely heard her name being spoken but, when she turned in the direction of the sound, she was startled to see a woman standing only a few feet away. It was Sheri Klein, her neighbor from across the street.

"Weird, huh? All this, I mean." Sheri swept her arm outward, the gesture meant to take in all the motionless vehicles around them. Her voice was higher-pitched than normal and strained. It made Kris think of a metal wire pulled so tight it could snap at any moment.

"Yeah." It was the best reply Kris could come up with, but she figured she was doing good to get that much out.

Sheri was a decade older than Kris, a short, round-faced woman whose kids were in middle school. She watched Danny from time to time and, while they weren't best friends, Kris was glad to have her for a neighbor.

"Do you think—" That was as far as Sheri got out before Danny pointed skyward.

"Look!" he said.

Kris didn't want to turn her head toward the sky. Something deep inside her knew she wouldn't like what she saw. But she looked anyway.

A few moments ago the sky had been a beautiful blue with a scattering of diffuse, blurry-edged white clouds. Now streaks of yellow—a sickly pus-colored yellow—threaded through the blue. As she watched, the yellow spread and expanded, the effect not unlike a high-school chemistry experiment where a yellowish liquid is dropped into a flask filled with clear liquid, the new color soon filling the entire container. The process was complete in mere moments, and when it was finished, all traces of blue were gone, and no clouds were visible. And although it was mid-afternoon, the light had dimmed, making it seem more like dusk.

Despite the dimness, the color made her eyes ache, as if she were staring into a too-bright light, and she felt a headache building in the back of her skull. The pus-sky filled her with a deep sense of violation, of *wrongness,* and her stomach twisted with nausea. She managed to keep from throwing up, but Sheri wasn't so fortunate. She doubled over, hands pressed to her stomach, yawned her mouth wide, and a torrent of liquid gushed onto the road. Kris expected to see stomach acid, bile, maybe chunks of partially digested food, but what came out of Sheri's mouth was thick and dark, more like oil than vomit. There were lumps in the foul muck, but once they hit the asphalt they began scuttling away on segmented legs or pushing themselves on distorted, uneven cilia. As bad as the sight was, the smell was far worse—a fetid combination of spoiled meat, rotting vegetables, and human waste. Kris almost puked at that point, but the thought that she might bring forth the same obscene mixture—or something even worse—helped her keep her stomach's contents where they were.

Danny looked at the dark mess Sheri had released and, rather than being dismayed or repelled by it, he gazed upon it wide-eyed. He didn't appear to suffer any physical distress himself, and he no longer seemed upset. Kris should've been grateful for that, but his reaction—or lack thereof—seemed wrong somehow, and it worried her more than the strange sky or Sheri's bizarre sickness.

She looked around and saw that many of the people who'd gotten out of their cars were throwing up. Some ejected the same oil-like substance as Sheri, but others appeared to be vomiting blood or far stranger things like clouds of flies, shards of broken glass, or small animal bones. A thought drifted through her mind, distant, detached.

Things are different now.

Not everyone was vomiting, though. Some were on their knees, sobbing and moaning. Some pounded fists into the sides of their heads, while others punched their cars, over and over, cracking glass, denting metal, and breaking bones.

The Eyes appeared then.

They filled the sky from horizon to horizon, blotting out the new yellow. They varied in size and type, but all were enormous. It was as if the sky were filled with planets, moons, and asteroids all crammed together. Some of the eyes looked more or less human, while others resembled those of cats, goats, fish, or lizards. Some were glossy obsidian, like insects', while others were orbs filled with swirling nebulae or alien starscapes. There had been times in Kris' life when she had felt small to the point of insignificance. Gazing down into the Grand Canyon. Standing atop the Empire State Building. Seeing the first sonogram image of Danny inside her. But those times were nothing compared to this.

Kris couldn't look away from the Eyes. She couldn't breathe, and she wouldn't have been surprised to discover her heart had seized up in her chest. She felt the Eyes' scrutiny upon her—upon them all— as a giant weight pressing down, as if the air pressure had suddenly increased. She felt a strange sensation inside her head. It wasn't painful, not exactly. It was an itching-tingling, as if hundreds of insects were digging around in the soft meat of her brain. She thought of what Sheri had expelled from her body and terror gripped her. Could there really be insects inside her skull, gnawing away at her brain with their tiny but oh-so-sharp mandibles?

And then, just as swiftly as they'd appeared, the Eyes were gone, leaving behind only the pus-colored sky.

Kris drew in a sudden deep breath, as if her lungs had forgotten how to work, and finally remembered. The tingling sensation in her head wasn't gone entirely, but it had diminished to the point where it was bearable. She looked at Danny. His face was red, as if he too hadn't been able to take in air, but he seemed to be breathing fine now. He continued gazing at the sky and she had the sense that he saw something there that she couldn't.

"They're coming down," he said. His statement was matter-of-fact, his voice devoid of emotion. Kris found it so disturbing she almost wished he were crying instead. That, at least, would've been normal.

Sheri had managed to stand upright once more, but her face edged toward gray, and her eyes were wide with fear. When Kris had been a child, she'd once picked up a small mouse she'd found in her parents' garage. She'd held it close to her face so she could examine it. Its eyes had looked like Sheri's did now.

"Who?" Kris asked Danny, her voice shaky. "Who's coming?"

Danny lowered his gaze until he was looking at her. His features were impassive and Kris feared he was in shock.

"The Masters," he said.

It was a simple word—*Masters*—yet the sound of it made Kris want to scream. Sheri did. She screamed at the top of her lungs, her voice raw and cracking, and Kris imagined her vocal cords tearing like overdone spaghetti. As if Sheri's scream was a cue, dozens of people near them began screaming, shouting, wailing, and moaning. *We're like animals*, she thought, *sensing danger and reacting without knowing why.* Terror moved up and down the highway fast as wildfire, and soon the air was filled with a chorus of fear and despair. The cacophony was so loud that Kris almost didn't hear Danny say, "They used to live here a long time ago. A long, *long* time. They left, but they're back now. And this time, they're going to stay."

There was an odd cadence to his words, almost as if he were repeating something that someone else was saying. Like he was a flesh radio broadcasting a signal that he, and only he, was receiving.

The screams intensified then, and people a half mile in front of Kris, Danny, and Sheri began running in all directions, as if fleeing something that had appeared in their midst. Kris heard the sound of metal twisting and bending, and her first thought was that one of more of the stalled vehicles had started working again and had crashed into those that remained immobile. But then she saw movement and realized that cars, vans, and trucks *were* moving, just not in the way they'd been designed. They were sliding together, compacting against each other, fusing into a single mass. Within moments, a large dome-like structure had formed. It covered all three lanes of the highway and rose twenty feet into the air. And still it kept growing. Lengths of metal—dozens of them—extruded from the central mass, grabbing vehicles as they came toward the dome and lifting them upward so they could be added to the nightmarish structure. Faster than Kris would've believed possible, the dome became a small tower, and it continued growing, rising fifty, seventy-five, a hundred feet into the air. It stopped there, and Kris estimated the tower topped off at 125–130 feet, although for all she knew it could have been even larger. It was more difficult to see distances now. Light didn't seem to travel the same way it used to.

Although there was no way they should work, given the crushed and mangled states of the vehicles, engines roared to life and exhaust began pouring into the air, thick, black, and acrid, drifting upward to coalesce into a cloud that formed a dark halo around the Tower's top. Headlights began to glow, gleaming far brighter than they should have been capable of, putting out so many lumens that looking at them was like gazing at dozens of miniature suns.

Danny stared at the Tower, eyes wide not with fear, but wonder. Kris felt an impulse to slap his face and demand he turn away from the obscene thing. It didn't belong here; was a *violation* in the truest sense of the word.

Most of the screaming had stopped as people's attention became fixated on the newly made Tower. Even those who had fled when the vehicles first began joining together had stopped where they were and turned back to regard it. The structure radiated a sense of … Kris supposed *presence* was the best way to describe it. It made you want to look at it, made you want to come closer. Kris found herself taking a step toward the foul object, then another. Danny reached out with both hands, as if eager to get close enough to touch it. Seeing her son yearn for the Tower like that brought her back to her senses, and she stopped walking. Danny continued reaching for the Tower, squirming in her arms, straining to wiggle free. She knew if she released him he'd go running straight toward the Tower, and so she held him even tighter.

She turned to Sheri, but before she could say anything to the other woman, Sheri started walking forward, a dull cast over her eyes, mouth open, lower jaw slack. She stepped into the black muck she'd vomited without seeming to notice.

"Don't …" was all Kris managed to get out before Sheri started running. She felt an impulse to go after her—*not* because she wanted to reach the Tower but in order to stop her—but she had her hands quite literally full with trying to stop Danny from wriggling out of her arms. And truth was, she was afraid to move a single inch closer to the Tower. No; more than afraid: *terrified*.

People passed them, most running as Sheri had, eyes wild, faces expressionless. Kris wondered what they were thinking, or if they were thinking at all. She looked to the northbound side of the highway. The north and southbound lanes of I-675 were separated by a large grassy median, and people—men, women, children, young, old—trampled across it now, rushing to reach the Tower. Not everyone from the other side of the highway was attracted to the Tower, though, just as not everyone on this side was. Some of those who hung back on either side stood around, looking shocked, lost, or bewildered. Others ran for the trees alongside the highway, many of them carrying young children. More people on the northbound side seemed to resist the Tower's influence, and Kris wondered if that was due to their being farther away from it. It made sense—as much as anything did right now.

She didn't try to tell herself that this was a dream, or that she was hallucinating, or that she'd been in a wreck and was delirious, maybe even in a coma and experiencing what seemed to be a living nightmare. She liked to think of herself as a serious-minded, no-nonsense person, someone who took life as it was, not as she wished it to be. And maybe that was part of why, frightened as she was, she hadn't turned away mentally and emotionally from what was happening, regardless of how bat-shit crazy it was. Then again, after learning your child has cancer, dealing with all the doctors' appointments, the surgery, the chemo, the follow-up appointments, and *then* learning your poor baby's body was once again being attacked from within—and this time there was an excellent chance he wouldn't survive—well, the end of the world didn't seem like all that big of a deal, really.

"Stop squirming!" she told Danny, but her words only seemed to goad him into increasing his exertions. He might've only been four, and his body slowly being taken over by a poison which would eventually kill him, but right now he was still strong, and she didn't know how much longer she could maintain her hold on him.

She looked to the right. There were trees on this side of the highway as well. Not woods, really, just a strand of trees that had been allowed to remain when the highway was put in to block the sight of traffic from the residents on the other side. She wasn't sure what lay beyond the trees. An apartment complex, she thought. Whatever it was, it was better than staying here to discover what the Tower was—and worse, what it wanted from them. She gripped Danny as hard as she could and stepped off the highway and into the grass.

"No, no, no!" Danny shouted. He thrashed and kicked, the heels of his sneakers pounding into the outside of her leg like hammer blows. She ignored the pain and kept going.

Others on this side of the highway had come to the same decision as Kris, and several of them—those not encumbered with young children or infants—were already halfway to the trees. They ran wildly, arms and legs flailing, driven by unreasoning terror. Kris could feel raw fear roiling just beneath the surface of her consciousness, threatening to burst forth any second and overwhelm her, and it was tempting to give in and let her rational mind be swept away so animal instinct could take over. But she couldn't let that happen. She had a son to take care of, and she had to retain her grip on sanity for him, if for no other reason.

She walked toward the trees at the best speed she could manage, and as she did, she saw that the grass was losing its green color and slowly turning white, as if the life was being bled out of it. But the grass began moving, swaying back and forth as if in a breeze despite the fact that there was no wind, and Kris knew the grass was still very much alive, maybe more so than ever. The trees began to change as well, trunks and branches lightening, browns and grays giving way to a clear crystalline appearance, the same transformation occurring to their leaves. Kris knew that what was happening was wrong, a corruption of the deepest, most profound kind, and yet she couldn't help finding the sight of white grass and crystalline trees to be beautiful, like a scene out of a child's storybook.

When the first of the runners reached the treeline, leaves detached from branches and sliced through the air toward them like shuriken made of glass. Sharp edges cut faces, necks, and hands, sliced through clothing to get to the tender flesh beneath. The wounded screamed and fell where ivory tendrils that were no longer grass extended from the ground, lengthening as they wormed their tips into bleeding wounds. The screams became shrieks of agony as the tendrils began to feed, their white becoming pink and then crimson as they drank deep.

It seemed the sky wasn't the only thing about the world that had changed.

Kris stopped running. For a moment she didn't move at all, fearing that the white grass around and beneath her feet would reach up, wrap around her legs, and pull her and Danny to the ground and begin feeding on them. But the grass did nothing, perhaps because neither she nor Danny was bleeding. Whatever the reason, she was relieved.

And then the birds came.

At least, she thought they'd been birds. But whatever the things had been before, they had wings, so they were birds as far as she was concerned. They flew out of the trees, and a number of them fell upon the bodies of those who were being drained by the white grass and began tearing at their flesh with crooked claws and twisted beaks. But others came gliding toward those, like Kris and Danny, who hadn't gotten close enough to the trees to be cut by the crystalline leaves. It didn't take much, a claw raked lightly against a cheek, a sharp peck on the back of a hand, but the instant that blood—no matter how little the amount—was exposed to the air, the white grass attacked, grabbing hold of legs and arms, yanking people to the ground where more tendrils could get at them. And when the grass began to feed, so did the birds.

Danny's struggles had ceased when the first people had been cut by the falling leaves, and now he hung motionless and limp in her arms. She didn't know if he was fascinated by the sight of these mutated predators in action or repulsed, but either way, she was grateful that he'd stopped fighting her. She was able to turn back to the road and run toward it without being slowed by fighting to hold onto a thrashing four-year-old.

She was within a half dozen feet of the road when something grazed her right shoulder, stitching a fiery line of pain across the muscle. The impact staggered her, made her stumble, but she managed to maintain her footing and keep going. She saw the bird—although the creature was as much lizard as avian, with a dab of mammal added for a good measure—that had struck her circle around for another attack.

She also felt small tugs at her feet, ankles, and calves, and she knew the white grass, attracted by the blood oozing from her shoulder wound, sought to bring her down. But the grass was too weak and she was moving too fast, and none of the tendrils were able to catch hold of her.

The bird came diving toward her face just as she reached the highway, and she threw herself toward the asphalt, angling her body to protect Danny. She landed on her left side and she felt more than heard a couple ribs crack. She took in a hissing breath, but otherwise didn't react to this new pain. Just because she had reached the highway didn't mean that she and Danny were safe.

She shifted to a crouching position—her injured ribs loudly voicing their protest—and kept her arms around Danny, who was now standing. As mother and son looked out upon the field littered with bodies encircled with white grass and covered with feasting winged monstrosities, they saw that none of the creatures came near the road. Kris turned to look at the northbound side of the highway and saw it was the same over there—crystalline trees, white grass, monstrous birds, and far too many dead bodies—but the asphalt seemed to act as some kind of magic barrier, keeping those who stood upon it safe. Kris knew it wasn't magic, though. Her guess was that the grass, birds, and trees understood the people on the highway had already been claimed by a far stronger power than they, and they knew to keep their distance.

So escape wasn't possible. What options did that leave her?

"Mommy?"

Danny's voice startled her. Not because there was anything wrong with it, but because it sounded so normal, so *him*.

She gently turned him around to face her.

"Can we go home now?" he asked. "I really want to."

His gaze was clear and he looked at *her*—not toward the damned Tower. She wasn't sure what had happened to return him to his senses. Maybe seeing so many people killed in such a gruesome fashion had shocked him back to full awareness. Or maybe the jolt when they'd hit the asphalt had done the trick. She didn't care. She was just glad to have her Danny back.

She wanted to lie to him, to tell him that everything was going to be okay, that they'd find a way to get home soon. But she'd never been able to lie to her child. She hadn't been able to pretend that Santa Claus existed, hadn't been able to keep the truth about his cancer from him. So how could she lie now, when he needed her to more than he ever had before?

She saw movement out of the corner of her eyes, and she turned toward it. People were moving between the cars, not heading toward the Tower but coming from it. She recognized some of them as people who had run past Danny and her earlier, only now each of them had puffy red marks on their foreheads, a strange squiggly symbol that looked as if it had been branded on them, except that instead of appearing to have been burned there from the outside, the marks appeared to have emerged from the inside. The symbol hurt her eyes to look at, and even though she tried to focus so she could clearly make it out, her eyes refused to cooperate, her vision blurring and becoming watery until she was forced to give up.

Someone came up behind them and stopped. Kris looked up and saw that it was Sheri. She had one of those marks on her forehead, making it difficult for Kris to look her in the eyes. When Sheri spoke, Kris expected her voice to sound guttural, bestial, as if she'd been possessed by some evil force. But she sounded perfectly normal—calm, rational, even caring as she said, "You need to come with me, Kris. Danny, too."

Kris kept her eyes focused on Sheri's chin as she said, "What will happen to us if we don't?"

"That will."

Sheri pointed toward the grass. Kris had seen too much already and she didn't know if she could take anymore, but she looked. She knew she had to.

Those who possessed marks were grabbing hold of those who didn't and forcing them to the edge of the asphalt. No matter how hard they struggled, the Unmarked couldn't escape the Marked, and they were pushed out onto the white grass. Birds abandoned partially devoured bodies and streaked toward the fresh meat offered to them. They struck, and when blood was let, the white grass attacked. New screams filled the air.

Sheri put a hand on Kris' shoulder and squeezed slightly. Her grip was like iron.

Kris nodded and Sheri removed her hand. Kris stood, took hold of Danny's hand, and the three of them started walking toward the

Tower. There were others being guided by the Marked, more than Kris expected. Then again, given a choice between an immediate and grisly death or living a few moments longer, who wouldn't choose the latter?

"Getting a Thrall mark isn't so bad," Sheri said. "Yeah, it hurts. Hurts like blazes. But the pain doesn't last, and when it's over you'll know what you need to do."

"Do?" Kris asked.

Sheri looked at her, and Kris had to avert her gaze from her mark. "To survive," Sheri added.

As they drew closer to the Tower, Kris had to squint because of the intense light blazing from the headlights. She felt pressure building inside her skull too, and from the way Danny whimpered, she knew he felt it as well. The smell of exhaust was thick here, and it stung her nasal passages, seared her throat. The Tower's engines were putting off a lot of heat too, so much so that she thought maybe she should start thinking of it as the Furnace. The engine noise was near-deafening, the sound buffeting them like a solid force. Most of the vehicles that comprised the Tower had been empty when they'd joined the mass—but not all. Blood ran down the metal in places, and arms, legs, and heads jutted between folded metal and shattered window glass. Although there was no way the people that had been trapped inside their vehicles when the Tower formed could still be alive after the horrible injuries they'd suffered, their body parts moved with jerky, erratic motions. Fingers curled into fists and uncurled, reminding Kris of fast-motion video of flowers drawing in their petals for the night and opening them at dawn's arrival. Toes wiggled, and eyes and mouths opened and closed randomly. The eyes darted this way and that, occasionally pausing to linger on one object or another. Kris expected those eyes to be utterly devoid of life, but they were not. Their gazes shone with a strange— and she couldn't avoid thinking this next word, although she really wanted to—*alien* intelligence.

At first she thought the Tower itself was one of the creatures— Masters, Danny had called them—that had gazed down upon them from the sky. The Masters had returned, as Danny had said, and they'd needed to form bodies for themselves. But while she could feel waves of power pouring off the Tower, she sensed that the structure itself was empty. The creature—the *Master*—was here, not inside the Tower but beneath it. The Tower was a façade, mere decoration, like a church.

It gave people a physical place to go in order to commune with the infinite and the unknowable. And maybe the Tower served the same function, but it was also possible its only real purpose was to announce to the world that *I Am Here.*

She thought then of the thousands of eyes—thousands upon thousands—that had filled the sky, regarding the humans below with the same detached curiosity those humans might regard a bustling ant hill. Had they all descended and found themselves lairs as had the one below the Tower? How many places like this were scattered across the world? How many similar scenes were playing themselves out at this very moment?

It's their world now, Kris thought. And maybe it always had been.

The eyes of the dead people gazed upon them as they approached. Kris could feel a single intelligence peering through those dead eyes, and she knew that the thing beneath the Tower looked upon them.

A line had formed in front of the Tower, and Kris, Danny, and Sheri took their place in front of it. It moved at a fairly good pace, and it seemed like it didn't take long for people to receive their Thrall marks.

Danny squeezed her hand so tight it hurt, but she didn't ask him to loosen his grip. Whatever becoming a Thrall meant, Kris feared that these last few moments might be the final time that she and Danny would truly be themselves, and she wanted to make them last as long as she possibly could. She thought of Kenny then and wondered how her husband was doing. Had he died when the Masters first arrived or had he accepted a Thrall mark, too? She wondered if she'd ever find out, either way.

Eventually, sooner than she wished, it was their turn. Now that they were at the front of the line, she could see a person—or rather, a hideous parody of one—standing at the base of the Tower. It had been formed from parts of other bodies, some male, some female, and its skin came from different races. It was made of more than flesh, though. Metal, plastic, and glass formed its body as well, and thick liquids oozed from its pores—oil, transmission and brake fluid, engine coolants.... A rusted fan jutted from where its mouth should've been, and spark plugs protruded from otherwise empty eyes sockets. Its large sagging breasts had battery terminals in place of nipples, and a thick cable emerged from between its legs, ending in frayed, sparking wires. More wires and hoses stretched from the thing's back, attaching it to the Tower.

She felt Danny begin trembling a half second before she realized she was doing the same.

Sheri leaned close to her ear and whispered and, despite the din of the engines, Kris heard her clearly.

"All you have to do is stay still and let it touch you."

The horrible conglomeration lifted its right hand—a thick-fingered calloused paw that Kris imagined had once belonged to a burly trucker—and reached for her forehead. But just before the rough tips of those fingers came in contact with her skin, she said, "Wait!"

The hand stopped but didn't withdraw.

"What are you doing?" Sheri hissed. Kris ignored her.

She had no idea if the thing—an avatar of some sort, she assumed—could see her with its spark-plug eyes, but she looked at them anyway while she spoke.

"My son ... He has something growing inside him. I'll serve you willingly, gladly, if you make him better."

She had no idea what the extent of this being's power was, but she had witnessed a number of remarkable, if nightmarish, transformations since the sky turned yellow. And if there was any chance the Master could heal Danny, she had to take it.

The avatar looked at her for several moments before turning its face toward Danny.

"Mommy, take me home. *Now!*" This word came out as a half-shout, half-sob.

Kris knelt down next to her son. Tears threatened, but she fought them back. She needed to be strong for Danny a little longer. After that, she could cry all she wanted—assuming she was still capable of it.

"We'll go home as soon as we're finished here." A pause, and then she added, "I promise."

She looked up at the avatar and nodded. The creature touched Danny's forehead and then drew back its hand.

Danny's body stiffened as if he were experiencing a sudden seizure. His eyes bulged and his lips drew back from his teeth. His fingers contorted into arthritic claws, and he hunched forward, a "Guh-guh-guh" sound coming from his mouth.

When he'd bent forward, his shirt had ridden up, exposing his lower back. Kris watched as the tender skin at the base of his spine began to swell, becoming darker as it tightened. When it had swollen to basketball size, the skin began to tear, and it burst open with a spray of blood. Danny screamed—once—before falling at the feet of the avatar and lying still. Sparks from the creature's cock-wire showered down on Danny's head like rain, setting his hair to smoldering.

Kris gasped in horror as the cancerous growth emerged from Danny's back, pulling itself free of his body with tiny limbs that ended in claws. The tumor had no features—no eyes, nose, mouth or ears. Its corrugated hide was a sickening dark purple, and it glistened with a coat of something that resembled mucus.

She turned to look at the avatar, and a single word sounded in her mind loud as a trumpet blast.

BETTER.

Then the fingers touched her forehead.

Kris walked down the highway, threading her way between rows of abandoned cars. Her Thrall mark burned as if it were aflame, but that was okay. The pain would lessen eventually. And if it didn't, that was okay, too. She kind of liked the sensation.

In her arms she cradled a slick purple mass. It was hard and cold, and the claws at the end of its thin legs dug into her skin. But she liked the way that felt, too.

Things were going to be different from now on. Much different. But as long as the two of them were together, everything was going to be all right. More than all right, in fact.

She looked down at the wet lump she carried and smiled.

Things were going to be better.

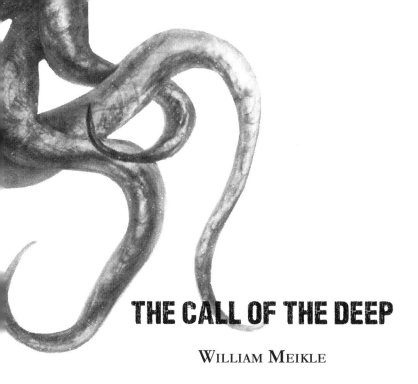

THE CALL OF THE DEEP

WILLIAM MEIKLE

Sam Green kicked the dead amphi over, sending it tumbling down the Embankment steps to drop with a soft splash into the murky river. It sank in a flurry of bubbles.

"How many was that?" John Ridder asked.

"Twelve," Sam replied. "And we didn't get them all. The buggers are getting more confident."

"Or more desperate," Ridder replied, harnessing his assault rifle across his back and lighting a smoke. "It's the heat, they say—and I can't say as I blame them. They've been down there minding their own business all this time, then we go and fuck it up for everybody."

"Speak for yourself," Sam said, harnessing his own weapon. "I'm from Glasgow, remember? A wee bit of warmth is just the ticket."

Humor was the only answer to what they were facing, and both men knew it.

The problems had been building for years—seas rising, storms increasing, and drought across vast swaths of the tropics. It took the Eastern Seaboard wipeout of 2066 for developed countries to finally sit up and take notice—but by then it was decades too late. The methane deposits in Northern Russia blew out in 2070, the Eastern Antarctic melted over the next decade, and the worst case scenario predicted in

143

the early years of the century came all at once.

London was getting hit hard—the river burst its banks regularly now, despite the new barriers at Greenwich and Tower Bridge. It was a constant battle to keep the old city above the waterline—when it wasn't baking in temperatures that topped forty centigrade.

Then the amphis started coming up out of the river.

Sam had laughed when he'd been told about them at the briefing, thinking it to be a joke.

"Come on, Sarge—the creature from the Black Lagoon? Really?"

Now that he'd seen them up close, he knew there was no humor to be had from them—they were vicious, relentless in their attacks, and fearless even in the face of automatic weapons.

Nobody really knew what the amphis wanted, only that they were weird, and they were pissed off. As Ridder had said, Sam would be pissed off, too, if some arseholes up top had screwed quite so thoroughly with his environment.

Besides, mine is not to reason why.

The first big attack had come off Scarborough last summer; two hundred locals dead before anybody noticed. But now that the threat was known, defenses were proving adequate—for the time being anyway. The amphis seemed to have habits and arrived in swarms. "Guard the city," was a simple enough order to follow, especially now that martial law had been declared and the boffins were guessing the location of the attacks on most nights.

The streets had been quiet last night—at least until the amphis came out of the river. The firefight along the Embankment was intense, but not long lasting. And finally the tide had turned; the threat of flood was receding, and the amphis had gone with it—for now. As the sky lightened in the east to bring the dawn, Sam allowed himself to relax—at least enough to join Ridder in a smoke.

He wasn't given time to finish it; his implant buzzed, he tongued the switch, and HQ came on the line in his ear.

"You're needed. Both of you. Right now."

That was another order that was easy to follow.

The briefing room in the Admiralty was already packed full when they sidled in and tried to look inconspicuous by the doorway. Ridder smiled, and Sam might have responded in kind—but the words from the General at the head of the long table brought all chatter in the room to complete silence.

"The Yanks have lost Washington."

Nobody spoke—they didn't have to. The battles across the ocean were common knowledge, longer and fiercer than any on the European side. But nobody had expected this. The General gave them all plenty of time to digest the implications before continuing.

"They've decided it's time for what they call the 'Hail Mary' scenario." He turned to look at where Sam and Ridder stood.

"That's where you lads come in. There's half a dozen scientist chaps downstairs that we need to get to Lakenheath Air Base—all in one piece and ASAP. The choppers will be leaving the roof in ten."

"Babysitting duty, sir?" Sam said. "We're of better use here, surely?"

"You're of use where I say you're of use," the speaker said, and Sam shut up fast. You learned quickly when an officer used that tone—this conversation was over.

Two minutes later he followed Ridder up onto the Admiralty roof to where the choppers were waiting. His implant buzzed and the General came on the line.

"I couldn't say, Sam, but this is more than just babysitting. The Yanks have a plan, but it's risky. You and Ridder are there to pull the plug on them if they try to do anything really stupid. We don't want a repeat of Boston. Understand?"

Sam understood only too well.

While the situation in London might be bad, at least the city was still habitable, in the main—Boston had been abandoned to the amphis last winter after an attempt to foul the seawater and kill the attackers had backfired and poisoned millions onshore. Just thinking about it gave Sam the cold chills as he helped usher a group of miserable-looking civilians onto the two choppers. He looked out the window as they banked up and away from Westminster, giving him a bird's-eye view over the partially flooded, almost deathly quiet city that used to be the heart and soul of the world.

Even despite Boston, a bunch of scientists with a risky plan might be just what is needed right about now.

He stopped looking out of the window after a while. There

was little to see but mile after mile of waterlogged fields, submerged towns, and abandoned vehicles, all punctuated by thick fog banks. The oppressive glare of the sun almost blinded him, and the same glare was also cooking the interior of the chopper meaning that the journey was not the most pleasant. Sam was glad when the pilot announced they were bearing in on Lakenheath.

As they landed, Sam's implant buzzed and Ridder came on.

"Hope you brought your passport—welcome to the USA."

Sam smiled thinly. This wasn't their first rodeo in these parts—and he liked the Yanks well enough. He just hoped that his role as 'cleaner of fuck-ups' wasn't going to be required.

The country around here was flat—good for an airfield, but also prone to flooding, and Sam knew that huge expanses of open water and reed beds surrounded the facility on all sides. On a calm summer's day in the past the air would have been filled with dragonflies, kestrels, butterflies, and the sound of bullfrogs. But now, under the hammer of the sun, there was just an oily heat haze and too-hot concrete. Sam was looking forward to some respite, and hoping that the Yanks had brought some of their fabled air conditioning with them.

They weren't given time to see the sights—everyone was shepherded in some haste into a hangar in the center of the airfield. Sam only had time to further note that the whole perimeter had been heavily fortified with gun towers and higher fences since his last visit, before the hangar doors shut and the lights went up.

The first thing Sam noticed was that the air conditioning was definitely on—it was still hot inside the hangar, but not so much as to impair his faculties. The room was a flurry of activity—massive screens showed scenes from numerous sites around the world, excited people shouted into headsets, and the holoviews glistened and roiled. Whatever was going on, it seemed important, but Sam and Ridder were only allowed to stand by the door and watch—it seemed they were to be excluded from any sort of explanation.

Sam tongued his implant and engaged the iris viewer; he heard the drone and whine in his medulla oblongata as the processor kicked in—that had taken some getting used to, way back when, but now it was as much part of him as his own eyes and ears. He let it process data for a while, then the soft voice of his companion spoke in his ear.

"It looks like some form of atmospheric system," she said. "High intensity ionospheric enhancement technology, of the kind utilized by the HAARP program in Alaska, but with a greatly boosted power input. There are scenes in the main screen from Egypt, Kamkatcha, and a point in the South Pacific. Logic processing gives a ninety percent probability of sites like this one at each of those areas—four corners of a quadrant."

"Yes," Sam whispered. "But what's it all for?"

"Rapid impact weather modification on a global scale," the companion said, her robotic monotone and matter of fact manner only adding to the fresh chill in Sam's spine.

The cleaner of fuck-ups might be needed after all.

The six scientists they'd brought from London were in a huddle at a corner desk. Sam set his gaze on them and told the companion to listen in. He only understood every third word but he hoped his listener would be able to condense it succinctly for him. There was talk of Polar Mesospheric Summer Echoes, heating-induced scintillation, and great concern over calibration of something called the fluxgate magnetometer. In the end, his companion did indeed boil it all down to a simple sentence.

"My first conclusion was correct. Weather modification," she said. "All across the planet. They're planning on a sudden lowering of the global temperature, and they're hoping to do it without putting any undue stress on the biosphere."

This wee part of the biosphere is bloody stressed already, thank you very much.

"So what's the big argument about?" he asked.

"They are considering just how much power needs to be applied," his companion replied. "The plan is to hit the ionosphere as hard as can be managed. There is a branch of opinion that the risks are worth the effort, but not all are convinced, and there is concern about the stability of the magnetic field and the tectonic plates, especially in the Pacific."

Ridder chose that moment to buzz in on Sam's implant.

"You getting all of this?"

"As much as I can manage," Sam replied. "Keep your wits about you. This has the feel of something that could go sideways PDQ."

As if to punctuate Sam's point, heavy gunfire started up outside, deafening even above the chorus of frightened chatter that rose up in the hangar.

Sam led Ridder outside. The source of the gunfire was two of the tall towers at the perimeter of the airfield. They sent volley after volley of heavy fire into the surrounding wetlands; from his current position Sam couldn't see any target. His companion whispered in his ear.

"Amphis—the base has been getting periodic attacks for several weeks now, hence the heightened security."

Sam became aware of a rising hum from the hangar behind him, a vibration that ran through the ground and set his gut tingling, like standing too close to a bass speaker at full volume. The gunfire from the towers faltered and failed until the hum was the only sound, getting ever louder.

Out in the fens beyond the fence, something—many things—answered, raising guttural voices in unison until it seemed that a vast choir wailed in the warm breeze wafting across the runways. Sam strode past the silent helicopters that had brought them here and walked over towards the nearest portion of the fence to look out past the perimeter.

Amphis, a horde of them, stood fifty yards from the fence in serried ranks, five or six deep, as if paused in their attack waiting for a signal. They had their heads raised to the sun, huge eyes staring upward, mouths gaping as song poured out of them, oblivious to the bullet riddled bodies of their kin lying all around them.

Then, as quickly as it had started, the hum stopped. The amphis seemed bemused, for all of a second, then turned away and were quickly lost from sight as they waded deep into the watery fens.

"What the hell just happened?" Ridder asked.

"Damned if I know—but if it's something that stops the amphis like that, we need to know about it. Let's see what the boffins have to say."

It turned out that the boffins weren't saying much of anything—at least, nothing that made sense to Sam, although the hangar was full of excited chatter, backslapping, and sporadic applause.

Sam's on-board companion spoke in his ear again.

"They think it has worked—after a fashion. They only used a quarter of the power at their disposal but readings show a distinct temperature drop across the North Atlantic—both in the air and in the ocean. They'll have to wait and see if they have caused any associated disruption elsewhere, but for the time being it's being considered a success."

"So now what?" Sam muttered. He wasn't thinking about temperature drops—he was thinking about the ranks of amphis outside, heads raised in song. He realized now what it had reminded him of—it had felt like he'd been in a church—it had felt like a hymn.

But a hymn to what god—what kind of god?

The rest of that day was spent in settling in and babysitting the scientists—not that they needed much looking after here, in what was probably the best-defended bit of ground in the country these days.

After a time Sam started to relax, at least enough to join Ridder for a smoke outside the hangar.

"All quiet," the other man said. "But have you heard the news from the Yanks?"

Sam shook his head—he'd been too preoccupied in trying to make sense of what was going on inside the hangar itself to worry about matters across the pond.

Ridder stubbed out his butt on the concrete before continuing.

"It's not just Washington they've lost; Baltimore, Philadelphia, and most towns along the Delaware have fallen. They're not calling them incursions now—they're calling it an invasion. And they're talking about using nukes if our little circus here doesn't get results in the next 48 hours."

In some ways Sam was happy to know that matters were being brought to a head—being baked in a slow oven wasn't any way for a man to go, never mind a whole planet. And it wasn't as if he was given any time to worry about it. His companion pitched in as he was finishing his own smoke.

"They're not waiting. They're going straight for half power at the top of the hour."

Sam checked he had a full load in his rifle. He had a feeling he was going to need it.

The hum from the hangar started up right on cue at the top of the hour, a bass vibration that pounded in Sam's gut and brought tension at his jaw and pain in his ears. His stomach roiled, and he was thankful he hadn't yet eaten as acid boiled in his throat. He saw that Ridder was in similar discomfort, but that was all forgotten when he had a look out beyond the fence again.

The amphis were back—in numbers far greater than before, a horde—an army—of them already starting to press up against the fence as the hum from the hangar went up another notch. They came forward in waves, singing as they approached. The guns on the watchtowers burst into action, but the press of the beasts was just too great—they were already swarming over the fences north and south as far as the eye could see. Even as Sam raised his rifle he knew it was going to be worse than useless. The tower guns fell silent as the amphis seethed over and around the watch positions. The fence collapsed—in three places—under the weight of the attack.

"The chopper guns," Ridder shouted. "We can still mow them down."

But even that thought had come too late. The amphis' song was louder even than the hum from the hangar as they came forward across the runways in a loping stride that belied their aquatic origins. Sam raised his weapon, but there was no immediate threat—every pair of huge, pale eyes seemed fixed on the hangar.

Their song rose again, filling the air with reverberating sound that once more reminded Sam of a church service, every voice calling out in praise and glory. He felt sudden tears at his eyes and wiped them away angrily as Ridder tugged at his arm, dragging him back to the hangar.

They reached the doorway just ahead of the approaching throng.

"Inside, quick," Ridder shouted, but as Sam turned for a last look at the amphis he saw that they had stopped. They stood in rank after rank, as far back as the perimeter fence and beyond, thousands, maybe tens of thousands of them. They had come to a standstill just yards from the hangar door, looking skyward, mouths open, the song pouring out of them in waves, washing around the airfield, setting everything—air, reeds, sky and clouds, all pounding to its beat.

Sam felt his head drift, as if he'd had too much Scotch. The ground underfoot seemed to swell and buck, like the deck of a boat in heavy seas, and he tasted salt water at his lips. His sight went dim, deep shadowy black and green obscuring the sun, and for the first time in weeks a cold chill ran through him, icy water gripping tight and seeping into his marrow.

He might have been lost there forever had Ridder not pulled him inside.

The hangar door slammed shut, and Sam's sight cleared, the sudden brightness of the overhead neon dazzling him momentarily. He realized he still heard the singing from outside, but now it was overlaid by the louder hum from inside the hangar itself.

"Sam?"

He heard Ridder shout, but didn't feel any strong urge to answer until his companion spoke loud in his ear.

"Is everything all right, sir? Do you require medical attention?"

The hum from the hangar cut out, and at almost the same instant the singing from outside came to a halt.

Finally, Sam's head cleared.

The hangar was once again a hive of activity.

"What just happened?" Sam asked.

Ridder was obviously as confused as he was, but the companion, as cool and calculated as ever, had been paying enough attention for all of them.

"They are saying that they have beat the ionosphere 'like ringing a bell'. The whole planet shook—temperatures are falling all over. Most of the scientists are declaring it enough of a success that they should immediately go for a full power hit."

"There are no doubters?" Sam asked.

"Yes—there are dissenters. There was a serious rise in tectonic activity in the South Pacific, near the base at the southernmost aspect of the quadrant. There is also a severe tsunami alert for New Zealand,

Hawaii, and as far north as Japan. But the USA in particular are saying that it is a price worth paying. And given that the invasion on their eastern coasts is gathering pace, the Western powers are inclined to agree with them."

Another thought struck Sam.

"And what about the amphis? Any reports of them massing—or singing?"

His companion wasn't capable of either mockery or sarcasm, so there was that to be thankful for, and the reply, when it came, sent a fresh chill through Sam despite the heat in the hangar.

"There have indeed been reports of singing. The consensus of opinion is that the experiment has a harmonic frequency that the aquatics are particularly attuned to and ..."

Sam tuned her out. His attention had been caught by fresh activity in the main control area. Several of the scientists—he recognized three of them from the chopper trip—were gathered in front of the world map. They no longer looked quite so happy.

He walked over to investigate. It took him several seconds to get their attention and several more to get them to talk one at a time.

"It's the harmonics," one of them finally explained. "We used too much power and the whole planet is responding—a ripple across the whole planet, and it's getting stronger by the second."

"Well, turn the fucking machine off, then," Sam said, before he saw their faces.

"We did that ten minutes ago," one of the scientists said, just as the sound of singing rose up again from outside the hangar, even louder than before.

By the time Sam climbed up into the hangar's gantry the whole structure was reverberating—it did indeed feel like being inside a giant bell. The scene outside did not improve his mood any.

From the height of the gantry he had a view of the whole airfield—and of the horde of amphis who stood on every inch of it. All of them had their heads raised high, mouths open in a single unified chorus of song that rang and echoed, seeming to fill the air, an almost solid wall of sound.

Once again Sam started to feel light-headed, starting to drift, and he had to concentrate to maintain focus.

He called up his companion

"Can I get an air strike out here, sharpish? We could take them all out at once."

"Negative, sir. It's the same all over—everyone is under siege and nothing is leaving the ground."

He could see it in his mind's eye—ranks of the amphis, around Westminster, around the old palaces, coming up out of the river, singing as they came.

Maybe the Yanks are right. Maybe we do need to use the nukes.

He couldn't watch any more— just the sight of the ranks of upturned, amphibian features made him light headed and queasy again. He made his way slowly down off the gantry, barely aware that his heartbeat had synchronized with the rhythm of the chant, not noticing that he moved like a dancer, keeping the beat with his feet.

There was an argument going on among the scientists.

"Look, we've been ordered to do it," an American voice said.

"No. *You've* been ordered to do it. The last thing this planet needs now is more gung-ho cowboy crap. We don't know how much damage we'll do."

"But we know we're fucked if we don't." An Irish voice this time, but no one was paying much attention, everyone intent on getting their own voice heard.

On the other side of the room Sam saw that the Yank guards were getting antsy, and to his right, Ridder's grip had tightened on his rifle.

We're only seconds from a firefight here.

He stepped forward and raised his voice.

"Okay—what's this order you're on about?"

The American scientist managed to speak up first.

"It comes from the Chief of Staff in NOMAD. 'Ring the bell again. Ring it hard.' It says we're to go full power."

"And what are the risks?"

"What are the risks if we don't?" the scientist replied, and Sam had no answer for him as the noise of singing outside went up another notch and every fiber of his being called out for him to join them.

"Just do it," he said, and the scientist turned away towards the controls. Two of the Europeans moved to stop him, but Ridder moved to stand in their way, and he wasn't a man to argue with in his current mood.

The whole hangar was already ringing and vibrating, even as the scientist spoke two commands into the mic.

The chorus of amphis swelled in a crescendo, the hangar, the ground, the air, Sam's whole body rang, a planet-sized tuning fork sending out a tone that could not be ignored.

They lost the Egyptian corner of the quadrant first—the Great Rift Valley tore wide open along its whole length, a three-thousand mile volcanic wound that sent a fresh scream all around the world and swallowed all the old civilizations of man as if they had never been.

The same tsunami that took out Japan and most of the Pacific Rim was three hundred feet high when it hit California. It washed L.A. and Frisco up against the Rockies just before all the big faults slipped at once, sending rock and water and earth and people seething and roiling in a boiling hell.

The folks in the hangar had a great view on their monitors from surviving satellites—for as long as it lasted. The amphis outside sang ever louder, with ever more fervor.

Something in the Pacific answered.

The sound seemed to rise up from the ocean itself, an answering ring to the tuning fork, but amplified now into something that shook the whole planet to its very core.

Sam's head spun, a dizziness that felt like floating. He tasted salt water again, and felt the chill as black ocean depths threatened to take him away.

He was only brought back by the voice of his companion in his ear, calm and eminently reasonable amid the cacophony and turmoil.

"They are attacking the hangar, sir."

He didn't really need to be told. The metal frame of the building creaked, bent and tore, like so much paper, as the amphis poured in. Even as he raised his rifle Sam knew it was too late—far too late—for everybody.

The huge monitor showed a final, zoomed in shot of the Pacific Ocean taken from satellite. It was the last thing Sam—or anyone in the hangar—saw: the ocean parting, great black blocks of strangely shaped stone rising from the depths. And out of the stone, something impossibly huge rose—wispy, almost gaseous, as if it was not quite fully present in this reality.

The amphis cried out in prayer.

The waking god answered.

The tsunami that came down the North Sea was five hundred feet high and washed most of Southern England away with its passing, but by then everybody was long past caring.

Sam floats.

We all float now. We are alone, in a vast cathedral of emptiness where nothing exists save the dark, the cold, the pounding beat from below and the song of our risen god.

Shapes sing in the dark, wispy shadows with no substance, shadows that caper and whirl as the dance grows ever more frenetic. We taste salt water, are buffeted, as if by a strong, surging tide, but as the beat grows ever stronger, the song gets ever louder, we care little. We give ourselves to it, lost in the dance, lost in the dark.

Lost, singing, in the sweet, cold dark.

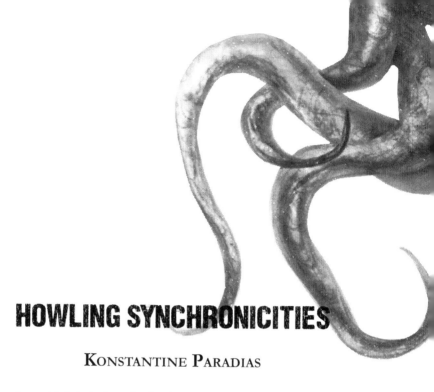

HOWLING SYNCHRONICITIES

KONSTANTINE PARADIAS

Anatoly couldn't help but think about the dog, even as he watched the world below him unravel.

Behind him, the great idiot face of the moon was infested with pulsing yellow tumors. Beneath him, the Soyuz shuttle drifted aimlessly in perpetual freefall. The sight of Wei's crushed face drifting past the porthole enveloped in a halo of broken teeth felt oddly familiar to him. Even in the all-encompassing silence, Anatoly could hear the soft clattering sounds that the teeth made, as they drifted by the controls and grated across the airlock. Like tiny pearls, a bounty worthy of Cleopatra. Through the sterilized air fed to him from the suit's tanks, Anatoly could make out the overpowering scent of gunpowder discharge. He was momentarily haunted by the sight of billowing black smoke hanging over the dog's blasted skull.

Anatoly checked the communications channel one last time. The people from Baikonur had long since stopped screaming. Belousov had kept going until the bitter end, spouting an endless stream of gibberish across every frequency. Houston had picked up on it, tried to kill the broadcast before it could reach any civilian networks. *Memetic attack*, they had called it. Killing words, like the hexes of the Mongol Tngri. Anatoly had read about them when he

156

was a child; he had adopted their practices. Barely six summers old, and he would sneak out in the dead of night to work the forbidden magic: he would get on his knees and dig through the dead Aral sea bed, burying clay pots festooned with nonsense syllables among the hecatombs of dead fish, wrap them in layers of rotted kelp to blight his mother's suitors.

They had sent the word out, those engineering braves, killed every channel they could get to before the word-virus would reach the civilian centers, their brains infected from the start. Anatoly heard their vocabulary devolving, their thought-processes tumbling down into dark dusty wells where the monkey that dwelt in every man mashed them to a pulp with jagged bits of onyx.

"Iä! Iä! Fhtaghn wghan'ahl," Belousov's message snaked through the cloud of static. Anatoly knew what it meant; his own understanding expanded as the gods reached out through him, extending tendrils of pure mind from their perch upon the moon to broadcast their message to the infestation of humanity: *Amen! Amen! The waiting's at an end!*

Anatoly had seen the gods reflected on the surface of the shuttle as they flew past the face of the sun: the great bloated things that moved in a solemn procession; titans infested with teeming city-states, crowns of hardy fungal fauna adorning their misshapen heads. He had no name that could ever accurately encompass their nature. He only knew them by virtue of their *presence*, of the cancerous black shadows that they shed upon the minds of every living thing. He knew them as locust-gods, swarming across the length and breadth of Creation, squatting in the orbit of stars to feast on the detritus that their gravitational pull sent into their waiting maws. Ravager-deities with virus-like intent, their minds laden with forbidden knowledge, driven by world-consuming appetites; hordes of supplicants chanting praise into their minds, themselves creatures broken and orphaned of the worlds that spawned them.

Anatoly didn't know why they chose him to be the vessel through which they would broadcast their message upon the Earth. The hungry gods could have found others better suited to their bidding. Looking through the hive-like structures that had become his eyes, his consciousness swimming through pitch-black oceans where the minds of arrogant sorcerers and zealots were mired, Anatoly saw mankind in its entirety, lone beacons of purity and genius flaring out among the masses. Wei, the engineering genius with whom he had shared this final trip had been a polyglot, immersed in the arcane faiths of the world. Hughes, their comms expert, had been burdened with a vast intellect, utterly lacking in empathy. A quick glance let Anatoly see the secret clusters of nihilists who had prepared for this moment, entire generations seeking to harness the power of the ancient, hungry things.

Anatoly's mind looked for someone, anyone that would share his burden: any living being on that ball of impure iron, broadcasting what shred was left of his consciousness down below to see …

The Prophet screamed at the heavens from his desert perch, a glistening red bounty in his hands. The wounds on his chest and back ululated madly, calling out to the gods of his fathers and their fathers before them. His legs shivered, his genitals were engorged and fully erect for the first time in years since he had long since abandoned all hope of sowing a scion.

Around him, the dead earth crackled and hissed and sputtered. Noxious fumes shot out into the air. Abandoned machinery hummed to life, wrought clockwork struggling to set cyclopean gear trains in motion. In the world below, the necropolises of the serpent-men, scions of the nothing-gods began to actuate protocols that would awaken their masters, themselves long since brought to dust.

"To me! To me!" the Prophet pleaded "I am the Chosen One! I am the Emperor of Earth! Kootooloo, K'tuugha, Cxaxuktuth! I bring red gifts!" he spat, lips frothing.

Was he not prepared? Was he not learned? He had lived three lives, sustaining himself with forbidden sorcery; his organs rested inside carefully hidden clay pots, beating away in the dust. He'd fasted for years, living off the hearts of crows and the juices of cacti. He had fathered hyenas, let carrion fester in his wounds. It could not be for nothing.

"Bring me your Fire! Bring me your Secrets! I kept the faith, Venerable Masters! Give me the word!" the Prophet whimpered, beating his chest, stomping his feet in the dust. With shaking hands, the Prophet raised his flute to his parched lips, hewn from the bones of owls and played the shrill song that would call his sky-steed. But the susurrus of membranous wings never came. When he beat his fists on the earth, the red worms would not come. The Prophet rattled his talismans, drew blight-signs in the dust under the unforgiving glare of the midday sun to call the Messenger. But the Messenger would not heed his call.

"To me! To me!" he howled one last time before a vessel in his brain finally popped and his life finally ended, unceremoniously, snuffed as he was about to step through the threshold of glory, denied of what he considered his birthright. Stepping out of their hiding places, the hyenas yipped joyously and descended on the meager feast.

"Too eager. Too greedy." Anatoly said. The Prophet had thought the charnel-gods could be reasoned with. Foolishly, he had not thought that on the day of their Coming, they would have no need for him whatsoever. He wondered how many others had suffered because of the Prophet and his fathers. Hundreds? Thousands? How many courts had bowed to their will, how many had died to serve their futile purpose? Anatoly had known, since he was a teenager that the world he inhabited was a small place, a tiny rock bobbing in the gravitational eddies of an uncaring giant. He had seen the stars from up close, when the man who married his mother took him to the observatory, taught him about the secret shapes of the constellations. Anatoly had known, then and there, that the night sky was a vast ocean teeming with life. That his life, the life of every human being, was inconsequential in the grand scheme of things.

Through the porthole of the Soyuz, Anatoly caught a glimpse of Hughes leaned over Wei's body, sinking his teeth into her flesh to rip at the soft skin, abandoning himself to the forbidden lusts that the end of the world had promised. In the shattered haze inside his skull, Hughes nursed a glimmer of hope. Perhaps he, in turn, thought that this was a show of faith to the venerable gods. That with this display, he would be spared their attentions.

But the void-gods had long since become jaded to atrocities.

Hughes' gift was in vain. Anatoly looked once more below, looking for an anchor.

Off the coast of Latangal, Aluses the fisherman was thrown off his boat as the basalt city erupted from the waters of the Pacific, raising a mile-high tsunami that swept across Namatanai, wiping it off the face of the Earth. His skiff skirted along the edge of the tidal wave, cresting over the top of it, slid over the rim. Over the deafening roar of the waves, he could hear the screams from Lihir and Konos and Tatau. For one terrible instant he could even make out the shrill cry of his wife before the wall of seawater broke every bone in her body and carried her all the way to the Bismarck Sea.

His skiff splintered into a thousand tiny pieces on the jagged rocks of the shore. His legs shattered with the impact. Aluses grasped a jagged edge, holding fast to an outcrop that *should not be there,* hanging from empty space. Above him, the city shivered and growled like a living thing, a behemoth composed of barnacle-studded obsidian. Centennial coral reefs cracked and rained down on the rocks, their edges slashing at Aluses' back.

The fisherman pulled himself up over the edge, looking blindly for purchase. His rough, calloused hands had borne him to the peak of Puncak Jaya when he was a young man. Back then, he was invincible. The entire world, it seemed, was his for the taking. These same hands strained as they pulled his broken body up on a perch, carrying him to safety just as a large section of the rocks began to shudder and split, hidden seams running across the face of the rock releasing a torrent of searing red light. The behemoth burst forth, blossoming outward like a newborn continent, branching like a lotus. Mighty windowless towers rose from its depths, coiled like snakes prepared to pounce. The terrible blighted light of the behemoth exploded outward into the heavens, spreading to envelop the moon and choke the starlight. Aluses started praying despite himself. It was a prayer his grandfather, a Greek whaler by way of Tangalooma, taught him. It was all that he had left the boy besides the skiff and his skinning knife. The words were gibberish but they kept him from succumbing to shock. A splinter of bone was poking out of his knee, pumping out blood in synch with the beating of his heart.

"Oh God, you are in Heaven ..." he began, the verse reduced to a string of babble. Behind him, the drowned city began to sing its war chant, a million voices welcoming the alien sight of dry land. Spiral spears, their hafts hewn from trunks of giant underwater kelp with jagged volcanic-rock tips, gleamed in the sun. It was a deep, terrible sound that shook the ocean bottom, sending tremors across the muddy bed of the Pacific. Aluses knew the words, a half-remembered rote that had been passed on unspoken through countless generations, surviving from the wriggling traditions of trilobites all the way to the dawn of man. It was the song of the return of the Masters of the Earth.

Aluses dragged himself along the branches of the surfaced city (whose name he knew, by virtue of having beheld it, was R'lyeh the Sunken, R'lyeh the Perpetual, R'lyeh the Patient and Holy). The pain in his shattered leg, which had long since overwhelmed his senses, reduced into a dull throb. Aluses' agony had subsided, transmuted into a ball of pure hate inside him. The ape in the back of his mind had wrested control. Pulling himself up the perch, knife in hand, Aluses grasped the ankle of one of R'Lyeh's soldiers: a towering thing with scales that glistened in the cancerous false-dawn. Aluses brought his skinning knife down into the thing's gills, watched in fascination as the blade slipped with ease into the flesh. He twisted the knife and brought it down on its neck, neatly cutting its head off in the process. Thin blood spurted out of the wound, coating his hands and chest. Aluses let out a hoarse, futile battle-cry. Bringing his knife-blade down once again blindly, he severed a fishman's fingers, cut through another's thigh. The edge caught into the brittle bone, the slick hilt slipping from the fisherman's fingers. Disarmed, Aluses was stuck by the spears of the warriors, pinned against the slick floor.

"Quiet!" the fishmen hissed through gritted teeth, twisting the points into his flesh. Blood welled up in Aluses' throat, choked him into silence. His thrashing ceased, the fishmen continued their blasphemous ululation. From the center of the city, the bald countenance of the arch-priest emerged, shedding murky sea-water as it went. Wriggling its tentacles, it called to the idiot face of the moon, beckoning its gods to come closer.

Aluses died on the rocks of R'lyeh and his body was divided among the fishmen. His flesh was bitter, however, tainted by the rictus of the slain fisherman. For in his final moments, Aluses had recognized the terror in the arch-priest's voice.

Anatoly ceased his contact with R'lyeh. He had seen enough. Across the length and breadth of the Earth, fear gripped the hearts of the living. In their resting places, the dead ceased their envy of the living and were finally still, content to slumber in the quiet dark.

The god-swarm pushed through the confines of Anatoly's mind, crashing against the face of the planet, a great unseen wave that swallowed the talented minds and set the brains of artists on fire. Driven by unholy fervor, these impromptu doomsayers ran to the streets to proclaim pointless gospel. Across the old whore that is Europe, the lakes boiled with newfound activity; simple-minded monstrosities crawled along the shorebanks, cilia flailing blindly. In the jungles of South America, half-forgotten tribes donned the masks of their ancestors to shield their eyes from the killing glare of resurrected machinery.

In Canada, the carnivorous gods of the Senijextee left their snowy perches to snatch at the newborn. Across Antarctica, shining cities winked into existence for brief moments and finally collapsed. North America set great atomic bonfires to hail the new masters. The Russian tundra disgorged its hidden fauna, prehistoric jungles infested with intelligent spiders monster-forming Siberia in the blink of an eye. Spreading outward from the Mediterranean, the waters of the world became poison, killing everything that they touched. The Earth was being shaped to the form that pleased its hidden masters. Anatoly looked down once again. Perhaps there was a pocket of sanity left in the middle of all this madness. Perhaps he could find the chosen few that would muster the waning forces of humanity.

Hila had gathered the men after the infighting had died down. Allai had burned fiercely and briefly, the men turning on each other, the women prostrating themselves blindly, offering their children to the invading gods. She was not a learned woman, but she was wise in the ways of the world and she had known that this was not the end, not even after the deadly cloud had erupted over Kabul.

"It was the Americans!" the men screamed. "No, it was the Jews!" said others, as they climbed up the mountain ranges, treading the narrow paths. Others blamed the Hindi; some said that the Russians had enacted a poorly planned revenge for the thrashing they had given them. Hila let them have their spats; she let them spit their poison and concoct their theories. Any explanation that the men offered would keep them occupied, stop them from turning against her and the children.

The children were what had saved Hila: the sight of her newborn gurgling out a string of nonsense, its eyes glazed as it was swept up by the rapturous presence of the invaders. No enemy of the Afghani had the power to destroy their minds in such a manner, to fill their pristine brains with poison this fast. Hila had smothered the child to keep it from spreading. If this damned her, so be it. She would cherish her next child, raise it to be a warrior worthy of standing up against the hell that it would inherit.

"Where are we going? How can we run from this?" Pamir, her brother-in-law, was the first to crack. He raked his nails across his face, forming deep red gashes along his cheeks. "There is no place to go! Nowhere they can't find us!"

Hila pushed past the children, ripped the ancient automatic rifle from Pamir's hands. Pamir was too caught up in his rapturous trance to notice as she unloaded half a clip into his chest, sent him hurtling down into the rocky outcropping below. "We have no time for fools or prophets!" she barked and they followed her lead. The children did not weep even as the men blubbered incessantly behind her. When they regained their presence of mind, perhaps they would kill her. No matter; Hila was more than willing to take this risk.

She led them across the mountain range into the secret cave systems that the Taliban had built. Hila's husband had been one of them, a zealot, overwhelmed by the rapturous promise of heartless fanatics. He had died with the rest, choked by American nerve gas pumped into the mountain. He still lay there among the desiccated bodies of his comrades. She found a family of sheep-herders huddled in the darkness. "Don't come closer!" the father threatened her, wagging his ancient revolver around like a witch's finger. Hila slapped it away from his hand, shook the man by his shoulders. The shepherd began to weep uncontrollably. She let him have this luxury.

"There is water here. We can drink it. We'll find food and shelter. We'll keep vigil until it all ends," she said to the cowering few that had joined her.

"And then? What will we do afterwards?" one of the children asked. A boy, barely three summers old. Hila had rocked him in his cradle while his father eked out a living as a taxi driver in Kabul.

"Then we go back. And we pick up the pieces. And we make something beautiful blossom from the rubble," she told the boy. It would have to do, for now.

Looking through the twisting corridors of time, Anatoly saw Hila's future: starved after a cave-in, trapped under tons of rubble when the continents would once again slam into each other. But she would bear another child to replace the one lost. And her pale get would sire a hardy generation in turn that would brave the blasted surface of the world and raise their fists against the cancerous sun. It wasn't much, but it would have to do.

Small pockets of sanity still remained. Anatoly did not look for them. He could not bear to see them, could not risk the chance of the gods finding them. They were an uncaring lot, but they gravitated toward fear.

Shattered hope was a rare delicacy to them. To keep them occupied, he turned inward, scanned the contents of his own mind, saw the entirety of his life unfold around him.

Anatoly was born again in Uzbekistan, his mother's home overlooking the dead patch of dirt that had once been the Aral Sea. Ravaged by the Soviets, it had destroyed the lives of the workers and the fishermen, driven the sane away. Only the hardy madmen and the paupers lingered. Anatoly played in the mud, digging for dead fish to keep his mind away from the rumbling of his belly and the moaning of his mother who gave herself to visiting officers to put food on the table. Anatoly hated the strange men; he wished he could bury them in the muddy ground, watch them go under the earth, where his father was.

Skipping through the years, Anatoly made it to Kirov, piggy-backing on the shoulders of an officer who had fallen in love with the hardy beauty of his mother. An air force man as cool and patient as the Urals. He taught the boy the secret of assisted flight, took him to see the jets come and go from the tarmac. Anatoly loved and hated him in the same breath.

The officer had a prize bitch. He called her Kuja, adored her almost as much as he loved Anatoly's mother, took her hunting in the forests and always brought back a bounty of fowl. Anatoly was a teenager aching to hurt the officer, but the officer was an impregnable fortress further shielded by his mother's devotion. The dog seemed like a quicker way to his heart. It was easy to make up an excuse. He would take the dog hunting. He was old enough to know his way with a gun and Kuja adored him. She never got wary of the boy even when he pressed both barrels of the shotgun against the base of her skull and pulled the trigger.

Anatoly could feel that he was not alone in his memories anymore: the gods dwelt at the fringes, reveling in the guilt, the fear, the horror of the moment. The dog died. The boy cleaned the blood from his eyes and threw up. Below, hunchbacked ghouls licked their lips and clicked their teeth as they shared the spectacle. They clapped their crooked hands as they felt his joy upon seeing the officer's expression. The dog's death had crushed him. But Anatoly remained unpunished. He was still loved—albeit from a distance—still trained and educated to prepare for Baikonur. The boy made it to the stars, borne on cruelty, on the day the officer's aching heart finally caved in his chest.

Now Anatoly knew why they had chosen him: for his lack of compassion, for his inhuman distance, and for his capacity for calculated cruelty. Out of all the Olympians and the sorcerers and the pious, he was the only one who could muster their presence in his mind. "Did I end the world?" Anatoly mused to himself. The Old Ones cackled, wriggled their tentacles in open mockery of the man. No, of course not. How could he end the world? He had only lingered at the threshold, held open the gate to let the nightmare take hold.

Below, the mayhem has ceased. Isolated pockets of chaos still remain, themselves swiftly extinguished. The planet spins on its axis, ancient and uncaring. Even it, in turn, is impervious to the Old One's sophisticated cruelty. In time, the wounds will heal. In time, even the immortal idiot gods will wink out of existence as mankind did. This is a cold and uncaring universe, after all.

Anatoly climbs back into the Soyuz, clears away the blood and the teeth, ejects Wei and Hughe's bodies from the airlock. The gods have abandoned him, having turned against each other to resolve ancient enmities. He turns the shuttle down, aims the thrusters at the flesh-forests that have choked China where formless maws gnaw at what's left of the populace. Looking through the vast oceans of possibility, he adjusts the course and launches into the atmosphere. With any luck, he should burn on entry, reduced into a clear ball of impure metal and reduce the horrors into ash in a display of apocalyptic force.

Above him, around him, below him, the gods scoff at the futility of his sacrifice. It is good. It means they've noticed him. The sight warms his heart. For a brief flash, he sees them frozen and lifeless, drifting in the desolate emptiness of heat-death. The sight sends them into a frenzy. Perhaps there is something that even they fear.

"No way out. Not for you," he tells them as he smashes his hand against the ignition. And all the way down, Anatoly is laughing.

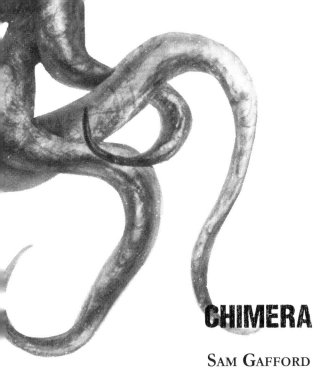

CHIMERA

Sam Gafford

"… and reports continue to come into the WCVB newsroom regarding outbreaks of random violence connected with mental health facilities. The CDC has become involved in the investigation to determine if the instances are a result of bacterial or pharmacological origin. Now here's Kelly Shapiro to give us a sneak peak of what's happening on today's edition of MASSACHUSETTS MORNING!"

"Shut that fucking thing off," Lt. Jeff Byers said as he poured himself another cup of coffee. The morning was supposed to be his quiet time, when he got himself mentally ready for work. As a cop, he never knew what he might run into on the streets that day, so those few minutes of peace and quiet had become precious to him.

"I'm watching it," said his wife, Teri, who was spread prone over the couch. Once, Teri had been a real bombshell, a beautiful blonde with big eyes and a shape to match. But time had not been kind to Teri, and the years had left their mark on her face and figure. Her hair was brittle now, with no luster or shine. Her robe was open and she was naked under it, but only out of indifference, not from any sense of seduction or sexuality.

Jeff slapped her hard in the back of her head and she quickly shut off the television.

"When the hell is that piece of shit son of yours going to get out of bed?"

Teri kept her head facing forward, not daring to make eye-contact. "He'll be up in a little while," she said. "He's going to the university for those tests today."

Shaking his head, Jeff put his coffee down and started heading upstairs. "'Tests', my ass. Just another fucking excuse not to do anything."

Afraid to move, Teri hoped that her son heard Jeff stomping up the stairs soon enough to get out of bed and out of the way of his stepfather. She couldn't risk moving, so just closed her robe and withdrew inside herself, wondering if she dared to turn on the television again.

Upstairs, Jeff walked down the hallway to his stepson's room and, not bothering to knock, threw the door open. The boy, William, was still asleep. If an art director had been asked to create a typical twenty-year-old goth-metalhead's bedroom, they would have created William's room. There were posters on the wall of bands with strange, foreign names. The window shades and curtains were tightly closed. A television in the corner droned on with music videos that few people would have recognized. William was lying face down on the unmade bed, on top of the covers. He wore all black, as usual, and his hair was dyed into a spikey, dark tangle. He had a nose ring and multiple earrings, along with weird tattoos that looked incomprehensible but had a sinister pattern. On his left arm was what looked like some sort of humanoid octopus with tentacles that wrapped around a circle with a symbol inside it like a cross between a hieroglyphic and a Japanese kanji. Basically, it was as if William and this room had been created for the sole purpose of pissing Jeff off and it worked very well.

Jeff grabbed William by the hair and threw him out of bed. "Time to get up, spaz," he said, "go out and do something for a change."

William lay in a pile of discarded snack bags and dirty clothes. He had knocked over an ashtray and the contents had spilled onto the carpeting, already making an invincible stain. "Fuck you, asshole!" he shouted.

Downstairs, Teri cringed as she listened.

Because of his training, Jeff knew just where to hit to not leave a visible mark and, because he had spent a lifetime hitting smaller people, enjoyed it as well. A quick punch to the side made William curl up like an armadillo but Jeff grabbed the boy's face and held it to his.

"I'm not telling you again, fucker. I want you out of my house. Gone. I don't give a fuck where you go but you'd better be out of here by the weekend or me and a couple of my pals will take you out by the river and settle this."

He shoved the boy back down and turned to leave when William asked, "Don't you ever get tired of being a stereotype, Jeff?"

The man snorted a laugh. "We all are, kid. Ain't nothing new in Arkham anymore."

"Dr. Madison, should our viewers be alarmed by this increase in violence?" the perky blonde newscaster asked one of the smaller talking heads on the screen.

"No, not at all; our evidence shows that only those with serious and previous psychiatric disorders are affected. This is nothing more than a case of 'mob mentality' and will pass soon enough."

Slowly, the sleep subjects were waking up.

One by one, they sat up in their beds, and attendants busily detached the monitor sensors and brought them cups of water. There were five subjects this time; the empty sixth bed was a painful sore that no one wanted to notice or admit was even there. Three women and two men sat there with body language that suggested a long, agonizing struggle instead of a simple night's sleep.

"There're more spikes," said Elaine Andrews to Dr. Munroe, head of the sleep lab at Miskatonic University. Munroe was a small man with crinkly hair that had begun to bald enough that he had finally started paying attention to male-hair-growth commercials on late-night television. He'd never been married and his glasses were thick. More than once, he had noticed the supple, full figure of his student assistant, Ms. Andrews, and at night, would fantasize about violating her in obscene ways. She, for her part, pitied Dr. Munroe when she thought of him at all.

"I can see that," Dr. Munroe said, looking at the brainwave printouts. Each subject had been closely monitored all night and their sleep patterns recorded. Not for the first time since he had started this study into 'night terrors,' Munroe noticed something that bothered him. "Look at this," Dr. Munroe said, taking the opportunity to lean over Elaine so he could smell her red hair.

"What am I looking at?" she asked.

"Here," Dr. Munroe pointed to two of the patterns. "Right near the beginning of REM sleep. See how these two are virtually identical? It's as if their brains are synchronized. Then, they're joined by a third. Finally, all five are sharing the same pattern, leading to this." He pointed at the graph which showed a huge spike in all five patterns. "They all spike together here and then break apart again. Then there's nothing for the rest of the night."

Dr. Munroe looked out of the observation window at the subjects as they were beginning to move about and head towards the restrooms. "Did you notice anything unusual last night? While they were sleeping?"

Elaine shook her head. "No; nothing, doctor. They tossed and turned like they always do. There was some whimpering but nothing major. No anguish patterns."

He looked at the spike on the printouts. It had to have been some sort of night terror—but were they all having the same one?

"I want to see the post-sleep interviews as quickly as possible. Oh, and remember that we have a new subject coming in today. William Byers. He's a replacement for … well, you know."

Elaine nodded her head. Together they watched the subjects shuffle out of the room like zombies mumbling for 'coffee' instead of 'brains.'

"Breaking news out of our foreign affiliates. An earthquake measuring a record 7.8 on the Richter scale was recorded this morning in the South Pacific Ocean. Tsunami alerts are being issued and initial reports state that a large new land mass has been sighted roughly 100 nautical miles from the island of Ponape. We will report any updates as they are received and now we return to 'The Maury Povich Show' currently in progress."

"Where were you last night?" Teri asked her son without taking her attention away from the television where a large woman was breathlessly anticipating the results of a DNA paternity test.

"Just out," William answered, eating dry cereal from a bowl.

She shrugged. "Fine. I don't want to know. Then I won't have to lie when the police come."

"Don't you mean 'Dad'?"

Teri smashed her cigarette out in the overloaded ashtray and lit another. "Son of a bitch isn't your dad. Don't call him that."

For the longest time, William had fantasized about rescuing his mother and taking her away from Jeff and this place. But now, standing there with a bowl of cereal that was dry because there was no milk in the house, he looked at her and felt, not for the first time, that maybe this was all she had deserved after all.

He'd never known his 'real' dad. William wasn't even sure if the man in the faded photo that his mother had shown him was really his dad or just someone Teri had screwed once. At the time, Jeff had seemed just as good a choice as any of the other men. At least he had a good job and a house and a car—but that ended up being all he had going for him. It hadn't taken long for a harsher side of Jeff to become visible until eventually that was the only side visible at all.

As the woman on the television jumped up and screamed at the results she didn't want to hear, Teri picked up the remote and idly flipped through the channels. She slowed as she got to the news channels and stopped on Fox News where there was a fierce debate about the state of mental health in America and a never-ending ticker of bad-news headlines passing by on the bottom of the screen while stock prices filled a banner along the top. "Cult massacre in Oklahoma elementary school," read one headline, only to be replaced by "Widespread rioting in European cities," "Oil rig explosion in Gulf of Mexico death toll reaches 100," and more painful news.

"Whole world's going to shit," said Teri.

"Who cares?" replied William. He put the empty bowl in the sink already full of dirty dishes. He looked back at his mother, trying to summon up any sort of emotion about her, anything at all beyond a pervasive indifference, but could find nothing.

"I'm going out," William said as he put on his jacket and opened the door.

Some sort of noise came from his mother, but he couldn't

decipher it, so he just left.

"You see, when three or more planets come together in a straight-line configuration, it's called a 'Syzygy' and that is what we are experiencing now." The well-dressed scientist appeared very calm as he spoke to the television newswoman, who could have been a model.

"And you believe that this is responsible for the outbreaks of violent behavior we've been witnessing across the planet the last few days?"

"Most certainly. Ancient civilizations knew the impact of this planetary alignment on tides, earthquakes and especially people. It was said that it would drive people mad through their dreams."

"What the fuck is this?" Jeff said as they stood deep in the Arkham woods, past the Aylesbury Pike where no axe had ever cut, and looked at something that shouldn't have been there.

A body had been burned and displayed in a way no one had ever seen before. It was a woman, or had been once, but age and ethnicity were impossible to determine now, as the skin was black and charred. Sticks had been inserted into her back to give the impression of spreading wings and she had been lifted into place and fixed to a tree by a large spike through her abdomen. Her arms were outspread, as if in supplication, and her legs positioned to look as if she were taking off or landing.

The crime-scene techs were staying back while Jeff and his partner, Mason Turner, inspected the body. "Who the hell found this?" Jeff asked.

"Some old fart called it in," Mason answered. "Said he was out walking his dog."

Looking upward, Jeff could barely see the tops of the trees. There was an odd, almost circular break in the branches near the top that was like an eye looking downward. He shook his head and went back to the body.

"Who'd be walking a dog through this mess?" he asked, more to hear himself speak than in anticipation of an answer.

"The old reservoir is just over the hill that way," Mason pointed off in the distance. "Says he cuts through here every day and walks around the lake with his dog."

Jeff nodded. "So that means this wasn't here yesterday or else he's the one who put her here. Fuck. I hate this shit. This is like something out of a TV show or something."

Turning around, Jeff put on his expensive sunglasses despite the interior gloom of the forest. "All right, they can take the pictures and cut her down now. Probably have to do dental records and check missing persons. I can just tell that this is going to be a pain in my ass."

Mason looked at the corpse as if he were searching for a hidden message or encrypted code in the blackened flesh and wooden wings. "But what does it *mean*, Jeff? It's got to mean something."

The detective looked at him and spit on the ground. "Shit don't mean nothing, Mason. Just some mean-ass fuckers is all. Every killer isn't Hannibal Lecter. Sometimes it's just some jackoff playing with himself. C'mon, let's get out of here. I hate the fucking woods."

"We're getting the first pictures of the new island that was created by today's earthquake in the South Pacific and, although grainy, they appear to show ruins and monoliths possibly indicating an ancient civilization. Dr. Thompson, could we be looking at the remains of Atlantis?"

The professor of Archeology glared at the newswoman with open contempt. "No," he said, "don't be absurd. We've no idea what this could be."

"William," Dr. Munroe asked, "do you know why you're here?" They were sitting in Dr. Munroe's office in the Miskatonic University Medical School. It was a typical office, filled with mahogany bookcases and comfortable leather furniture. It could have been a psychiatrist's office on a movie set.

The boy shifted uncomfortably in his seat. "Yeah, I guess. I was told you would pay me to sleep or something."

The man in the lab coat smiled slightly. "Well, that's part of it. You do realize that your psychiatrist recommended you for this program?"

He nodded.

"Do you know why, or what we do here?"

He shrugged.

"I see," said Dr. Munroe. "Basically, I am conducting a sleep study to show the effects of 'night terrors' on adults. I understand that this is something that you've had some experience with?"

He nodded.

After a moment where no response was given, Dr. Munroe spoke up again. "Could you tell me about it?"

He shrugged again. "No big deal. I've had nightmares all my life. Makes it tough to sleep sometimes."

"What kind of nightmares?"

He shuffled in his seat and wouldn't make eye contact. "Sometimes, I get attacked by these things. They're dark figures with wings and tails but no faces. They chase me and then grab me and fly through the air. Sometimes they'll toss me around. Then there are other dreams where I am running over a bunch of old rocks and there's some huge *thing* coming after me. I can hear it coming and this ... this thing is like the size of a mountain and it's looking for me. Right before it finds me, I turn around and see it and that's when I wake up screaming."

Munroe nodded and made a few notes. "And you've been on medication for these nightmares?"

"Yeh," William said, "but it doesn't help much. Some nights it's better. Some nights it's worse."

"How have they been lately?"

"Worse than ever."

The doctor leaned forward and tried to make eye contact with the youth. "William, I'd like you to join our study. I believe we can help you and you can help us."

"How?"

The leather chair creaked as Dr. Munroe sat back, still trying to keep William's attention. "We're trying to chart how the brain reacts during night terrors. My theory is that we can identify the period of REM sleep in which it occurs and, with medication, prevent it from occurring. Our work here can be of great help to others in the future."

William finally asked the only question he cared about. "Does it pay?"

Munroe sighed. "Yes, William. $25 a night. So are you in?"

Finally, William showed signs of life and nodded 'yes.'

"Fine," Dr. Munroe said, "Let's get your paperwork started."

William was quickly passed off to attendants who took his personal information, his vital statistics and had him sign the waiver exempting Munroe and the Miskatonic University from any liability. Now William was a member of the 'Dream Team'.

"We now join the press conference by the Chief of Police for Oklahoma City who is addressing yesterday's cult massacre at the Oklahoma City Municipal High School."

The impeccably dressed man in uniform walked up to the microphone while a line of officials stood stoically behind him. "Yesterday at approximately 1:35 pm, five assailants entered the U.S. Grant High School on S. Pennsylvania Avenue. They began shooting almost immediately. The students of four classes were herded into the gymnasium which was then barricaded. There were a total of fifty-six students and six teachers and teacher assistants confined in that room. The five assailants then began a systematic, well-planned program of ritual executions. When police responded to the alarms and were finally able to gain entrance into the gymnasium, everyone was dead including the assailants, who killed themselves at the end."

The room was silent.

"Investigation at this point has been unable to determine any connection between the assailants or any known terrorist or cult groups. The five men range in age from 19 to 54 and have been positively identified. We are not releasing their identities at this time but we have conducted search warrants on their places of residence and are currently evaluating evidence that has been seized from these locations. We will continue to pursue all avenues of investigation in this matter. Thank you."

Jeff hated his partner. Mason was the kind of officer who had gotten degrees from college and spent time going to classes and reading textbooks and probably marched in peace rallies if they still had those types of things. Jeff had come up through the ranks, starting as a beat cop over in North Arkham where the rich and privileged were afraid to go. There had always been the attraction to police work for Jeff. Not because he had the desire to protect the innocent or to make sure that justice was served. No; he wanted to be a cop because it was a way to beat others legally. With a badge, he could punish people as much as he liked, and with impunity. That he was actually a pretty good cop was simply a happy accident.

"Got the coroner's report on our Jane Doe," Mason announced, walking into the detective's squad. "Female. Estimates the age to be about 20 years old. The burning was post-mortem. Cause of death was a slit throat. Looks like she was bled out."

Jeff leaned back in his chair, a toothpick dangling in his mouth. "There were no signs of fire in the woods or blood, so she was probably killed somewhere else and then mounted on the tree later."

Mason handed the photos to Jeff, one by one. "This type of thing takes time, Jeff. And planning. There's more than one perp here."

"Just like the old fucking days," Jeff said, aimlessly looking out the window a few desks over. From there, one could see the beginning of the hill that the university sat on like a large, squatting toad.

Mason didn't catch the reference. "What do you mean?"

Jeff shrugged. "You wouldn't know. You're not from Arkham. My grandfather used to be a campus cop and he told me some wild stories—even one about a break-in at the library. A fucking library! Someone stealing a book, for crissakes. Got themselves killed by a security dog, of all things."

"What's that got to do with any of this?" Mason asked, not seeing the point.

Jeff sighed. "Listen, what I'm saying is that Arkham is different. Lots of weird shit has happened here over the years. Salem's got nothing on us."

"So you think this could have been witches or Satanists?"

Flipping through the pictures, Jeff stopped and looked intently at one. It was a close-up of the charred face. Something about it looked familiar, but he couldn't place it. "Nah," he said, "we wouldn't get that lucky. Hey, tell that fuckwad coroner to check for tattoos, just in case."

"You see something?" Mason asked, looking at the pictures again himself.

"Just a hunch," Jeff said and looked out the window again. There was a large storm cloud coming in from over the hill, and it sat there over the university building, glaring with menace.

"So we're only hours away from the highly anticipated planetary alignment. As we can see from this computer model, five planets are aligning along with Earth's moon. By early this evening, we will see Mercury, Venus, Mars, Jupiter and Saturn form more or less a straight line along with our moon."

"I guess that leaves us as the 'odd planet out', right, Dr. Mike?"

Laughing, the weatherman replied, "I guess you could say that, Phil. Earth will be sticking out like a sore thumb to anyone watching! Might as well just draw a line straight to us!"

The other members of the 'Dream Team' began to drift in after 6 p.m. The program was not one that required the residents to stay at the facility all day, and in fact Munroe preferred that they didn't. Not as if anyone could make a living on this money, anyway. There were five of them, and Elaine introduced William to each as they came in. There was John, the 54-year-old morbidly obese accountant who mumbled when he talked and looked as if the sight of a mouse might scare him to death. He sat down on his bunk, opened his laptop and quickly began working on his spreadsheets. Alicia was a 32-year-old divorcée who was working as a call-center rep for a phone company. Every word out of her was painful to speak or hear. Simone was 19 and was some sort of New Wave punk with the right piercings and tattoos in the prescribed places. She spent most of her time listening to her iPod, which she had set at an ungodly level, and her spiked hair had several distinct colors. Don was a misplaced redneck who wore a baseball cap with the logo of a tractor company and a kind of flannel shirt jacket. Last was Priscilla, who was a psychology student at the university and was taking part in the study as part of her course work and for the extra money.

Elaine had placed William in the sixth bunk, the one that had been empty earlier, and explained the procedure. "We'll be attaching these electrodes to your head," she said, "and these will measure your brainwaves. Lights go out at 9 p.m. and you'll be monitored at all times. Before then, you're free to walk around, talk, watch TV, whatever you like, but you can't leave this room for any reason other than to use the facilities."

"Why not?"

She smiled at him, used to how her smile could make others simply go along with her wishes. "It's just part of our controls for the experiment."

As she walked out, Simone carefully came walking over to William, never taking her eyes off Elaine as she did so. She motioned for William to be quiet and positioned herself with her back to the reflective glass wall. "They don't like us to talk to each other," she said, "cross-contamination. They don't want us to influence each other. What are you here for?"

William shrugged. "The money."

"And the nightmares," Simone added. "We all have them. You're sitting on his bunk, you know. Alex's bunk."

"Who?"

Don spoke up loudly, not caring who heard him. "Alex Kintner. That was his bed until three nights ago. He used to dream about sharks attacking him."

Starting to become wary, William asked, "What happened to him?"

Don went silent. Simone's eyes darted back and forth. "Guess the sharks got him," she said. "There was a lot of blood. See?"

She pointed on the floor near the corner. There, nestled in the cracks of the antiseptic tiles, were a few tell-tale lines of dried blood that could not be reached by brush or mop.

"Got any weed?" Simone asked.

"What we're seeing here is dramatic footage of the violent rampage now taking place in the Auburn Mall in Auburn, Massachusetts. Details are still coming in but early eye-witnesses have described a mob of, and I'm quoting here, 'insane people screaming crazy words' who have armed themselves with any weapons they can get and started murdering indiscriminately. At present we have no information on the origin of this mob or where ... I'm sorry, as you can see by our helicopter camera, riot police have begun to storm the mall and you can hear the screams and gunshots. What is that sound? Is that ... chanting?"

Over the sound of screams and gunfire came the cry of dozens of voices calling all at once, "Cthulhu fhtagn! Cthulhu fhtagn!"

"Coroner for you on line five, Byers," said one of the other detectives.

"Go for Byers," Jeff grunted into the phone.

"Yeah, Lt. Byers, this is Dr. Dexter Wilson, the assistant coroner. Dr. Pagliaro asked me to give you a call about that Jane Doe. We haven't found a match for the dental records yet but we were able to recover several tattoos on the body. I'm surprised you thought of checking for these. Luckily, tattoos penetrate below the epidermis, so even though the outer skin was cooked, we can recover the tattoos if we dig deep enough. She had some pretty intricate designs on her arms. Color is pretty faded, though, but I'll fax you the photos."

A few minutes later, someone brought Jeff a few pages of faxed photographs. He grunted without even looking at the other person and grabbed the pages. He sat there and looked at the pictures, not believing what he was seeing. There was the same tattoo that he'd seen every day for months and which pissed him off without his understanding why. On her left arm was what looked like some sort of humanoid octopus with tentacles that wrapped around a circle with a symbol inside that looked like a cross between a hieroglyphic and a Japanese kanji. It was exactly the same as the tattoo on his stepson, William.

"Son of a bitch," Jeff said and grabbed his coat as he ran out the door with Mason in quick pursuit.

"Reports are coming in from Antarctica about a new and startling discovery. Seemingly overnight, an entirely new mountain range has been discovered along with the ruins of an ancient city. Although several pundits have claimed that these appearances are due to climate change and the melting of the ice caps, archeologists disagree."

"This is not a case of ice retreating," said Dr. Felton, head of the National Geological Society. "Those areas have been well charted years previously. The mountains and the city just suddenly appeared there. Just as if they had opened a door and stepped through."

"You're gonna tell me where that worthless prick of a son of yours is, and you're gonna tell me right the fuck now!" Jeff yelled at Teri who stood with her back against the wall, still wearing the same robe from that morning. Jeff's fist was raised and ready to strike.

Mason stepped forward and tried to grab Jeff's arm. "Jeff, for crissake's!" he yelled. "What the hell do you think you're doing?"

Jeff pushed him off. "This little bitch's kid has a tattoo on his arm. The same fucking tattoo our BBQ case has, which means that he's mixed up in this, and I'm going to make him tell me what's going on."

Remembering his 'hostage situation' training, Mason put himself between Jeff and the frightened woman and tried to speak in a slow, evenly measured tone. "Ok, Jeff, let's just take this easy. Your wife will tell us where he is and we'll go talk to him. Ok? Everything clean and above-board. Right?"

Jeff nodded. "Yeah, yeah, you're right, Mason. Clean."

Then he punched Mason hard in the face and Mason crumpled to his feet, unconscious.

"Now," Jeff said as he grabbed Teri by the throat and pushed his face into hers. "I'm going to be all calm and nice. *Where the fuck is he?*"

Crying, Teri remembered and sobbed, "He's at the university. He's doing one of those sleep tests, remember?"

Jeff did remember, but he punched her anyway.

"We're getting some unbelievable images from our plane over the new island that formed after the earthquake in the South Pacific. Frank Simpson is our man in the plane. Frank, can you confirm for me what we're seeing here? Is that actually a huge door?"

"Yes, Jane, that's exactly what that is. It's difficult to get bearings on the island's landscape. It's like looking at an Escher painting come to life but I don't think that there's any doubt that we're looking at a massive door that, our experts are now saying, opens from the inside!*"*

Far above, in the vacuum of space, vast planets moved without knowledge or luster or name, coming into an almost perfect alignment. Left aside, conspicuous in its non-conformity, was a tiny blue planet. Vast and dark figures flew through space, guided by the aligned planets like a car driver measuring his journey by the lines painted in the middle of the road.

"We interrupt this program for a special report: Worldwide episodes of mass hysteria, rioting, murders and suicides are occurring at a cataclysmic rate. London is aflame in the worst case of destruction seen there since the days of World War II, while communication with France is intermittent and almost gone. Scientists and doctors have been unable to identify the source of these outbreaks. And we've just received word that the President of the United States has been evacuated to a secure and secret location."

In the sleep lab, there was no contact with the outside world. No one knew the chaos that was unfolding. Dr. Munroe had banished all cell phones from the lab, feeling that they would be too disruptive to not only the patients but the staff as well. Normally, it would just be Elaine and maybe one other attendant monitoring the sleepers but, this night, Dr. Munroe had decided to stay himself. It was just Elaine and him in the booth, which made Elaine uncomfortable, but for once, Munroe had little thought for his attractive assistant.

Together they watched the sleepers and charted the brainwave patterns. The synchronization began sooner than before, but this time was different. William, who had never been present before, was now the base pattern. First Simone matched him, then John. After a short pause, Alicia joined the group, and then Don. Priscilla seemed to resist joining.

"Look at her pattern," Munroe said, "she's actively fighting it. She's locked in an 'anguish pattern.' I think she's actually trying to instigate a nightmare to break her out of her sleep."

"Should we wake her up?" asked Elaine.

The doctor shook his head vigorously. "No, no, not yet. We have to see what happens next."

Suddenly captured by a new thought, Munroe barked, "Quick! Get me the printouts from last night!"

Elaine ran to the side of the room, grabbed the binder and hurried back. Munroe flipped the pages back and forth, not understanding what he was seeing.

"I thought so … but I don't understand how this can be happening."

"What is it?" Elaine asked, not seeing whatever Munroe was seeing.

"Here: the pattern that they all synchronized to last night? It's William's pattern. They were matching his sleep pattern even though he wasn't here."

With a start, Priscilla's pattern finally locked into the group.

"Where am I?" William asked. Everything shimmered around him and the landscape was a barren firestorm.

"You never remember, do you? After all the times we've done this and you still don't remember," said Simone.

They stood around him, in honor. They were all naked, and on the left arm of each one was a tattoo of what looked like some sort of humanoid octopus with tentacles that wrapped around a circle with a symbol inside that looked like a cross between a hieroglyphic and a Japanese kanji.

"He'll remember now," John said. "His day draws close."

"I'd have thought he'd have remembered the sacrifice, though," said Alicia. "We did it for him."

Above, in the skies that rained fire from red clouds, horrifying things flew through the air. Things with pointed tails and no faces.

Don smirked. "Can't blame him. Dope don't even remember who his dad really was. Neither does his ma for that matter."

"I don't like this," Priscilla said, "I don't want to be here anymore."

"You can't back out now, Priscilla." John said. "It's preordained. Remember what we did to Alex when he tried to leave?"

"I don't understand any of this. What's going on?" William said.

Priscilla began to cry, but the others looked at William the way you look at a child who still can't comprehend something he's been told a hundred times.

"This is the world yet to come," John said. "You are its herald. Through you, the Old Ones will come again."

"The Old Ones were," Alicia said.

"The Old Ones are," Don said.

"The Old Ones shall be," Simone finished.

There was something pulling in the back of William's brain. Some memory that he couldn't quite access but should be able to. Slowly, it was becoming clearer but was still unfocused.

"That which was set in motion decades ago is coming to fruition," John said. "Yours is the most important role. Feel yourself becoming."

William's skin began to blacken and pain began to emanate up and down his back as fibrous wings broke free. Slowly, painfully a pointed, spiked tail began to emerge.

"His form is many for he is vast," John said.

"Yog-Sothoth knows the gate," Alicia said.

"Yog-Sothoth is the gate," Don said.

"Yog-Sothoth is the key and guardian of the gate," Simone finished.

Priscilla could not stop crying. "I didn't know it would be like this. I don't want my baby to be born into this world."

With great pain, William managed to speak. "What is going to happen to me?"

"You will rise and open the gate. The Old Ones will pour through you and remake the world in their image."

"Man rules now where they ruled once," Don said.

"They will rule again where Man rules now," Alicia said.

"Past, present and future are one in Yog-Sothoth," Simone said.

"As they are in you, William," said John.

The boy screamed in pain as he was remade into the key and the gate.

The door to the monitoring room flew open and Jeff burst into the room. "Lt. Jeff Byers! I'm looking for William Byers. Where the hell is he?"

Both Dr. Munroe and Elaine jumped away from the controls in fear and shock.

"What's this all about?" Munroe demanded. "William's my patient."

"I don't give a shit, Doc. He's a suspect in a murder case, and it's taken me all fucking night to find him and you, so *where the fuck is he?*"

In reflex, Munro and Elaine looked through the window into the lab room. All six subjects were asleep but the needles on the brainwave printouts were moving wildly up and down.

"I won't go on with this!" Priscilla screamed. "I won't! I don't want that world anymore!"

"It doesn't matter," John said, "you can't stop it now. No one can. He comes. They are coming. Like the girl last night that we sacrificed through our dreams to give William strength, you will light the way."

In her dream, Priscilla's body spontaneously erupted into flames. She screamed, and instead of trying to help, William watched dispassionately through his new eyes.

In the sleep lab, Priscilla screamed and suddenly erupted into flames. She leaped from her bed and ran straight into the observation window and began clawing at it. The fire alarm began to blare and the sprinklers exploded, drenching the room in water. None of the other sleepers woke up or even moved.

Smoke began to fill the lab room.

Without a word, Jeff opened the door and Priscilla leapt onto him, knocking him back into the monitoring room. Munroe and Elaine backed away, terrified. Still on fire, Priscilla screamed horribly as Mason ran into the room. Thinking quickly, he grabbed the fire extinguisher off the wall and covered Priscilla and Jeff in foam.

A mix of charred flesh and foam, Priscilla rolled off him and whimpers in pain.

"Jeff!" Mason yelled. "Are you all right? What the hell is going on here? Have you heard the police band? The whole city's going crazy!"

The detective hauled himself to his feet, ignoring the burns on his hands and face. "Don't give a shit about the city," Jeff said, "I'm gonna kill this fucking bastard."

Jeff lumbered into the lab room, which was still filled with smoke. Slowly, the water dissipated it enough to see what was going on. There were four people standing before him, protecting a dark figure that was huddled in the back. Behind Jeff, Mason and Dr. Munroe slowly edged into the room. Elaine stood as far back as she could where she could see through both the window and the door at the same time.

"Time's up, asshole," said Jeff as he drew his gun.

The four patients parted like the Red Sea. Two men on the left and the two women on the right. Jeff looked past them and could see what used to be William stumbling to get up. His wings spread tentatively, searching for purchase. William's skin was completely dark now with an absolute absence of light. He was the embodiment of the dead girl from the woods.

"Hi, Jeff," William said, "I'm glad you're here at the end. But let me show you something first. I want to share with you what tomorrow will bring."

Like a wave, the vision swept over them all and suddenly they could see everything. They could see the world wiped clean and terrors walking the Earth. People screamed in torment in a world that had become a literal hell. Mason stumbled backward and crawled out of the room in a useless effort to escape the scenes before his eyes. Munroe felt his bowels give out as he fell senseless to the floor, while Elaine's mind shattered.

William floated over to Jeff. Looking in his eyes, William said, "I should kill you now, but letting you live will be more painful." The walls of the building began to fall away, and William had started to move through them when he stopped and looked back at Jeff. With the last semblance of his mind, Jeff emptied his gun at William but the bullets melted as they hit William's flesh. "I've changed my mind," William said and gestured at Jeff, who flew apart like a meat balloon filled with blood.

This is the Emergency Alert System. The United States is currently in a state of Emergency. Citizens are encouraged to seek refuge in their homes or secure locations. All trains and air travel have been suspended indefinitely. 911 and emergency alert systems are no longer available. National Guard and Army members are ordered to report to their emergency posts immediately. Anyone traveling on the roads without authorization may be shot. Stay tuned to this channel for further updates.

Mason Turner, after leaving the Miskatonic University lab, went home where he shot his sleeping wife and two young daughters to spare them what he had seen. Afterward, he sat down in his living room and put his favorite movie, *It's a Wonderful Life*, into the DVD player. Near the end, in between his tears, he swallowed his gun.

Dr. Munroe violated Elaine in all the ways he had always fantasized about and, when he was done, began to eat her flesh while she was still alive. Her mind had shattered with the first vision, and whatever was left bore little resemblance to what had once been Elaine.

William rose into the sky and opened himself up to the outside. His flesh rippled like water and tore like paper, but he held strong and the gate opened wider, allowing the first to come through. After that, the way was easier for the others.

On an island in the South Pacific, two mammoth doors opened and a mountain walked into the burning air for the first time in centuries.

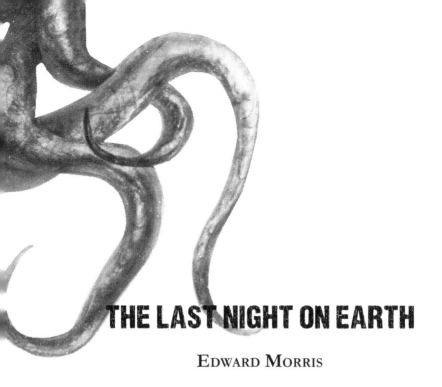

THE LAST NIGHT ON EARTH

EDWARD MORRIS

Look. In the sky. (A hushed whisper meaning Not To, an awful twisting of the gorge perpendicular to the head.)

Fungi the size of a man, with moist, wet wings, their every mandible cold and pitiless as the grave, making landfall on the cobblestones of Allegheny Street, on the Town Diamond, on the Courthouse lawn,on the horizon. POP. POP. POP. Not fireflies. Not Perseids. Not aerial phenomena.

Not bedbugs. Too big. But… Like that. Moving like that. One mind. One chewing, crawling Space-Invader mind that always needs batteries. Hungry. More batteries. More…

Not very many people screaming in the streets, really. More in the houses. Among themselves. There's nothing left to do.

It's never been now and that's it, and that's why it's the end. I'm tired. Someone left the water running in the kitchen. Not me. Not fixing it. Not going in. Again.

Even before I woke up, the starlit stream of hours through the sky grew progressively red and my room grew way too hot. I heard people shrieking here and there, out in the rotting suburban roofline of fish-eyed houses that gave no quarter and asked for less even on nights that weren't tonight.

Two of the shriekers sounded like men. It was all far away. But even before the dream, everything was off, off far beyond my dream-plagued childhood that brought this curious lack of fear, this wonder now. This Now.

The dream said it was the last night on Earth. But not from something that came from somewhere else. Not completely. Part of it would. Part of it was called from beyond the curved rim of Space itself, but there was more to it than that. I saw a lot, in the dream. A lot of things, and what those things carried under their wings.

Things. It felt like a tide. One part gets drawn, one part recedes. Diffusion. Something moving from an area where that something is highly concentrated…to an area where it isn't. Or isn't much.

It was no other country that this doom came from, no hurtling missile missive from any region NORAD could yet track. Not the way any previous nightmare had gone. The nightmare came in the simple racing thoughts before waking. A voice saying things would stop. The closing of a book, frightening and numbing by turns

Diffusion. The hills called them. The Allegheny Mountains, and all the mountains everywhere ever, inhaling-exhaling the way they do with shadows at night-time, just that natural, wordless, *not involving us.*

("We don't deserve it," Mom told me when I was still waking up, still just outside in the dew, "We don't not deserve it." I hadn't even seen her come out on the porch, but all I could do was clutch myself as I observed that which didn't last very long. That which didn't stay Mom very long, and eventually got up and went back inside.

She left her face on the grass. Her Mom-face. In wax. I won't touch it. Won't.)

I dreamed it was the last night on Earth. And I woke up and it was. So I got my notebook and just got dressed real quick and it is so bad this notebook is all I have until.

Until. People have been nuttin' up. Dad shot himself. Just a bit ago.

I heard the Ruger. I'm still scared to go back in the house or he'll get up and bitch me out. There's weirder stuff happening. Humor me.

It wasn't a big movie-type dream. I remember gray storm clouds opening up on the stars, the words, the simple words. This is the last night on Earth. Last. Night. Only the mysterious part of what that phrase meant, but no other kind of mystery about it. Just worse.

Lots worse. My Dad shot himself when the thing fell in the yard. Because it talked to him. Through the window. I heard all its chompers buzzing on the glass. It was asking something. Something Dad didn't want to give over. I heard all this from the front yard. Just moments ago.

Everybody dreamed it at the same time. Just like that. We could all tell. We all knew. It was going to be the last night on Earth. The night that nothing came before and This came after. The last night of our world.

The neighbor lady had a wax face for a face when she came back out, after the screams. Mrs. Long. That was also just now. But she didn't stick around, or speak. Even before anything fell out of the sky, I knew that it wasn't just creatures from outside.

It felt local. And old. It smelled all those things. The wind. The wind told me before I was even all the way awake.

Everybody dreamed it at the same time. The wind said that the hills called them, too, in a pact that was … *interplanetary*, rather than just *extraterrestrial*.

I dream a lot. Sometimes I remember words like that. Like *Mi-Go*. That means "Crustacean." I'm pretty sure I dreamed that part, too. Mom always says I should be a writer, but there's no time now. Except I'm writing this down. When I can. In bits.

I remember waking up and not going downstairs at first. Looking out my window, and seeing the old black man walking in the streets. He didn't look happy. He didn't want to look at anyone. He was so tall, so skinny, he looked like something out of a movie. But human. And black. Not African-American. *Black*. Staring into the stars. Stretching his stretchy hands toward the sky.

That frightful buzzing. That shocking smell. Calling them in. Calling them *back*.

189

Any tune. Any words. Any tune now but those thousand mewling voices from the hills, from the caves in the hills, up on Chimney Rocks, where there's barbed wire and rock salt close but you can still smell the smell, the smell, worse than cliff-diving at the Blue Holes mere feet above Model T Fords, gangsters melted in caustic soda, flippered babies with bricks tied to their necks ...

The hills called them in, from brooding gulfs beyond the Zodiac's course, fused into one terrible swift drone. No chants to weird gods or beating old gongs. Just a wind. A call. A *time.*

It had to have been Time. We were pretty gnarly to begin with, anyway. There had been some sort of pact, some sort of blood spilled.

A covenant with that formless star-spawn from the remotest gulfs of Space, in an earlier age that made the wind rise backward from the caves of the planet we were all fool enough to call home. The wind that gave this wisdom at the end to the last one holding a pencil. Me. The wind in the hills.

The wind sounds like it's trapped in a jar. Like a soul trapped in a jar. Like the screams that stop. And stop. And cap off. And even worse, that one family at the end of the block, the ones that dress like Mennonites or JW's but different, sort of, the ... whatsit, Akeleys.

They're worse. Mom and Pop Akeley are both out on the porch, waiting. The children ... The children have been restrained to accompany them. They ... It's ... Duct-tape. They're crying. But not making any noise.

No noise. There are too many to fight. We must have deserved it, because we can't withstand it. No way we can.

Above me, across the void and through the space-hung screens, the stars are doing things no stars should, but even that's no weirder than the squirming non-dreams that fold their wings, and turn the leechdisks of their faces toward the porch, antennae moving as one in soft pink stone with all those chompy claws up and down, up and down the rippling slime-mold of their off-Earth flesh.

No eyes. One of them is looking at me without eyes. I'm hooped. The whole world's dead. I'm dead.

I'm going out to them. I may be back for this notebook. I can't hope. Because I understand—

[*remaining pages are blank*]

THE INCESSANT DRONE

Neil Baker

It had been four months since the first wave of Thrashers had phased across North America and destroyed every capital and industrial city on the continent. By the time the Euro-Asia Coalition had formed, the landmasses that had once been Canada, the United States and Mexico were no more: half a billion people gone—crushed, liquefied, roasted or eaten. Cities were flattened, terrain was leveled, and waterways drained as the monsters took control. The desperate scurrying of the world's think-tanks had provided no answer, other than that the Thrashers were precursors: ground troops preparing the way, cutting a path for their masters. This had been ascertained during the razing of D.C., when an air-to-air missile from one of the last remaining F-22s hit a Thrasher just as it phased out. Its impermanence, coupled with the energy from the blast, had briefly opened a rift—*a window*. For a split second the creature's world was visible ... and recorded. The playback revealed blasted deserts under roiling skies and legions of vast, crab-like beings waiting to enter and claim their spoils. These creatures were twice as large as the Thrashers, which themselves were a mile high.

It hadn't taken long to give the invading behemoths their moniker. Each of the Thrashers that phased into our world purely to level it was identical to the last; a vast column of gray putrescence atop two stubby legs that stamped across the land in quarter-mile strides. Two long limbs extended from the torso, just shy of the top, and each limb ended in a collection of fleshy tendrils as thick as redwoods that clawed at planes in the air and tore buildings from their foundations. The creatures had no face to speak of, just a gaping hole where features might have sat, and from this fleshy abyss poured emerald-green flames in mighty spouts that turned everything to ash and glass. The only discernible difference between the Thrashers themselves was their *halo*; a collection of symbols formed from orange fire and held in a ring by spindly plasma webbing. These ghastly crowns rotated slowly above them, and no two were alike. The symbols were more complicated than mere runes, with intricately woven designs enclosed within erratic shapes. Once in a while, before a city fell to one of the monsters, a recognizable symbol would be spied and recorded: a pentagram here, a magical sigil there. It was only after three months of fruitless investigation by the world's leading surviving linguists that the research was handed over to students of the dark arts, who had been clamoring for an opportunity to work with the data, and they eagerly huddled over the reconnaissance photos with their crystals and questionable tomes. A month later, still no translation had been offered, and meanwhile the Thrashers had started materializing across Europe, starting in Germany and expanding their paths of destruction toward every compass point until only the outlying countries remained relatively unscathed, the United Kingdom among them.

Jasi inhaled deeply, filling her lungs with the oxygen-rich air mixture being fed into her flight mask. She held it for five seconds and felt a calmness wash over her, then exhaled sharply and eased the throttle forward, a familiar invisible hand pushing her back into her seat as the Eurofighter Typhoon hit Mach .75. A field of green stars exploded in her HUD, but a cursory glance out of the cockpit window was all the confirmation she needed to know that she was still in the midst of the pack. The airspace around her was thick with fighter planes, even more so now that they had caught up with the group of MiG 31s and H-Xs that had been given a head start. The background chatter, a Babylonian soup, was set to the lowest volume, which allowed her Wing Commander's voice to cut in with sharp clarity.

"Mandrake, Rollover, take the lead. Pinball, Sixer, bring your fives and sevens around, cover the old girls."

An assortment of affirmations peppered the radio stream and then Jasi watched her comrades peel out of formation to their assigned positions. She knew the WC, Moses, would bring her along for the frontal assault, served her right for being so damned good.

Moses' voice sounded grim in her earpiece, "Squid, Hot Stuff, you're with me on point. ETA sixty seconds. Brimstones up."

"Roger that," Jasi replied, banking left to squeeze between a pair of F-15s.

A deep voice rumbled in her ear, "This big boy's mine."

"Dream on, Squid," Jasi barked back, "I'm on a roll."

"That was a lucky shot last time, Hot Stuff."

"That's enough." Moses' voice cut them both off. "Target will be phasing in eighty seconds. Be ready."

Jasi refocused to scrutinize the landscape ahead of her. Lake Windermere flashed below, a ribbon of silver, and then the Yorkshire Dales briefly bobbed up and down on her left like the nubs on a chameleon's tail, before she banked slightly right, following her WC toward Liverpool. The brass had no idea why phase-signs had been detected on the outskirts of that particular city; its docks lay dormant, its streets empty of football fans and Beatle-worshippers. Phase-signs were never wrong, though. Two hours before a Thrasher materialized, the ground would become statically charged to a point where the very air crackled. Plastics became unwieldy and metals uncomfortable to touch, which made evacuation of threatened populaces more chaotic than usual. She recalled how the phase-sign warning had been suppressed before the attack on London, the brass believing that a panicked populace trying to evacuate on such a scale would have been devastating. *More devastating than what was approaching?* That was why the air-coalition had fought even harder, tried new tactics, and eventually brought the Thrasher down over Kent by focusing their attack on one leg, decimating a square mile of countryside. The monster had phased out as it toppled but its leg remained, a vast lump of meat as long as an oil tanker and as wide as a stadium. Immediate studies revealed the severed limb was hollow and filled with whirling clouds of silica that shredded the first investigative teams and destroyed analytical machinery.

Jasi had been one of the pilots whose missiles had slammed into the Thrasher's thigh, and she had every intention of doing the same again.

A static burst, then a chirp. "It's a privilege to fly with the nation's sweetheart, Hot Stuff."

"Shut it, Squid."

He was right, though. After the capital had been saved, the online rags had plucked Jasi from the ranks to serve as the face of the *Saviours of London*. She was a reluctant figurehead, doubly so when the journos discovered her call sign. One small consolation had been the brief moments of hilarity back on base, at Jasi's expense.

"Seriously though," said Squid, "someone should tell 'em you got your call sign for your madras, not for your looks...."

"Can it, Squid," Moses barked in their ears, "visual in five."

Jasi checked her position—perfectly on Moses' seven. Squid was equally precise; a mirror-image wingman, while their WC formed the tip of the arrow. Behind them, the rest of the squadron formed up, twelve more Typhoons, *the spear*. Further back was the rest of the coalition; Russian MiGs wingtip to wingtip with French Rafales, German Tornados zipping between lumbering Chinese H-Xs, on loan from the People's Liberation Army, and the last remaining American F-22s bringing up the rear, laden with fiery death, nothing but bloody vengeance on their agenda. Eighty-six planes in all.

As one, the coalition banked right to approach the city from the North, the setting sun pouring orange through canopies and throwing the cockpits into violet gloom. Static flashes bounced between wisps of cloud and touched down in the green waters of the Mersey Estuary and the very air itself seemed to shimmer, blurring the world outside. Jasi frowned as her HUD winked out, then sputtered back fainter than before, and then the Thrasher phased in, one mighty leg in the churning port, the other in the middle of the ferry terminal which collapsed like a sandcastle. It was directly in front of them and barely had time to raise its flailing arms before the planes were upon it.

Moses' voice thundered in every earpiece, "Brimstone markers and hail! Right leg!"

Jasi swooped in tight formation with Moses and Squid, and let loose.

"Enemy engaged, sir."

Group Captain Redcarr nodded at the young officer who had appeared at the open door of his room, and reached for his jacket, "Inform the AC I'm on my way."

"Yes, sir," replied the woman, already out of view. A few months ago such informality would have cost her dearly, but that was a different time. He buttoned his jacket and straightened his tie. Redcarr might have let standards slip a little, but Air Commodore Grant would still chew him out if he wasn't dressed for battle. An hour of sleep had done nothing to alleviate his fatigue and everything served to make his march toward the command center miserable: the bright, overhead light strips, the stench of sweat and coffee and nicotine and the bitter Icelandic air that seemed to penetrate the corridors of the airbase with awful ease.

Keflavik was small, but it would suffice. The air station was once home to the U.S. Air Force, but had been returned to the Icelandic coast guard many years ago. Now it bustled once again with pilots and engineers; rescue helicopters shunted to one side to make way for fighters and bombers that jostled for space on the tiny runways, spilling out onto the surrounding fields. Redcarr knew that their tenancy was to be short-lived; it seemed that no sooner had the coalition taken root than a Thrasher would appear to spoil the party. Humanity was dealing with a ruthlessly intelligent foe.

As with everything on the base, the command center was cramped and filled with frantic personnel. Redcarr squeezed through the bodies hustling around, relaying information and status updates, and returned quickly snapped off salutes as he made his way to a raised dais at the rear of the room. A huge metal desk squatted in the middle of the platform from which the Air Commodore barked orders at an endless stream of subordinates. AC Grant was a big man, half as wide as his desk, and he acknowledged Redcarr's arrival with a curt nod.

Redcarr saluted, "Air Commodore."

"Sit down, George," snapped the AC, dragging a wooden chair to the side of the desk. He angled one of two monitors that were connected to a solid, gun-metal slab of a laptop so that Redcarr could watch the feed: six different views of the battle—live images from cameras mounted beneath a half dozen support planes.

Redcarr sat and craned forward, scanning the six quadrants of the monitor, trying to get his bearings. Each of the feeds was a mess of activity. He might as well have been watching a live feed from the mouth of a hornets' nest. Six tableaus, grainy and chaotic, taking turns to freeze in an impressionistic splash of pixels. Six images showing the utter one-sidedness of the battle as wave upon wave of fighter planes strafed the monster, whirling around it like a nursery mobile as the Thrasher flailed its colossal arms and swatted them from the sky. Tiny pinpricks of light dotted the creature's body, evidence that missiles were finding their targets, but still it rampaged, incinerating the docks with its fiery breath, seeding the ground with golden blooms. Even as Redcarr watched, two of the images turned to static in rapid succession.

"Too damned close," growled the Air Commodore, "what are those fools playing at?"

"They are under orders to capture the moment the Thrasher falls, sir," said Redcarr, fixated on the monitor, "the EAC wants to capitalize on the momentum of London."

"This is a fucking war, George, not a TV show."

"Those lines were blurred long ago, sir."

Another live feed winked out, and suddenly the remaining three showed the same image, albeit from different angles: fifteen fighters in tight formation, streaking towards the monster.

"This is it, sir," Redcarr said, pushing forward in his seat, his voice rising with excitement, "the Typhoons!"

Grant motioned to a comms officer standing at the base of the dais. The officer looked up, his hand still pressed to the receiver in his ear.

The big man yelled at him over the loud hum of the command center. "Tell them Godspeed. Bring that bastard down!"

The officer nodded and relayed the message into his mic as his superiors settled in to watch the conclusion of the battle.

"Markers away!" Jasi corkscrewed her plane between the whipping tendrils of the Thrasher, keeping her WC in sight through the spirals of black smoke and ash that swirled around the monster's torso. A bright flash to her left, then a violent shudder through the cockpit as an F-22 spun wildly overhead to crash into monochrome flesh. Moses was already long past the danger zone, his own laser markers firmly embedded in the creature's thigh, and Squid was hot on his heels.

Jasi's HUD showed ten of the original formation had survived; Pinball along with both of her wingmen had been vaporized, Sixer had bailed after being clipped by an arm and Mandrake's seven had been hit by a friendly. Nobody would be blamed for that, such was the confusion in the sky.

Moses' voice came through clear and calm. "Good signal from homing markers. Hot Stuff, Squid, on me. Mandrake, shepherd Sixer's support and provide cover. Rollover, take your boys around and flank from the south. Brimstones up!"

By the time the wing commander had finished his orders, the Typhoons were already a third of the way to Manchester. In perfect formation they turned around, three peeling off to the south, the remaining seven forming into a tight wedge as they screamed back toward the enemy. The weapon stations nestled beneath each fighter wing retracted their safety locks and dim lights blinked on the launchers, each one carrying three brimstone missiles. *Fire and forget,* they were called.

Within seconds the battle was in sight.

The Thrasher had not taken another step. Instead it appeared to have rooted itself, one leg in the water, the other surrounded by rubble and fire. The top of its torso had curved over and the gaping maw was spewing verdant flames in a roaring column that utterly destroyed all it touched. Its limbs were raised, protecting its 'face', flailing in all directions and occasionally sending a plane to join the heap of twisted metal and death below. All around this monstrosity flew the remainder of the coalition, half of the original force. Each country was still represented, but only one H-X remained to bomb the creature in swooping runs, flanked by a gaggle of Tornados and Rafales. The American F-22s and F-15s looped around the monster's head, tearing out globules of flesh with their cannons and the remaining MiGs darted in-between the meaty whips of the Thrasher's fingers, peppering its trunk with air-to-air *Vympel* missiles. The distractions appeared to have their desired effect for the Thrasher kept its limbs aloft, exposing its legs, upon which seven Typhoons now descended.

Jasi stayed tight on her WC's seven o'clock position. She thumbed up the trigger guard.

Six bursts of yellow from beneath her leader's wings signaled the attack as his voice boomed loud in her headset.

"Missiles away!"

Jasi fired simultaneously with Squid, and twelve more trails of white smoke joined the six already inbound to the creature's right leg. Seconds later another eighteen trails appeared in the sky over the sea as Rollover's group joined the fray.

Again, Moses' voice thundered in Jasi's ear, "Impact in seven seconds, get over the water!" She watched him bank hard and ascend, and then he exploded into glittering dust as one of the thick tendrils sliced through his plane.

"Fu—" was the last sound Squid made as the limb continued its sweep, pulverizing his cockpit and sending his Typhoon to the shattered dock below. Jasi fought the steering column as she twisted her plane away from the tendril and barely had time to seek an exit before the brimstones hit. The Thrasher's upper leg erupted in a colossal ball of bright flame, and charred meat blossomed like a grisly firework. Instantly, the main torso of the creature began to shimmer and fade as the severed leg folded in on itself, tumbling into the water in a cloud of smoke, silica, and gore. The force was overwhelming and Jasi could feel her face burning through her visor as the momentum of her turn propelled her into the dematerializing torso. Her plane seemed to dissolve around her, and then she felt nothing.

AC Grant pushed back from the desk and stood, rolling his shoulders in an exaggerated display.

"George, I want an operational report in one hour." He stepped down from the stage and grabbed a mug of coffee from an adjacent table on his way out of the command center.

"Yes, sir."

Redcarr watched Grant leave and then turned to the comms officer. "Bring the reports to me here, I'm staying to re-watch the feeds." He typed in a handful of commands and loosened his tie. "And tell the interpreters in the basement to come up here. I want to speak to them."

The officer barked into his headset as Redcarr began to watch the recordings, rewinding and re-watching that one particular moment when a crashing Eurofighter Typhoon appeared to *phase out* alongside the fallen Thrasher.

The light hurt her eyes, but there was no sun in the sky. She felt the wind on her face, freezing, shredding. The sand beneath her feet shifted and rippled; the dunes, colored green and brown and blue, rose no higher than her ankles. Jasi brought her hands to her face but could feel nothing save a dull pressure that soon dissipated in the relentless chill. Squinting, she peered around, looking for a semblance of normality, but received no reward, just an endless vista of undulating sands beneath sepia clouds that chased and clashed overhead. She dimly recalled a life. She saw faces, tasted food and lovers on her tongue, heard whispers—a name that might have been hers. Jasi raised her right hand and gazed at it, surprised that she could not focus on her caramel skin despite every grain of sand stuck to her fingers being crystal sharp in clarity. She considered an emotional response—fear? Sadness? Neither seemed appropriate. As her eyes grew accustomed to the light she opened them further, and then she could see structures on the horizon: towering black spires that thrust into the clouds. One of the spires moved.

I will go there. The words percolated inside her until she began to walk.

The two people standing before Redcarr had already surprised him by not being freakishly dressed weirdos. They further surprised him with their findings.

"As far as we can ascertain," began Madeline King, the lead researcher on the alternative linguistics team, "the *halos*, as they have been dubbed, are an amalgamation of known symbols and mathematical patterns...."

"But so intricately entwined that they cannot easily be identified without being broken down into their purest forms," interrupted her partner, Phillipe Montenegro, unaware of her admonishing glance.

"Indeed," King continued, "we have identified cipher runes dating back over a thousand years."

"Elder Futhark," added Montenegro.

"Yes, Futhark derives from Old Norse, but these have been married to unverified sigils from The Book of Azathoth."

"The book of what?" Redcar sighed, rubbing his face.

"Azathoth," repeated Montenegro, "and these, in turn, have been broken into simpler forms using hyperbolic tessellation fractals and then rendered…"

Redcarr cut him off with a hand in the air. "Simplify. Give me something I can tell the AC without him shooting me."

King placed a manila folder on the raised desk. "The contents of this won't be much use to you then, Group Captain. Just tell Grant that by working backwards, we think we can decipher a basic meaning to the symbols."

"Don't let me stop you, then," said Redcarr, picking up the folder. "Get back to it."

As the two interpreters left the room, they parted to allow a red-faced young man who was barreling toward the dais, a scrap of paper in his hand.

"Group Captain Redcarr!"

Redcarr jumped down from the stage and snatched the paper, scanning it quickly before yelling at the comms officer. "Get AC Grant back in here! We have a new phase-sign on the edge of London!"

How long had she been walking for? Minutes? Days? The spires on the horizon had not grown at all; many of them had uprooted and disappeared over the distant curvature of the desert. The sand continued to shift beneath her feet and the air had grown no less frigid. Jasi thought she had been deafened by the constant rush of wind past her ears—surely that rushing noise was her own blood in her veins—but then a new sound came, so high and intrusive it stopped her in her tracks. It was a whining, buzzing sound, mercilessly aggravating, growing louder. Jasi turned slowly, scrutinizing the air for the source of the irritation, and then she spasmed as tiny pinpricks of pain riddled her body. She spun wildly and then she saw them. A cloud of tiny insects, swarming around her chest and waist, biting, stabbing with their stingers. Jasi tried to run, but the sand offered no purchase and so she stood and swatted at her antagonists with flattened palms, hoping to knock them to the ground. As the insects attacked her she was able to squash them against herself, feeling nothing as she slapped them against her numb skin. Despite the bug numbers dwindling, the buzzing grew louder, to the point where she could no longer function rationally. She flailed wildly, all thoughts of reaching the spires receding as she fought against the biting flies and their constant, awful drone. She stumbled forward, brushing insects from her eyes, and then she saw new shapes in the sand: tiny towers of dirt and glass dust arranged in clusters between the shallow dunes. Their nests. Even as she watched yet more insects poured from these structures, and Jasi lumbered forward, determined to stamp their homes into the dust.

Air Commodore Grant blustered into central command, purple and steaming. "Bring me up to speed!" he roared, stumbling to his seat behind the desk, reeking of Scotch.

Premature celebration, thought Redcarr as he shared the monitor images with his superior. "Second Thrasher attack, sir. It materialized south of the Thames about ten seconds ago. Hardly any phase warning."

"Damn." Grant pawed at a stack of notes next to the laptop, "Where are we?"

Redcarr checked the screen. "The London defense is already engaged, sir. Mostly all gone. I have what's left of the EAC refueling in route to the location. ETA four minutes."

"Armaments?"

"Looking rough, sir. I've made Rollover—Sgt. Wallis—the acting WC. According to his reports they've next to nothing left in the pipes save cannon rounds and a handful of air-to-airs."

"God help them," said the AC. "Bring me those fucking freaks in the basement. I want to know why this thing has attacked so soon."

"Yes, sir." Redcarr passed on the order and returned his attention to the monitor, grimacing.

You have done well. The thought welled up from deep within and caressed her warmly, antiseptic words that made the stinging fade away. Jasi knew the commendation had come from the horizon, and she looked up from the crushed mounds at her feet to see the spires moving toward her. So vast were they, so massive their strides, that they were upon her in moments, resplendent in their liquid-pitch carapaces, their sinewy, hinged claws sinking into the desert sending silica waves spouting skyward. Jointed, cylindrical appendages sprouted from slits in the central spires, and Jasi caught the shimmer of lustrous black hair within: a writhing veil over multitudes of milky orbs. The closest forelimb reached out for her, and Jasi smiled as the point of one bristly pincer pushed onto, and then through her, drawing her out of the cold wind and into the warm dusk of a late summer. *Mission accomplished.*

King and Montenegro stood before Grant's desk, the looks on their faces indicative of the roasting he was giving them. When he had finally spluttered his last and wandered off claiming to need another drink, the pair turned to Redcarr.

"Apologies," said Redcarr, motioning for them to join him on the stage, "he's under a lot of stress."

"Aren't we all?" said King, gathering back her folder from Redcarr's pile.

Montenegro stabbed at the screen, "Is this live?"

"Yes," said Redcarr. "We can't fathom why London is getting hit again."

"Strategy," replied King. "The Thrashers are cutting off supply ports, communications, and all potential threats before the final invasion."

"Much the same as we would," added Montenegro. The young man suddenly snapped his head forward and peered at the screen. "Group Captain, can you rewind that?"

"Of course." Redcarr tapped the keypad until Montenegro waved his hand.

"There! Freeze it there!"

Redcarr paused the image. The frame was filled by the top half of the Thrasher. In the background a fighter was spiraling to the ground.

Montenegro toyed with the arrow keys until he was satisfied with the clarity of the picture; the halo was plainly visible and sharp against the darkening sky.

"Maddie, look!" the young man pointed excitedly at the fiery symbols now frozen mid-revolution.

His partner gazed at the image. "I see it."

"What do you see?" said Redcarr.

Montenegro pulled open his file and started to rifle through his notes. Redcarr caught glimpses of hastily scrawled passages surrounding crude drawings of runes, mathematical formulae, and photocopies of ancient rubbings. The interpreter suddenly yanked out a sheet and held it up to the monitor screen.

"There! It's the same! We have just deciphered this one!"

As Redcarr scanned back and forth between the images he noted the similarities: concentric circles containing four distinct geometric shapes, those same shapes repeated, twisting into the center.

"We believe it means *substance*," said King, referring to her own notes, "*elemental form*."

"*Material*," said Montenegro excitedly, "we saw the same shapes in the halo of the New York Thrasher."

"So, you can decipher the rest?" said Redcarr.

"I think so," said King.

"Just a simple case of reverse-engineering the symbolism," said Montenegro, already sketching the adjacent sign and scribbling furiously next to it.

Redcarr looked at his watch. Rollover should be close to engagement by now. He was itching to resume the feed, but had no intention of interfering with a potential breakthrough. "Well?" he pushed. "Can you read it?"

The interpreters spoke as one, their words tumbling over each other.

"*Fire*," said King.

"Not fire, *burning*," retorted Montenegro, "it's a descriptive rune."

"Burning, then," said King, "*burning matter*."

"What the hell does that mean?" said Redcarr, angrily, "That just describes the bloody halo."

"No, sir, wait," said Montenegro, "we can continue to simplify it."

He returned to his notes and King did likewise, as Redcarr heard the unmistakable rumble of his AC returning down the corridor.

"Quickly," said Redcarr, snapping his fingers, "give me something good."

Montenegro slid his working notes over to him and Redcarr followed the linguistic equation as it cascaded down the page, simplifying yet becoming more complicated as it reached a conclusion that was not good.

Two words.

Hot Stuff.

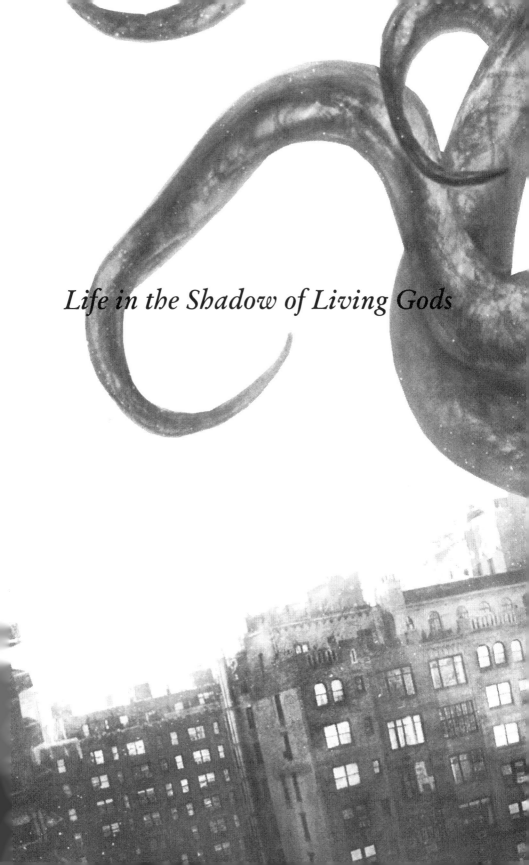

Life in the Shadow of Living Gods

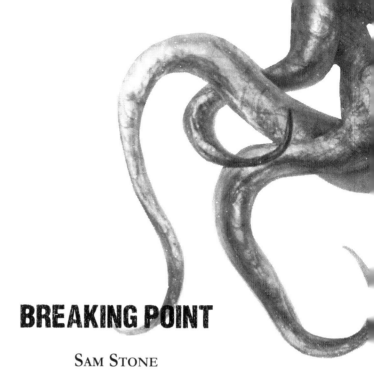

BREAKING POINT

SAM STONE

Kerys and Mai huddled down behind the remaining dried husks of trees and watched as a group of men loitered by the rusting slide. They were smoking something. It might have been the remnants of tobacco-filled cigarettes, difficult to find, or some of the new stuff that was favored among the scavengers because of its hallucinogenic properties. Kerys didn't know. She didn't care. All she cared about was that she and Mai weren't seen.

These were dark days. The end of all eras. A fall from grace that could never be rectified. A cold and vicious wind swept through the deserted land. All signs of life were fading, as trees shriveled from their roots upwards, weeds no longer thrived unchecked and the patches of grass looked like dried, charred wasteland.

In what used to be a children's playground a dried bush, ripped out by the roots, rolled with the airstream like tumbleweed. Dull clouds loomed overhead. There was an absence of noise. The world was afraid to speak; even the wind's whistle was subdued as though it were scared to draw any attention to itself.

The swings nearby creaked gently in the breeze. The roundabout had long since rusted, unmoveable, and the slide was caked in filth— ash and acid rain that fell intermittently from the poison-filled sky.

Kerys and Mai had ventured out from what had been a safe hidey-hole down by the docks. It was early morning, though the light remained dimmed. The need for food had pushed away their natural fear of the outside. It wasn't just the cold, harsh weather or the days that never quite got light; it was the *others* they feared the most.

"What should we ..." Mai began.

"Shush...." Kerys cautioned.

The wind howled around and through the woodland as though attempting to reveal their hiding place. They couldn't move. To try to leave would reveal their presence; there was nothing they could do but wait.

They didn't have long.

Driven away by the cold, the group of men began to shift. Cigarette stubs were dropped, still burning, to the dried and cracked soil. Loud raucous chatter followed them, and it made it easier for Kerys to track their progress as she and Mai lingered.

Patience was something they had learned the hard way, though the waiting was always difficult, especially when the fear kicked in. And there was always fear. It was on the air, they could taste it in every ash-tainted breath they took, in every mouthful of scavenged food. In every drop of rain that fell.

"Come on," Kerys said finally.

"But where?" Mai complained.

"That way," Kerys said, pointing towards the remnants of the town ahead.

"Not there ..." Mai was afraid.

"We have no choice if we want to eat tonight."

"We could scavenge. That's what others do."

"We'd have to fight for every morsel. Besides, that's why the scavengers aren't surviving," Kerys pointed out, "and we are."

Kerys hurried across the playground, Mai tried to keep up. Exposed places were always the most difficult when it came to dealing with other scavengers or, worse still, *them*, but it was a risk that was unavoidable.

Hunger clutched at Kerys's stomach; it growled as though it were responding to the wind. As they reached the other side of the open space, Mai gripped her hand and whispered harshly into her ear.

"I can't do it. I'd rather starve than let another of them touch me again."

"No, you wouldn't. You'll do what they want. We both will. Then we can get back and feed the children. If not for ourselves, we'll do this for them."

Mai fell quiet. She knew what this trip meant more than most. Her pretty, petite figure was always a draw. It was why Kerys brought her along. So few Chinese women had survived. Mai would make good trade, but Kerys would do well, too. Perhaps even better than her friend, because of her unusual scars. *They* liked to see the damage that had been done by the battle at the end of days. Suffering in any form delighted *them*.

They reached the outskirts of the town unaccosted, then skirted around the edges, avoiding any humans if they saw them. They passed the high-street shops with their shattered windows. A food store had its doors ripped from their hinges, the contents long since looted. The streets were full of waste, animal and human, but the animals were fewer now, as the scavengers caught them for food. The smell was awful.

A roar in the distance brought them both to a halt. One of the Old Ones was out. Hunting down humans to enslave, or kill; it didn't matter which, as both meant death in the end.

Mai huddled against the side of the old library building, afraid to go on. Kerys took her hand once more. She pulled Mai to her feet. The Old Ones didn't concern them. They had made a deal, and they would survive because of it. But first they had to reach the half-breeds.

Kerys and Mai had visited the lair before. It was the journey that was always such a challenge. The half-breeds paid well for what the girls had to offer, and the commune would be able to survive for several weeks on what they would bring back. But it was a horrible thing to face. The prodding, the staring, the couplings that left them bruised and battered. Then that vague moment of what Kerys chose to think of as *kindness*, when the girls were given a cart of food to take home.

"Almost there," Kerys said, but her words were unnecessary.

Mai was shaking so hard that Kerys heard her teeth chatter.

"I won't survive this time," she said. "I'm not as strong as you."

"You will," Kerys said. "You have to, or we all die."

Kerys took her hand. They had reached the entrance. Above the door was a broken and cracked sign. The name was gone, but the underground symbol still remained. They began their descent down into the bowels of the old tube station.

Kerys let out the breath she had been holding. They were safe now. Outside they could have encountered anything. The Old Ones, the scavengers, or worse still, the broken ones. No one ever survived an encounter with them.

They had barely crossed the threshold when Mai squealed. A thick, slimy tentacle had brushed against her bare calf. The playing had already begun.

"You know why we're here," Kerys said, trying to sound braver than she felt.

The same tentacle brushed across her breasts. She tried not to move. The thing shuffled backwards; she could smell its stink on her though, that awful odor of rot that accompanied the creatures. And although they never spoke, they always seemed to understand the intent of the women. Or maybe, the half-breeds, their masters, could somehow tell them telepathically. Kerys didn't know. It was just one of those mysteries that she often pondered.

They passed down an unmoving escalator. Although there was no electricity, a greenish glow filled the corridors to light their way. Kerys had expected this: *they* didn't want their playthings to injure themselves in the dark. A waft of warm air rushed around them, another testing of the goods, probably, but the air stank of breath exhaled from a rank mouth that held nothing but rotten, decayed teeth. Kerys forced back the urge to gag, and as she heard Mai begin to heave, she dug her nails into the girl's palm, hard.

"Ouch, why did you …" Mai complained, but soon realized that Kerys had once again taken her mind away from the awful situation.

At the bottom of the escalator the corridor on the right illuminated, and the women turned and made their way further down. This one sloped, and it felt as though they were entering the bowels of the Earth.

They reached a former platform. Below, where the tube once ran at break-neck speed, the tracks were churned up; a hole lay in the center. Something foul moved inside the hole. Kerys pulled Mai back from the edge as a vicious appendage lashed out towards them.

The women pressed up against the tiled wall, keeping back from the crevice as a misty illumination led them onwards towards the side of the platform and down into the tunnel. Kerys glanced back at the hole. She wondered where it led. The center of the Earth, perhaps, or some dark dimension that contained the remnants of the evil that had destroyed and corrupted them.

Mai's hand gripped hers tighter, and Kerys could almost feel the hysteria bubbling up inside her friend. The fear was not irrational, even though they had been through this countless times.

Once there had been three of them.

Kerys pushed aside the memory of Amanda, but not before the flash of thought delved into her final moment. She barely quelled the sight of Amanda's insides seeping from her torso, as though she were nothing more than a stuffed doll bursting its seams.

"It won't happen to us, will it?" Mai said.

Kerys didn't reply. Ahead of them the old train carriage waited. She saw one of the half-breeds in there, but more would come.

"I'll go first," Kerys said.

She climbed up into the carriage with Mai at her heels. They could both hear the shift of movement outside as the others were drawn to them, like moths to flames. Only it was the women who were the moths; the half-breeds the flames that would burn them if they weren't careful.

Inside the carriage was a filthy mattress. It was there for the comfort of the girls, not for the monsters, who didn't need it. Though Kerys didn't know if these things even slept.

Kerys slipped out of her clothing and lay down on the mattress. She tried not to look at the half-breed—not seeing them made it easier—but the smell was stronger on this one than most. It wasn't just filth—the stench of body odor was something they all lived with—it was something else. Vile, poisonous, they smelt of disease and death. They were like the plague personified.

His appendages explored her, touched the scars. And in her mind she concentrated on that; the puckered flesh was unattractive, but not to these creatures. They liked scar tissue, and this one suckled on it as though he had found an erogenous zone. One of the limbs pushed her legs apart and she lay, accepting the probing, until the thing pushed up inside her, forcing a grunt of pain as it began to move. The thing chuckled in its throat. Giving pain pleased them.

She lay there until it was done, felt the awful flood of its seed filling her; then, as it moved away, she stood on shaking limbs. Waiting in the corner, she looked down while another one did the same thing to Mai.

Mai cried, though, and she heard the awful titter of pleasure her tears brought to the one abusing her, and she felt the excitement of the others waiting in the doorway. The tension in the air made the hairs stand up on her naked skin.

The vile seed slid down her legs, escaping when it failed to work on her, and then she was encouraged onto all fours as another one of them used her. This one grunted like a human man. Kerys kept her eyes closed, forcing herself to imagine that it was only a man after all. The pummelling wasn't as painful as what the last one had done, and a ripple of excitement flooded her loins as she tried to enjoy it. But the creature didn't want that, and so another appendage wrapped around her and pinched one of her nipples hard, until she cried out. Her pain brought the half-breed to his climax. Kerys collapsed under the weight of its final thrust.

Standing again she saw Mai, pressed against the window of the train, while a monstrosity pushed itself into her from behind. Through the window she saw several shapes watching. She looked away. How many would they let loose on them until their poor, battered bodies gave them what they needed?

Another picked her up, wrapped her legs around a place that could have been its waist, she squeezed her eyes closed as it lifted and lowered her on to itself. She couldn't bear to be face to face like this, feeling its hideous breath blowing onto her cheeks.

Outside the carriage a fight broke out. The thing holding her became more excited and finally finished. Its orgasm burnt her insides like hot wax. Her eyes opened to see what the commotion was and she came face to face with it. Snout crumpled, sharp, dangerous teeth gleaming in the dark, the multiple bloodshot eyes. It leered at her like a hungry wolf. Bile rose in her throat.

I won't be sick. They would like that too much.

Pain and suffering was a drug to them, and they enjoyed human flesh too much, which was why there were so many survivors left alive. Anyone willing to make a deal by selling themselves at least had a chance of survival. The rest would just be picked off one by one by each other or by the gods themselves.

Mai was left to stand in a corner. They waited. Nothing happened. She groaned and sobbed as she was pulled down onto the mattress again.

"Please," she said.

This brought more laughter, Kerys wished that the girl could just remain silent. She always made it worse for herself by showing so much fear and emotion.

Kerys took her turn in the corner. She could smell the frustration of those still waiting to use her. All hoping that they could continue. It would be such a small thing that would end this for both her and Mai. She hoped that next time would be the last for Mai, at least.

One after another they came for them both. Kerys ached from head to toe, Mai cried until her eyes were swollen, and then Mai's respite finally came.

In the corner her naked belly twitched and began to swell. One of them had finally impregnated her and the thing inside grew rapidly. Kerys was pushed aside. Mai was placed once more on the mattress until she birthed the thing, a mass of black tentacles that seemed to claw its way out of her, while she screamed with the worst pain yet.

Afterwards another mattress was brought in. They left Mai bleeding; the half-breed was taken from the carriage, and Kerys's torment began again until she, like Mai, had given them another monstrosity.

The things backed away from the carriage then, though one brought them some foul cocktail that the women were forced to drink. They knew that it would help them heal somehow and so did not fight. Kerys and Mai were used to this process. After all, it had taken place once a month since the beginning of the end.

When they were sufficiently recovered, Kerys got up and began to dress. Mai remained still on the mattress. The birthing always seemed to take more out of her, and the recovery, despite the medicine, was slower than for Kerys.

"Come on Mai, we need to get back," Kerys said.

Mai didn't answer.

Kerys pulled her tee-shirt over her head, then she went to the second mattress. She was sore, but healing rapidly. It was a shame that they didn't know what the potion was; it could possibly help them all heal from other injuries.

Mai turned her head towards the window. Kerys glanced there, saw that some of the creatures were still lurking. Perhaps these would be first in line next time. But they were safe for now, and they would be allowed to leave as easily as they had entered. Those had always been the rules.

Kerys helped Mai dress—she was slowly recovering her faculties. By the time Kerys pulled on her shoes, Mai was fit to leave.

"Let's go," Kerys said, supporting Mai with an arm around her waist. They struggled back through the corridors and up the escalator. At the entrance they found the cart. It held cans of all sorts of food, some half-rotten vegetables, and a few bottles of water, cola and lemonade.

In the shadows, scavengers shrank back, allowing them to pass. Kerys had always thought it peculiar, though, that the scavengers didn't try to rob them as they left. In fact, no one ever came near them on the return. They had been through as much as anyone could endure; now they were given safe passage. Or maybe it was because they both reeked of the monsters that had used them. They were feared because of their association.

As they reached the outskirts of the town, both of them felt a return to peak fitness, but mentally, they were shattered.

"I can't do this again," said Mai.

"You can and you will," Kerys said.

"How can you be so brave? How can you bear it?" Mai said.

Kerys knew the hinges of Mai's mind were at breaking point. Her own was teetering on the brink of insanity. It would be a blessing when they both finally snapped.

"We didn't burst," laughed Mai realizing belatedly that she had survived. "We spewed out their brats and we didn't burst...."

Kerys looked at the food in the cart. It seemed meager for the effort. But they would live another month. What other choice was there left to them? It was live or die: the Old Ones ruled, darkness consumed the light, and their offspring brats forced a new breed from the bellies of any remaining women willing to sell their souls.

Death might be a better alternative, Kerys thought. Others had taken that road.

"We're already in hell; nothing could be worse on the other side," Mai said.

Kerys barely noticed that her friend often spoke aloud her own thoughts.

The docklands were a fair distance from the town, but they reached them just before full darkness came down. The potion was starting to wear off, and Mai's energy was failing. Kerys took over pushing the cart herself.

They arrived at their hovel to see the door wide open.

Kerys pushed the cart inside, then closed and locked the door. The former warehouse was full of dust and filth brought inside by the wind coming in from the sea.

Mai was on the brink of collapse now, and Kerys set her down on the floor beside the cart.

"I'll check on the others," Kerys said.

She hurried away. Inside the former offices Kerys found the children. They were all sitting nicely around the table, just as they had left them.

"Food is here," Kerys said.

The children didn't reply. They waited as Kerys went away again and returned with Mai, who had recovered her breath, and the cart full of food.

Kerys helped Mai to a chair. She opened one of the cans, which contained some kind of meat. Then she spooned it onto Mai's plate.

"You have to eat," Kerys said.

Mai glanced around at the children. They all stared at her with glassy eyes. Then she began to eat her food. It was all for their sake, after all.

Kerys went from one to the other, feeding them scraps of food. "They are always so quiet," Mai said. "It's just not normal."

Two more children had joined the group in their absence.

I hope the food will last, Kerys thought.

Then she sat down and lifted her t-shirt. One of the new arrivals latched on, its long black appendages wrapped around her, pulsing like a boa constrictor. Mai squirmed as the second newborn crawled towards her, its slimy arms clawing at her chest. But she, too, lifted her top and let the monstrosity suckle.

After that the other children took their turn, though some now ate scraps of protein from their plates.

Kerys sang a lullaby as she nursed the last one. She placed a small kiss on the creature's cheek. The flesh was soft and squishy, its head like the bulbous body of an octopus. Bottomless black eyes stared back at her from an expressionless face that vaguely resembled a small child's. Kerys smiled. A mother's love was a strange thing indeed.

She looked up at Mai and saw the other woman staring at her as though she were insane.

"We are never going to be free, are we?" Mai said.

"Why would you want to be?" Kerys answered, the smile back on her face as she rocked the child in her arms.

She had been to breaking point and beyond.

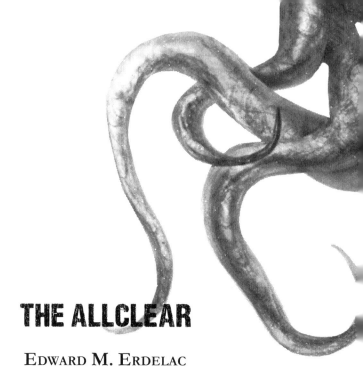

THE ALLCLEAR

Edward M. Erdelac

Two hundred and fifty six Scouts had come and gone since the Pox Eclipse, when the enemies of Usgov walked the Path O'Jen and brought the Bleeding Cough, and Potus of Usgov and the Joint Chiefs of the Staff called the sky bullets and planted the holy mushrooms to try and burn the sickness from the Upper World. But the mushrooms turned the enemy into Ray Dio, and the Upper World became the Hellabove.

Baxter, the last of the Scions of Tist, had led the people down to the bunker, to Greenbriar; two thousand all told, and they'd buttoned up and waited there in the gray steel rooms, eating cans and sleeping through the endless horrors of the New Clear Winter, the riots of the idiot blind, and the raids of the gutmunchers and all the ones burned by Ray Dio.

But Baxter had prepared. He'd known the cans and the jugs would run out one day, so he'd taught the gardeners the sacred ways of the Hydraponix and Ree-Sigh-Clean, and he gave the people a way to live without killing.

Then Baxter had burned the books and papers, and smashed the old idols of Teevee and Ray Dio, them whose worship he said had brought about the Pox Eclipse as much as anybody, and he taught them the Ways, and appointed Alberta first Scout.

The Scout was the offering to the Hellabove. Baxter knew that it was in the nature of man to be discontent even with the paradise of Greenbriar; that eventually they'd unbutton and go see the Upper World, to try and find Potus of Usgov.

The Hellabove, Baxter said, was a place of fire and cold and Ray Dio's sickness and black darkness. It was not a place a man could go and return from, at least not until the Allclear day came, that prophesied time when the ash clouds blew away and the snow melted and the poison of Ray Dio was no longer active. Only then could they venture out and reunite with Potus of Usgov.

Baxter had known he would not live to see the Allclear day, so he had begun the tradition of the Great Reckon in the year of Alberta, the first Scout.

Every September a man or a woman was elected Scout. All that year, Scout was more important than the Scion of Tist who kept Baxter's writ, even. More important than the Lord of Ops or the High Gardener, or the Armsmaster. The Scout could eat and drink as much as they wanted. They could fuck whoever they wanted. They were Vee-Eye-Pee. The year itself took its name in their honor.

Because come next August, the time of the Great Reckon, what some called the Reckonnaissance, would come due, and Scout would write his or her name on the wall, and take the ride up Elly Vader. Scout would unbutton. Scout would sacrifice him or herself to Ray Dio, so that the people wouldn't unbutton and abandon Greenbriar to die in the Hellabove for want of the Upper World and Usgov.

In the morning, Nougat would go up Elly Vader. She would see the Upper World, smell it, feel it. Probably she would taste the poison of Ray Dio, the last communion.

She wasn't too scared. She had prepared for a year, a very good year. The year of Nougat. She had filled her stomach with the best spinach and avocado, she had drunk as much wine as she liked. Yet though she knew she had her choice of the best of the men, men like Cannikin the Pipe Tech and Storax, the High Gardener's apprentice, she had never exercised that right.

Part of it was that she didn't want to spend the year of Nougat pregnant, or go to Ray Dio with a baby in her belly, or the guilt of a dead baby on her soul. But also, she knew Cannikin was Julin's man, and she remembered the year of Plum Bob only too well, when he had barged into their quarters and taken her right on the table in front of Latchkey, and neither of them had been able to say a word against it because it was the law. Things had been different between her and Latchkey since. Colder.

She hadn't wanted to inflict that on anyone else. Besides, despite what had happened, she still loved Latchkey, who was one of the Holy Radmen.

But old Uncle Buster-Jangle, the current Scion of Tist, claimed no favorites. He said the name of Scout came to him always in a vision on the night before the Reckon.

She had never had a vision in her life.

But as she lay against Latchkey's naked chest, listening to his breathing and the beat of his sweet heart, feeling his sweat cool on her cheek, she closed her eyes, and had her first.

She was standing in Elly Vader, and she knew as the doors opened that it was the Upper World, for why would she be in there otherwise?

The doors slid into their housings, and she saw before her all the Scouts she had ever known. Sculpin and Cresset, Wei Wu and Jancro, Basinet and Heathrow and a dozen more whose names she could not recall. All of them, except Plum Bob.

They were all standing in a field of green under a blue sky, like the one in the picture she had found deep in the bunker while cleaning in Uncle Buster-Jangle's quarters.

Uncle Buster-Jangle had told her it was a picture of the Upper World, as it used to be in the Long Agone, before the mushrooms and Ray Dio and the Path O'Jen and the Hellabove. It was a sacred relic of Baxter, and on the back, he said, was written a love letter to his wife, Blessed Sheila Baxter, who had been a Scion of Tist in the faraway bunker of Pindar. It had never been sent, and it was called Baxter's Great Sorrow. She couldn't read the words herself. No one in Greenbriar could. Only the Scion of Tist could untangle them into thoughts. The picture though, was beautiful, so vibrant and full of colors, and she knew the Upper World wasn't like that anymore, but in her vision it was, just as it had been in her secret hopes all this past year, when she had prayed with all her heart to Potus that she would be Last Scout and be the one to ride Elly Vader back down and unbutton the people.

But though they stood in that happy place in the ceremonial red jumpsuits and Scout regalia she had last seen them in, the Scouts weren't happy. They looked pained and desperate, and their eyes were gaping sockets as they stretched out their hands to her all as one and said;

"Don't let him in."

They said it all together in one voice and then some dark shadow fell across them and they all looked up at once and opened their mouths and bared their teeth and screamed, but instead of human voices it was the loud, blaring Klaxon of the Drill Ritual that came out, the machine wail of distress that the Scion of Tist said meant that Ray Dio had found a way down into Greenbriar, the catastrophe they re-enacted every month, stripping naked and running into the scouring showers while the Radmen acolytes rushed to their holy lockers and donned their yellow rubber vestments and black masked hoods and passed their crackling wands over everything, warding the seams and corners of the bunker against Ray Dio, all to the primal song of the Klaxon.

She opened her eyes again, and flinched.

Latchkey stirred.

"Are you all right? Bad dream?"

"No," she whispered. Because it was no dream. It had been a vision.

"I love you," Latchkey whispered.

"I love you, too," she said, entwining her hands in his.

"I keep praying that this won't be our last night together," he said.

She said nothing. What was the point?

She pretended to sleep, not wanting to face his tears or to shed her own.

In the morning he was gone.

Gone to his locker to dress early for the Great Reckon.

He had left her favorite salad on the table, with fresh cherry tomatoes and a piece of grilled corn.

She left it there.

She donned the red jumpsuit, and took from her locker the Scout regalia. The Scout bore into the Hellabove an offering from each of the Departments in the Kit of Emergence. One pistol and a clip of bullets from the Armsmasters. Four days' worth of soy bars from the Gardeners. A thermos of clean water and a purifier from the Pipe Techs. Matches, a folding shovel, and a knife from the Lord of Ops, representing birth, burial, and commissary, the three domains of Ops. A crackle wand from the Radmen. A box of bandages, sutures, and medicine from the Medicis. And finally, a Book of Instruction, the Scout's sacred hymnal, prepared by the Scion of Tist himself.

She donned her Scout's mask, fastened it to her head, and opened the Book of Instruction ritualistically, though she could not actually read the words, to recite the Mystery she had committed to memory at the beginning of her year as Scout.

"The primary goal of Feema is to protect lives and reduce proper tea loss from Dizzasterse and Emergence. To accomplish this, Feema works with state and Lokullguvminz to help them deliver more effective Emergence Manijmentsurvisses across the whole spectrum of hazards both natural and man-made."

She bowed her head, and recited the next passage in reverent singsong.

"This publication provides basic preparedness guidance combined with specific measures useful in Nash-null Secyuri-tea Emergence. Chapter one. The Effects of New Clear weapons...."

The recitation of the Book of Instruction into the mask had left her feeling lightheaded. Euphoric. The mask had a sweet smell of frankincense, and she detected a hint of the blessed marijuana the Gardeners grew in the Grove of Joy.

She passed down the corridors on her procession to the Elly Vader room in a kind of ecstatic daze as the people of Greenbriar gathered on every side outside their quarters and cheered and applauded her, and the children blanketed her way with rose petals.

She heard people call her name, but the mask made things muffled, and she could not discern friends from mere acquaintances.

At last she came to the Elly Vader room, and Gordon the High Armsmaster, waiting at the door with his two honor guards, their machineguns held to their blue-painted chests, asked the password, which was her own name.

When she had spoken it, they saluted and stepped aside, and she passed into the room. They closed it behind her, being forbidden to enter themselves.

This was the Holy Airlock. The Porch. The door from the bunker, from the safety of the world of Greenbriar to the Hellabove.

The Radmen, all faceless in their yellow suits and masks, lined her way to Elly Vader, a silver cylinder on the other side of the room. The wall into which it was set had the names of all the previous Scouts scratched into it, with the month and day of their departure.

Uncle Buster-Jangle waited there in his pure white coat, hands folded benevolently before him, a peaceful smile on his face.

Nougat breathed in the scents of the mask and walked slowly through the lines of Radmen. Latchkey was there somewhere, and she was happy to know he would see her off.

When she came to stand before Uncle Buster-Jangle, he raised his withered hands in benediction.

"Scout Nougat, it is our intent to send you forth via Elly Vader, it is our intent to send you into the Hellabove in the hope that Ray Dio is departed. It is our hope that you will return to us the way you came, and lead us to the promised land of peace."

"Scion of Tist," she answered, "it is my intent to ride Elly Vader to the top. It is my intent to face the Hellabove. I look for the departure of Ray Dio, and hope that I may bring the Allclear and lead Greenbriar to the promised land of peace."

She took out the knife given her by the Lord of Ops and put its sharp point to the gleaming wall, to etch her name beneath that of Plum Bob. Long she had studied under Uncle Buster-Jangle's tutelage. He had taught her again and again how to make the marks that meant her. A thrill passed through her as the point ground the first mark, the 'Enn,' into the wall.

"Scout Nougat, look for the bright sky and the clean air, be mindful of the sores that boil, of the cough that bleeds, of the air that burns...."

She had just moved to the 'Jee,' her favorite mark to make, when Uncle Buster-Jangles stopped short in his prayer and craned his neck to the steel ceiling, to the lights inset there.

The Radmen were stirring too.

Then she heard it.

The groaning of machinery.

Elly Vader was lifting of its own accord.

Uncle Buster-Jangle ran to the panel and opened it, slapping the controls in confusion and shaking his head.

Nougat stood behind him, and one of the Radmen broke ranks and came over.

She thought she recognized Latchkey's voice as he said;

"What does it mean, Scion?"

Uncle Buster-Jangle could only shake his head.

"I don't know.... I don't know!"

He stared at the controls. There was a display there, showing Elly Vader's progress as it moved far up to the Upper World.

"I can't recall it," Uncle Buster-Jangle admitted.

Nougat wavered in place. What could it mean?

The light that was Elly Vader stopped.

The sound of the machinery ceased.

They stood there in silent confusion.

Nougat stared at the doors of Elly Vader. They looked the same as before, but Elly Vader was not there. How could that be?

A light changed on the panel and Uncle Buster-Jangle sucked air through his teeth.

"What is it?" she asked.

"The doors of Elly Vader have opened."

The light winked off again.

"I'm frightened," she admitted.

She felt fingers grip her own gloved hand, and she knew for certain the Radman was Latchkey.

She squeezed him back.

Then the drone of the machinery started up abruptly again, making them all jump.

"It's coming back down!" Uncle Buster-Jangle exclaimed.

He backed away from the panel, stumbled, and then hurled himself at the door.

To their shock, he opened it and called for the Armsmasters to enter.

Gordon stood there dumbfounded until Uncle Buster-Jangle took him by the bandolier and pulled him in. The two guards followed, and he shut the door behind them again.

This was an unprecedented breach of ceremony. No one was supposed to be allowed in this chamber but the Scion of Tist, the Radmen, and the chosen Scout.

Uncle Buster-Jangle returned to the panel and stared at the light which showed Elly Vader descending.

"Get your guns ready," he said.

"Scion?" Gordon stammered.

"Get them ready!" he ordered, and pointed at Elly Vader's doors. "There. Safeties off."

The three Armsmasters leveled their weapons at the doors and their thumbs made some kind of clicking sound. They were bound by sacred oath to obey the Scion of Tist's every command.

The machinery grew louder as Elly Vader neared, and then there was a slamming and great knocking as the machines stopped again.

Nougat held her breath and moved closer to Latchkey as the doors slid open with a hiss. Those doors were supposed to have opened only for her. The chamber beyond was supposed to be empty to receive her. She felt a pang of jealousy, though she knew it was foolish. She had been only a simple cleaner in Ops before today.

A figure stepped out of it.

A Scout.

The red jumpsuit, the Kit of Emergence, the mask, all identical to her own. For a moment, she thought she was looking at herself somehow, and her mind quivered like a tense wire.

The other men in the room gasped.

The Scout stood there, until the doors shut behind.

Then it raised one hand, the Armsmasters tensing, put it to its mask, and removed it.

She shuddered.

It was Plum Bob.

He looked the same as the day he'd departed a year before. The same as the day he'd … she didn't like to think of him like that, of him leering over her, sweating on her, groping her, tearing her clothes. She didn't like to think of Latchkey sitting in his chair, gripping the arms of it with white knuckles, of the thin line of blood leaking from his lips.

He'd gotten up to leave and Plum Bob had ordered him to stay seated there till he'd finished.

That same balding head, the long, scraggly brown hair down to his shoulders behind, that little mustache, grown to hide the cleft scar the Medicis hadn't properly repaired at birth.

He leered now, as he had that day, and she wanted to reach into the Kit of Emergence, pull the pistol and shoot him.

He raised both his hands, palms outward, as Uncle Buster-Jangle had done during his prayers.

"Allclear," he said.

"What?" Uncle Buster-Jangle said.

"Allclear," Plum Bob repeated. "I have been to the Upper World. Look at my flesh. I am not burned. Listen to my voice. I do not cough.

See my clothes. Touch my hands and feet. Ray Dio is no more, and he has taken the Hellabove with him. It is Allclear."

Gordon the Armsmaster was the first to lower his gun, and fall to his knees, grinning and laughing excitedly. His guards followed suit.

"Wait," said Uncle Buster-Jangle. "What if this is some trick of Ray Dio?"

"It is no trick, Scion. There is no Ray Dio, if there ever was. Tell the Radmen to use their crackle-wands on me. I have nothing to hide."

He turned in place, and Latchkey let go of her hand and took his wand and passed it over him. It made no sound she had not heard from it before.

The other Radmen tried. Each one that did, and found nothing, fell to their knees alongside Gordon and the guards.

Plum Bob raised his hands into fists and shouted.

"Allclear!"

Gordon and the other armsmasters lifted their guns and took up the cry.

"Allclear!"

The Radmen took off their hoods. They were smiling. Some of them crying.

"Allclear!"

They got up, crowded Plum Bob, touching him. They took off his gloves and felt his hands, took off his boots and socks and felt his bare feet, and laughed and cried out;

"Allclear!"

And it was like that that he led them out of Elly Vader's chamber into the outer corridor.

Nougat did not follow, but she heard the cries of astonishment from the gathered people, heard the excitement spread through the bunker with each new shout of 'Allclear!'

It became riotous. A jubilation like they'd never known in Greenbriar.

Nougat stood in the chamber of her averted destiny. Even Latchkey was gone, caught up in the celebration.

Only Uncle Buster-Jangle remained alongside her. He stooped and picked up Plum Bob's boots, turned them over in his hands, and frowned deeply.

She took off her mask. She had been afraid to take it off in his presence. She didn't want him to know she was the next Scout. She dropped it on the console.

She breathed in the cool air of the room. By rights, the next breath she was supposed to take after removing her Scout mask, should have burned her lungs.

She thought about the vision she'd had. She wanted to tell Uncle Buster-Jangles, but would he believe it?

He was mulling over Plum Bob's boots.

Then he glanced up at her, as if he hadn't realized she was there. He cradled the boots and left the chamber without a word.

Nougat wandered out after him, back into the dull grayness of the bunker.

The rest of Greenbriar was ecstatic. The children were laughing, their parents were in tears. She saw people leaping about and kissing. It was Allclear. After two hundred and fifty six Scouts, the Last Reckonnaisance had come. Plum Bob and those that had seen him step out of Elly Vader were spreading the word like an uncontained fire.

Nougat's thoughts were troubled. She was glad that she was not going to die, but she couldn't believe that Plum Bob had returned. She couldn't believe providence had chosen a man like him to unbutton the bunker and lead Greenbriar to freedom. Had Baxter foreseen him?

Then there was the vision she'd had.

"Don't let him in," the Scouts had said.

Had they meant Plum Bob?

She wandered aimlessly for hours before she went back to her quarters.

Latchkey was there. He was packing his things into a duffel excitedly.

When she entered, he dropped what he was doing and held her, lifted her off the ground, spun her, and kissed her.

"Allclear!" he exclaimed. "Isn't it wonderful? I told you! I prayed and Potus heard me."

"What are you doing with your things?" she asked, unbuckling her Scout belt and sliding off her pack. She slung the Emergence Kit into a corner. She supposed she wouldn't need it now. She should return the pistol to Gordon.

"Packing to leave, of course," he chuckled, and went back to it. "Plum Bob says he will lead us out into the Upper World in the morning."

"Do you believe him?"

He slowed.

"He's the only Scout to ever return. He spent a year in the Upper World and is unmarked."

"Where was he?" she asked.

"He says he traveled the land, trying to find Potus himself. He ate sweet fruits from trees taller than the generators. He says he drank cool water from a trench in the ground. The water was bubbling up from stone, and moving like down a pipe. He says there were animals swimming in it. And wild algae. Can you imagine it?"

"But…Plum Bob?"

He stopped, and looked uncomfortable.

"I know. I wish it had been you to come back down Elly Vader with this news. But what does it matter? I mean, there has to be a price for our faith, doesn't there?"

"Why?" she asked.

He frowned and went back to packing.

"You should eat your salad."

It was still on the table. Her last meal.

"It's wilted," she said, and left their quarters.

She needed to think.

But it was impossible to do that in the tumult and frenzy that Greenbriar had become. She was jostled by ecstatic pilgrims, all packed and rushing to the Porch to line up outside, to be the first to breathe the fresh air of the new world.

They were blessing Plum Bob's name, using it in the same breath as Potus.

But all she could think of was the line of spittle that had dribbled from his lips onto her naked breast as he'd heaved into her that day.

Did she want to be part of a world where Plum Bob was the messiah?

A hand gripped her arm, and she nearly struck the owner.

It was Uncle.

"You have to come with me, Nougat. It's important."

He turned without waiting for her reply, and she followed, wanting to do anything other than return to Latchkey or fall into Plum Bob's exodus.

Uncle Buster-Jangle led her through the happy, singing throngs deep into Greenbriar, to his cloisters, the Great Lab. Only his acolytes and the chiefs ever came back here.

He took the gilded card of Baxter, which bore the image of Baxter himself, the symbol of his office, from the chain around his neck and passed it through a slit beside the heavy, ominous door, and a green light shone on the panel and the door opened.

The Great Lab was all polished silver and glass reliquaries set into some complex mystic order she could not guess the purpose of.

But Uncle did not stop there. He led her between the altar tables with their silver sinks and burners, and took her to a windowless door at the back of the room.

He passed the card through a slot again, and held the door for her. She went inside.

"What is this place?" she whispered, catching her breath at the sight of Baxter and a smiling, bespectacled red haired woman standing beneath the tallest tree she'd ever seen. Was that Blessed Sheila Baxter?

"This is the Chamber of Baxter."

She reeled. She had never known this room even existed. There was a desk against one wall, and a flat, slate-black plate sat in the middle of it. A lustrous green glass lamp stood on an ornamental brass stand, the finest electric light she had ever seen. There were more pictures on the wall, some of them displaying only paper sheets with writing on them.

She reached out and touched one, her finger cutting a path in the thick dust.

Then she stiffened, for Uncle went right to the desk and sat down in the soft, wheeled chair.

"Why have you brought me here?"

"It is the will of Baxter," said Uncle, and he turned to the dark rectangular plate, and opened it like a book. On the bottom half were buttons with letters and numbers, which she knew. The top half was blank.

Or was, until Uncle touched one of the keys and a tiny motor whirred to life somewhere in the plate. The blank space began to glow.

"What is this?"

"Baxter passed down a secret tradition, known only to the Scions of Tist," said Uncle. "I have borne it all my life, and my replacement would have borne it, too, as it has always been borne."

"What tradition? Why are you telling me this?"

"Because Plum Bob is false. He is a servant of Ray Dio. A servant of the Old Ones."

"What?"

"Nougat, I have to tell you something. I have to tell you the truth about Allclear, and the Hellabove, and about Potus and Usgov and the mushrooms and Ray Dio."

It was pouring out of the old man, almost as if he couldn't stop it, as if it were a sickness he needed to expel.

He turned to the electric book as a white box appeared on the blue screen. He tapped in some mystic manner at the buttons, and stars appeared in the box.

Then the blue screen disappeared and, instead, she saw a static gray and black and white picture. It was moving, trembling, and that terrified her.

"What is that?" she asked fearfully, wanting to look away.

The picture was of a lonesome light shining out from a doorway, looking out onto a vast empty space. That wide black emptiness frightened her somehow. It was bigger than any space she had ever seen, and yet it was entirely empty.

"It is as I feared," said Uncle. "It is the Contingency."

"What is that?" she asked again.

Uncle looked back at her.

"An electric eye keeps watch above the door of Elly Vader, where it opens into the Hellabove. This is all it sees. An empty land of black ash."

"Then it is not Allclear?"

"Nougat, there can be no Allclear. Not ever. Baxter invented the Allclear to give the people hope, to keep them going through the years."

She felt her heart tremble in her chest, and slide down into her stomach. She wanted to vomit.

"But Ray Dio ... and Potus of Usgov. The Path O'Jen and the mushrooms ..."

"Potus was the ruler of Usgov, the Upper World, yes. And he and the Chiefs did plant the mushrooms to stop the enemy. The Path O'Jen was a disease, a living, thinking disease. That was the route by which the Old Ones came. Baxter knew them, because he brought them to this world. They existed beyond our perceptions, incalculable creatures of ferocious power. They whispered to him in dreams and through the insidious boxes of Teevee and Ray Dio. The Old Ones manipulated him into bringing them forth with ancient math magics and experiments, fooling him into believing it was his own inspiration. That was the Outbreak. The Path O'Jen spread everywhere. Baxter couldn't call it back. And those infected became hosts for the Old Ones so they could take physical forms and conquer Usgov and the lands beyond. Potus and his Chiefs ordered the sky bullets to plant the mushrooms to destroy them, to cure Usgov as the worst infections must always be cured: with fire. But it did not stop them. It tempered them, baked them like cakes. Baxter took everyone he could find down into Greenbriar to escape. That was why he burned all the books, broke all the records of what had happened. The Old Ones made the Upper World into the Hellabove, so that they could thrive. Baxter and the survivors wanted them to forget us, and for us to forget them, so that we would never meet."

"But Plum Bob?"

Uncle tapped the electric eye screen.

"Look at the ground. Ash. And Ash in the sky. But there was no ash on the soles of Plum Bob's boots or on his clothes."

"How can that be?"

"Baxter warned us that this might happen. That one of the Old Ones might find Greenbriar, come to us as one of the Scouts, or maybe enslave a Scout into luring us out. He thought of everything."

"Last night, I had a vision," she said, and told him everything.

"It's a sure sign," Uncle said, eyes wide. "We must enact the Contingency."

"What is the Contingency?"

"Plum Bob must not unbutton Greenbriar. Plum Bob....must die."

"I still have the pistol from the Lord of Ops," she said. It was in her quarters, but she had it. She would like nothing better than to shoot bullets into Plum Bob. That it was part of Baxter's plan only made it sweeter.

"Many of the people will believe Plum Bob. They will kill to protect him."

Uncle reached into the pocket of his coat, and brought out a ring of keys, much like the one the Lord of Ops carried on his belt.

"And this," he said, taking the talisman of Baxter from his own neck. "It will get you into any room the keys do not. It will get you into the Armory. Into the Splo-sieves room where even Gordon cannot go. The Splo-sieves are in pieces. You must bring the components to me so I can assemble them."

He took a pad of yellow paper from the drawer of Baxter's desk and drew a picture on it. He pointed out each component. The block of soft gray matter. The coil with brassy needles stuck into the block. The box with numbers, into which the wires ran.

"What about Gordon?"

"Gordon and the guards follow Plum Bob wherever he goes. Gordon has abandoned his duties. The Armory is empty."

"What do we do then?" she asked.

"I will take the Splo-sieves into Elly Vader, set the numbers to counting, and send it up. This will destroy Elly Vader, so that Plum Bob cannot unbutton."

Uncle was right. With all the excitement, none of the guards were at their posts, and the way to the Armory was clear. It was nothing to unlock the door and slip inside. The Armory had been cleared of weapons. Gordon must have taken everything for the unbuttoning. But the old door at the back, the one no one could open, did open for Baxter's talisman.

It took her some time to find the right components, and even then, Nougat wasn't exactly sure she had the right things, so she took extra and slid it all into a pack Uncle had given her.

She put the heavy pack on her shoulders and returned to the Great Lab.

She almost walked right into Gordon and the guards, but she ducked back behind the corner before anyone saw her.

She peered around, and saw two Medicis emerge, carrying a bloodstained stretcher, and Plum Bob walking behind them, smiling.

"It was the will of Potus," he told Gordon, wiping blood from his Scout's knife on the sheet and putting it back on his belt.

She knew it was Uncle under the sheet, and that she was alone.

Did Plum Bob know she knew? He hadn't seen her under the Scout's mask. Had he made Uncle tell?

She didn't have much time.

She fairly ran back to her quarters.

She found her Scout's pack, got the pistol and slipped it into her pocket.

She spread the Splo-sieve pieces out on her cot. She'd taken three of everything, and after much fumbling, she thought she had one assembled as in Uncle's drawing. She slipped it into her Scout's bag. The second came easier. Much easier. It fit together like a puzzle. The brass needles sank into the soft clay-like block. The other ends clicked easily into the number box.

She was reaching for the third set of components when the door opened and Latchkey walked in.

"What are you doing, Nougat?" he asked. He was sweating, and his eyes had a strange look.

She couldn't hide the components on the bed.

She stood.

He took a step closer, closing the door behind him.

She drew the pistol from her pocket. She didn't know just why.

He stared.

"Plum Bob lied. It's all wrong. It's all lies," she stammered. How to tell him everything now? She barely had it straight in her own head.

"How could he lie? He returned from the Upper World."

"There is no Upper World. There are these things. These things that live in the Hellabove."

"What are you talking about?" he said, coming closer, holding out his hand. "Give me that."

She thumbed off the safety as she had seen Gordon do.

"Don't," she warned him.

"Plum Bob wants to see you."

She sucked in her breath.

"What?"

"He wants to see the last Scout."

"You told him it was me?"

"Why wouldn't I? There's nothing to worry about. He's sorry for what he did. He wants to apologize."

He lunged.

She pulled the trigger.

The sound was incredibly loud and she dropped the pistol after it bucked in her hands.

Latchkey knelt on the floor in the center of their quarters and blood spread out between his knees. He gasped once and fell over.

She sobbed, but went back to the cot and hastily began putting the last Splo-sieve together.

She heard footsteps in the hall.

She dropped the last one into her Scout bag and slid it under Latchkey's cot.

The door opened, and Gordon and his guards stood there,

machineguns pointed at her.

She raised her hands.

She wasn't in the cell long before Plum Bob showed up, still in his Scout regalia, hand on the knife that had killed Uncle.

"Funny that the old man picked you after me," he said. "Maybe Latchkey couldn't live with what happened that day. Maybe he put your name in Uncle's ear."

She didn't say anything.

"The year of Nougat. Funny that I spent much of the year of Nougat thinking of you. Missing you."

He came close enough to the bars that she could see his bloodshot eyes.

"Why didn't you die in the Hellabove?" she asked.

"You think the Hellabove kills the Scouts?" he grinned terribly. He shook his head. "Nope. None of the Scouts are dead. They're all alive. Even Alberta. She keeps them, you see. Keeps them safe. Suckles on their memories, their emotions. And Baxter's kept her fed all these years. Even long after he killed himself. I know. I saw it. I seen everything the Scouts have seen. You can't help it. All our minds mixed like in a soup."

"Who? What are you talking about?"

"All except me. 'Cause I told her she could have all the rest down here. All she had to do was let me go. That's my payment. Greenbriar. All to myself. But I'm gonna need company."

He leaned in closer, and slid his hands into his pockets.

"Do you remember how it was with me?" He closed his eyes and grinned.

She backed away against the wall in disgust as he moaned to himself, rising in pitch and vigor until he was finished and gasping.

"It's going to be like that again. I'm going to leave you here, Nougat. And when I've brought the last of them up, then I'll come back here for you."

He put his hands on the bars again, and blew her a kiss.

"I love you," he said.

Then he was gone.

When she heard the outer door close, and she was all alone, she stood and took the ring of keys from around her neck, where she'd hung it with Baxter's talisman.

It only took five minutes to find the right key to open the cell, but considerably longer to find the one that opened the door out into the corridor.

She had never known Greenbriar to be so quiet and still. Her boots resounded on the floor of the empty corridors, all the way back to her quarters.

Latchkey's blood was turning orange on the floor, and there were drag marks from where they pulled his body out.

Her pistol was gone, but they hadn't found the bag or her belt with the knife. She took these, and a hooded sweater, and left for the Porch.

She was shocked at how few remained in the corridor, brightly chatting as if they were in line for Chef's red onion soy burgers. There were maybe a hundred people.

There was only Gordon and one guard at the door.

When she began to move ahead of the line, eliciting protests, Gordon came over himself, smiling.

"Say there! Wait your turn! The Upper World isn't going anywhere."

There were some nervous chuckles.

Gordon didn't see the knife coming. She stuck it under his chin to the hilt and he fell, spluttering blood. His machinegun nearly slipped from her bloody fingers, but she lifted it and killed the guard before he could react.

She took back her knife and waved it and the gun at the people in line. She fired off a couple more shots to get them running, and even then they kept looking back.

She went to the door, used Baxter's talisman to open it, ready to kill Plum Bob and any guards inside.

A bullet whizzed past her face and she killed the shooter. He slumped against the controls to Elly Vader, a guard.

The Radmen started to rush her, but when she shot one they fell back in terror.

She ordered them out and locked the door behind them, shooting the door panel for good measure then dropping the empty gun.

She went to the controls. Elly Vader was only just beginning its descent.

She used the time to get out one of the Splo-Sieves. She realized with a panic that she didn't know how to make the things work. She pressed a few buttons on one until the numbers blinked red and began to count backwards. She tried to stop the numbers again, but couldn't figure out how.

It didn't matter. The numbers were at eight and counting back to one the long way. She had time.

She went to stand before Elly Vader and prayed to Potus, if he existed at all, that Plum Bob or the other guards didn't break the door in behind her.

Elly Vader clanged to a stop and the doors slid open.

Plum Bob, faceless in his mask and gloves, jumped out at her, startling her. They wrestled for a moment, and he flung her hard into the cylinder, but she pulled him along by his belt. The Splo-sieve tumbled between them.

The doors closed and with a lurch, Elly Vader began to rise again. The dead guard must have fallen on some switch that made it rise and descend automatically.

Nougat pulled the mask from Plum Bob and clawed at his face and he cursed and struck her hard. His hands went to her throat and squeezed.

She gasped, but he was pinching her airway shut. She couldn't breathe, and her eyes bugged. His face loomed over her, rabid. Just like that day. The veins standing out alongside his temples, his bloodshot eyes wild, teeth gnashing, drooling.

"It doesn't have to be you, I guess," he said, leaning so close his breath was hot on her face. She knew it was rancid, but she sucked hungrily at it anyway, desperate to breathe.

He smiled as her eyes began to roll and blackness encroached from every side. Her hands scuttled down his face, his shoulders, to his waist.

He pressed his lips to hers, forcing them open with the tip of his salivating tongue.

Then the pressure was gone and he was trembling. She gulped air and kicked him off of her.

He rolled on his side. She had stuck him with his own knife and dragged it halfway up his torso until the blade lodged against his sternum and his guts sagged out of the ragged vertical cut.

She crawled the rest of the way out from under him, coughing over his own last breaths.

She scrabbled for the Splo-Sieve. The numbers were at three something and it was pinned under Plum Bob's body and she couldn't stop it.

The whole room shook and clanged and she realized with a jolt of terror she was at the top of the shaft. The doors would open and she would choke on the air of the Hellabove.

She found Plum Bob's mask and pulled it on. It reeked of his breath and something else, some sweet something not the same as whatever had been in her own mask.

The doors slid open, to a world of ash and darkness.

She could see something beyond the threshold of Elly Vader, more than the electric eye, which she spied perched above the door, glass circle with a red light, could discern.

The Hellabove was not empty. It was filled to brimming with clouds of whirling black smoke. Two hundred and fifty-six years' worth. It was like murky water, that air, but it was not hot. It was cold. Very cold.

And in those murky clouds, things moved and swam. She caught only glimpses of strange, writhing shapes, immense beyond reckoning and also crowds of scuttling things, tiny as fingernails. Other things glided through the thick air, and other things crawled along the ground, inching through the mounds of ash like the earthworms the gardeners used. There were lights out there too, fading in and out.

It was not quiet.

Upon the opening of the doors, her ears had been assailed with a cacophony of yammering, wild cries and mad speech. There was music, or it was all together a kind of music, without rhythm or pattern. Just jabbering chaos and confusion. Chirps, wails, squeals, howls, and weird piping, as if in those impenetrable black depths an orchestra of madmen played upon the elicited shrieks of the harried damned, strumming exposed nerves with clawed fingers and beating upon living brains with bloated fists to play a blasphemous symphony of instruments human and inhuman.

The Splo-Sieve was at one, leering at her through Plum Bob's blood.

She panicked, and leapt from Elly Vader as the doors began to close.

She fell on her hands and knees in the soft ash and moments after the doors closed there was a flat, heavy sound and a rumble beneath her and the doors crumpled outward. There was fire behind them, but they didn't blow off.

Greenbriar was sealed.

It was safe.

Why had she done that? Why hadn't she thrown out the Splo-sieve and retreated into Elly Vader and saved herself, used the other Splo-sieve to destroy the exit?

She looked, and through the lenses of the Scout mask she saw the tracks of all those that Plum Bob had already led up here. They disappeared into the black cloud.

Something had called her. She could feel it. A voice. No, two hundred and fifty-six voices. The same voices that had told her,

"Don't let him in."

Only now, they called:

"Mercy."

She stood on unsteady legs, and waded out into the cloud, stepping in the tracks of those who had gone before.

She went toward the lights.

They swelled and contracted in a hurried but definite rhythm, as of a heartbeat. As she got closer, she saw whorls of moving bioluminescent tendrils, attendant to a series of faraway globules, as though they were caressing these nodes high atop some unknowable vast form, a mound of pulsing, living matter.

What was this thing? Did it have a name? She felt it must, and also that were she to learn it, she must not speak it. Yet this was just one among many horrors moving unseen in the ash that blanketed the world, she knew. The Paradise she had longed for in Baxter's postcard was not here. Here there was only the Hellabove. Greenbriar had been Paradise. She just hadn't known it.

This thing, this Old One, nested here atop Greenbriar like a great bloated parasite, a mandarin wastrel, imperious and stupefied in its gluttony, yet still malevolent, still cunning, and ever-voracious. Maybe Baxter had known its name. Maybe he had fed the Scouts to it over the years, made some bargain with it, or maybe it was just the thing's luck to have drifted here on the burning winds.

As she stood wondering, something whipped out of the darkness, bathing her in that same sickly, pulsing light, probing her with it. Then it tightened around her. She was jerked into the air, and brought rapidly toward the top of the thing. Particles ticked against her mask, and it was difficult to see up here in the whirl of ash. She felt strangely at ease, even when she looked down and saw the glowing barbs piercing her torso wherever the tendril touched her.

Her brain flooded with euphoria, and she fancied that the veins of her wrist, just visible between the end of glove and sleeve, were glowing too.

But then that nagging multitude cried out again for mercy, and she saw the source.

Inside the globules.

Outspread human silhouettes, like paper dolls held against a fluorescent bulb.

None of the Scouts are dead. They're all alive. Even Alberta. She keeps them, you see. Keeps them safe. All our minds mixed together like in a soup.

Mercy.

They had touched her somehow. Deep down in Greenbriar. They had pooled their dissipated consciousness into one and plunged desperately down to the home they had been tricked into vacating, and they had found her.

It was hard to care, but it was also hard to be afraid, so there was that. The cold was making her sleepy. Was it the cold?

She reached back into her pack and came out with something in each hand. Her fingers were growing numb. She fumbled at the blocky objects, nearly dropped them, and so hugged them close to her, as if she were keeping them warm.

As she was thrust toward a dome of pale, throbbing light, she smiled to see the red numbers pop to life in either hand. Maybe she couldn't kill this thing. It had been born in fire, matured in hell, and it wallowed in ash and grew fat upon misery. But maybe she could cut off its food supply.

Two.

One.

And then the chorus.

Thank you, Nougat.

Light and warmth. All that she had hoped for from the Upper World, and left behind.

THE KEEPER OF MEMORY

Christine Morgan

"The gods, once, were kind."

Laughter greeted this, but the old woman merely smiled.

"Oh, yes," she said. "They were different gods then. Kind gods. *Our* gods. The gods who made and loved us. We spoke to them in prayers and praises, and they heard, and answered."

The laughter turned, for the most part, to smirks. *We may be young, but we are not fools,* their looks—again, for the most part—declared. *Kind gods, indeed.*

Still, they'd gathered eagerly enough around when invited. It was a change from the sameness of their chores, a reprieve from cutting reeds and dredging mud, gutting frogs and hauling water. Entertainment, novelty, and rest were rare. Already, these children knew that all too well.

Some of them might have never in their brief lives seen outsiders before. Let alone outsiders who traveled with hide-covered huts built on sledge-rafts, pulled by harnessed many-legged beasts. Outsiders who wore strange garments and stranger ornaments, who brought strange things from stranger places.

Who brought this old woman, with her wizened head and matted strings of pallid hair. A knobby hump of flesh rose above her bent

241

neck; a loose skin-wattle drooped below it. From her fingertips curled long nails in thin and yellowish chitinous spirals.

"I am Mema," the old woman said, "though you may call me Grandmother, if you like. I am the Keeper of Memory."

She sat on an upended, water-worn stump put to use as a chair, its roots cradling her limbs. A canopy of broad-fronded leaves held up on bent poles provided some shelter from the steady dripping of the mist.

"This is Nemon, my granddaughter's daughter, who will become Keeper after me."

Nemon dipped her head as she poured mossbark cups of juice pressed from lilyberries. Just as they—she and Mema, their fellow travelers, their sledge-rafts and their tamed, harnessed beasts—were the objects of scrutiny, so too did she examine with interest the crude village and its inhabitants.

Irregular hills rose low from the morass, topped with clustered dwellings made from sticks and mud. The shape of them was like that of wader-birds' nests overturned, or the lodgings of oil-furs moved to higher land. Meandering paths of stepping-stones crossed slow-coursing waterways. Fresh catches from fish- and frog-traps hung on lines, near bundles of harvested reeds with pulpy, fibrous tufts.

"In the time of my grandmother's grandmother's grandmother," Mema went on, "our people were numerous, and powerful, and strong. We held this world and ruled it, and our gods were kind."

Again, her words were met—for the most part—with those smirking looks. *Silly old woman and your fancies, your made-up tales of a never-was.*

The children who did *not* sneer and smirk, however, Nemon watched with close attention, but discretion. The ones who listened to Mema with attentiveness, with curiosity ... whose expressions showed something more ... something *other* ... those were the ones she made note of.

The ones who thought, and questioned. The ones in whose minds lived something other than necessity and survival.

"They granted wishes and gave us gifts," said Mema. "If we were hurt or ill, they healed us. They protected us. They provided us with bounties of food and clean, clear water."

"What did they look like?" asked a little boy called Lut.

242

Yunnig, a larger boy, nudged him, nearly knocking him over. "Don't be a hoot-head. Everyone knows the gods are indescribable."

"That's not true," said Tesya, who wore her hair woven into several thin braids. "The Mindless in the Dark-Between has no head and no body."

"You can't describe something by saying what it hasn't." a girl named Anith said, then looked to Yunnig as if for his approval.

"My papa told me that the deep-folk by the ever-waters say their god is bigger than hills upon hills, with wriggling feelers like handfuls of worms where a mouth would be." Paulph held a hand against his lips and wiggled his fingers to demonstrate.

Nemon, observing the boy's wide-set bulging eyes, supposed that his papa might have come by that lore at first hand.

"And the Over-Seer of the Under-Seers is all shiny slime-bubbles and glow-bulbs," Tesya said, persistent.

"Our gods were beautiful," Mema told them. "They looked much like us, because they made us in their own shape and image."

"This is *gone-world never-was* talk," Yunnig said, scoffing. "You'll be telling us about fire and fairies next."

Tesya threw a mud-clod at him. "I want to hear."

A few of the others voiced their agreement. More joined in when Chayg pointed out that it was better than going back to their chores. Shurg, his twin, asked if they could have more lilyberry juice as well, and that convinced the rest.

Meanwhile, over by the largest of the mud-and-stick dwellings, the usual trade negotiations were being helped along by the sharing of a foamy brew made from pounded yeast-roots soaked in stone troughs. The travelers had picked it up at one of their previous stops, and, judging by the jovial tone, its heady effect was already taking hold.

"Well, then," said Mema, as they settled themselves on hummocks of damp grass. "Much of what I know has been passed down to me from my grandmother and her grandmother and her grandmother before that. It was a very different world, then. Before the new gods came, bringing the mists. When we knew night and day, *real* night and *real* day. When there were seasons other than warm-steam and cool-fog."

The children laughed again at this, at the very idea. And, again,

Mema merely smiled her toothless, indulgent smile.

"There was a sky beyond the mists, and lights hung in that sky. Lights so very bright and brilliant, brighter than anything you could imagine."

"But lights hang in the sky now." Paulph peeked from under the leaf-canopy, up toward pulsating lambent orbs within dark shadow-shapes.

Dark shadow-shapes, undulating in slow courses through murky striations of gray-upon-grayer clouds ... the under-seers with their under-eyes ... never blinking, never closing to sleep ... sometimes shedding forth gleaming beams, sweeping back and forth ... eternally watchful, but for what?

"Yeah," Yunnig said. "and if you look too long, they'll reel down their suckery ring-toothed tendrils and pluck you up for a snack."

The younger children squirmed and hid their faces; even some of the older ones made sure to avert their eyes from the cloudy expanse overhead. Lut hunkered beside Mema's stump-root chair. "I don't want the under-seers to eat me," he said. "I don't want the lights in the sky."

Mema patted his tousled hair with her long-nailed hand. "Not those lights, no. I meant the lights from before the mists. Oh, such wonderful lights. Why, when the sky was blacker than black, they say a pale shining stone would float high up in it."

"Stones don't float," said a girl named Oalthi, rocking a hollowed bark-log in which her baby sister slept.

"This one did, for it was a great stone of magic. Sometimes it would be round like a paddler's egg, and sometimes only the thinnest curve, like a shard of egg-shell. The Muen, it was called."

"*Muen*," Tesya murmured. She, as she listened, had idly plucked many long blades of grass and was experimenting with ways of twining and lacing them together.

A weaver, Nemon thought. The girl with the intricate braids might one day become a weaver, a maker of baskets and cloth, an artist of patterns and design.

"There were also points of light," said Mema, "thorn-sharp, dotted across the black sky, like a vast swarm of fireflies, but motionless, white as bone, clear as water."

"Stars!" cried a boy who, up until that moment, hadn't seemed to be paying attention in the slightest. "The stars were wrong, so the gods waited and waited, and then the stars were right and the gods came!"

Nemon caught her breath, but Mema remained calm. "What was your name, child? I don't think you said."

He didn't answer. Sticking his grubby fingers into his mouth, he resumed staring off at nothing.

"That's Zath." Anith rolled her eyes and heaved an exasperated sigh. "My stupid little brother."

"Were they stones, too?" Oalthi asked, when Zath showed no signs of speaking further. "The stars?"

"No one knows, dear girl," Mema said. "No one knows. But, the brightest light of all, so bright it dissolved the sky-blackness into the clearest and most beautiful blue, was called the Sunn. Which was more than bright …" Mema leaned forward, pausing with each word. "It … was … *hot!*"

Paulph tilted his head. "What's 'hot'?"

"Hot is like warm," Oalthi told him. "Hot is warmer than warm."

"Like at the spitting pools," Shurg said. "Our uncle fell in once."

"That's how he got those scars," Chayg finished.

"Shh," said Lut. "I want to hear about the Sunn."

"It was hot," Mema repeated. "Hot enough to *dry*, children. Why, there were places so dry, the mud went away, and rain didn't fall for days on days, and water sank far beneath the ground."

They fell silent for a moment, pondering this. Even Nemon, in all of her knowledge and all of her training, could barely just begin to imagine what it must be like to be *dry*, fully *dry*. Or to walk on sand, not clammy silt-mud sand but Sunn-heated *dry* sand.

Nor could she quite envision some of the other truths Mema had taught her, truths of places colder than cold, so cold that lakes turned to stone. She did not *doubt* them, but such a reality would not fit well into her comprehension.

"Never-was stories," Yunnig said. "I told you she'd be talking of fire and fairies next."

Or fire … Nemon didn't know what fairies might be, but Mema *had* now and then spoken of fire, that it *was* real, that people had once possessed the secrets of stealing it from sky-storms or springing it alive out of wood and stones. Fire, also bright and hot like the Sunn, also with the magic to *dry*. Fire, which ate and consumed, which had to be fed, but which could be controlled, and killed.

"I'm only telling you of our once-world," Mema said. "When the land itself was larger, and the waters not so deep. Much of it, I learned from my grandmothers down through the ages. More, as I said, we have learned in our travels. Why, we have been from the fog-forests of the mountains to the rocky salt-shores. We have seen the hoof-prints of the goat-folk stamped into the soft black loam, and we have seen the deep-folk swimming toward the endless waves."

"Ohh," Paulph said.

"And we have seen the immense clay-mounds formed by the colonies of one will and mind, clay-mounds ever-growing in chambered tunnels around the rugose and oozing nodules of their Masters. They devour their own dead, you know. All waste is cast into the rendering pits, and flows into the food-trenches. If babies are born thought-deaf, of no use to the colony, they too are thrown into the pits. Yet, even they—even *they*, dear children—were once like us. Oh, yes. Long ago, when we were of one people, and this was our world."

"Our world," Tesya said, sounding wistful. "Was it pretty?"

"So very pretty. Plants of so many kinds … flowers of every color, flowers that smelled sweeter than sweet-nectar … fruits too big for one person to eat … trees as tall as the clouds …"

"Were there animals like now?" asked Lut.

Mema patted his head again, ruffling his matted curls. "Far more than there are now. Some ran faster than anything. Some had fur, not wet and oily fur but thick and soft. And there were birds, not just paddlers and waders but birds that flew all the time, flew high and far—"

"Without getting snared by the under-seers?" Paulph's wide eyes widened further.

"There were no under-seers then."

"You can't know any of that," Yunnig said.

"But we've seen them, in ancient make-arts, and in the relics." Mema's old eyes twinkled. "Would you like to see, my dear ones?"

"Yes!" Tesya bounced up and down.

"Pleeeeeease!" Lut added.

Those two were the most eager, capering in their excitement.

The others ranged from interest to skepticism, but they did crowd closer. Only Zath, sitting slack-mouthed with a vacant stare, appeared oblivious.

"Now, let me see …" said Mema, rummaging in the folds of her voluminous scrap-hide robe. She drew from within some inner pocket a small item, pinched in the yellow spirals of her nails.

It was the figure of a bird, unmistakably a bird, but like no bird any of them had ever seen. No squat pond-paddler, nor gangly stick-legged wader … this bird was sleek-bodied, feet curled into claws, head cocked, beak hooked, and wings outspread in magnificent sweeps.

Even Yunnig, the most skeptical, was momentarily dumbstruck. They all simply gazed at the bird, at the intricate precision of detail, each feather, each tiny eye, so lifelike they might have expected it to flap and flutter in Mema's grasp.

Tiny flecks of pigment in the deeper crevices suggested it had once sported full glorious plumage, but the colors had been weathered away by the ages until only the shape remained, the shape in its strange substance and solidity, its strange uniform opacity.

She held it out to Tesya, who hesitated and curled her hands shyly against her stomach.

"Oh, it's quite all right, child," Mema said. "You won't damage it."

The girl, emboldened, extended cupped palms and let Mema drop the bird-relic into them. As she examined and felt it, her confidence grew, and she looked up at Mema with wonder.

"It's so light!" Tesya said. "But so strong! Not wood, not stone, not … I … try it, touch it," she added, turning to the others.

When those brave enough had tested their nerve, Mema brought out another figure. This was larger, vaguely hound-like in form, but with upright points of ears, an erect posture, un-bowed limbs, and a tail resembling the bushiness of a chaff-frond about to go to seed. More pigment remained on this relic than the bird, showing a gray hide with whitish undersides and darker grey markings.

She showed them still others: a lizard that went on two strong hind legs and had gaping, toothy jaws … a graceful-looking creature with flowing hair along its neck and a single twisting horn … a chubby figure with huge round head and eyes, a pale face and belly, and the faded vestiges of dark stripes.

"So, you see," said Mema, "our people knew all these animals, and many, many more. More kinds than you could count. Some were hunted for food, yes, like now. Some were tended for their eggs, the way you might visit a paddler's nest again and again. Some even gave milk that people could drink!"

"Eew!" chorused several of the children. "Milk from *animals*?"

"Milk from animals. Others did work, the way our beasts pull our sledge-rafts, and some let people ride upon their backs. Still others, people kept as friends and companions, and taught them to do tricks."

"Oh!" Tesya clapped. "I found a little oil-fur once, all lost and alone. I wanted to bring it home, feed it, take care of it ..." Her face fell. "But everyone said no."

"Where did they all go?" Lut asked. "All the animals?"

"They died and drowned and got eaten by the under-seers," Yunnig said. "Tff. Hoot-head. Duh."

"Many did, that's true," Mema said. "But, there are places, my dears ... magic places, wonderful secret places ... hidden far beyond the reach of the new gods. In these places are chambers filled with seeds, and pods, and eggs, and sleeping unborn babies of every animal that ever was ... waiting ... waiting for a time when the stars change again."

She paused, glancing at Zath, but the boy still seemed far off in some secret place of his own. Then she continued.

"When that happens, the mists will lift ... the lands will rise from the waters ... the Sunn will shine in a blue sky by day and the Muen in a black one by night ... and the world will be renewed."

"You mean, the gods will go away?" Paulph's voice wavered like a strand of sea-kelp caught in an uncertain current.

"And our own gods will return?" Tesya added. "The kind ones who love us?"

Anith snorted. "The gods that look like *people*! Sure they will!"

Mema brought forth another relic, the torso of a goddess-figure, one who could be none other than a goddess of eternal beauty and youth. Ideal, ideal to perfection and beyond ... high-breasted, the narrowest tapering of waist, smooth loins. Where a head might have been was a slim neck ending in a rounded knob. Empty sockets showed at the shoulders and hips.

"We've found many of these, across the land, from the mountain edges to the salt-shores," Mema said. "None complete, but all identical in form."

The color of the idol's substance was a vivid peculiarity for which Nemon never had found fitting words. It reminded her of the innermost surface of a speaking-shell, or the fleeting blush at the heart of a just-blooming lily, or the raw-meat slice of a wader-bird's flesh.

"Our goddesses looked like *that?*" Yunnig glanced from the idol to the girls around him, raising his eyebrows. Anith flushed, tugging at the front of her knotted sedge-grass dress.

"Identical?" Oalthi asked. "How can that be? No two things are *exactly* the same! No two leaves, no two stones, no two seed pods—"

"No two twins," Chayg put in, and Shurg nodded.

"—or frogs … *nothing* grows that way!"

"They didn't grow," said Tesya. "They were … made."

"Nothing is made that way, either," Oalthi argued. "Nothing *can* be! No two mud-pots, no two stick-houses—"

"These, we believe, were hero-gods," said Mema, bringing out two smaller figures. "Mighty warriors, fighting evil. You can see how very strong they were, how muscular and powerful."

Anith stuck her tongue out at Yunnig. "Our *gods* looked like *that?*"

Tesya traced the supple curve of a design upon one of the figure's chests. "We … we had *symbols?* Of our *own?*"

"His looks scary," said Lut, pointing at the other.

"Like the wings of a gloom-gaunt," Shurg said. "Our uncle saw one, once."

Chayg nodded. "It had little horns that stuck up like that, too."

"Our own symbols." Tesya shook her head, amazed, thin braids swinging. "Did we have … were we allowed … *books?*"

"Oh, stop it." This time, it was Yunnig who threw a mud-clod at her. "It's only stories, no more real than the Cities of Lines!"

"But the Cities of Lines *are* real," Mema said. "We've seen them. What remains of them, their ruins. Cities of the gone-world, *our* gone-world. The waters have not yet claimed everything. Structures rise above the shallows, structures of stone and stuff harder-than-stone. Crumbling, yes. Rotting like carcasses from strangely-bleeding skeletons. But real. In some places, paths can be seen, paths that do not meander for hill or hummock."

"In …" Paulph swallowed, throat making a thick gulping sound. "In *lines?* You don't mean, they really *do* go in lines?"

"In lines," she said, nodding gravely. "In *straight* lines that meet in right-angles and squared corners. There are steps, steps stacked one atop another atop another, climbing toward the clouds."

They listened, some agog and some askance, as Mema continued describing the ruins of the old-places. Bridges and towers, circles and arches, and other words all but meaningless. Even for Nemon, who had seen for herself, much of it sounded impossible. That there had been such cities … that there could ever have been, and were … cities built by the hands of *people … their* people … people who had *symbols* … idols and art and lore of their own …

That they could have had all that, and done all that, and lost it forever …

She watched as the full, awful extent of that loss and horror sank into Tesya's eyes like a stone dropped into a deep pool. She watched Lut's chin began to quiver, his lower lip down-turning.

Those two, yes, those two. Their minds could envision, could imagine, could invent and create. Could think in clever ways and try various ideas. It had not yet died from them, not yet been pressed and crushed by the drudgery of simple survival.

If they lived, if they were allowed to live and to grow, and to thrive … if that difference of other-thought lasted …

It would be them, ones like them, who'd be chosen. Who'd be led to the secret places of which Mema had spoken, the chambers filled with all the waiting treasure-troves of the world's renewal.

Zath, who had been quiet since his earlier outburst, staring vacantly off into the mists, voiced a sudden shrill cackle. It made the rest of them jump, even Mema.

"Cities!" he cried. "Rich cities, sin cities, great vain folly cities! Lines and order from chaos, nature cut to man's whim! Sky-scrapers, sub-ways, transit-stations! Palaces of crystal and streets paved with gold! Chicago! Paris!"

Uneasy shudders crept through Nemon with each of the boy's utterances. His words tingled along her nerves and in her marrow-bones, resonated in the deepest caverns of her mind.

"Miami, Cairo, Istanbul!

"Hush, now, child." Though she tried to sound soothing, Mema's voice stretched taut with tension. "Hush, now. That's enough."

"Are those ... *names*?" Tesya asked.

"Machu Picchu! Quebec! In their houses at Parliament, at Congress, they die dreaming! Tokyo and Boston! The wheels on the bus go 'round and 'round and all roads lead to Rome!"

Oalthi's baby sister began to wail, waving tiny fists. Paulph backed away, eyes nearly bulging from his head, rubbing fitfully at the flap of skin between his forefinger and thumb. Tesya trembled from head to toe.

"What's wrong with him now?" asked Shurg.

"He's not making any sense," Chayg said.

Nemon saw that Mema had taken on a sickly pallor, the sagging wrinkles of her skin hanging from her skull. At the old woman's temples and in the center of her forehead, veins pulsed like unearthed worms. In the sunken hollow at the base of her throat, something seemed to throb.

"They come from Memphis and Madrid. They go to Sydney, Dubai, Saigon! Next stop all aboard! Vienna!"

Yunnig gave Anith a dig in the ribs. "He's *your* brother, make him stop!"

"Za-a-ath, quit it!"

"The city, the city, the city that never sleeps! What happens in Vegas stays in Vegas! London bridge is falling down, falling down!"

"I mean it, Zath! I'll tell—"

Ignoring his sister, he turned to Mema. His smile was pure innocence, but something rippled in his eyes. In them, or behind them. A shifting, shimmering veil. "Did you think no one would notice you, old woman?"

Mema went paler yet, clutching at her thin chest. "Wh ... what?"

"Moscow nonstop New York! Did you think you were unknown, unseen?"

"He's scaring me," Lut said, clinging to Mema's knee.

"*She* means to steal you from your home, you and Tesya there, steal you from your home and take you away forever, but *I* am scaring you? Copenhagen, Glasgow, Buenos Aires! Look on ye works, o mighty, and despair—"

"Zath?" Anith asked, sisterly severity giving way to genuine worry.

"I don't think he's Zath right now," Tesya said.

"Stop him," said Mema, in a harsh whisper. "He must be silenced."

Nemon took a step toward the boy, but before she could take another, he sprang away. His strange, rippling gaze met hers with an intensity that stunned her to the core. For a moment, he seemed calm, even reasonable.

"It was too late in Babylon," he said. "*Much* too late in Athens."

"What was too late?" Nemon heard herself ask, as if from very far away and through numb lips that did not feel like her own.

"No, Nemon! Do not listen—"

"It was too late already in *Jericho* and *Ur!*" With a final cackling cry, both hideous and triumphant, Zath clawed at the sides of his head. His fingers sank in knuckles-deep, popping through the skin.

The children screamed, stumbling and tumbling backward. Nemon felt mired in cold, sludgy mud. She could not move, could not even look away, as Zath worked his fingers deeper into his own flesh. The noise of it was a wet squishing; fluid too dilute and pale to be blood spurted from the wounds and trickled down his neck.

He peeled off the wholeness of his face like the rot-softened rind from a decaying fruit. Underneath was not a raw, flayed skull ... nor a gaping hollow ... but a slick mass of slimy bubbles and myriad glowing orbs. They oozed, bulging and receding, moving over and around each other in a strange, oily effluence.

More screams erupted all around her, but Nemon still could not move. She stared at the spreading horror birthing itself from the boy's collapsing form. Its smell was both bitter and sour, insinuating itself into her nose, coating her tongue and throat with a lingering foulness.

Above them, the gloom-darkened clouds grew even darker as immense shadow-shapes converged, and shifting lambent beams wavered through the mists. The air seemed to have thickened, become clammier with a tangible, gelatinous chill.

The beasts went mad in their harnesses. Some broke free and fled, crashing through mud-and-stick dwellings, trampling anyone in their path. Others fell, half-entangled, tipping sledge-rafts, kicking and biting.

Villagers and travelers alike succumbed to shrieking panic. Nemon saw from the corner of her eye Chayg and Shurg running in opposite directions, Anith on her knees sobbing, Oalthi abandoning her howling baby sister, Paulph diving into a much-too-shallow pond,

Yunnig on the ground with his arms over his head.

The thing that had been Zath loomed up before her, bulbous and writhing. In its faint, vile sheen, Nemon saw herself reflected untold times, reflected in mockeries and distortions. Mouthless now, voiceless, a loathsome gurgling hiss was its only speech … yet, somehow, she understood.

"You know what will happen if you do what she wants. They will die, you will die, in the end you all die. Why make it worse? Why such torment, such poison suffering? Let it fade. Let it be forgotten. It is the only kindness you have left, the only true gift you can give. Remembrance is pain. Hope is cruelty. Spare them."

All at once, Mema was there, Mema terribly illuminated in the questing rays of the under-seers, looking more ancient and haggard than ever. Tesya and Lut were by her side, each clutching precious relics of the gone-world tight in both hands. They, alone among the tumult, looked serene … hypnotized, almost spell-struck.

"Did I think no one would notice me?" Mema asked. "That I was unknown, unseen?" She laughed, fearless in the face of the monstrous entity before her. "You noticed, but you did not comprehend. You thought you knew, but you were wrong. You saw … but you did not *see!*"

The Zath-thing recoiled in uncertainty. Under its slimy iridescence, orbs rolled and bubbles roiled. In the mist-thick clouds above, the coursing shadows hesitated. More of their beams converged, bathing the gloom in a seething, murky light.

"Take the children," Mema said, pushing them toward Nemon. "You are Keeper now. You know where to go."

"Where we took the others," she said, hefting Lut onto her hip and grasping Tesya's arm. Neither child resisted. "But, Mema—"

"Our comprehension is beyond yours, greater than you guess!" came another noxious, gurgling hiss. *"If you had left them in dull nothingness, we might have let them live out their lives!"*

"Nemon, go!" The old woman suddenly stood taller, straighter than it seemed the bowed hunch of her spine should allow, and cast aside her scrap-hide robe.

"Instead, let them be consumed and dissolve a thousand years in the mindless madnesses Beyond!"

Nemon turned to run, pulling Tesya with her. Their feet slipped on rain-slick grass and splashed in sloppy mud. They hadn't gotten more than a few paces before the sounds of ripping meat and cracking gristle reached their ears.

"They *will* remember!" Mema cried from behind them. "They will rebuild, and they will *renew*!"

A keening screech of otherworldly agony split the air. Almost despite herself, Nemon risked a quick glance over her shoulder, and wished she hadn't.

The knobby hump on Mema's back had split apart, bones forced up in jagged quills strung with glistening strands of slime. From her temples, her brow, and the base of her throat, wormlike segmented lengths extruded, black eyes opening wetly at the ends of whip-thin stalks.

"And as for you—" The thing that had been Mema laughed again, as the thing that had been Zath writhed dripping in her grasp. "Now that you've revealed yourself, O Over-Seer, you are *mine*!"

SHOUT / KILL / REVEL / REPEAT

Scott R Jones

The *Hassan-i Sabbah* touches down / crashes / sexually assualts / makes landfall on the shores of the Mad Continent in the last hungry minutes of the Hour of the Spastic Mandala. The shiftship quakes like a palsied geriatric and yowls in obvious pain / pleasure / indifference / surprise. The sound / colour and vibration / texture are enough to wake me, or at least bring me up to what passes for human consciousness in this, the Time of the End, the Eternal Finishing of the World, the Age of Dead Stars.

"Greetings from sunny R'lyeh," I whisper / mindlessly chant in a guttural tongue I barely recognize as mine / gasp with my last breath as I gaze from a porthole onto a sea like phosphorescent corpse-clogged black gelatin, a sea that washes and foams onto a spit of so-called land that looks like a migraine made of granite / oozing egg sacks / other, brighter migraines.

I would order the shiftship to immediately begin repairs on itself, but a quick glance at the telltales in my sleep chamber tell me that would be unnecessary; the *Hassan-i Sabbah* had etheric conduits draining strange matter from the ancient alien stone of R'lyeh since it cleared the event horizon in the early hours of a grumbling dawn. Her protests have nothing to do with her state-of-being and everything to do with where she is.

"Good girl," I whisper, and place a palm on a bulkhead that quivers and warms to my touch. The *Hassan-I Sabbah* used to be several whales, sperms and greys and humpbacks, but that was very long ago, before the hexentechs went to work on her, before I took command. She's old. I don't know what she is now, but she's a she. A capable she, a she that's delivered us safely.

We are here. We have arrived. Other telltales indicate that our payload is safe, our hearts resolute. My crew is well-trained, healthy, at least thirty percent sane, and most importantly, prepared. We have had centuries to prepare.

I open a channel to greet them.

"You all know what to do. Boots on the ground in twenty."

I close the channel / murder a small bird with my bare hands / masturbate my secondary organs until they bleed / finish penning this narrative / weep for a mother I can't remember, then prepare to go ashore.

Before setting my feet for the first time on the schizophrenic ground of the Dreaming Lands, I pay a visit to the upper deck to check on our payload.

Nestled in the concave bay of its hangar, the ruddy light of the clinker sun glistens from its surface like mother-of-pearl, like Hope. A team of hexentechs call out to each other as they work. *Hoist that line, Bob! Get that coupling secure, Emily!* The order believes adopting the ancient names of their ancestors will somehow strengthen the human life wave. The names are clunky, empty things that bruise my ears, and yet somehow I recall each and every one of them, so perhaps they're right. The hexentechs swarm around the massive globule like the ants they are, attaching Hoffman-Price field generators to its carriage of steel and bone.

I marvel / shudder in fear / shrink away in disgust at the sight of it. I know that within its esoteric depths lies a hermaphroditic human form, a painfully beautiful androgyne body that houses a Perfected Human Soul, the shining result of generation after generation of artificially-induced reincarnation. We were never able to figure out how the Yith had migrated their entire population across space and time into new bodies, but we understood enough of their abandoned mind-transfer technology to reverse-engineer our own crude devices and move a single mind from one dying body into a freshly conceived one.

Over and over again, and then again. Again. Again. A thousand years to shield one individual consciousness from the madness of the world in the deepest chamber of the Voorish Domes. A thousand years for the hexentech priesthood to refine whatever it is we are into its purest, most energetic form. Now that form rests, a saviour, waiting to fulfill its dread purpose, to do what saviours do. To save us.

Grantha waddles to my side, and I try not to let my eyes rest for too long on his twisted features.

"Is it ready?"

"Yaz, yaz, Captain. Zhe's ready, ready, ready for that jelly, straight up." The hexentech High Priest's voice is a glutinous, wet thing that slops unpleasantly into my ears / licks the fingers of my left hand / lays eggs in my dermis. "That's the last of the field generators now. You get the anchor where it needs to be, and we'll deliver our shining Little BoyGirl here. Right into his throne room. We'll drop hir right into his abominable lap. *Who's a shiny baby?* he'll coo. *Who's a morsel? Who's tasty?*"

"We'll get there. We've trained for this."

Grantha smirks and gurgles. "Oh, sho nuf, son. You're the best. Best of the best of the hand-picked beasties and no mistake, none." His head does a repulsive little jig on his shoulders, and he points a scabrous chin to the pearl. "Still. Makes ya think, don't it? Puts your own monstrous existence into some kinda horrible perspective."

"I don't follow."

"Look at it there. A Perfected Human Soul. A being of pure enlightenment. Conduit for untold kilotons of Universal Energy. Or whatevah, whatevah. I'm sayin' it's cold, homes. All our work and striving, all the love and death and blood-soaked evolution, from the second we climbed down outta the trees, a million years and change of the Struggle, and *this* is all we're good for?

"The best and highest thing we can ever be is a bomb, Captain Strunk."

"A bomb to take out a god, hexentech. That's something."

"Maybe, maybe. Or take out its balls, at least. If it has any." The grisly little gnome sniffs, kicks at a loose bolt at his feet, sending it clattering over the side of the ship. "Good luck, in any case. Waiting on your signal."

"You'll get it."

He puts his back to me and waves a hand in a vaguely disrespectful manner, starts barking at his acolytes.

The best and highest thing...

Atomics couldn't do it; the Thing That Should Not Be and its impossible spawn weren't made of our matter. Harvesting asteroids from the Kuiper Belt and dropping them on their insane cities couldn't do it; the shrieking fractal architecture received them like kisses, incorporated them into its mass. The re-purposed tech of the extinct crinoid things in Antarctica, poorly understood and poorly implemented, did little more than annoy them.

And all the while, with every attempt to cut them, to disintegrate them, to collapse the weird space-time bubble that housed their foul continent and send it back where it came from, we went mad. Our dreams, our every thought and feeling turned against us, as surely as we turned on each other in rage and confusion. Our minds losing all cohesion as surely as our genes. Our very existence on this plane becoming multiple, a constant flux of forms and actions in a temporal stream that thrashes and buckles and splits every second, only to merge again every other second.

How long has it been since I did *one thing* only?

We became monsters. Monsters in a world ruled by greater monsters, rulers who didn't even acknowledge our presence, except to scoop up a handful of us when they got peckish. And there are very few of us left to scoop.

So. Let this mission I lead be my last. Let it be my one true and singular thing, my pure deed in an impure world.

I cast a last glance / scream until my throat's raw / faint / do a manic jig to entertain the unseen being at the core of Grantha's bomb before going below to check on the engines.

"Are they fed?" I ask before she can say anything. "I want them happy and fueled and ready to pulse the second we get back."

My chief engineer has a terrible speech impediment. Even with the inhibitor collar anchored by flexible spurs to the cartilage of her throat, her voice is still weapon enough to make eyes bleed. Without the collar, Silattha Parv could ask your pineal gland to come out through the front of your skull for some air, and the thing would do it, too. Another child of the hexentechs: a Speaker to the Hounds.

"They're *never* happy, Captain." Her eyes roll alarmingly in her head, and she grinds her teeth with such force her breath carries with it little chalky puffs of enamel. She pats the side of the perfect sphere that is one of the two Tindlosi Drives.

Without the neutered Hounds suspended in grav-harnesses within the plasteel casing, the *Hassan-i Sabbah* would have broken up into shrapnel, cetacean meat, and good intentions before the sun had set on the first day out from shore. Slaved to the ship and the navigation system, the Hounds provide power, and let the ship slip along angles outside of Time, avoiding the worst of the distortion waves that tsunami their way across the planet from R'lyeh.

"They are Foulness and a Contagion from before there was a Universe and they are lean and athirst, as ever, Captain, but they. Are. Never. Happy." Silattha hisses to the floor. Paint peels around her feet. "But fed. Oh yes. My babies are fulla babies."

"I don't know how long we'll be gone..."

"Yup. Time gets funny here, I get it. Got my dogs on an automatic three squares a day of ripe abortions. The hopper's full, so quit your worrying."

The early research that led to our payload on deck revealed a terrible truth: there *was* such a thing as a soul, though as a descriptive term "soul" was woefully loaded and inaccurate. A discrete packet of energy, then, unique and unchanging, that accessed this dimension through the medium of flesh. Sometimes the flesh failed or was ended before it had a chance to really dirty that energetic cocktail: miscarriages and abortions. The hexentechs knew enough about their cannibalized Yithian machines to begin the harvest of these small but potent packets from the depths of the past, but with no purpose other than the pure science of it, the so-called souls were put in storage and stayed there. Until we caught our first Hound in a grav-sink, that is.

"Poor things," I say. Silattha whips her head around at me at the words, and I can see her merciless ghoul ancestry leering at me from the lines of her face.

"Poor things? *Poor things?*" she snarls. "Man, you don't know what they experience! They were never going to live, Deimos. They were dead already. Shit, they've been dead for *millennia*. And now they serve us. The dead should serve the living." Her eyes flare wide enough to show white all around, her irises flexing wildly.

The best and highest thing...

"Is that from your cannibal bible? Dagon's Teeth. Are you *high* right now?"

Her face cracks wide in a sloppy canid grin. "You know it, Captain." She lifts the mass of her yellow-grey mane to reveal an intravenous slug strapped to the back of her neck. She taps it. "New Jack Lao on a steady drip, cut with a little hexstacy to take the edge off."

I know it won't affect the mission, but it irritates me anyway. I don't say anything, but then I don't have to.

"Don't get pissy, D. I'm five by five. Still feeling mad aggro though. You said boots on the ground in...?"

"Twenty. That was eight minutes ago."

"So it's a quick fuck then." Silattha turns her back to me, places long palms against the milky translucency of the Drive. "C'mon. You know how a ghoul likes it."

Her orgasm sounds like a dirge. From the impossibly compressed space inside of the sphere, a livid blue tongue lashes out to trace a spastic trail of sizzling ichor where her curves press into the plasteel. She hisses, and her own tongue mirrors the action. I shudder / compose a haiku / half-recall a play I once saw or acted in, I'm not sure which / climax, and then pull away from her.

"All ashore who's going ashore, Sil." She whimpers something affirmative in response.

She's still licking the sphere when I leave.

On the slick, nauseous pseudo-granite of the shore, littered with the aromatic remains of dead sea life, the massive vantablack tetrahedron that is the Hoffman-Price anchor sits in a chassis, studded with grav-harnesses waiting for activation. Around it, a dozen makeshift altars have been set up, for those inclined to make religious observances before heading inland.

The hexentechs use ceremonial graphite crystal blades to remove thin strips of flesh from their forearms or abdomens, according to their rank. Worshipful tongues click in dry hexentech mouths while braziers cough a greasy pungent smoke into the air as the strips are consumed in offering to their obscure Render, Daoloth.

Silattha lifts a juvenile dhole's skull to her mouth and drinks from its contents: a heady liquor brewed from the worm's fermented seminal and lymphatic fluids. She toasts her charnel gods with a wordless curse thrown to the boiling sky.

Other prayers are made. Piotr Tillich, my science officer, lifts the lid of a black lacquered wooden box and with unmoving lips hums to the glowing thing inside, his buzzing quickly moving below the range of hearing into the subsonic. I don't pretend to know what passes through his Yuggoth-cultured mind; Mi-Go meatpuppets are eternal observers, detached, inscrutable.

Grantha's faith is ancient and foreign; he stamps on a trigger-pad to generate a holographic representation of something he calls a *curb*: a dull grey rectangular slab of some porous stone, complete with small tufts of weedy plant material leaping from the cracks, and the suggestion of odd sigils cast upon a ghostly wall that float in the air behind the curb in traceries of neon light. The hexentech High Priest roots around in a satchel at his waist and produces a bottle of amber fluid, which he empties out onto the virtual object.

"For my homies," he says, not without a certain reverence.

"I hope your old gods are looking out for us, priest," I say as he waddles past me on his way to the gangplank. He grunts.

"Homies got better shit to do, I'm thinking. Can't hurt, though, straight up. What about you, Captain?"

"Prayer doesn't work, Grantha. It never did. And the gods that could listen choose not to."

Piotr pauses in his humming to look up. "Perhaps the very one we go to destroy this day, Captain. Why is that, do you think?"

"Why is what, Tillich?"

"Why do the Old Ones not speak? We have made our attempts, over the centuries, to send ambassadors. To open a dialogue. To come to terms with madness and filth, degradation and horror. With the true state of the Universe. To dream its dreams, and survive the experience. Yet not once has it spoken."

"We've had this chat before."

"Hm. Yes. You know my views, then, Captain. Since my abduction by the...well, you know my history as well. The trick to communication

261

with the alien is knowing when you've got one on the line. For instance..."

He drops into a sudden crouch and aggressively probes the carcass of some deep-sea abomination with a finger. In moments he pulls a foul R'lyehian grub from the red mess, its thrashing asymmetrical length all random pincers and eye stalks. Grantha huffs and makes his grumbling way back to the ship, while his hexentechs and Silattha gather round for the demonstration.

"Look at this creature. It has no conception of me as a being, does not even know in any more than a rudimentary way that it is held between my thumb and forefinger. It does not even know what fingers are, or a hand. It has no language, other than perhaps the silent firing of its own nervous system. We are utterly unalike, it and I.

"Now, say I wish to communicate with it. To tell it something. Relay some small truth about existence to it. How may this be done?"

Before anyone can answer, Piotr drops the grub to the stone at his feet and crushes it beneath his heel. There is a sound of crumbling chitin and a strong acrid tang as the guts of the thing are exposed to the air. Piotr looks at us all, a strange expectant light in his hybrid eyes.

"Do you think it misunderstood me?"

Silattha smirks and licks her lips. "But they haven't killed us. Or at least, not all of us."

"True. But then, whom the gods would destroy they first make mad, Parv. And are we all not such, after our various fashions? Only minds as functionally insane as ours could survive here." He presses his heel into the stone again, twists it, rendering the pulpy tissue into liquid. "Perhaps *our* ultimate revelation awaits us still."

"That's enough, Tillich," I snap. "You want ultimate revelation? It's up on deck, waiting for us to get that anchor to the coordinates."

"Of course, Captain. Of course. Our final statement." He lifts his dripping heel and grins horribly at it. "Which may amount to little more than a pinch from a grub."

"The early bombs in the Severn Valley did for the Old Ones there, Fun Guy," Silattha scoffs. "Same goes for the Wind Walker, *and* the Voltigeur King in the North Atlantic. Those were low-yield devices, but they bulked up the human life-wave enough to drive the beasts back."

People, I almost correct her. Low-yield souls. Perfectly enlightened, weaponized souls.

"Minor deities, all," Piotr counters.

"And this one is major, right? Well, what kind of *fhtagn* difference does it make? Okay, so, we bring it some major ordinance. This is the biggest bomb we've got!"

The meatpuppet laughs, a sound like stones clicking together at the bottom of a well.

"What *difference*? My dear, look around you. Look around. This is *R'lyeh*. To say that the rules here are different borders on comedy."

"Enough, Tillich." I signal to the hexentechs, who scramble to activate the grav-harnesses that support the anchor and our supplies. The loads lift into the distorted air with a dull thrumming.

"We're here to break a few rules."

Forty-one minutes into the Hour of the Itinerant Showman, the hexentech Jeff Thurman crumples to the ground with a shriek. Before anyone can get to him with a hypo of sedative, he manages to rip out his tongue at the root / disembowel himself with a graphite blade / shatter his own spine with a single self-induced convulsion. As he lies dying at our feet, he lists a number of concerns with each ragged expulsion of breath.

"I'm worried about my kids. Little Sarai and Tim-tom.

"Those who Sit Above In Shadow have your number, Captain Strunk, and it's not one you can count to, not in the whole of Time's vast expanse. Didn't you get the memo?

"I'm pretty sure I left the gas on at home. I don't know what that means.

"In his House at R'lyeh, he waits, awake. He dreamed us, but now he's awake, and the dream is over, and we are nothing but sleep-grit the Prime Minister of Horror flicks from the corner of his terrible eye. A microbe on the grit. Gritty stuff, Captain.

"People. There aren't any, you know. I don't have any kids. Tell my non-existent wife I..."

Poor bastard. His fellows strip him of gear and rations, then roll his corpse close to where two massive blocks of stone meet in a headache-inducing angle. The weird physics of this place do the rest, and the hexentech slides away into an impossible oblivion, the shape of him dopplering into the distance at speed while his colour and the outline of his bones remain to leave a print on the rock. Piotr is at my elbow suddenly, a still presence of unnatural calm.

"That's one down. Madness takes its toll."

"We've enough left to manage."

"Hm."

"The simulations prepared us for this. Everyone here has clocked years in the Tryptamine Baths, mastered the Oneiric Steeplechase at elite levels, run every track at the G'hnath-Carter Angles. There is nothing this place can throw at us— physically, mentally, spiritually—that we haven't anticipated."

"And yet..." Piotr murmurs as we watch the last of the dead man fade into the ravenous stone.

In the Hour of the Fleshless Mask, in a claustrophobic canyon of columns that throb and glisten with an ichor that reeks of kerosene and rotting uranium, we turn a seemingly endless corner to be greeted by a R'lyehian citizen, the first of many, and I am forced to remove Silattha's collar. The spurs exiting her flesh drag gobbets of meat at their tips.

The ghoul-girl begins her serenade. Not everyone gets their hearing protection on in time, and these join the star-spawn in the wholesale dissolution of their molecules. It's a slow process, accompanied by much screaming, and the delirious howl of an ancient, unkillable thing violently changing state, painting the walls of the canyon in a phosphorescent gore-mist.

When she's done, Sil clamps her deadly mouth shut and signals for her collar. The air hums with the last notes of her attack and the lingering consciousness of the beast that still permeates the spaces between space, seeking ingress. I slide the spurs back into her seeping wounds with gratitude. Then I empty my guts on the stuttering tiles and bas reliefs to the sound of the hexentechs mourning their fallen.

"Quite the solo," I manage after a few minutes. Sil pants with happiness at my small praise.

"I had an appreciative audience. Can you believe I had to target *all* of its hyper-chakras? Just wow. Wait," she says, her voice dropping to a whisper. "Okay. Okay, it's still here. I don't know if I'm up for an encore."

Piotr looks up from the strobing displays that hover in a holographic coil around his head. He nods, confirming what we all feel. "We should move, Captain."

The air and rock of the canyon split at his last syllable. For half a moment, the thing finds physical form again. A maelstrom of viscid flesh and hissing pinwheel claws with multiple entry points into reality. I'm raked across my dorsal plates and fall to the ground. The hexentech MaryJo Cherry is split from neck to groin by a whip of spikes. Silattha and Piotr dive below a pistoning limb that strikes the anchor, reducing four of the device's grav-harnesses to sparks and dust.

The moment passes, and we're alone again with our wounds and the dead. The anchor lists to the right, the harnesses on the left side shrieking in protest, and impacts the wall with a sickening crunch.

Our curses ring out and return to us strangely echoed by the maze that is the Dreaming City, the First City. R'lyeh.

"This fucking place. Worst spot on the planet," Sil sighs. The remaining hexentechs are frothing at the mouth with despair as they adjust the grav-harnesses.

Piotr snickers. "There's decent evidence that it's not actually *on* the planet, engineer. Such efforts to get here, after all. Your doggie-powered engines, just as an example. The old records state that R'lyeh wasn't here before. The sea floor at these coordinates was sea floor and nothing more. And then it *was* here.

"Massive, an entire continent. Ancient cities of primal evil. Infinite suburbs of existential mirror-muck, sprawling slums constructed of discarded, croaking anti-languages, laced over with living circuitry telepathically transmitting a constant insect-chitter stream of flash-cut reverse-universe pornography! I can't be the only one who watches the broadcasts on the back of his eyelids, so don't give me that look.

"R'lyeh! Suppurating districts of unspeakable shopping malls that give ferocious new meaning to consumption. Thumping hyperdimensional everlasting-night clubs, every bouncer a shoggoth, every dancer a coruscating chaos of perversion and alien sensuality!

"R'lyeh! Suddenly, it had *always* been here, because it had never left. The stars were right and there was nothing for us. Nothing but what the Old Ones gave us. Nothing but their gift."

Sil hisses and hawks a bloody mass from the back of her throat onto the stones. "Dagon's Teeth! Listen to him with the fuckin' poetry! The Fun Guy *loves* the place. You're sick, puppet. You've got spores for brains."

Piotr smiles and winks. "Such a literalist, Sil."

"You can give your guided tour some other time, Tillich," I say. "We all know the stories."

"Hm. Stories which *suggest* that R'lyeh occupies, or somehow *is*, a highly artificial bubble of space-time. This place could be their ship, occupying multiple points in the Universe but only manifesting at certain times. When the stars are right, they plunge from world to world."

A hexentech appears at my side and whispers into my ear. I don't like what I hear. I cut him off and address the team.

"Enough speculation. The anchor's in the air again, but it won't be for long. We need alternate transport, and that means your specialty, Piotr."

Tillich rubs his hands in glee / tears at his hair / consults a holo-readout at his wrist / spontaneously bleeds from his eyes and smiles. "Move with a purpose, people."

It takes half a day to haul the limping anchor to the nearest shoggoth midden. By the time we arrive it is already the Hour of the Guarded Quotation and the setting sun is a rusty disc in a lowering grey cobweb sky. We are bone-tired and psychotic: Sil paws at the ground like a muttering animal, Piotr is skittish with wild eyes on constant scan, I'm full of remorse and anger. The sight of the midden does nothing to help our dispositions.

"They're not like that in the simulations," Sil whines.

"They're not like this anywhere," Tillich affirms. "Not even on Yuggoth. So calm. I'd say this is hibernation, but look at the colour spectrum. They're awake but there's a lack of autonomy here." He punctuates his statements by vomiting down the front of his armour.

"We need one, Piotr," I clip.

Tillich grimaces and wipes at himself with the edge of a hand. "It's a single mass, Captain. It's a pit. Two clicks wide and who knows how deep and...it's a *single* shoggoth-mass. I don't..."

I glare at him in utter fury, and for once he seems perturbed.

"I'll scout around the edge. See if I can locate a young one." He cracks open a supply pod, begins strapping equipment to his back and arms, places an enhancer circlet on his scalp. "The fresher the bud, the more susceptible to command."

"Just make it happen."

A hexentech fires up a thermal plate and we gather round for warmth, assuming various meditative positions and practicing our *ujjayi* breath. The stone beneath the plate begins to seep oil and blood as it heats; the smell of petrochemicals and scorched honey fills the air like cancer. We quit the *ujjayi* in discomfort and instead watch Tillich move around the midden, the spastic perspective shifting him near and far, reducing him to a collection of sticks, a bloated mass, a cartoon. He pauses, or seems to pause, and there is a frenzied frothing in the pool of sentient plasm near him. In moments, the sound of his screaming reaches us. I key my radio on.

"All good, Tillich?"

More screaming, a terrific wail of complete anguish, but cut with eerily calm assurances. "Five by five, Captain. In negotiations." Further anguish ensues, so I key the radio off.

Sil slides close to me, leans in to my neck to nip at an ear. There's a rasp in her throat as she speaks and I can feel the quills on the side of my head sizzle and crisp.

"Did you imagine it would be like this?"

"Like what, Sil? Like the maddest madhouse to ever be built. Like a revolting graveyard of the Universe. Like the worst nightmares wrapped in perfect truth. Yeah. Yeah, I pretty much always imagined it to be like this."

"Not that," she sighs. "That feeling you've got. You know?"

"What feeling? Nausea? The near-constant urge to murder everything?"

"Yeah. Only...you don't have it? That feeling like you've been travelling your whole life, homesick since the day you were born. When I turned that spawn into powder back there, I just..."

"It felt like coming home, finally. Like I'd just turned a corner in the road, and there it was. I want to do it again and again. Does that ev—..."

She doesn't finish. R'lyeh pulls one of its messed-up physics tricks and Tillich is back with us in one stride, a fetid mass of sentient gelatin towering above him. He's missing his left arm. There's a twitching stump of bleeding mycelial tissue where it used to be and his face is a rictus of pain.

"Negotiations complete. I could use some cauterizing. Painkillers." The hexentechs shriek and scatter to the medpods. In seconds, there's a dirty pink bubble of analgesic foam where the stalk was.

"What happened there?" I say.

"Show of faith. The master-slave relationship with these things is complex." Tillich sips from a tube held to his mouth. "Give a little, get a little. I am it and it is I." He wets his lips, whistles something in a minor key. The shoggoth heaves and with oozing grace slips its stinking bulk underneath the anchor. It lifts the device as if it were no more than a shell, or a small rock stuck to its hide.

"It's why they came here. To serve."

The beast expels jets of befouled air from a hundred ventricles and it sounds like a hissing *tekellliii-lliiiiii*. We choke and gag while Tillich chuckles.

"That's right. *Tekeli-li*, motherfucker.

"Now, mush."

The gutted remains of the violated moon lie heavy and fulgent in the blood-black night as we crest a final rise and look down / cast our eyes upward at the sickening crag formation / abyssal flood plain that lies at the centre / on the perimeter of R'lyeh. We have walked the Maze That Is Not A Maze, come close to this point a thousand times, only to be shifted away by disobedient angles, monstrous lies of the light, chuckling spacial corridors, minutes that cross-dressed as millennia. But we are here, finally. R'lyeh. You tease.

This place can only be called a landscape with tongue firmly in cheek; there are shifting planes of agitated stone folding in and out of perception, vast blocks of masonry behaving like water, like plants, and a conniving horizon that refuses to separate ground from air from sea. The whole is awash in an emerald fog of peculiar and malevolent density that soaks our skins and armour, slides with intention down the back of the throat to raise bile and fear.

It is the Hour of the South-most Pinnacle, and we are on his doorstep, finally. There is the fabled door, near and far at the same time, slightly ajar in its twisting fractal frame set in the side of a mountainous slab of dripping stone, the bas reliefs leaping and foaming like a river on either side. I am thinking of the first dead hexentech and considering my next step.

"So, do we, I dunno, knock?" Sil growls.

"I thought it would be here," Tillich says. "I've corrected for every deviation we've been through. These are the coordinates. I thought we'd see it."

"It doesn't have to be here. It's probably below," I say. "Or between. Off-planet, even. It's free now. Has been for thousands of years. Would *you* stick around if you had to?"

Tillich's face is blank, a bloodless mask of indifference.

"You're making assumptions about a being you can't possibly understand," he says. "And so am I. But in answer to your question, no. No, I wouldn't stick around."

"Wherever it is doesn't matter. This place is its throne. Every insane ley line on the planet converges on this spot. The high priests agree: we detonate here, and R'lyeh collapses. The event horizon we crossed to get here contracts, taking everything inhuman with it back to where it all came from. Back to hell."

"What about us," Sil whispers.

"We're human. Enough." She glares at me like I've whipped her.

"We're human enough."

We pick our way across the migraine canyon / plain, every step threatening to become a fall into the sky, an orthogonal slide into a higher dimension, a stumble into a compressed lifetime of agony. The hexentechs prod the shoggoth with makeshift pikes and the perverse thing moans and whistles with delight at each assault. I get on the radio to Grantha.

"It's time."

My stomach drops as I say the words and my feet follow, rushing away beneath me in a single vertiginous plunge. A moment later and we are at the door, our vertebrae cracking and quaking with the effort to keep upright, our eyes bleeding. One of the three remaining hexentechs gives us a cheery thumbs up and proceeds to reduce the front of his skull to slurry on a bas relief.

"Dreams for the Dreaming Lord! Courtesy of *me! Jesse A. Oster!*" His laughter becomes a wet red gurgling as his head rockets back and forth into the stone. It's over in seconds. His fellows and Sil and Piotr stare at me in mute horror as I key the radio again.

"Send it through, Grantha. Full Oppenheimer. Repeat, we are at Full Oppenheimer."

"Activating Hoffman-Price bubble now, Captain Strunk. Deployment of Little BoyGirl in ten, nine, eight..."

The anchor gasps once, twice. The vantablack coating makes it difficult to see the contractions in the angles of the tetrahedron, so that when it happens, it seems to happen all at once. The anchor condenses, pops out of existence to leave an oily bubble of nothing hanging in the air. A sizable chunk of the young shoggoth goes with the anchor to wherever it went; the beast yowls with sick pleasure.

The void sizzles in anticipation, warbling shafts of light and scenery coming into view: the deck of the *Hassan-i Sabbah*, Grantha's misshapen mug in a silent anticipatory leer, another sky, a different time. Another moment of this and the bomb is here, shedding light and polymer plates like a lotus blossom sheds petals.

The shoggoth roars and changes state in an effort to escape, becoming steam and memory, leaving Little BoyGirl to hover in the air. Green mist recoils and pulses in a peripatetic rhythm at the periphery of the golden light that builds and builds. Tillich is passive in the glow, the hexentechs have tears in their eyes. Sil is on her knees, openly weeping, with her long hands palms up on the stone between her knees. Worshipful.

"So beautiful," I hear her say.

She's right. The footage of the early bomb tests did no justice to the experience of being here, at Ground Zero. The bomb is the most beautiful thing I've ever seen. Little BoyGirl shines like a beacon from heaven as zhe rises, the darkness sloughing away from hir like scales, like a bad dream after waking. Gravity, despair, madness, all the things that could pull hir down to the tormented earth; these have no hold on hir. Zhe shines like the sun, no, better than the sun. Pure in a way the sun could never be. Zhe shines like the Platonic ideal of the Sun, with a light that welcomes the eye instead of burning it away, a light that is Life and Hope. Zhe is clean-limbed and symmetrical, perfect in hir form, with a noble forehead and graceful hands, a golden mane of hair in a halo around hir head. Hir generative members are aroused and pleasing to the eye, thick and moist and swelling with the potential for life, human life, the real *human* lifewave that has been gone from the world for so long and I am weeping now, weeping with the others in this awful place, my hands outstretched to the floating being, this bodhisattva, this gorgeous creature who will sacrifice itself for us, for our future. I want to touch hir face, to tell hir *thank you*, to press my deformed mouth to hir perfect lips and know the grace of hir accepting smile for a single second, know the warmth of hir enlightenment on my wretched wintered skin before zhe saves us all with her glorious ignition. I cry out, once, an inarticulate sound of longing, a longing to be consumed, to be ended in hir light...

My cry is answered.

The emerald mist begins to howl. In the air, on the stones, streaming from our fingertips and filling our lungs: each drop of it begins to vibrate and scream, and not with fear or anguish or rage. This scream is one of lust. Triumph. And worse, a species of gleeful indifference.

Little BoyGirl halts in the air for a moment, and casts hir shining eyes down to the monsters below, to us, hir worshippers, the monsters zhe is here to save. A fleeting cloud of concern passes across hir beatific features before it all comes to an end.

The mist condenses in a thunderclap. It was everywhere: here, across the impossible length and breadth of R'lyeh, and in our dreams and our history, in our genes and our philosophy and most especially in our hubris. It was everywhere, and it had always been. It had never died, only dreamed, and had awakened long ago, and would now, at the birth of stranger new aeons, conquer death. The mist condenses, becomes a mountain that walks, stumbles, screams to end the world.

We answer it, all of us. Sil, Tillich, the hexentechs, myself. Little BoyGirl screams too. The bomb screams most of all as the mountain plucks it from the air with limbs I know are not limbs, only the suggestion of limbs, only seeming to be long muscular feelers to my lower-order mammalian eyes. Little BoyGirl is plucked, and dissected, and raped across all levels of reality, hir perfect soul and hir weaponized enlightenment rendered into a mewling paste. It takes seconds.

There's not much left of hir, but what is left is extended to me, speared on the tip of a writhing pseudopod. A parting gift of awareness. I grasp the contorted remains—a head, part of the upper torso—with numb hands and pull hir to my chest. A golden eye looks up at me from a face made insectoid, reptilian. The perfect lips, smeared into a jackknife smile of derangement, crack and hiss into my ear. The mountain is already moving away, its vast bulk blacking out the moon and the reeling stars, but the words I hear surely belong to it, siphoned through a mouthpiece it has already forgotten it owns.

Captain, Little BoyGirl says. *Captain, do not all the old texts state that this would come to pass? The time would be easy to know, for all men would be as we, shouting and killing and reveling in joy. This is the foretold holocaust of ecstasy and freedom. We shall teach you new ways to shout, kill, revel. Enjoy. Your friends are.*

In the distance, Piotr is dropping the waxen mask of his humanity and assuming his ideal fungoid form. The hexentech Laura Lambert lies convulsing at his feet, obscene mycelial cultures bursting from her mouth and soft tissue. Chris Loan is pinned to a slab while Piotr feeds the glowing growth from his ruined shoulder down the hexentech's throat. Piotr hums while he works.

There is a sound of tearing fabric and I feel a sudden searing pain in my core. I look down to see Sil between my knees, my secondary generative organs dangling from her crimson teeth. I drop the saviour's remains at my feet and cuff the ghoul-girl across the mouth. She laughs in derision as her cheek bounces off the slimy rocks with a crack.

"Don't be pissy, Deimos. I'm five by five, still, your Sil, your servant. Stay with us." She moans and twitches and dances like a dog cornering prey. "The dead should serve the living, and there was never anything as alive as the Lord of Dreams. Stay and serve him."

She's not wrong, says the head of Little BoyGirl. *You're already here, after all. So many times. So often you visit. Look. Look and see.*

I look, and I see the ghosts of every other attempt we've made on the Lord of R'lyeh flicker in and out of view. Bodies and bombs strewn and ruined and draped across the land in a carpet of gore and failed detonations and detonations that *were* successful but made no difference. We are legion, and nothing. The eternal dirt from which nightmares grow. Not even the dirt. Crawlers in the dirt. Mites on the crawlers.

Enjoy, enjoy, enjoy, Little BoyGirl coos. *You must work at it, though. The best and highest thing you can be is me, and you've a long way to go. Shout. Kill. Revel. Repeat.*

The Hoffman-Price bubble is contracting rapidly, but I throw myself through anyway, knowing I'm too late. As it closes, I can hear the mouthpiece speak to a laughing Sil...

Do you think it misunderstood me?

On the deck of the *Hassan-i Sabbah*, I spend a moment in contemplation at the loss of my lower legs, and take some small comfort in the thought that Sil is likely making a meal of them even now, prayers remembered from her cemetery catechism dropping from her mouth between red bites.

I drag myself past the spot where Grantha has propped himself against a bulkhead. He is delicately removing his own eyes with a graphite blade, slice by quivering slice.

"Homie don't do that," the gnome mumbles. "Homie can't see *shit*. Straight up the *wgah'nagl*, coming at ya right straight up."

"Carry on, High Priest," I say, giggling at his futile efforts. There's still the pineal to be seen to. "The stars are right."

"That you, Captain? Mission aborted? Heh. Stars. Son, they ain't never been *wrong*.

"You're right there, at least. I'm sorry about your acolytes, for what it's worth, priest."

"All lost? Well. I liked 'em, but whaddaya gonna do when doom falls like the night, ai'aight? Y'all be keepin' it R'lyeh, now." He returns to his self-butchery, a wiser man.

I go below, seeking my one true and singular, pure thing. Of course I don't find it, no matter how many corridors I careen down on the stumps of my ruined legs, no matter how many blubbering crew members I tear apart in absent glee. I don't find it.

Instead, I sit in my sleep chamber / confess my sins to the ship / strip naked in front of a mirror, those manifold tusks, that prehensile whatsit, I'm a thing of rare beauty even with the red ruin at my crotch oh yes / paint myself in bloody sigils / execute a decent pirouette for the gathered ghosts, thank you thank you I'll be here all aeon / make my way to the engine room of stuttering blue light / paint myself again, this time in the weak chakra-glow of depleted abortions retrieved from the overflowing waste hopper in back of the Tindlosi Drives / begin penning this narrative / place one hand on the icy curve of a sphere while the fingers of my other hand drop to a command pad, keying in the sequence that will crack the seal on the sphere.

It is the Hour of the Virginal Appraisal, appropriately enough, and my mind is as clear as the air around me is clouded with the hiss of approaching death. I know what the mountain said at the last, but I respectfully disagree with its assessment. And I may have my one pure thing, now. The best and highest thing I can be.

"Here, puppy," I softly whistle. "Who's a good boy. Who's tired of kibble. Who wants a real meal?"

STRANGERS DIE EVERY DAY

CODY GOODFELLOW

The first time he showed up in the U-Haul lot on East Comanche to look for work, the other guys, Mexicans and Central Americans who'd paid in blood for the corner, knocked his Dunkin Donuts coffee out of his hands, beat the shit out of him, and threw him in front of a passing car. When he came back next day, someone somehow had found out what he did and what he was. That morning and every day thereafter, there was a tall Dunkin Donuts coffee on the furthest stretch of curb from where the other pick-up laborers waited and flagged down cars.

Miracles and wonders, Tobin Thrush thinks, drinking his coffee. *It's supposed to be different, now.*

Some things are different. Every once in a while, a car slows down without pulling into the rental lot, the driver looking lost in more than just this dead industrial wasteland neighborhood. And they roll down the window, and if they ask him to help them move, he pretends not to speak English and asks way too much, because he hates moving. But he's good at other things, things that, now, everybody needs, sooner or later.

Just before sunrise. "I need help with a … I heard you … I …" They can never just say it. He gets into the passenger seat of the Volvo station wagon. "What kind of job?"

The driver pushes his glasses up his nose. "Somebody took our daughter."

"How old? Is she a virgin?"

No hesitation or outrage. "Yes, and she's eleven."

"Has she had her first period?"

"I don't ... how would I...?"

"You want to call your wife? It could be important. Show me a picture."

He shakes his head. "She's ... she took it hard, she's at her mother's. I can't ...." He spaces out.

"Picture," Thrush says.

He reflexively goes for a phone, then takes out his wallet, shaking his head. "Everybody still does that, you notice?" No phones, not much TV and hardly any computers. Thrush never had a phone. He misses the news. He misses knowing and seeing it live when cities fall into the sea.

A school Xmas portrait. Brilliant smile, eager to please, not a self-satisfied or a rebellious bone in her birdy, blossoming body. Ash-blonde hair, fine as feathers. Thrush smells the picture, pockets it. "Where and when did you lose her?"

That almost makes him argue, but he's smart enough not to take the bait. "Out of her room last night, sometime between two and four. I'm a night owl and my wife's an early bird, but neither of us heard anything...."

"Drive," Thrush says, and they pull away too fast. "Where do you live?"

"Bishop Creek. It's not the Heights, but it's gated."

"So you have money."

"Well, not really ... The house is my wife's family. We don't have anything left, we're down to selling furniture. I don't see why they'd pick on me...."

No point in explaining that kidnapping is just something to do for a lot of people now. They don't check the means of the victim's family. A lot of times, they're just desperate to get anybody and collect the ransom in a hurry to pay the ransom on the loved one someone took from them....

"No ransom note?"

"No ..."

"If you don't hear from them by noon, then it probably wasn't a kidnapping."

The driver nods. Even he knows that.

"You know what I do?"

Pretending to watch the road, the driver nods but shrugs. "I don't ... I just heard you can ... bring people back."

"Sometimes," Thrush says. "I know some people, and a thing or two. I could help, but if it's what you're afraid it is ... Why so sure? Didn't you talk to the cops?"

"We can't afford the cops. Not the real ones ... We already pay a fortune for security, not that they're worth a shit—" They're driving in circles around downtown and the mostly dead blocks around it. "It's just, they said it was the end of everything, and it ... I guess it's not the same for you, is it? You people got what you were praying for...."

"Just drop me off by the payphones there, in front of the post office. I'm gonna need a hundred ... and fifty, uh, deposit, and, uh ..."

Mouth turned down, he says, "I was told what to bring," and hands Thrush a sandwich bag.

Thrush gets out and goes to a payphone and picks up the receiver. "Ursula."

Her thick wet breath. "I'm working, Tobin." Bathroom-tile reverb, low red whisper. "And he's not making it easy."

"I need the car. I have a job...."

"That's great, hon. But so do I."

"How far along are you?"

"Not even conceiving yet, damn it."

"Give him his money back."

"*You* get paid yet?"

"I *need* the car."

"Get over here."

"Come get me."

"Walk."

He runs.

A lot of Thrush's people, they were angry all the time, like the sun was supposed to burn out, all their enemies were Raptured away, and nobody would ever have to work again. Like everything was supposed to change, like the stars were supposed to run on their schedule. That was the old thinking. That was why things were running down, but nothing changed overnight. The Oklahoma Sink just outside of town was ten miles across and had no bottom, but nothing much had come up to say thanks for all the countless offerings cast into it. The seas had risen and washed away about a fifth of the world's population, and sent the rest scurrying to fight for food and shelter, but after all the sensitive types went mad and offed themselves, the line had gone dead. Maybe somewhere they were ravening for delight in the streets, but shit is pretty much the same as it ever was here in Norman. Thrush thinks of the poster on the wall in the U-Haul men's room, next to the Snap-On Tools calendar. It says, IF YOU'RE NOT THE LEAD DOG, THE SCENERY NEVER CHANGES, and the picture is a close-up of a husky's asshole.

Some things did change, though. They still have to eat, still have to work. But now, at least, they don't have to hide.

He finds the apartment by listening for Ursula's voice. She's arguing with the client. "Listen, I don't make the rules, bright boy—"

"I just don't see why I can't just in vitro it...."

"Give him his money back," Thrush says through the screen door. "Stay out of this, Tobin."

The door is locked, but the cheap tin frame comes apart at the merest tug. He rips it away, batting at rusty screen and comes in.

The client stops pacing, glaring at him. He's wearing torn-up black Levi's and a faded shirt that says HARRY CREWS on it but has a picture of a bunch of pissed-off chicks on it, horn-rimmed glasses taped together. Books and empty bottles everywhere.

The hairs all over Thrush's body stand out, pushing through his shirt. "What the fuck is wrong with you?"

Ursula spills out of a sprung loveseat, face bloated with tears, choking down snot as she digs around in her purse. "Take the damn keys and go."

"You don't know what you're doing, do you? What do you even want a monkey for?"

"None of your goddamned business. Look, I want my money back, and I want you both to leave...."

Thrush pulls his t-shirt down over his gut, wipes the sweat out of his eyebrows and kicks the front door shut. "We're keeping your money one way or the other, because you made her come all the way over here and you made her cry. But whether or not you get your money's worth, you're gonna understand something."

The client puffs up. "Get out of my fucking house—"

Thrush goes over to sit on the arm of the loveseat. "This woman was marked from birth to bear the offspring of an Outer God whose name alone would strike you dead if you heard it. Her womb was consecrated with blood sacrifices to host the new gods who would eat the sun and bring the Night of All Days. To bring forth an army, David!"

"Dennis ..."

"Now ... Can you imagine how it must feel to live for such an exalted destiny, and to have a gift like she has, and then to have to squander it on the likes of a peckerwood fuckup like yourself for goddamned rent money?"

Ursula's sobbing ratchets up to a gobbling, whinnying sound almost like a lumberjack's saw being played with a bow. A monkey like a stick insect scuttles out from between her quivering breasts to feed on her tears. The smell of her grief makes Thrush's knuckles tear the fabric off the threadbare loveseat.

Burgundy, acne-pitted cheeks, sweat pooling on the insides of his glasses, the client sits down on the swaybacked recliner. "I'm sorry. I ... never thought of it like that."

"Now, we don't care what you want one for. If it's for a slave, or a proxy to lift a curse, or just for the organs, or what. But you gotta lie with her to make it work. It's not just your seed. It needs your sweat and your blood and the breath and ecstasy of the act itself. It's no less a ritual, no less a magical act, than making a real baby."

He squirms at that. "I just ... I wasn't ready...."

Thrush crosses the room and faces the guy down. Draws his knife so it flashes in the client's eyes. "You don't have to like it. You don't have to like her. You don't even have to go through with it. Lord knows we all have better things to do. But you don't get to make her feel bad. She's the consort of a fucking deity."

Somewhere in there, Ursula's blubbering turned to giggling. Rolling off the couch, cradling the cantilevered hammock of her bra. Her knees pop like gunshots under a pillow. "Take the fucking keys, Tobin."

"Pick you up at two." He dumps her purse out on the glass-topped coffee table and swipes the keys and her fertility fetish and a damp, sticky twenty.

"Who is this asshole, your husband?" Rediscovering some trace elements of testosterone, good deal.

Thrush is out the door and slams it, but the wadded-up throw rug fouls him, hanging open so the sound of her forced laughter follows him all the way down to the car.

The car is full of monkeys.

The old books call them homunculi. Thrush can't read Latin, but alchemists made them for all kinds of things. Ursula can make them. Her church got blown up by a Xian militia and the Million Favored ones never manifested to make god-babies with her, but the first time they did it, she got sick and in a couple hours, she made a little manikin that looked just like Tobin Thrush. It had Tobin's eyes, anyhow, but no mouth to speak of. Thrush got scared and stepped on it. It happens every time they fuck, and sometimes, when she's angry or sick, she hatches a litter with no heads, hands at both ends, or just long, eyeless serpents. Couple times she hatched something that looked like a chicken, but it sure didn't taste like it.

She got real big after that, and unfit for any other work. Some would pay a couple thousand for her services, and what happened after that was nobody's business.

"What about when They come?" he asked, that first time, when they were teens in a refugee camp. She'd laughed at that, and it wasn't her fake laugh. He asked every few years, and she never stopped laughing at him.

Eight of them creep out from under the backseat once he gets the old Celica moving. He throws a crushed tin can at them, fights them for control of the stereo as he drives.

Puffing a crooked blunt of Plutonian Gold, Thrush plays 52 Pickup in his head.

The AM station is local, but weird sounds crowd the newsreader out of the frequency: the mating cries of the unborn, the death throes of mirror universes. The stories are passed from station to station, sifted out from the gibbering cosmic asylum of the shortwave bands.

Somewhere out west, they're feeding the last self-professed Xians to the sea. Somewhere down in Mexico, the priests cut the hearts out of a hundred men every day to keep the world turning.

He passes the old Trinity Baptist, now mint-green and rebranded the 1st Ophite Church of Christ & Bible Museum. The sign out front promises tonight's sermon, HOW EVE DECEIVED THE SERPENT—GNOSTIC GOSPEL REVEALED. A naked man hangs by his ankles from a gibbet over the rock-garden frontage, blackened and swollen to bursting from thousands of rattlesnake bites.

In Egypt, some prophet calling himself Mahdi Nephren Ka has declared victory in his war on Islam, and now orders his Fedayeen armies to destroy the rival prophet bearing his name, who broadcasts from the glowing ruins of Jerusalem.

He slows down on Kansas to watch the cheerleaders drilling on the football field. Two cops are burning a truckload of unclean chickens in their cages out front of the flea market in the old central-library ruins. The occult symbols on their hoods wink in the sun. Thrush feels their eyes on him and slows, nodding like he knows them, like they have faces. The one with the flamethrower makes a gesture at him that makes his heart pound faster and everything he was ever ashamed of comes gushing out of his skull, and he waits for the fire to splash across the side of the crippled Toyota, but he crawls past them and they just keep incinerating chickens that shriek *Tekeli-Li!* as they burn.

Somewhere in China, there's a city getting ready for the first visit of the Lama of Leng. In accordance with his edicts, nearly fifteen million people put their own eyes out so as not to see his veiled form.

In Norman, it's not so bad. Books are illegal, writing and recordings of any kind are anathema, because nothing written comes out true; every recording is corrupt, a trap, or a door. So they stopped teaching kids how to read and write, but nobody around here misses it. TV is a different story, but you can't ever trust them. Thrush's friend Forkboy says it's because there're embryonic Outer Gods swimming in the sun, and the sunspot activity transmits their dreams. Whatever the hell it is, nobody has seen one for years.

It's not illegal to be famous, but with what you can do with just a name nowadays, it's not a good idea. The cops, nearly all public servants, wear masks, hoods, veils. They still have elections, like any democracy.

Tomorrow, the town will choose their new mayor from between two anonymous rich gentlemen in identical hooded ceremonial robes. Regular folks are mostly real polite because they're scared shitless of each other, because nobody's got anything to lose. Strangers die every day, and there still seems to be no shortage of people.

A Jeep overstuffed with neighborhood militia cuts him off on the right and runs through the intersection, clipping a pedestrian who caroms off the hood of the Celica, which knocks them down and they don't get up, but the cop waves at him like a ref saying *play on*.

Some people got everything they prayed for.

While he drives, he opens the little paper bag, crisp brown bag like somebody's lunch is in there. He pulls out the sandwich bag and opens it, digs out the clump of pale blond hair. A lock of hair would be prettier, but he ordered the client to clean out all her brushes. When it's tugged out, the roots come out, and the roots contain DNA.

Absently listening to the radio, he wads the hair into his mouth and lets it marinate on his tongue.

In the South Pacific, there's an island that wasn't there before the waves smashed the west coast. It's covered in clouds and fog, and the one or two satellites still working have never seen it clear, but there are sixteen thousand ships, boats and rafts tied together in a junk-continent around the island, waiting. No one has set foot on the island and come back since it surfaced, and bloody internecine wars sweep the fleet whenever someone tries to mount another expedition to the new holy land. Seven years, and nothing has come out of the fog.

A few blocks further down, he sees what he's looking for.

Thrush is half Toxodo. American Indian tribe local to Oklahoma, they believed they emerged from a hole in the ground on the First Day, forsaking the ruins of a subterranean empire more advanced than modern white society today. Massacred by Cherokee and Choctaw forced into Oklahoma by Andrew Jackson, the Toxodo's numbers dropped into the double digits before they were officially denied protected status by the U.S. government. Their genes had more in common with Olmecs than with Indians, though later sequencing efforts pegged them as closest to a tribe of Greenland Eskimos that went extinct shortly after the first contact with European explorers, but whose DNA survived in artifacts and apparel Vikings made of their skin and hair.

Tobin's mother took him out to California and they drifted up and down the coast until she found someone who took her in and kicked him out. He was a debt collector and weed dealer in Buttonwillow when the Big One leveled California and the whole Imperial Valley became an inland sea again. Lost in the mass migration of refugees fleeing the demolished coastline and the unbelievable horrors that emerged from the vengeful sea, Tobin heard white people gibbering sounds exactly like the little fragments of the Toxodo tongue his mother taught him, just before they died of hemorrhagic fever. He would've joined one or another of the bizarre cargo cult sects that sprang up in the camps, had he not found Ursula. Together, they made their way back to Oklahoma, because he heard about the Sink.

For all Tobin Thrush knows, he is the last of the Toxodo. The blood of the shamans of the Shapeless Sleeper runs in his veins, the rhythm of the Backward Path pounds in his ears, the legacy of K'n-Yan is his birthright.

All of which means he knows where to score drugs.

Horace "Forkboy" Labrador comes out from under the awning of Hideaway Pizza and jumps in his car. They drive around the corner to a burnt-out duplex on Asp, across the street from the curtain wall of the college.

Between his mules out of Mexico and Texas and the college labs, Labrador can get most anything—hydroponic weed, DMT, ayahuasca, mushrooms, peyote, amphetamines, even coffin salts and Snakeladder, if you're that far gone.

Labrador is one of a handful of people who can get in and out of the old OU campus, now a walled forbidden city run by a mob of mad grad-student monks. Labrador says they kept all the dangerous books after the big burns, and they're doing things behind the walls that would get them all burned at the stake themselves, if anyone found out.

He shakes his head at the photo as he fires up a joint and passes to Tobin Thrush. "Nobody's into young stuff in there. Necromancy is a waste of time if your dead don't know anything. 'T'aint the meat, it's the humanity,' as they say...." Then he catches the look on his customer's face. "What?"

"I'm not saying eating people is bad," says Thrush, "it's just stupid. Wasn't mad cow from cannibals eating brains in New Guinea or some shit?"

"That's what they want you to believe, man! Don't buy their

bullshit!" Forkboy bogarts the hotboxed joint, using it like a leash on Thrush's rambling attention. "Behind every taboo, like, there's a secret they don't want you to know. That's why the big scare campaign around LSD and weed, like, it was because they alter your perceptions so you see through their bullshit, and you slip right through their controlling fingers. Same exact thing with cannibalism."

He doesn't eat the whole body, he explains. The med students render most of the corpses they get into salts when they're done dissecting them. Not everybody's into salts; it's a dangerous trip because when you snort it, you trip on the holographic memories stored in their organic matter. Forkboy just eats the brains. Photographs his teeth and takes careful skull measurements daily to chart his devolution into a ghoul.

Thrush finally gets the joint back and hits it hard, trying to remember what he wanted to ask about. "I can see it, man," he chokes out amid a storm of smoke. "It's totally happening, dog."

"Fuck off, Toby. Whether or not, man, next semester, I'm going down there. You should go with me, dude. Fuck, your people came from down there, right?"

Thrush flicks the roach at Labrador. "I'm from right here, asshole."

"Gotta be somewhere safe; there ain't gonna be no shelter on the surface, soon...."

Thrush shakes his head. "I hear Mexico's fucking nice now, if you get across the desert."

"Must be; they'll shoot your ass, you try to cross the river."

"It ain't gonna change."

"Fuck, man. *Everything* changed. I was a fucking Econ major when the Thunderbird Sink opened up.... But like ... sure, maybe the Sink is just a fucking hole. Maybe it's just we fracked so much shit into the ground that it broke. Maybe we dumped so much shit in the ocean that it just threw up. Like ... maybe Cthulhu isn't a real thing, like a shark or Godzilla, maybe he's just a name for all the shit we don't understand...."

"They're just another crutch. If a giant foot came down out of the sky to crush us like bugs, most folks around here would be dancing in the street and lining up to kiss that foot."

"Maybe it's stinky thinking like that that's keeping them away...."

He drives aimlessly for another hour, stops at a couple places, runs down a couple pimps on the street. Norman isn't such a big town. Word gets around about anything, even something as ordinary as a kidnaping. The Esoteric Order of Dagon in the old Rotarian Hall officially rejected human sacrifice to pick up a broader flock, but were known to drown a drifter or ten in the river on the holy days. The pyramid weirdoes in their shantytown, where they almost built a mosque back in the day, they like to set offerings on fire and make them dance to those crazy, skirling flutes. Thrush has seen them dance till there's nothing left but ashes and smoke. But their god likes young men and boys. Out on the reservations, they go for the old gods in a big way, but they'd never come into town and take a white girl out of her house. Even now, such a thing just isn't done. The Mexicans, steadfast suckers for Catholicism and Santeria, still try to get by on red wine and chicken blood.

He ends up cruising the gated enclaves along Oak Tree, near the golf course. A woman on horseback with an English saddle asks him if he isn't lost. He mumbles in Spanish until she directs him to the landscaping depot. His infallible senses have led him back to the family's house. He sees the Volvo tucked in the open garage beside a Hummer and a Lexus SUV. Two trucks are parked on the driveway, one from a catering place, and the other from a party rentals place.

He slows down as he passes, puts on a toque from the floor. It wouldn't help to get spotted outside the one place where Megan isn't. Davenport would be stupid not to assume Thrush was casing the place, himself, and Oak Creek security, unlike the cops, excels at their job.

Nice place, but far from impregnable, as was proven last night. People come in and out all the time, invisible to the residents, so long as they work. Just like someone must've come in to paint the street numbers on the curbs, because it sure doesn't look right here, like curb feelers on a Ferrari—

He's almost to the corner when it registers. He hits the brakes and turns around, clips a mailbox, and stops out front of the Davenports.

A golf cart screeches to a halt in front of him and two rent-a-cops in ragged flak jackets with badges painted on jump out.

"Get out the car!" one screams at him over and over while his partner cracks the Celica's windshield with his truncheon.

It's a time-honored suburban grift. Spray all the curbs, then guilt the money out of the rubes. A perennial favorite of cults, churches, and bogus charities.

They're not allowed to carry guns around the plantation, but sure to drag him off to the fairway to be murdered by a driving-range firing squad, if he gets out.

As quick as he can, which is still infuriating, sub-glacial, Thrush climbs out of the Celica. Billy Club thumps him about the head and shoulders while his partner hauls out the pepper spray and douses him like a dog in flea dip.

It's starting to get on Thrush's nerves. In a few minutes, it's gonna start hurting. "You boys are pretty tough now. Where were you last night when the Davenport girl got snatched?"

The mercenaries look at each other and laugh. Pepper Spray lets him have another faceful. His vision foams over. Billy Club works the body. Somewhere, another golf cart pulls up. "Goddamn it, Toby, whyn't you get the fuck out of here when you had a chance?"

Tobin Thrush wipes the foam out of his eyes and spits. "Can't you see I'm interviewing for a job?"

The fresh paint numbers are black on mint green.

He shivers, shaking off sweat, suddenly frigid, even though Pepper Spray is tasering him now.

"Cut it out," Thrush yanks the taser ramrod off his feet by the wires, facefirst into Thrush's fist like a punch-balloon. Billy Club gets tangled with his friend and Thrush doesn't even have to push them over.

"Fuck off out of here and don't come back. Nobody's selling what you're buying."

Makes as much sense as anything else today. Thrush stumbles to the Celica and falls behind the wheel.

The last people in the world he feels like dealing with. Still the nastiest, blood-simple cult on the block.

Xians.

Just after sunset, he pulls into the church parking lot, among a dozen other junkers. The mint-green paint is so bright it almost glows. All the windows are boarded over; there's no seeing inside. A fiery preacher's sermon blares out the open door, hot and flat from blown-out speakers, loud even over the growl of their generator.

Thrush drops a piece of goat cheese in the bowling bag in the passenger footwell, then stubs out his joint and pops his knuckles, his neck, his shoulders out of and into their sockets, limbering up. These jobs are a hassle enough without getting physical.

Usually, assuming they have the one he's looking for, he'll just go in and negotiate first. Most of the idiots who do these things are just confused sex fiends or deluded losers trying to appease their own failed lives with someone else's blood. They never understand that you don't trade blood for making something better; you have to shed it to keep things from getting worse.

These kind of people are the worst to deal with. The ones who think they know what they're doing. Thrush has traded a couple times— take me instead. Hurts, but if you do it, you can take the rest of the week off.

He zips up the bowling bag, checks his shitty old .22 target pistol. No bullets, but if they're not scared of the sight of it, shooting them seldom does much good, anyway. He tucks it into the pouch of his hooded sweatshirt. No pass-by, no lights; only lanterns hanging on porches, candles in windows. Somewhere out there, a man battles an accordion, and loses.

He listens to some screwball yodeling cowboy on the college station and waits. A slash of cold cobalt light spills out of an open door on the back of the museum wing of the church. A hulking brute in filthy overalls drives a couple of feral children away from the dumpster, then dumps a trashcan full of scrap lumber and moldy drywall.

Thrush flips on his headlights and throws the Celica into gear. The hulk turns and flashes a big K-Bar pig-sticker that glints in the light.

Thrush floors it. The bumper clips the goon just above his knees. He bounces off the windshield and roof and hits the pavement. Thrush reverses and parks on the body. Never bring a knife to a car fight.

Thrush gets out and kneels by the corpse. A piledriver of stench wafts out over him, but he tastes her sweat, tears....

These idiots are either pouring innocent blood into an empty hole, or they're unknowingly feeding something they can't name, and they'll never stop regretting when it answers their prayers.

Thrush goes over to the door. There's no knob on the outside, but it's not locked, standing out an inch from the frame. He presses his ear against it and stills his breath, stops his heart to listen.

Blue-white china screams, breaking on garbled red words. He throws the door open and pounces on the space. Blue light so thick it drips off him. Shadows you could drown in.

Just as his eyes begin to adjust to the darkness, the lights come up to reveal a cyclorama of boundless indigo sky and clouds like ghostly funeral barges crawling with headless cherubs and winged eyeballs. Muted red, gold and blue lights nestled behind the trees.

Not trees ... crosses.

One door, artfully hidden, leads to the gift shop, while another goes into a massive plaster serpent's mouth. This is where the noise is coming from.

The robed man comes out of this and throws a trashcan, knocking Thrush on his ass.

The man comes at him, and his loose, floppy robe swirls round him. He's naked, swaddled in rippling curtains of skin. He must've weighed five, six hundred pounds, back in the day.

A head taller than Thrush, the zealot tackles him, throwing an arm round his shoulder and another between his legs, crushing his balls. Thrush braces himself, grabs his opponent, but it's like grabbing an empty waterbed slicked with bacon grease. He's resisted stronger men, but the naked man hoists him nearly over his head and flings him across the exhibit hall.

He flies backwards and slams into a cross. The knotty 4X8 pine splinters and snaps at the base. Thrush flops around, trying to catch his breath, to find the gun, but his pocket's empty.

The naked giant kicks the pistol away. Thrush rolls over and over, grabs a cord and yanks on it, swinging a Skilsaw over his head like a lasso. The giant swats it down, catches the cord, yanks Thrush off his feet and face first into the big man's knee.

Dazed, smothered and sinking into musky folds of skin closing over mouth and nose so he inhales only sweat and smegma until he just decides, fuck it, and stops breathing.

He wakes to bad breath, and a piercing falsetto humming "Were

You There When They Crucified My Lord," and nails going into his flesh at high velocity. He tries to stop it, but his arms are tied down with nylon rope, secured to the wings of the cross he knocked down.

Something that stinks like a fish kill in August shuffles over to lean in close. "Is this the Serpent, come at last," it croaks, "bearing forbidden wisdom?"

"Naw," growls the naked, flabby man, "it's just some shitheel from over to the U-Haul."

The naked man does the yodeling refrain part and his voice goes up somewhere dogs can't hear, and he nuzzles the nail gun into Thrush's left palm and punches a ten-penny nail into the sinewy gap between the middle and ring fingers, then one through the ball of tiny bones in the heel of the hand, then he snaps off a salvo of them up Thrush's forearm. Some go through the gap between radius and ulna, but more than a couple stab right through the bones. The muted splintering sound when he twitches is like ice cracking.

Then they cut his clothes off. "Were you there when they rolled away the stone," the fishy man tunelessly gasps, vestigial gillflaps spasming in his bloated neck-sac. Rheumy eyes behind nictitating membranes like grimy glasses, but it'll dry up and die in the dustbowl rather than be what it is. Its blood would be worth money to some people, who have the fool notion that transfusions will let them change and go down to the sea and live forever.

Thrush strains with all his might to smash the bastard with his other hand, pops his shoulder and twists and strains until the nylon rope saws through his wrist. The naked man stands on his forearm and goes to town on the right arm. He stops to reload, then does the feet with twelve nails each onto a little ledge on the board.

Thrush mumbles and moans for them to stop, please, and everything else he can think of, but the pain sweeps him off his nut and into the darkness that is his birthright.

He's just drooling when they hoist him upright and stand the cross up in a posthole in the middle of the room. The stink of the other crosses' occupants is lost on him. When the crowd files in from the church, the flabby man and the fishy man stand by in cheap Roman centurion costumes, handing out rocks.

Embittered die-hard Xians, they couldn't quite bow down to a monster, but they had a funny way of loving the Lord, lately.

The preacher's mic is a bullhorn. "Behold the prophet of submission and false hope, his hour come round at last!"

A big chunk of sandstone hits Thrush's face, crushing his left cheekbone, forcing him to smile.

"Hold, brother!" The preacher howls and rails at the crowd, laying all their thwarted hopes, all their crushed dreams, all their unanswered prayers on Tobin Thrush's head, until they all hold their rocks up, some old folks staggering under the weight, some kids jumping up and down with one in each hand. "And for his too-little, too-late Rapture, brothers and sisters, we ask only the boon of replying in kind!"

This goes over their heads, and he has to cast the first stone. Then they all come flying, and everybody goes back five, six more times, until the unrecognizable sack of shattered bones nailed to the cross is buried up to its ankles in rocks, and the crowd seems to wear out without satisfaction, somehow, because though they've broken every bone in his body and he's a swollen purple-black rag, they could not make their failed savior shed a single drop of blood.

"Cast this pathetic demiurge from your hearts and your memories, brothers and sisters," says the preacher, leading them out of the room through a hole in the horizon beyond which dinosaurs snarl and prowl in their stalls in the belly of Noah's Ark. "At the end of our tour, you shall bear witness to the invisible glory and terrible beauty of the true savior of this world, waiting only to be born—"

Why fight it?

You were never cut out for this civilized, day-labor, upright-walking bullshit. Who were you trying to fool?

Just give up and let go.

Go back to the beginning and start again—

Let yourself fall back into the arms of your ancestors, into the memory of your blood, into the abyss that your people mistakenly crawled out of twenty thousand years ago. Go further, give it all up. Forsake the sun and stars for the eternal womb of the Earth. Abandon the land for the primordial sea.

What do you have to lose?

He surrenders to the fatalistic gospel of the god whose unspeakable true name was corrupted into the tribal name of his people, gives in to the slower, deeper pulsation of his blood. Thrush can't come up with an answer, can't come up with words to defend himself. How truly stupid and useless words are for one who never has to beg, never threaten—

All of the forking paths of his life and all those lives behind him rise up in a thicket, a forest of wrong turns and evolutionary misfires. We fell from grace long before the Garden. We fell when we left the sea, when we arrogantly rose up on spinal towers, when we gathered together into colonies of cells. Before, it was better … it was all so simple.…

Thrush's body is in shock, a slug in salt. Every twitch, every breath, carves up his insides with bony knives. But he is powerless not to contort and throb in time with the quickening rhythm of the Backward Path.

The crowd has moved on into the recesses of the museum by the time Thrush comes around on the cross, but he is so far from conscious that his actions are only a retreat from pain and confinement to liberty. Free is all he knows, all he wants.

He tries really hard to remember what he's doing here, but the Backward Path is calling, the slippery coil of sweet devolution sucking him down. He tries to fight it, thrashes, tearing his flesh on the nails and shattered skeleton, biting at the monkeys swarming up the cross to gnaw at his wounds, even though it is his only hope.

He convulses and upchucks his lunch and breakfast, then his bones.

The naked man stomps into the Golgotha Room to crack open the fuse box and push a circuit breaker, when he notices the new cross is empty. Growling in alarm, he goes for the gun on the floor where Thrush dropped it, and steps on something that jabs through his foot. It's a shattered rib. Stumbling backwards, he falls on his ass amid the wreckage of Tobin Thrush's skeleton. Puzzlement and disgust and terror set him scrambling almost backwards, the need for a wall at his back trumping all other concerns, when he feels tiny claws climbing all over him, up into the folds of his baggy skin, climbing him faster than he can claw and swat them off.

He hears someone whispering above him, and he looks up, mouth gaping so wide that Tobin Thrush falls right into it.

"Behold! The mother of us all, and the author of our grief!" Even with his bullhorn, the preacher has to shout to be heard over the drums.

The spotlight falls on a girl standing under a tree with red luminous apples hanging from it. Plastic grass covers the floor. She wears only a green G-string with fabric leaves sewn to it, and a serpent. Adam stands next to her, a strapping Caucasian youth with a fig leaf painted on his featureless plastic pubic arch.

"Condemned for her sin, branded with her madness with none of her hard-won wisdom, you writhe in night soil like serpents and worms yourselves, and all for the sake of her!"

Everyone in the crowd is holding a snake. Timber rattlers and cottonmouths twist in the trembling hands, placated, seemingly hypnotized by the pounding rhythm and the rivers of gibberish flowing from the mouths of every member of the congregation.

Only the fishy man takes any notice of the flabby man when he comes back into the Eden room, but all he can do is stare. Naked and restored to morbid obesity, his partner waddles through the Garden, shoving ecstatic rednecks out of his way with the blunt prow of his turgid belly.

The preacher stands above her on a riser, holding a rattlesnake that spills out of his arms and drags on the fake grass. He's a handsome silver-haired man, vaguely familiar, with a big, perpetual grin that belies the venom spewing through his bullhorn. "An eternity of suffering for all humankind for the failure of one … until tonight, brothers and sisters! Let her taste the sting of damnation, and let our souls be cleansed and restored to the innocence of Eden!"

Two of the quivering flock stumble towards Eve with their snakes upraised like daggers and crash into the plexiglass wall just before the flabby man runs into it.

"Who among you is worthy to claim the wisdom of the serpent?"

The drums fall silent. The preacher lays his snake on Eve's shoulder. The flabby man pounds on the plexiglass, making it buckle, smearing it with sweat and blood.

"Now consider," the preacher says, "that most blameless victim of the conspiracy of Heaven and Hell, the most magnificent of all God's creations, in its wisdom superior even to man, that did walk even as a man, that did spread its wings to fly even as the eagle. Condemned for eternity for its part in Eve's temptation to grovel in dust and mud and to be trampled underfoot by the author of its disgrace. Behold the glory and splendor of the serpent, before the betrayal of Eden! Behold!"

The preacher tears open his linen robes. The congregation begins screaming.

Behind him, men and women writhe as the vipers in their hands strike again and again at necks, faces, shoulders, arms in a frenzy. Some throw down their snakes and stumble towards the gift shop exit, but nobody makes it. The tangle of spastic limbs, glassy eyes, bloated, blackening faces is knee-deep from the glass wall to the exit.

"Not a mother-loving one of you," the preacher sourly concludes. When he's not looking directly at you, his handsome face is just a cracked old Halloween mask of one of the old-time presidents. The rattler glides across Eve's shoulders and slithers down her arm, no more interested in her than she is in it.

The flabby man bulldozes through the plexiglass wall.

"What'd you do with Francis?" the fishy man gasps. He shambles around the mountain of corpses, pointing Thrush's gun at him.

"I just come for the girl," says the flabby man. "She's wanted at home."

The fishy man pulls the trigger again and again, then throws the empty gun aside. "Shit, who's gonna help me clean up this mess now...?"

The preacher laughs and says something to the fishy man in a tongue composed entirely of varieties of Y and S. "Just take her, then. We don't want any more trouble." Going over to help the fishy man collect the exhausted snakes from the dead rednecks' hands, he spitefully adds, "Never should've let her come with us in the first blessed place...."

The Davenports are hosting a party. Security lines the driveway, and even real hooded police stand by the front door. A valet tells Thrush to drive around back and meet Mr. Davenport there.

Thrush gets out in the backyard and scratches his back against the bark of a twisted oak in the back driveway, ripping off the last chunks of the flabby man. He's still doing it when Davenport and a bodyguard come strolling up.

"Congratulations." Still shedding copious gobbets of necrotized flabby man, Thrush staggers over to the Celica and pops the trunk.

"What for?" Davenport slurs, tosses a highball glass into a shrub.

"You're the new mayor, ain't you?" He had to fold down the backseats to fit the rolled-up area rug into it. He pulls it out now, careful of the hank of blond hair sticking out one end.

"She's all right," Thrush says, "in case you're wondering." Brushing back the bodyguard, he shoulders the area rug. "Where d'you want this?"

"Uh … follow me." Davenport leads him down a path through Italian cypresses and box hedges into a backyard big enough to hunt poor folks for sport in. Somewhere, off by the house, a party is in full swing. Folks are dancing on a banquet table, swinging red banners, and fucking in the hot tub. Davenport leads him up to a guest house, unlocks the door, and flips on the lights. Thrush carries the area rug in and lays it not ungently on the Spanish tile, then kneels over it, subtly pushing Davenport back. The bodyguard comes forward with his hand on the automatic in his shoulder rig, but Davenport tells him to go get a cola.

"We still have to settle up, don't we?" Davenport goes into the hip pocket of his slacks and hands Thrush a fat wad of cash and ration coupons. "Gas, meat, medicine … and they spend like cash money most places. So … where was she?"

"Right where you put her."

Davenport flushes, but he didn't win a mayoral election in a shit-stain town like this by losing his cool every time some mouthy nobody gave him shit. "Friend, I don't know what you think, and I don't much care. I asked you a simple question.…"

"She was with those folks painted your curb the other day. Maybe she went off with them, and maybe you set it up, but she had to get out of here so your wife wouldn't take her before election day."

"I don't take your meaning, boy."

"Everybody knows, sir. About how the quality people around here show they have what it takes. About how bargains get done out at the country club. I heard all about how some folks will offer up their first-born at a banquet … usually if it's a girl, and all the other rich folks come pig out. Nobody blames you for taking the belt-and-suspenders approach."

Davenport's slow smile made his face look like the preacher's rubber mask. "Oh, you know, do you? You boys share stories at the U-Haul lot when you're not doing deals over at the courthouse? You know what it's like to be left holding this monumental bag of shit when the goddamn music stops? To try to hold it together so the few decent people left in this world don't go batshit crazy and eat each other? You know what it's like to see something going down the street you know damn well ain't even a human being, but you can't say or do anything because you don't know for good and all how many of your own people you can count on. You think this fucking mess has knocked us all into a cocked hat and we're a big joke, don't you? Well, let me enlighten you, my subhuman scavenger friend. We were cutting throats just to keep the lights on around here since before we took this shithole back from the Indians. Don't matter if your tin-shit toad-god crawls up out of that hole at the edge of town or the stars fall from the sky. We know how to keep order around here, and we'll keep on doing it."

Thrush sighs, holds out his hand and takes Davenport's money. He gets up and shuffles towards the door. "I suppose you're right. I'm sorry I didn't get her here in time for your big to-do...."

"Davenport shrugs. "We got a local girl and bleached her hair."

"I hope your friends were fooled. Your wife must've left because of what you were gonna do, but you had it figured out all along, didn't you, Mr. Mayor? Now she's outta your hair, you run this town, and you get to keep your daughter as a hole card for the next time you need a blood sacrifice to get out of trouble."

"You're not as stupid as you look. You should come work for me regular...."

"Folks're talking up a range war with OKC pretty soon. They outnumber us a bit, but we got the college, and lord knows those freaks know a thing or two about warrin'. Big boy like you could write his own ticket, end up a rancher with a spread."

Thrush shrugged, wiped dead skin out of his eyes. "I don't much care for regular work, truth to tell. Probably going to go home and sleep for a month now."

"Well, you've earned it," Davenport says, back already turned, kneeling beside the rug. The toes of a pair of scuffed-up Converse hi-tops stick out of the other end. He fondles the hair, smells it. "My man will see you out."

Thrush goes out, pulls the door shut. Davenport can contain

himself no longer. "All the trouble you caused me … you could've ruined me, but you don't even understand … well, now you're gonna know, you little—"

The area rug unrolls across the red Spanish tile and a dozen angry homunculi leap out of the nest of dirty girl's clothes to feast on the mayor's face.

Thrush parks the Celica in the weeds by their double-wide Airstream because there's a primer-red Charger in the driveway. He goes over to the garden hose and turns it on full blast and showers, scrubbing out his hard-to-reach spots in full view of the neighbors. Then, looking back at the Celica, he goes in.

He has to step over the guy in the Harry Crews T-shirt, who sprawls from the front door to the dinette and has soaked right through the cleanest portion of their carpet.

A pistol is slowly, laboriously cocked just behind Thrush's ear.

"What's for dinner, darlin?" Thrush says. "We can get take-out. I got paid…."

Ursula rolls slowly forward on the couch, into the light from the neighbors' bonfire. Sniffling, she says, "He came back … You know how sometimes, they … they …"

Yeah, he did, especially the ones who wanted a monkey to do for them what they were too chickenshit to do for themselves. Suddenly, after making a day-baby with her, she became their Earth mother savior, and their only reason for living.

Thrush turns to look at the monkey perched on the knickknack shelf next to Ursula's crystal unicorn collection. The misbegotten thing is little more than a cat's skull and a pair of stunted arms and something that could be a leg or a tail. It's wrapped around a 9mm Glock. It has its father's pustular complexion, and Thrush wagers it can't see for shit.

"He tried to get it to shoot me," Ursula says, "can you imagine?"

"Yeah, maybe we ought to see about getting you a different line of work."

A shadow falls across the screen door. The monkey wheezes and twists the gun to point at the intruder. Thrush takes the gun. The thing lunges at him, but he raps it with the butt of the gun and knocks it on the floor with the others.

"Who's that?" Ursula struggles to pull herself up.

"It's just this girl I saved today."

"You sure didn't save her hair."

"Long story. Tell you sometime."

"Well, she can't stay here; we don't have nothing to eat for dinner as it is."

"Well … Maybe tomorrow I'll go see if the crazy snake-handling church I got her from wants her back. But for now, whyn't you just sit there and think real hard about a twenty-pound turkey full of stuffing, and try not to make it look like me."

He pushes open the screen door, but stops the dazed bald girl from coming in. "Come on and help with this," he says, dragging the dead loser out of the trailer. "Get the feet."

She's not much help, but she tries. He drags the surprisingly heavy jackoff through the Russian thistle and wild cucumber around back of the trailer, with the girl holding one or the other of the dead man's ankles, lifting them up over hidden pieces of lawn furniture.

Around back and twenty paces from the porch, they come to the edge. He tells the girl to go back to the trailer. There's a fence around this stretch of the Sink, but the section behind the trailer collapsed and fell in a few months ago. It isn't growing too aggressively, but every so often a good chunk of land will fall in without ever making a noise. Ursula keeps nagging him to move them into town, but Thrush doesn't feel any urgency.

A sound comes out of him like the sound of his voice when he was a rag of meat inside the flaccid void under the flabby man's skin. "Iä, Tsathoggua."

He rolls the dead boy off the edge and waits, watching the moon, for the sound of something hitting the bottom, or climbing to the top.

Contributor Bios

Neil Baker is the owner of April Moon Books, a small press based in Ontario, Canada. He has published several well-received books including *The Dark Rites of Cthulhu, Flesh Like Smoke,* and the 'Short, Sharp, Shocks' series. His own stories can be found in a clutch of great anthologies including World War Cthulhu and Atomic Age Cthulhu, and he has several more stories due for release in the coming year. Neil lives with his wife and two kids in a perpetual state of confusion.

Glynn Owen Barrass lives in the North East of England and has been writing since late 2006. He has written over a hundred and thirty short stories, most of which have been published in the UK, USA, France, and Japan. He has also edited anthologies for Chaosium's Call of Cthulhu fiction line, and writes material for their flagship roleplaying game. To date he has edited the collections *Eldritch Chrome, Steampunk Cthulhu* and *Atomic Age Cthulhu* for Chaosium; *In the Court of the Yellow King* for Celaeno Press; and *World War Cthulhu* for Dark Regions Press. Upcoming books include *The Eldritch Force, The Summer of Lovecraft,* and *World War Cthulhu II.*

Tim Curran is the author of the novels *Skin Medicine, Hive, Dead Sea, Resurrection, Hag Night, Skull Moon, The Devil Next Door, Doll Face, Afterburn, House of Skin,* and *Biohazard.* His short stories have been collected in *Bone Marrow Stew* and *Zombie Pulp.* His novellas include *The Underdwelling, The Corpse King, Puppet Graveyard, Worm,* and *Blackout.* His short stories have appeared in such magazines as *City Slab, Flesh&Blood, Book of Dark Wisdom* and *Inhuman,* as well as anthologies such as *Shadows Over Main Street, Eulogies III,* and *October Dreams II.* His fiction has been translated into German, Japanese, Spanish, and Italian. Find him on Facebook at facebook.com/tim.curran.77

Edward M. Erdelac is the author of ten novels including the acclaimed occult Civil War thriller *Andersonville* (Random House), the Judeocentric Lovecraftian weird western *Merkabah Rider* series, and *Monstrumführer* from Comet Press. His fiction has appeared in *Dread Shadows in Paradise, World War Cthulhu, Star Wars Insider Magazine,* and dozens of other places. Born in Indiana, educated in Chicago, he now lives in the Los Angeles area with his family and a trio of felines. News and excerpts can be found at his Delirium Tremens blog at http://www.emerdelac. wordpress.com

Sam Gafford has been published in a wide variety of anthologies and publications. His fiction has appeared in such collections as *Black Wings* Volumes I, III and V, as well as *Flesh Like Smoke, The Lemon Herberts, Wicked Tales*, and in magazines like *Weird Fiction Review, Dark Corridor, Nameless*, and others. A lifelong Lovecraftian, he has written critical articles that have appeared in *Lovecraft Studies, Crypt of Cthulhu*, and more. An expert on the life and work of pioneering science fiction writer William Hope Hodgson, Gafford is currently working on a book length critical biography of Hodgson. Recently, he wrote *Some Notes on a Non-Entity: The Life of H. P. Lovecraft*, which is a 120-page graphic-novel biography of HPL, with PS Publishing set to release it in 2017. Gafford has a collection of short horror fiction, *The Dreamer in Fire and Other Tales*, coming from Hippocampus Press in 2016. He recently finished writing his first novel and hopes to have it published by 2017. A pop-culture junkie, Gafford has probably watched far more TV than recommended. He lives in Rhode Island with his long-suffering wife and three ambivalent cats.

Cody Goodfellow's previous collections *Silent Weapons For Quiet Wars* and *All-Monster Action* both received the Wonderland Book Award. His latest, *Rapture of the Deep & Other Lovecraftian Tales*, is out now from Hippocampus Press. He wrote, co-produced and scored the short Lovecraftian hygiene film *Stay At Home Dad*, which can be viewed on YouTube. As a bishop of the Esoteric Order of Dagon (San Pedro Chapter), he presides over several Cthulhu Prayer Breakfasts each year, from Comic-Con to the Queen Mary. He is also a director of the H. P. Lovecraft Film Festival in Los Angeles and cofounder of Perilous Press, a micropublisher of modern cosmic horror.

Scott T. Goudsward is a New England-based writer, tethered to a cubicle during the day. At night he listens to the voices in his head and writes them down. Scott has been writing seriously since 1992 and in that time, written two novels, *Trailer Trash* and *Fountain of the Dead*, and several non-fiction books with his brother David, including *Horror Guide to Massachusetts* and *Horror Guide to Florida*. He has also edited or co-edited the anthologies, *Traps, Once Upon an Apocalypse*, and *Wicked Tales*. Scott's short fiction has appeared in *Wicked Seasons, Atomic Age Cthulhu,* and *Snowbound with Zombies.* Scott is one of the coordinators of the New England Horror Writers and belongs to two writers groups. He is working on a new novel, a new non-fiction book, and new anthologies.

Scott R. Jones' fiction and poetry has appeared in *Broken City Mag, Cthulhu Haiku 2, Cthulhu Fhtagn!* (Word Horde), and Australia's *Andromeda Spaceways Inflight Magazine,* among others. His story "Turbulence" was awarded an Honourable Mention in *Imaginarium 3: The Best Canadian Speculative Fiction.* He is also the author of a non-fiction work, *When The Stars Are Right: Towards An Authentic R'lyehian Spirituality* (Martian Migraine Press), and has edited three anthologies for that press, *Conqueror Womb: Lusty Tales of Shub-Niggurath, Resonator: New Lovecraftian Tales From Beyond,* and *Cthulhusattva: Tales of the Black Gnosis.* He lives in Victoria, British Columbia, with his wife and two frighteningly intelligent spawn.

William Meikle is a Scottish writer, now living in Canada, with twenty novels published in the genre press and over 300 short story credits in thirteen countries. He has books available from a variety of publishers including Dark Regions Press, DarkFuse and Dark Renaissance, and his work has appeared in a number of professional anthologies and magazines with sales to *NATURE Futures, Penumbra,* and *Buzzy Mag,* among others. He lives in Newfoundland with whales, bald eagles and icebergs for company. When he's not writing he drinks beer, plays guitar, and dreams of fortune and glory.

Christine Morgan recently relocated from the Seattle area to the Portland area, beginning a new, more-social phase of her life among the local horror/bizarro weirdo creative community. They like how she brings baked goods to readings and events. In addition to her several books and dozens of short stories in print, she's a regular contributor to *The Horror Fiction Review,* the editor and publisher of the *Fossil Lake Anthologies,* and dabbles in many and various other writing-related projects. Her other interests include history, mythology, cooking shows, crafts, superheroes, gaming, and spoiling her four cats as she trains toward eventual crazy-cat-lady status. She can be found online at christinemariemorgan.wordpress.com/

Edward Morris is a 2011 nominee for the Pushcart Prize in Literature, also nominated for the 2009 Rhysling Award and the 2005 British Science Fiction Association Award. His short stories have appeared in *The Starry Wisdom Library* (PS Publishing;) *The Children of Gla'aki* (Dark Regions Press), and *Eternal Frankenstein* (Word Horde Books.) He is currently writing a superhero novel called *I am Lesion* for the National M.S. Society and finishing a science-fiction horror meganovel called *There was a Crooked Man*, which Barry N. Malzberg pronounced "fit to stand on the same shelf as *Earth Abides* and *The Day After*."

Konstantine Paradias is a writer by choice. His short stories have been published in the *AE Canadian Science Fiction Review*, Atelier Press's *Trident Magazine*, and the *BATTLE ROYALE Slambook* by Haikasoru. His short story, "How You Ruined Everything" has been included in *Tangent Online*'s 2013 recommended SF reading list, and his short story "The Grim" has been nominated for a Pushcart Prize.

Stephen Mark Rainey is author of the novels *Balak, The Lebo Coven, Dark Shadows: Dreams of the Dark* (with Elizabeth Massie), *The Nightmare Frontier, Blue Devil Island*, and *The Monarchs*; over 100 published works of short fiction; five short-fiction collections; and several audio dramas for Big Finish Productions based on the ABC-TV series *Dark Shadows*, featuring members of the original TV series cast. For ten years, he edited the award-winning *Deathrealm* magazine and has edited anthologies for Chaosium, Arkham House, and Delirium Books. Mark is an avid geocacher, which oftentimes leads him to discover creepy places—and people—that wind up in his horror stories. He lives in Greensboro, NC, with two precocious house cats, one of which owns a home decorating business. Visit Mark's website at stephenmarkrainey.com.

Pete Rawlik, a longtime collector of Lovecraftian fiction, in 1985 stole a car to go see the film *Reanimator*. He successfully defended himself by explaining that his father had regularly read him "The Rats in the Walls" as a bedtime story. His first professional sale was in 1997, but he didn't begin to write seriously until 2010. Since then he has authored more than fifty short stories and the Cthulhu Mythos novels *Reanimators* and *The Weird Company*. He is a frequent contributor to the *Lovecraft ezine* and the *New York Review of Science Fiction*. In 2014 his short story "Revenge of the Reanimator" was nominated for a New Pulp Award. In 2015 he co-edited *The Legacy of the Reanimator* for Chaosium. Somewhere along the line he became known as the Reanimator guy, but he fervently denies being obsessed with the character. His new novel *Reanimatrix* is a weird-noir-romance set in H. P. Lovecraft's Arkham, and will be released in 2016. He lives in southern Florida where he works on Everglades issues and does a lot of fishing.

Brian M. Sammons is the weird fiction line editor for Dark Regions Press and the Chief Editor for Golden Goblin Press. He has been a film and literature critic for over twenty years for a number of publications and has penned stories that have appeared in such anthologies as *Arkham Tales, Horrors Beyond, Monstrous, Dead but Dreaming 2, Mountains of Madness, Deepest, Darkest Eden, In the Court of the Yellow King* and others. He has edited the books; *Cthulhu Unbound 3, Undead & Unbound, Eldritch Chrome, Edge of Sundown, Steampunk Cthulhu, Dark Rites of Cthulhu, Atomic Age Cthulhu, World War Cthulhu, Flesh Like Smoke, Return of the Old Ones, Children of Gla'aki, Dread Shadows in Paradise*, and more. He is currently far too busy for any sane man. For more about this guy that neighbors describe as "such a nice, quiet man" you can follow him on Twitter @BrianMSammons

Lucy A. Snyder is a four-time Bram Stoker Award-winning author who wrote the novels *Spellbent, Shotgun Sorceress*, and *Switchblade Goddess*. She also authored the nonfiction book *Shooting Yourself in the Head for Fun and Profit: A Writer's Survival Guide* and the story collections *While the Black Stars Burn, Soft Apocalypses, Orchid Carousals, Sparks and Shadows, Chimeric Machines*, and *Installing Linux on a Dead Badger*. Her writing has been translated into French, Russian, Italian, Czech, and Japanese editions and has appeared in publications such as *Apex Magazine, Nightmare Magazine, Pseudopod, Strange Horizons, Weird Tales, Steampunk World, In the Court of the Yellow King, The Library of the Dead, Seize the Night*, and *Best Horror of the Year, Vol. 5*. She lives in Columbus, Ohio and is faculty in Seton Hill University's MFA program in Writing Popular Fiction. She also writes a column for *Horror World*. You can learn more about her at lucysnyder.com and you can follow her on Twitter at @LucyASnyder.

Sam Stone began her professional writing career in 2007 when her first novel won the Silver Award for Best Novel with *ForeWord Magazine* Book of the Year Awards. Since then she has gone on to write several novels, three novellas and many short stories. She was the first woman in 31 years to win the British Fantasy Society Award for Best Novel. She also won the Award for Best Short Fiction in the same year (2011). Stone loves all types of fiction and enjoys mixing horror (her first passion) with a variety of different genres including science fiction, fantasy, crime and Steampunk. She currently resides in Lincolnshire with her husband David and their two cats Shadow and Freya. Her works can be found in paperback, audio and e-book. sam-stone.com

Jeffrey Thomas is an American author of fantastical fiction, the creator of the acclaimed milieu Punktown. Books in the Punktown universe include the short story collections *Punktown, Voices From Punktown, Punktown: Shades of Grey* (with his brother, Scott Thomas), and *Ghosts of Punktown*. Novels in that setting include *Deadstock, Blue War, Monstrocity, Health Agent, Everybody Scream!,* and *Red Cells*. Thomas's other short-story collections include *Worship The Night, Thirteen Specimens, Nocturnal Emissions, Unholy Dimensions, Doomsdays, Terror Incognita, Aaaiiieee!!!, Honey Is Sweeter Than Blood,* and *Encounters With Enoch Coffin* (with W. H. Pugmire). His other novels include *Letters From Hades, The Fall of Hades, Beautiful Hell, Boneland, Subject 11, Beyond the Door, Thought Forms, Blood Society, Lost In Darkness, The Sea of Flesh and Ash* (with Scott Thomas), and *A Nightmare on Elm Street: The Dream Dealers*. His short stories have been reprinted in DAW's *The Year's Best Horror Stories*, St. Martin's Press's *The Year's Best Fantasy and Horror*, and Undertow Publications' *Year's Best Weird Fiction*, and he has been a finalist for the Bram Stoker and John W. Campbell awards. Thomas lives in Massachusetts.

Tim Waggoner is a Shirley Jackson Award finalist who has published over thirty novels and three short story collections of dark fiction. He teaches creative writing at Sinclair Community College and in Seton Hill University's MFA in Writing Popular Fiction program. You can find him on the web at timwaggoner.com.

Don Webb teaches high school, has shot fireworks professionally, and is an expert on the Greek Magical papyrus. He has had one rock-'n'-roll song recorded, designed games, and has two cats than are smarter than he is.

Made in the USA
Middletown, DE
26 November 2017